PRAISE FOR 'THE UNTHINKABLE SHOES'

A moving, sensitively written story. The setting and time of 'The Unthinkable Shoes' (with its echoes of 'unsinkable', a word proudly and confidently bestowed on the Titanic) is expertly evoked and the leisurely pace is exactly what is needed. — B L

I loved it. The opening is fantastic, starting at 'The End' with Finn's stats of life imprinted at the top of the page. It's brave writing. The use of language is gorgeous. Lovely, really sumptuous. And the shoes are a lovely metaphorical thread – really clever. Lovely! — D I

Brilliant writing. I loved it. So much to admire about it. I loved the narration of the ghost of Finn. A pleasure to read. — E J

One of the loveliest description of love I have ever read. — L G

Really excellent, quite superb. I enjoyed it thoroughly. The flow is perfect and the sense of place is excellent. — R W

I loved it – absolutely loved it. The language is rich, engaging and yet economical. I found the characters real and vibrant and the dialogue a delight to read. The characters were completely grounded in their time, and the settings are authentic. I was swept away by it. A real pleasure to read. — B L

Very evocative writing indeed, it literally made me cry. Well-written and emotional. I loved the use of language. It conjured up all sorts of scenes and I felt the hardships. — M G

What a winged tale it is. A stream of consciousness power excellence. A pair of innocent shoes says it all... more poignant than words in itself. The portrayal is perfect. — S G

The writing is captivating and full of emotion. As I read, an Irish family came to life before my eyes. — A H

Beautiful. I found the pure emotion almost overwhelming. The characters are beautifully (there's that word again) portrayed making them easy to visualize. — D D

Perfectly lovely and a heartbreaking story. An excellent job of painting Finn's "before" picture as well as hinting at what's to come. I'm fascinated and engaged. I especially admire the author's use of sensory details so I felt like I was there, and, even more than that, her use of language. I actually "heard" an Irish lilt in my head as I read. Just beautiful. Love the first line 'I drowned three times'. I like the inclusion of the countdown. Excellent. Heartbreaking. The full scope of love. — C B

Beautifully written with convincing characters and depth of thought. I love the way it was grown from the seed of a visit to a museum. — P R

Great writing. I love the first line — "I drowned three times." Blunt, concise, shocking. The writing style is beautiful and authentic. I heard the Irish accent in my head as I read which is really cool. I was struck by the references to explanations of Finn's mother's grief over the loss of Michael. I thought that was handled heartbreakingly well. — KT B

Highly enjoyable concept, well-executed. The concept is intriguing, and well-presented. Finn offers a fascinating and unique perspective, which is conveyed successfully to the reader. I certainly felt that this was a boy with 70 years of witness and development, rather than a national boy written with an adult voice.

I would recommend reading this, such was my high level of engagement with the characters and plot. — MD

The narrative voice of Finn is very convincing both as a child's voice and that of an Irish child.

I got a real sense of place: the cold and damp, and the poverty in which the family lived. The descriptions are excellent. Mam's character comes through brilliantly with her utterances of religious fervour and mourning her first son, Michael.

Poor Finn, you do get a real sense of him being the middle child, stuck between his dead brother, who can do no wrong, and a younger sister.

I loved the style of the writing. — MTM

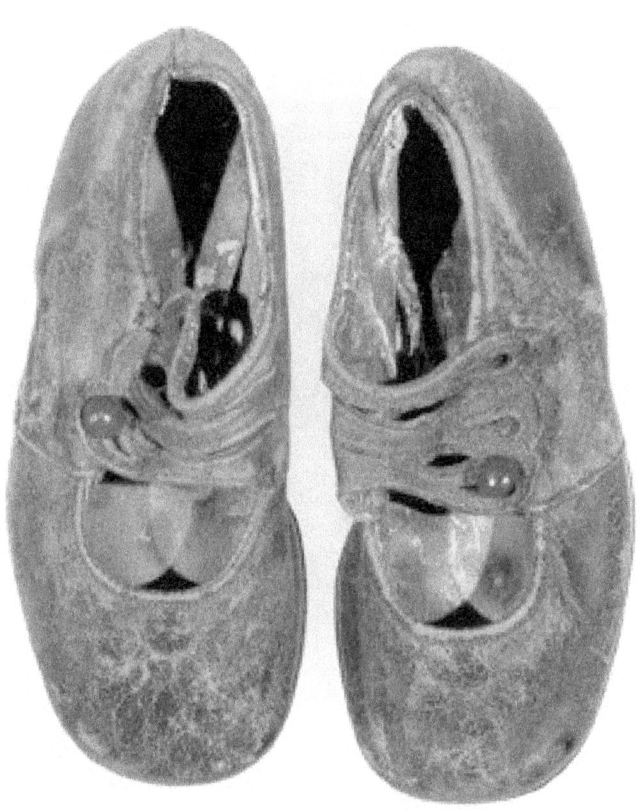

THE UNTHINKABLE

SHOES

SAVE OUR SOULS

V KNOX

for SARAH and DAVID

Library and Archives Canada Cataloguing in Publication
Knox, V ., 1949-, author
The unthinkable shoes / V . Knox.
Includes index.
ISBN 979-8445718888 (paperback)
I. Title.
PS8621.N695U57 2016 C813'.6 C2015-908012-6
Editor – Silent K Publishing
Cover design – Veronica Knox
Typeset in Times with Gatsby display
Fourth Edition
Printed and bound with KDP

Silent K Publishing:
Vancouver Island, British Columbia, Canada
https://veronicaknox.com
e-mail: veronica@veronicaknox.com

DISCLAIMER

Although the historic dates of the *Titanic* disaster are accurate, **'The Unthinkable Shoes'** was written as a psychological, supernatural profile of the real event.

The child's shoes that inspired this story are on display as part of an exhibit of authentic *Titanic* artifacts in the Maritime Museum of Halifax, Nova Scotia.

The grave of the unknown child strewn with toys may be visited in the *Titanic* cemetery in Halifax.

All of the characters, museums, and place names (other than Halifax), are fictional. Any resemblance to real people or places is entirely coincidental.

— *Veronica Knox* – April 15, 2023

TABLE OF CONTENTS

FINN
CLEARY
1907 - 1912

"We shall not cease from exploration.
And the end of all our exploring
will be to arrive where we started
and know the place for the first time."

– T.S. ELIOT

1

THE END

FINN – APRIL 10, 2012

I drowned three times. First, in the relentless rain of Ireland, second, in the deep gloom of mourning that settled over my mother, and third, in the freezing waters of the North Atlantic.

Even when the sun blazed down fierce as the devil there was the bleakness that settled in our bones like a great damp. Once in a blue moon Mam would pull me into her lap, rocking and singing and hanging on to me for dear life, calling me Michael, her wee angel, and ask me where we were going because sweet Jesus she was lost at sea.

It's sad, how in moments of despair when all a body wants is hope, a still small voice will tell you the truth you don't want to hear. Because, you see, I'm NOT Michael! I'm Finn, and it's sad how precious-few blue moons there are.

Yes, those are definitely *my* shoes, there in the museum case. Now who would have thought the likes of me would be famous for their shoes. And such a sad pair as that. I wore them the day I stepped onto the Titanic and the day I floated free of it, April 15, 1912.

I'm not sure if I was five or almost six when it happened, but after my death I discovered that time is an inexact measurement. Time raced ahead of me, pulling me backwards and spun me around so I met myself arriving. Even now, as the centenary of Titanic's maiden voyage approaches, it continues to fling me forward, years speeding past me until I come to a full stop without growing an inch or aging a single day. I've never felt more like a child, but I've never been wiser. I've never been more me. And now, I'm almost free. I have five days to keep a promise. Five days to break a spell.

Visitors come to marvel at the miracle of my shoes, awed that a pair of innocent shoes survived the terrifying chaos when hundreds of people perished. The little shrine of the shoes celebrates a moment in time, but not what they imagine. I know their secret. You'd think a dead child's shoes would make them grief-stricken, entirely. But then I've known miracle shoes before, and I know how they can capture a soul with magic. I've seen them cast a spell. I've seen them break a mother's heart. I can't go back to Mam shoeless. Sure, she'd skin me alive. Losing my shoes is a sin and I lost TWO pairs in the one day.

My shoes have their own life now, Mam is with her sainted Michael in heaven, and my age of innocence is over.

I've outgrown my shoes. Hindsight is the key to navigating random events that were meant to happen. And if I've learned anything, it's that time is a paradox of frozen promises and fluid reckonings. I'm accountable for the promises I made in childish haste, the selfish ones I *tried* to keep, and the selfless ones I had no *intention* of keeping. For these and my most recent accounting of posthumous sins, I face my fair share of penance – hopefully reaping the benefits of a death well-spent by seeing things through to the end. An end that may not be as bitter as the living are led to suppose. That is why I must stay on to tell my story.

Remaining in spirit form close to the living is like being kept after school. Not as a punishment but the timely intervention of a well-meaning head teacher who administers a necessary course correction, innocent shenanigans aside, so the likes of me might reach heaven.

It's graduating with honors on a level playing field where I'm both a naïve five-year-old schoolboy and a scholarly professor of advanced years. I can't always control which one will speak. I sometimes use words like paradox and conundrum and vicarious to show off, but I prefer the words nearest to my former life. And now, only an unearthly headmaster has the authority to release me from detention.

I've only ever had one grownup understand me. Two if you count Lacey. We did everything together. But I always think of her as a child because we met when we were young and I watched her grow old.

Essentially, humans are homing pigeons. We head for the nearest thing to home we can remember. For me it was a person rather than a place. It was Mamie Broughton. We'd only just met but sometimes a chance meeting with a stranger, changes everything. Life is a surprise that turns on a breeze. The pendulum swings, and then... 'worse things happen at sea'.

I used to be plain Finn Cleary before I found fame as the unidentified lost child from the Titanic and my shoes were enshrined as an object of wonder. As if no-one else ever had shoes!

2
THE BIRTH OF MEMORY

FINN – FEBRUARY 14, 1912
countdown – 60 days

I'm standing watch on a hill, facing Cork Harbor in the rain. Beyond Spike Island I can make out a thin blue band of the Atlantic Ocean on the horizon. Perhaps I only see it because I know it's there, always calling. And I pretend I'm the lookout on a grand ship like the ones Da builds in Belfast. Below me are the rooftops of Ballymore. The gulls screeching over the morning's catch in the inlets along the harbor unnerve me, and I can almost hear the waves crashing all the way from the Statue of Liberty. The wind blows through me as if I'm a boy hanging on Mam's clothesline.

I think it's my birthday because it's raining. That's all Mam can remember but maybe even *that* was part of the birthing fever. Da was away, working the shipyards of Harland and Wolff, and when he returned, there I was, and time had wrapped its arms around my coming. The life and times of Finnegan Cleary were well into the third month of wailing and hunger and the smell of peat burning in the hearth. Mam says if we hadn't lived so close to the town she would have died and we'd both be in heaven with my brother Michael, eating bread and jam without a care in the world. But Mam's friend, Mrs. Donovan, had looked in. Seeing no smoke from our chimney, she'd climbed the hill and found us in a terrible state. Mam, and me inside her, both of us fighting for life.

Mam told me how she'd wandered off to the gates of heaven several times during that night where the sunshine was glorious on her face but she always came home. Even from the gates of heaven she could hear me crying, she said, and it was me, the new light of her life, who brought her back. So, I was more than a helpless wee lamb. I was her guiding light like the white towers with the beacons that showed the big ships where to steer clear of the rocks and reach Queenstown.

The rain works itself up from a drizzle until I stand in a downpour, imagining my birthday surprise of scones with cream and jam. I wait long enough for Mam to set the table and race home, but there's only cold soup, and Mam is a huddle of sadness and pain under the blankets waiting for the new baby to come.

MARCH 4, 1912
countdown – 42 days

Maybe it always rains when new babies come, for my Bridie was born on a rainy morning with Mrs. Donovan poking our lazy fire into flames big enough to heat the turnip soup, and curse Da who was off again, needed at the shipyard, and wasn't it like a man to have the freedom whenever a shipyard called or he took a shine to wander. And I don't understand for the life of me how freedom can shine in all this rain but it's a comfort that I'm still a lighthouse for Mam and now for my Bridie. Mam says she's seventeen days old. She knows for sure because each day she's made a cross on the wall, like a calendar. I look at all the crosses. That's my Bridie's life there on the wall.

Michael remains the only hindrance to my future happiness. As ever, his presence dampens even the wettest days. But Titanic is about to save me. In the shake of a lamb's tail I'll be in New York. Michael can keep his corner and good luck to him. He can haunt all the corners in Ballymore with me on the other side of the Atlantic Ocean.

Dates of birth are less important than if a baby survives its first year. And even *then* a child's years are suspect. Michael died before I was born, after he'd grown all the way to eleven. He'd broken Mam's heart for she cried a little whenever she dressed me in the blue pullover she knitted for him. It was too big for me and hung down to my knees, and Mam would bury her face in it and inhale its magic before she pulled it over my head.

All I know is that when I entered the world in 1907, Titanic was being born on bits of paper amongst a team of designers and engineers. That makes us distant cousins. And when my sister Bridie was born, Da was away to Belfast, riveting the side of Titanic's starboard hull. But I had real cousins and aunts and uncles in New York who put the finishing touch to Da's notions of America as our only chance for survival. And the entire joy of it was that I'd be going to school at last.

But today on the cliffs of County Cork, when I can barely make out the Atlantic as a ribbon of darker blue, I know it's the spring of 1912 and that I'm *almost* five years-old or already heading for seven, and the possibility of it being my special day fares better than the summer, and that the wind's bony fingers are pulling at the loose strands of navy-blue wool in Michael's old sweater, making the holes bigger.

Even with the excitement of leaving Ireland our conversation remains dreary. Rain beats the slates on the roof, droning Bridie to sleep in her cradle. The slow ticking of a mantel clock times my parent's tasks of concentration so they don't have to argue. Da polishes his boots by the fire. Mam washes laundry at the sink, up to her elbows in greasy water. And while neither of them are looking at each other, their activities seem to be having a conversation of their own. It's as if they're in separate rooms talking to themselves.

Da shivers and asks Mam if she can stop up the draft with rags. Mam says when a body shivers someone's walked on their grave. I see an image of Michael's gravestone under a shade tree and send Da a look of panic. "Molly, don't be frightening the lad," he says. "Can you not recall a single memory of the gentle breezes of summer, woman?" He remembers but she's forgotten.

Mam sends him the ghost of a smile. He's forgotten but she remembers. She tells a lot of stories. Mostly about sea monsters and banshees and the spirits of the dead who died too soon, and the holy terrors of hell and being watched and judged and the consequences of being found lacking, and how I'd better watch my P's and Q's. So I'm that careful to look over my shoulder even when I'm being good.

Da tells me on the quiet, Mam's stories have been stormy ever since Michael left the world and not to mind so much about the angry winds. They tell him different tales and will blow us clean across the ocean to New York any day now.

The sound of everyday chores draws a battle line between my parents. Mam scrapes a shirt against the washboard, keeping time to Da's polishing. The scent of shoe polish and coal tar soap mingles with the excitement of going to America. If it wasn't for Michael in the corner, my life would be perfect.

My heart beats faster. Michael will be left behind. I will be free. I hug my knees and turn red from being too close to the fire. I can't stop smiling, but I don't want to be upsetting an apple cart again. We don't have an apple tree or a cart but Da says I do this all the time.

Da describes the size of the Titanic. Its length and the tonnage of coal it will take to cross the Atlantic. Mam holds my best blue shirt under the water and lifts it covered in suds. "Larger than life," she calls out, shaking her head. I think that if the wind could talk it would sound like Mam's sigh when she washes our clothes in a fog of sadness. Her words make me shiver. Larger than life is too big. I'm undersized for my age and everything important to me is enormous.

I pipe up ignoring the apple carts. "Da, is Titanic bigger than the dragon ships that brought the giants to Ireland?"

Da laughs. "My boy you've too much of the imagination about you," he says. "Sure you're a born storyteller like your mother."

It's the wild fables Mam tells that I hanker after, and sure enough they grow with each telling. Especially the ones invented a thousand years ago, so far back that they've grown into monstrous fibs to explain the world of stars and magic.

Da's hands are a blur over the brown leather. "Some stories are larger than life all right," he says. "Especially the ones your mother likes to tell."

I'm delirious with leaving and so I ignore the apple cart looming in the corner with Michael. "Larger than Titanic herself?"

"Aye. Larger than the miracles of saints," Da says.

"Heaven preserve us," Mam says.

Da ignores Mam and continues. "I'll tell you a tale I heard at the shipyard... and it's true. The ship we're going on is named for a race of giants called Titans who, once-upon-a-time, ruled the likes of thunder and lightning and the destinies of us wee men."

Da has my full attention. "It's powerless puny we are in the face of giants. Isn't it Da? And were the giants Irish?"

"It's powerless puny we are to an ocean," Mam tells a different shirt that she's scrubbing into another rag.

Da explains, his eyes lit like candles. "The Titans lived on a Greek mountain a long way from here and a long time ago. It's like wee David we are, and we have to use our wits to slay the likes of Goliath."

Mam's words blow around the room. "David had God on his side," Mam tells the ceiling.

I ignore the word Greek. It's a new word. I know because I treasure each word Da says. Sure he's a genius. I've heard Mam call him that even though her voice had a wee scorn of laughter in it. "But we have Saint Michael don't we Da? Sure Saint Michael could kill a giant as easy as a dragon."

Da and Mam's eyes lock across the room saying things I can't hear. "Aye, son. We have him, sure enough."

Da is finished. He lays his boots by the hearth and makes the fire jump with the stained newspaper scrunched into the flames. For a while the room is silent but for the crackling fire and Mam's concentration on a collar stain. The leap of firelight sends her shadow larger than life on the wall. I shiver because although my face is flushed from the fire my back is freezing. I don't dare shiver out loud as I don't want to think of strangers walking on my grave. I wonder if Michael can feel us when Mam lays wildflowers at his feet.

I unlock my knees and prop my feet on the fender. Da stares from the flickering pattern glancing off the sheen of his boots to my bare feet. He's lost in thought and I think he's like me, dreaming of America. But he sits up, struck by a new thought. A decision. "You can't be meeting the likes of rich cousins with charity shoes. Sure, even Saint Michael himself would never present himself to New York in second-hand shoes. Finn, you'll be needing a pair of store bought shoes."

Mam wrings the dirty water from the shirt and slaps it into a basket. "And will Saint Michael be providing the money for the new shoes?"

Da pats my knee and leans closer to my feet as if they can hear. "He will."

Mam plunges the last shirt, deep into the murky water. The bar of yellow soap scrapes up and down.

"And Molly, you'll be wearing a new hat, my girl."

"Sure, and that will impress the ocean will it?"

The fire coughs out a cloud of earthy steam. I savor the powerful-sharp aroma of Irish soil. "No charity shoes, Molly," Da repeats, extra-loud. He stokes the fire with a fresh slab of dried peat. "We'll not be shaming the Cleary name when we say hello to America." He chuckles. "God but we've a plethora of time to do that later."

Plethora is Da's favorite word.

In April we're going to America on the RMS Titanic. I don't know what RMS means but Da says it's the most important ship in the history of ships entirely, which means every ship that's ever sailed the seven seas from Queenstown to

Australia and around the tail of Africa. The Titanic will steam into New York harbor like an enormous black swan, so she will, with brass bands and fireworks, surely making history, and more than that, my story will begin and Mam will notice me and forget the sadness of Michael and all the damp dreary saints and sputtering candles that fill Ballymore Church, and feel the sun of America blessing her face. Da says I'm forever upsetting apple carts and to be careful in front of Mam. What I say could topple her into a huddle of fear and heaven knows I don't want to do that.

It rains a lot in Ireland and there are an enormous number of babies. A plethora of babies, Da says, and plethora means more than a few. Plethora means entirely too many.

3
BABY STEPS

FINN – MARCH 12, 1912
countdown – 34 days

Our house is still as a church. Mam's shawl slips to the floor but she doesn't notice. She's listening, staring over the box in her lap with a far-off look. Maybe she can see the statue of liberty. If she wasn't cradling the box tightly with both hands they would be trembling from the sadness. Her shawl has spooled to the floor with her rosary. I pull the wool back over her shoulders and she stirs, smiling a little from the comfort. She takes her hand away from the box long enough to accept her rosary. Her fingers begin to worry the beads I press in her right hand. I know she's thinking of Michael because it's the morning mass for the 'box-of-Michael' when time stands still and Mam prays over a relic so sacred it's kept in a place of honor next to a statue of Saint Michael himself.

I've seen the ritual dozens of times and I'm sure there are hundreds I don't see. Mam has most of her Michael moments when Da is away.

It's my job to rouse the fire at first light even though most mornings the sun is lost behind a wall of rain. Mam tells me, "Finnegan I love you and Bridie, I do, but Michael that's gone is with me still. He whispers to me. He's whispering now. Can you hear him, Finn?"

"I can't."

Mam's sitting there with her bare feet in the draft. I want to make her tea with sugar but the fire's crumbled to warm ashes and we're out of tea and sugar. On goes a slab of peat from the corner, and I prod it into life. It catches into a curl of brown steam. "Will I fetch your slippers Mam?" I say. Her slippers are three pairs of Da's socks, one inside the other. They're still damp, hanging beside the dying hearth. In our cottage drying and dying loom larger than life.

The word 'slippers' startles Mam. Her face goes dark and frightens me for she takes one hand from the box, and there go her beads on the floor again, and she grabs my arm, gripping too tight. "Finn, you must promise me a promise," she says. "Do you understand?"

"I don't."

"Keep every promise you make," she says. "A promise is a grand thing, so it is. God hears your promises and He will hold you to them. It's the devil you'll pay if you lie to God. Do you understand now?"

"I do."

She squeezes her eyes as she grips my arm, and when she opens them they're wet with tears. "Never make a promise unless you'll move heaven to keep it. Promises are all a body has to hope on."

This is all about our Michael. He was Mam's shadow. Da told me how their heads were always together and not a communion wafer could come between them. "Your Mam was different then," he explained. "I remember the laughter. The two of them near drowned in the pure joy of each other. We've had our fair share of hungry days but the light in your Mam's eyes was poured into Michael to save him and I believe she would have if she hadn't had to close them for a while. Your Mam believed Michael would never leave her. He promised her that."

"Mam says God hears my promises."

"On his last day, Michael made the promise he couldn't keep and your mother believed him. And so he's with her still. If she talks to Michael it's the truth he's beside her. You're not to worry. She's not off with the fairies, Finn, she's with your brother, and it's not for us to think different. It's a strange thing between a mother and her first child." And then he confided something I didn't want to know. "Michael died as your Mam sat beside him, drowsing. She had to, son. She was that exhausted. When she woke, he was gone. And the worse of it was, she didn't cry. Not once. She was silent, all through the prayers and masses and the churchyard. I never heard her grieving but she's never forgiven herself for falling asleep even though she held your brother's hand the whole while. She never let go. Not of his hand then, nor his spirit now. Part of your mother went to heaven with Michael. Finn, he was the sun to her, but even the sun has to set, and the consumption came. It came to families, taking one and leaving the others. And it took our Michael. Her beloved Michael."

For the longest time I believed Saint Michael was named after my brother.

The ritual of the box continues. Mam sings to it and rocks it like a baby – the same song she sings to our Bridie but with a distant look in her eye. Mam is no longer in the room; she's off in a dream of Michael. The click of her rosary beads make the sound of a clock ticking backwards. Today he's two, she says. By now I'm too sad to be terrified of her. I want to be a good boy so Mam will have the joy of me too, so the likes of a communion wafer can't come between us. I ask her to tell me the story of the night I was born. That night when I was the light of her life who called her home, but it's the 'day of the box.'

"You should have seen him, Finn. Your big brother, two years old, bright as an angel, walking across this very floor, so he did, and your Da was that full of Michael that he spared himself the drink and bought him a pair of new shoes. One's first shoes are a grand thing Finnegan, so they are. A baby's first steps are a blessing. It's a brave thing a child does to stand up and walk across a floor." She points to the far corner where I've stacked the peat nice and tall. "Michael was over there."

She stares at the spot and looks up, through me, a twinkle in her eyes. "And I was right there," she says, gesturing to the sink.

She is still there. And Michael is still a baby in the corner about to change the world entirely. It must have been a grand day because Mam is beaming like the sun that has no intention of setting.

"We made a game of counting his toes," she says, "before we wiggled them into the shoes. That day he was a rich baby with kid leather shoes."

Delight fair radiates from her face and I smile too. I can almost see the brother I never knew, there in the corner listening to the shining tales of his glorious babyhood.

Mam opens the box slowly. A snowy cloth holds something sacred inside. Michael's first shoes, worn soft from two pairs of feet for they were mine as well. So I knew Mam loved me. She'd given me the gift of Michael's shoes and it must have pained her to see me totter over the same floor.

I'd like to say I remember her holding out her arms to catch me, for I know she did, but I wouldn't be telling the truth of it. I have no memory of the shoes other than the 'Michael Days' when out they came with a story or two. I learned to count to six on those shoes. Three buttons on each shoe.

I sit close to Mam and wait. "I remember the day," she starts, and I lean in, my head on her shoulder. Her voice is gentle with a smile inside. "Ah Finnegan, he loved his shoes, so he did."

She polishes a shoe on the hem of her skirt.

"Were they mine too?" I ask, even though I know I'd worn them. "Did Michael give them to me?"

She hugs me. "He did."

"Can I hold them?"

"You can."

Mam places them in my hands, cupping them gently the way one holds a butterfly. Sure the shoes fair purr in my hand. It's wild to think my great feet ever fit in those perfect wee shoes because it was the end of the new shoes. Michael mostly went barefoot after that or in knitted socks. Later he wore misshapen charity shoes to school until he was big enough to clomp about in a pair of Da's old work boots stuffed with newspaper in the toes.

"Will Michael give them to my Bridie?" I ask.

"He will."

Mam is proud of Michael. When I ask her she says *pride goeth before a fall*. She looks up at the ceiling as if God were there, ready to bless her soul, or give her a scolding if she gets it wrong. I know what falling is, and Da explained about pride as me being too full of myself, but I can't get my head around the word *goeth*. It comes from Mam's black book with the cross that Michael read to her, him having been to the local school and learning the entire alphabet. Michael, who never had to be full of himself because Mam was full of him enough for the pair of them.

My brother is a brighter beacon than the tallest lighthouse. Sometimes I wish he was alive so he could teach me the rest of the letters in my name, including Cleary, and Mam would knit me my own sweater. The color red would do nicely for me.

I think being dead makes you more loveable. Sometimes I wish I could die of the consumption and stand in the corner and hear stories about myself when it's Bridie's turn for the shoes. Sometimes my insides churn after the shoe stories. Sometimes I hate Michael.

I love my Bridie, but wee baby girls are never short of the attention. Da says I'm an *in-between*. He's sorry but there it is. I must work harder. I must show Michael in the corner how proud I am to be his brother. And tell him that after I go to the school in New York, I will write poems and entire books and never use 'goeth' once, and never be so full of myself that I'll fall short of being a boy Mam is proud of, and catch her if she falls like Michael himself, walking across his heavenly floor.

All-in-all, goeth is a silly word. It doesn't show its face in normal conversations. Da has never used it, and he has a plethora of words in his head.

Mam kisses each shoe and gently eases them into the box as if she doesn't want to wake them. She tucks them in like a baby, and closes the lid. It's like the shoes are in a nursery and Mam has just blown out the candle and closed the door. I expect her to say goodnight. The box is placed next to our chipped statue of St. Michael. Da says he's the patron saint of mariners and that he can kill a dragon quick as wink. So I know there must be two saint Michaels: my sainted brother and the angel dragonslayer.

Mam grabs my shoulders and turns me to face her. "Will you promise to look after the shoes when I'm gone?" Her eyes are wild for the answer. "Finn look at me now."

"I will."

She searches my face and nods her head, satisfied.

Promises are not light things to Mam. They're *cross-my-heart-and-hope-to-die* things. So my life depends on it. And it's a lifetime later, with my new heart and soul, when I realize with a sickening feeling that I've had it wrong the whole time. But the worst of it is it's all a lie. I'm a wicked boy. I deserve to be forgotten. How could I have been so blind?

4

AN OLD BEGINNING

FINN – MARCH 15, 1912
countdown – 31 days

It's midnight dark in the early morning when Mam boils water for tea. The dawn is being strangled by the March rain. I'm awake because we all sleep in the one room and Da is leaving again. One last trip before we leave Ballymore for a drier life.

The wind is raw. It howls, whistling around the cottage, driving the rain hard against the stonework, prying the slates from the roof. Fingers of it poke under the door and worry the curtains. Mam says it's moaning because it wants Da to stay. It wants us *all* to stay. I say if it wants us to stay it should blow warm and gentle, and pat us dry.

The wind tells Mam lots of things. Most of her wild stories begin with stormy nights and God blowing the fates of men to kingdom-come who think they're too good for Ireland. Because Da has his heart set on America. And the wind knows it's only a matter of time before the money in the post office will buy passage for the four of us. If the wind had been to school it would blow down the post office and scatter our hopes like dandelion seeds.

"The Atlantic is a woman with a powerful temper," Mam says, stirring extra sugar into Da's tea. She looks out the window where our only tree is being uprooted by the minute. "Something's made her angry."

Sure as rain there'll be something called consequences.

The sugar is Da's breakfast. He says he's not hungry and he'll eat something on the train but he won't. He saves every penny for his dream of the tickets.

Mam slips a heel of bread in Da's pocket when he kisses her goodbye. He gives my Bridie a kiss. She's an angel asleep in her cradle. Mam's stories don't keep my wee sister awake in fear of the consequences, and Bridie loves the moaning wind. It's as good as a lullaby. Da ruffles my hair and tells me to be a good boy for Mam and to remember it's my job to take care of her and my sister. I'd like Da to kiss me too but as man of the house I'm too old for kisses. I can't cry over every spilled apple.

The door closes behind Da, heading into town for the train that usually takes him away for months at a time. But this time he'll be back in a week. I wonder why he's bothered to polish his boots when he'll be sloshing through a mile of mud and puddles.

Mam leans her forehead on the door and slides the deadbolt. "Twice before," she says, "we packed our things for America. Your daddy wanted to go right after Michael... after Michael left us. But God wanted us to stay." She shakes her head, addressing the rain on the window. "Third time lucky," she says and crosses herself. She and God want us to stay. The statue of St. Michael wants us to stay. Even Michael in the corner wants us to stay.

Me, I'm all for going. I say it's best to leave Michael and move on. Mam has *me* now, and soon I will reach eleven and take Michael's place. These terrible thoughts have me crossing myself to ward off the dreaded consequences, and my P's and Q's are flapping all over creation.

Mam returns to the table and refreshes the teapot. She glances over at her new hat with the blue feather. The hat she said was too grand for the likes of her and wasn't she full of herself thinking it would make leaving easier. She makes a sound in her throat I don't like. A low growl. A draft catches the tip of the feather. I imagine the hat is alive and that it's blowing her a kiss. The hat wants us to go to America. But Mam isn't listening. She's not having any of it. "Mark my words Finn," she says. "The Atlantic is a mother with a powerful temper."

APRIL 8, 1912
countdown – 7 days

I help Mam pack for the ship. Our best clothes are rolled into bundles. One of them contains St. Michael. He of the chipped china. I'm happy. Mam must love me because the first thing she puts in the bag is my new blue shirt, spread on the bottom. In goes the book with the lock of Michael's hair, but not before Mam opens to its page. Something new is there. A shamrock flat as a sheet of paper. "It's from his grave," she says. She closes the book and stares at the gold cross on the front. After a while she kisses the book and settles it into the cloth bag with the wooden handles.

The box with Michael's shoes is too big, so, out comes the shoes wrapped in a white handkerchief. Mam ties them with a blue ribbon and lays other bits and bobs around them so they won't be crushed.

Suddenly Mam is gone again, sitting down hard on the bed, clutching her belly. She can't breathe.

"What is it? Shall I fetch Da?"

She shakes her head and pulls me into a hug. She rocks me in her lap. She's trembling, racked with sobs that stay locked inside. "I can't leave him," she says.

She means Michael of course. My brother, laid to rest in Ballymore's churchyard.

"He'll be coming with us, so he will," I tell her.

She tousles my hair. "You're a good boy, Finn. But he's here telling me not to go. What will I do?"

Da puts his head round the door, whistling. It's time to leave for Queenstown where we will stay with a friend of Da's who lives near the docks. He sees Mam, thin as the ghost of Michael and enfolds her in his arms. "It's blue skies where we're going, Molly," he says, and Mam's sobs break free. Da looks over her head at me, closes his eyes tight and tells her. "Sure and it's Saint Michael himself who watches over the ships that's coming with us."

I try to be helpful. "And just in case, we've got him packed in our bag too," I say.

It's good that Mam cries. She looks sad but Da says he can see roses in her cheeks. I look, but all I can see is her cheeks the color of stormy water and the redness of roses is around her eyes.

Da's looking forward to a few last pints with his friends. I'm looking forward to the glories of fish and chips that I know will be waiting for me in Queenstown because Mam promised me they would and she keeps her promises on account of God. Bridie is always happy. It's only Mam who is looking back at Michael, two years old in his new shoes, toddling across the floor.

Last week, a day in Queenstown was like the Christmas's in the stories with the gifts and miracles. I'm mad for the shopping. Brown shoes and a blue shirt for me. The blue socks and matching bonnet for Bridie. A hat with blue flowers for Mam and a blue ribbon for Michael. Blue is Mam's favorite color.

"No matter how hungry we are, behind the rain, the sky is blue," she says.

Da hushes me. I think he can see inside my head because he puts a word in my ear about the weather. "Sure we know the world is full of grey rain, Finn, but even fools know that New York has the bluest skies."

"Every day?"

Da nods and gives me a wink. "It does."

APRIL 9, 1912
countdown – 6 days

A poor child's feet grow wrapped in stray rags tied with string. It's lovely they are for the freedom of the hills. Wet cloths drying at night on the hearth, warm and hard as leather in the morning. My Bridie is too small for Michael's shoes; she wears knitted socks, blue as her eyes.

All proper shoes are brown. Mam and Da have proper shoes. I help with the polishing. Tonight I have three pairs to polish, ready for the ship. Tomorrow we're going to New York.

We'll not be shaming our cousins with scuffed shoes. My fingernails are stained with the brown paste. Mam shakes her head with a soft shushing sound. "It's clean hands that'll be making the good impressions," she says. "You look after those new shoes now, or I'll skin you alive, so I will."

5
ON YE GO

FINN – APRIL 10, 1912
countdown – 5 days

It's April 10th – the big day of leaving.

"Don't be dawdling now," Mam says. "Sure there'll be hell to pay if we're late. Your father's already there on the dock waiting for us all. We don't want Titanic to leave without us now do we," she says, pulling my sleeve. She's avoiding the corner where I'm sure Michael stands telling her again, not to go.

"We don't."

"Take Bridie," Mam says. "Make sure her new socks are in your pocket, now."

Bridie likes to kick them off and Mam is determined she'll reach America wearing two blue socks and a bonnet to match. All thoughts of Michael are pushed aside in her haste not to upset Da.

Mam grabs the two bundles of everything that's precious to us. "The White Star Line won't wait for the likes of us, so it won't." She looks over her shoulder – a last look into the corner at Michael.

She doesn't want to go but I know she will. "I promised

your daddy we'd be there on time," she mutters to herself every few minutes. So I know we'll go. I glance into the corner squinting and imagine the fuzzy shape of a boy standing there. "You'd better stay or we won't stand a chance," I whisper to him. But I don't send him the whisper so much as throw it like a brick.

The three of us are entirely too early. There's not a tinker's chance of being late. It's all in Mam's head. It's slow going but we're well-fortified with tea and bread for breakfast. Mam gives me a pained smile and takes deep breaths that sound like sighs. I glance up at the white clouds blowing like summer cobwebs. "It's a grand blue sky," I say.

Mam's face is frantic as we board the tender that will take us clear of the harbor to Titanic. The Atlantic is a rolling field of grey oil, the color of Mam's cheeks.

My first vision of Titanic is a black castle with turrets flying a red flag with a white star, and the water sparkling and frothing around her like a lace hem. There's a cruel wind and it's windier still when we leave the shore. Mam moans like a sheep. The sounds all around me are wild with colors. Blue sky, yellow clouds, and a thin gold line painted onto the side of the ship. Mam explained once how ears can see colors as sure as the eyes can hear music when looking at the stars.

Noses are clever too. I can always smell the salt in the air of Ballymore. I lick my lips. It's the salt of Ireland. I close my eyes and say goodbye. I do what Da tells Mam and I don't look back. Da tells me we will stay in a cabin far below that gold line.

My new shoes squeak like a wee mouse. The pain of each squeak fair keeps me on my toes. Da says by the time we get to New York, I'll have worn them in and own a couple of grand callouses as tough as his leather belt, but I don't want to lose the squeaking because when I walk, I hear my shoes singing *new shoes new school* with each step that brings me closer to New York and my cousins who go to school who have bacon and eggs and new shoes every week.

My heels are raw as the bloody nose Ciaron Feeny gave me for saying his sister was a wee baggage which didn't seem like such a terrible thing because I'd heard his friends say it. Mam says only hooligans repeat what other people say when they don't know what it means, and I tell her that I *did* know, and all it means is a small suitcase. Mam gave me a thick ear to remind me of keeping a civil tongue in my head.

I try to get a rise out of Mam to cheer her by telling her our bag with the wooden handles means we're taking 'wee baggage' with us. She's feeling sad, again, after leaving Michael in the churchyard. She doesn't smile. She works the rosary beads in a way that scares me. If they break Mam will die. I know she keeps my brother with her in the beads and the lock of his hair in her book of miracles. Da told her to pack only what she couldn't bear to leave behind. Michael's shoes tied in blue ribbon and a lock of his hair will comfort her in America. I have to be especially good so that she sees me. If Michael is in the boat with us, Mam can't see him because her eyes are squeezed shut, as tight as her grip on her rosary. And she can't hear him either. The noise of the boat's motor deafens the cloud of shrieking seagulls that follow us.

I was hoping to get a rise out of Mam with the wee baggage remark. A thick ear now and then is well worth my while, and the pain of mice nibbling my heels only reminds me how lucky I am to have the shoes and the shoe polish and the two brushes that stick together like a pair of hedgehogs.

HER LADYSHIP

FINN – APRIL 10, 1912
countdown – 5 days

Until now, I've only seen Titanic's true profile on a postcard. The glorious silhouette of her four black smokestacks and the red flag with the white star fixed on a frozen sea, printed there on a scrap of paper. But now, as our ferry approaches her, she's alive, and Da says, "well, what do ye think of her?" but it's not a real question, and now I know why they call ships females because I'm that in awe of Titanic that I want to light a candle to her like Mam does to Our Lady.

The postcard water foams to life and slaps at her sides. Three of her four funnels billow with blue smoke that bluster the white clouds into a grey dragon riding the wind across the sky. To me, the ship is breathing. The dragon turns into a long wispy shape and disappears so there's no need to call on St. Michael who is safe in our bag.

There's a great flurry of activity as we line up to board. A crewman takes Bridie from me and another almost carries Mam up the swaying ropes. When it's my turn to climb the ladder the ship is lost to me. I never see Titanic again. Not properly. She's too big and I can only see parts of her. I'm three-foot-ten-inches-tall, perhaps as old as six, over-excited, and my new shoes are full of wee knives. But I catch the excitement from the white decks in the spray above me. I hear, orders being shouted and there's a blur of joyful waving.

A cheeky wind threatens to steal my cap, and I keep hold of it under my arm until I can stuff it into the pocket of my coat. Da says not to look down, and it's all I can do not to laugh. For there's only the wonders of a floating palace above me, and looking up is grand. Da keeps close behind me so I don't fall. I gaze up at Titanic and the sky is filled with the portholes on either side of me, and as high as I can see there's a black wall. Da points to a round button called a rivet and says, that's my work, son. He's smiling fit to burst and I grin back at him, proud to be part of the great ship through the miracle of Da's powerful rivets.

From inside the ship I feel Titanic is restless to be away. She creaks and groans, straining at her anchors. Da and I leave Mam and Bridie in our cabin and go for an explore. "We're on an adventure," Da says. I've never seen him so happy. The walls start to clank, and I almost fall but Da catches me by the collar and shows me how to widen my feet for the balance. Soon I'm walking like a real sailor.

"That's the propellers you can hear, big as Ballymore church," Da says. "We're on our way. Listen to the floor, now. There's an entire row of giant furnaces beneath our feet, bigger than the propellers, they are, and men feeding them day and night with a thousand tons of coal."

I listen to the ship's thunder roaring clear through my shoes. I imagine being inside a hungry dragon who breathes fire through the funnels of the ship. But the most enormous thing of all is when Titanic says goodbye to Ireland with a blast of sound that picks me up and shakes me like a terrier with a rat. It feels as if the bell is inside my heart, ringing me.

From steerage I can't see the promenade decks or imagine the gleaming silverware and flowers and the scalloped blue and gold porcelain with the red flag and white star. These things are above me in every way. But everything I *do* see is clean: spotless floors, bunk beds with white sheets and folded grey blankets. The whiteness of the walls is blinding. Mam and Da's meagre bundles look out of place in the corner where there's no room for Michael: one cloth bag with handles, a pillowcase of clothes, and Da's bag of tools for his new job in New York. The only thing that looks at home are my shoes. Shiny and new. Polished but for one wee cat-scratch from kicking a last Irish stone on the Queenstown wharf. I got a thick ear from Mam for my trouble. No worries. It will be no bother to fill it with the brown polish, good as new.

I perch on the highest bunk, my long grey socks dangling over the side, grazed knees slightly above and stare at my shoes on the opposite bunk where my best blue shirt lies folded beside them. I'm in heaven in a world where my shoes have their own bed. Mam and Daddy and Bridie sleep on the main floor, with me king of the castle, lording it above, with the smell of something entirely mouthwatering floating through the corridors.

Da says we have our own dining room, but Mam doesn't seem to care. She's wobbling from side-to-side like Da after a few pints, and just as green about the gills as she used to describe him in the morning.

"I've left my sea legs back on the dock," she says. "Now, get some sleep darling boy. I'll be right here beside you." She steadies herself by closing her eyes, and forces me to lie on my side. Mam called ME her darling boy. I'm floating with happiness. She opens her eyes and stares wildly at the floor.

"Darling boy," she says again in a whisper. She kisses my cheek and I see that her eyes are with her sea legs back in Ireland.

Some wicked-cruel demon makes me ask her before I can stop my tongue. "Mam, is it Michael you can see there in the corner? Is he here?" That makes her cry and I'm sorry for upsetting the apple cart yet again. I'm forever upsetting apple carts. I'm even sorrier that Michael was born.

I glare at the corner in case he's thinking of showing himself. I scream in my head. "Michael, if you're here, be gone with you now to your Ballymore grave and leave us alone."

Da is off exploring and Bridie is fussing in her baby dreams, down below. Mam's fingers still cling to the bed rails, her hair and eyes wild as a storm. When she can breathe again she fetches Bridie and tucks her in next to me to keep her quiet. Mam gasps for air. "Michael," she says, "Rest now."

I want to tell her it's me, Finn, but I can read her face. Michael is in the room. It's Michael who's her darling boy.

"I'll stay right here," she assures me. "Watch over your sister now. Will you do that for me? Keep her to the wall... and don't be rolling out yourself." And then she grabs her mouth with one hand and I hear her heaving into the bucket in the corner, and I look down at her like an angel from heaven and see her fall into the new white sheets. She looks the same way she did the night Bridie was born. Small and sad, but lost under new grey blankets, the same color as her skin.

From my vantage point I'm eye-level with my shoes. They mock me. They pain me.

The creaking of the ship lulls me and my Bridie. The engines drum Titanic's steady heartbeat, and the Atlantic tries to rock me to sleep. But I'm too excited to sleep and now I think the ship is upset because I hear it whimpering. Bridie doesn't wake, and when I look down to ask Mam what's wrong with the ship, I realize the sound is Mam moaning into her new blanket. She's crying her prayers, her book open to Michael's curl, so I kiss Bridie and try to guess what the delicious smell is, preparing itself for our breakfast. Michael grins like a demon in the corner.

I whisper so as not to disturb Mam. "Damn your eyes Michael!" This thought fills my head with a serpent's hiss. I'm that angry. But along with the anger is fear. I've gone and torn it with God, and this disturbs me enough for my lovely adventure to sink into despair. Michael will be in New York, every day in a new corner. He's no longer a baby waddling in his new shoes, he's a big lad standing his ground, lording it over me. Now he rules the middle of the room and it's me in the corner, face to the wall for being too full of myself. Now God is going to show me the back of his hand for sure.

Under the covers my heels throb with the soreness, wishing they were a leather belt. But it had been grand for a while, walking in new shoes that squeak with the thought of walking to school. Mam says one day they'll be supple, and when I asked her what it means she says it's when shoes become part of your feet. The whole notion disturbs me entirely. Barefoot is glorious for digging the toes into sand and shoes in the bed is not something that's been encouraged. But Irish shoes have to behave like American shoes, so it's best not to worry my five-year-old head about it even if I might be six.

Arragh. It's no use. I lie awake with the holy terrors of blasphemy on my soul. I've damned by brother to hell. What manner of a brother would do such a thing? Maybe God will forgive me but Mam says He hears everything. "I'm sorry. Cross my heart and hope to die," I mutter. It will have to do. Sure I can't harm Michael since he's already safe in heaven. A place I'm not likely to be going.

I lie awake with a fierce secret. I know Mam is lying. She wants Michael to go. She says rest in peace often enough to his lock of hair. It's Michael who wants to stay. And here's me thinking heaven is a wonderful place and why wouldn't everyone want to go there.

I pretend I'm forgiven – a saved boy with the expectation of a fine breakfast. Maybe the grand sort of egg Mam told me about, and something called soldiers. I'll be eating an egg sitting in its own tall cup with a teaspoon and the white bread soft enough to cut into soldiers for the dipping. I think Mam knows of such miracles from books but she only has the one and when I ask her she says she can't read but holding a book is almost as grand, and it was her friend Katie Halloran who once did the cleaning for the archbishop in Dublin, and she'd seen the empty eggshells and the silver cups and thin slices of white bread thick with salted butter and cut into strips and the special long spoons for the sugar, wide spoons for the jam, fat round spoons for the soup, and tiny fairy spoons for the salt. I'm hungry to read about all manner of eggs and spoons and my insides rumble thinking of soldiers and jam, but then I'm always hungry.

Da had used the last of his wages to buy Mam the hat with a feather and me a blue shirt and my shoes for America. Mam told me they were not to be kicking shoes. Not until I was safe in America after the first impressions with my uncles and aunts, and then I could be kicking the likes of anything resembling stones with my cousins. I'll be kicking up my heels, Da says, overhearing us. And I can just feel the comfort of my leather-belt-heels, kicking American stones and cabbages and footballs on my way to school.

Still, I can't help but worry about powerful consequences. I may be kicking stones and cabbages all the way to hell, eternally stained as a boy who damned his own brother. Heaven's gates may be forever barred to me. But I may be wrong. Maybe God requires a boy in heaven who's wickedly disobedient – that full of himself to set a bad example for the good of the others.

When Mam goes to the dining hall for tea I shout GOETH AWAY into the corner. It sounds so silly I almost laugh but I need to be heard. I HATE YOU MICHAEL CLEARY! I HATE YOUR BLUE SWEATER! I HATE YOU AND YOUR DAMN SHOES! I shout until my face is hot and my head aches. I'm sorry I've woken Bridie and made her cry. I'm sorry my throat scratches. I'm sorry for throwing a fit. I'm almost sorry for everything, but if I go to hell for cursing, at least I've kept my promise to tell the truth.

Somehow all this anger makes me sleepy. But in the morning I'm feverish. A lovely egg breakfast means nothing. My shoes wait for me, daring me to accept their torture. I will put them on later because I deserve the knives in my heels. Every step will remind me of what I did. Every step will bring me closer to heaven for the suffering I'm supposed to have to deserve a place there.

I take my sore head outside, beyond caring. I'm that beyond saving I run gloriously barefoot, releasing a hooligan yell that trails after me until I stub my toe on a fierce bit of metal. I see a blur of red sky over a red ocean. I curse the ship. Then all hell boils inside me. I'm a cauldron. Rage spills out of me. I curse New York and my painful shoes. I curse Mam. I hate her! Finally, I lurch forward to hang limp as a rag over the railing and spew a stream of sickness over the side.

Strong hands grip my shoulders. "Seasickness is no shame, lad," a man says in a comforting Irish brogue. "Steady on now. Sure it'll all be over soon enough. Will I take you to your mother?"

I'm embarrassed. And I'm that ashamed to have reduced the ocean's vast majesty to a slop bucket. But when I can breathe again I send it my thanks for having no corners where jealousy and pride can haunt me. Still, losing my temper felt good. One day I'll have the courage to lose it in front of Mam and she'll be sorry. I think I'm growing up. I must be six. I wonder what's for breakfast. Sure, I could eat a horse.

MAMIE

FINN – APRIL 11, 1912
countdown – 4 days

Our dining room bowls are made of heavy china, finer than any I've seen, pure white with a White Star flag on the bottom and a red stripe running around the rim that reminds me of the gold line on the ship. I look for the eggs in cups but there's only porridge filling the bowls with the red stripe, and mugs of sweetened tea. Mam takes her tea back to her bed and I sit eating my porridge with an ordinary spoon. The room seems foggy with light. It feels cozy. I'm safe here. The anger is over, but eggs are too good for the likes of a boy who wishes his brother harm.

I'm thinking how much porridge a dragon would eat when a beautiful princess sits down at the table and asks if I mind. "Is this seat taken?" she says, and her smile lights up the room already filling with tobacco smoke.

I'm that gobsmacked I can only shake my head, no. "There might be eggs," I say, to be helpful.

"Well, I like eggs," she says, will I get you one?"

My eyes open, round as saucers. "In a cup?"

"I'll see what I can do. My name's Mamie, what's yours?"

"Finn Cleary, missus."

"Mamie Broughton-Smith." She corrects herself and shakes my hand. "My friends call me Mamie," she says. "We're going to get on like a house on fire." And she flashes me another princess of a smile, and when she gets up I see that she's going to have a baby.

Mamie brings back a miracle. A tray with three eggs in cups, three glasses of milk, and a stack of white bread, and I see what all the fuss is about butter. And then Mamie performs another miracle and lops the heads of the eggs, and slices the buttered bread into strips and calls them soldiers. So Mrs. Halloran hadn't been telling stories.

"Do you know about spoons?" I ask her, bold as a crow.

"I happen to be an expert on spoons," she says. "What would you like to know?"

"Are there fairy spoons for the salt?"

She makes a small measurement with her fingers. "Upstairs in first class," she says, "salt is served in tiny bowls with silver legs, one bowl for each person. And butter sits on the table in a silver dish with a lid like a hat and the butter is shaped into seashells and there are at least four spoons for everything."

She tells me about long-handled spoons for digging into tall glasses of pudding and something called ice cream, spoons with wee saws for the grapefruit. I don't stop her to ask what a grapefruit is for along comes the stories of the forks for digging into the tails of lobsters and salad forks and cake forks until she has me thinking she's a grand storyteller.

And then it's my turn to tell a story. "I'm going to school," I say. "And learn the entire alphabet and read a plethora of books."

Mamie's eyebrows show me she's surprised. "Plethora is a big word."

"I know two letters. F is for Finn."

She takes a pen and a Titanic postcard from her handbag and writes F-I-N-N on the back. "There, that's you."

I'm speechless, holding my name in my hand. "And can you write Cleary, missus?"

She takes back the postcard and writes more letters and pushes it back to me. She points to each letter and sounds them out. M-A-M-I-E. "Unless you call me this, I won't spell Cleary for you."

"I will."

"Do you promise?"

"I do."

"I didn't hear you."

"I do, *Mamie*," I say. "I promise on my boiled egg. Whatever you want. Cross my heart and..."

"Nobody should hope to die," Mamie says. She writes C-L-E-A-R-Y and then a row of letters. "There's your alphabet, I'll teach them to you at dinner and tomorrow you can try reading."

Somewhere on the paper are the P's and Q's I'm supposed to mind. I recognize the other letter I know. "M is for Michael."

She pats my hand and taps the M with her spoon. "M is for Mamie."

I learn B for Bridie while drinking the second glass of milk.

I'm on air with the entire alphabet in my hands and thinking about America where I'll have my own bowl of salt with silver legs and a fairy spoon and I think I'm in first-class heaven with the boiled egg and a princess teacher who knows about butter and soldiers and how to read. I tell her Mam is grey from the heaving ship and Bridie is crying so much that Da says he wants to jump overboard, and Mamie says she knows all about babies because that was her job as a nanny to an entire nursery of babies and children the likes of me.

"I couldn't find any jam," Mamie says, "but I have something better."

I think she means butter, but no, she means better. She brings a wee jar from her bag. "I always bring honey with me for my tea," she says. "And it's glorious with bread and butter." So one-by-one my soldiers are dipped into the second egg and I save one for the honey and I think there's nothing to beat the butter and the egg but then the honey takes me straight to heaven and for a moment I'm jealous of the baby growing inside Mamie and I wish she was my mother. There'd be no Michael, and I'd live on honey and books.

I fold the postcard in half and slide it into my pocket. A shadow pass over me the way it feels when the sun goes behind a cloud and I'm ashamed of being so full of myself. I'd cross myself but that's a private thing and there's Mamie smiling at me as innocent as a princess lamb. She'd never think such evil thoughts about *her* mother.

"Do you have a brother?" I blurt out.

She shakes her head, no. "But I grew up with half-brothers and sisters on a farm. Now let's find your mother and we'll see if we can't tempt her with honey in her tea."

Mamie has something called peppermints that calm the seasickness. I'm excited to show off my Bridie, and Mam will feel better for the honey in her tea and the peppermints and someone who knows about babies. M is for Mam. M is for Michael and Mamie and Me.

8

THE UNSUNG CHILD

FINN – APRIL 14, 1912. 8:20 P.M.
countdown – 3 hours 20 minutes

Three nights later, Mam says it's about time I cleaned my
shoes and got well rid of that hideous scuffmark, sure it's
getting on her nerves, but when I get out the hedgehog
brushes and open the polish Mam is clutching her insides and
telling me to stop filling the room with the foul stench of boot
polish or she'll skin me so she will. And it's too late to fetch
more peppermints from Mamie, and too late to move the
polishing to the dining hall. Da says after dinner, the place
turns into a tavern and I'm not to go down there unless it's an
emergency. And not a 'Bridie-crying emergency,' but that
water is fair gushing in through the porthole we haven't
even got.

APRIL 14, 1912. 11:40 P.M.
the collision

I'm dreaming about bowls with legs and eggs wearing shoes,
dancing at the end of my bed, when my shoes fall to the floor

with a crash and wake me. Were they dancing without me? Have they jumped? But Mam's new hat with the feather and all the things on the floor are sliding into the bucket corner and my first thought is that I want to save my shoes from the terrors of the bucket.

I know I'm night-dreaming when a harpy pokes me with her bony finger, *"get up with ye, Finnegan me lad. Look sharp now... and be putting on yer new shoes."* I pull on Michael's sweater, and she tugs at the hole in the shoulder with the same icy fingernail that just clawed open a vein in Titanic's belly and grins at me with red teeth. *"Not this old thing. It's a special occasion,"* she hisses. *"We've arrived. Tis the blue shirt for America, ye want to be wearing now. Don't keep New York waiting."*

The bells in the passage are ringing like it's three Sundays all at once. Mam can hardly stand, but fear brings her sea legs all the way from Queenstown and she's swaddling Bridie into every blanket in sight. Da leaves us to make a plan with his new friends. He comes back inside the shake of a lamb's tail, red with anger. There are no white vests for the likes of us, he says. And the gates are padlocked. It's entirely my fault. God has barred the gates of heaven for all of us on account of my sins. Da's face is turning white as the vests as he lifts me down from the bunk in heaven.

Not to worry. He knows the ship like the back of his hand. Soon the gates will be opened. Mam shoves Bridie's blue socks into my pocket and a small bundle into my arms. I recognize the blue ribbon. "Take these for me," she says. "I'll not be leaving them behind." I shove it inside my shirt. I hope the peppermints are in there too but I remember Mamie didn't have any that last time we met. I'm dizzy. I can't feel my feet. I feel Mamie's postcard quicken in my pocket and throb against my heart. An unearthly voice surrounds me, and I realized it's me, calling for Saint Michael. Da carries his knapsack of tools and drags Mam behind us and we slosh through freezing water, but he's blue with cold now, and when my eyes meet Mam's I feel an icy grip on my heart. She's smiling, listening to Michael, and she's happier than I've seen her in a good long while. And then her rosary beads break and scatter to kingdom come.

APRIL 14, 1912, MIDNIGHT
time stops

My boots are that heavy with the water I feel dragged into a pit. And then Da grabs my head and kisses it once and I feel a blow of white light behind my ear. Da forces my head under the water. I'm too surprised to struggle and by then I'm half mad with the cold so I call out for Mamie and dark water gurgles down my throat making me light-headed. And instead of sinking, I rise from the icy water and slip through the bars, easy as a cat. And I look down to see that Da is crying, holding onto something beneath the water that looks like a boy wearing my best blue shirt.

I hear Mamie calling me and it's easy to find her. She's splashing her arms in the water with her head looking for all the world like it's sitting on a white plate but I know it's the life jacket under her chin. She's fighting to stay afloat. I see a red lump that's pulling her down and I shout to her to let go of it and take my hand.

She refuses and I turn to leave because I don't want to watch her drown. But the lifeboat flips. Over she goes and slaps the water. The crewman rowing, clambers on top, king of the hill, and he reaches for the women and children splashing alongside. I shout to Mamie again from inside the sailor. "Grab my hand," and she does.

The crewman heaves her onto the upturned boat and the red thing comes with her, and Mamie is so pleased she smiles at the night sky even though she can't see me and her labor pains begin. She has saved the red bag and now she can give birth, but her fingers are frozen around the handles and she lets it comfort her that she's connected to something from Titanic when 'she' was a grand palace, and herself a princess, chosen from steerage to walk the upper decks and bring me things to eat and milk for Bridie and the peppermints for Mam that worked so well she prayed to them like a holy relic. Saint Peppermint, I teased Mam, and she smiled. "I'm feeling grand," she'd said. "Thanks to Mamie, and you being my lighthouse that Mamie couldn't resist."

I'm sad because Mam will never reach the land of the peppermints.

Titanic lowers herself into the sea. All that's visible is a great river of passengers running like mice around the decks and a ship that is sinking progressively deeper in the water.

I can't be sure if I'm in a nightmare. I'm alone. Dreaming in my bunk. But dreams aren't real. Dreams are crazy stories. I don't know how I know so much more than I did yesterday but I need to make sense of what I see and what I refuse to see. Wherever I am it's surely between heaven and hell. I hear hymns and angels singing but then there are the screams and the fear that hangs over everything like a foggy morning. I see the lifeboats against Titanic. Fairy boats. I hear mermaids singing with the angels.

Mam has fair beguiled me with terrifying stories of sea monsters and waterhorses that steal children who stray too near the shore. The world is full of trickery: fairy boats of hope, ghostly music, and the moon round as a clock, and here's me, flying in the sky. Swimming in the sky. And then, Titanic flickers like a candle and sputters out.

Titanic is diving like a waterhorse. Her long neck beneath the water. Her tail lies black on the surface. She snaps in two and her last funnel hits the water. The fairy boats bob in her wake.

The sky is wild with candles, all pushing and shoving to be the brightest star, and they melt where they touch the horizon in a fog of despair. The Atlantic reflects twice as many points of light reminding me of midnight mass in Ballymore church. It's as cold as Christmas. Titanic's funnels gasp their last and the soul of the ship leaves the water. A thousand passengers holding hands exhale their final warm breaths together, and the whole of it, the darkened ship and the music and the passengers, leave a holy haze over the empty ocean in the shape of a ghost ship. They hover there like a band of angels before they race off to heaven.

Below me is a shimmering bed of water with sleeping passengers pale as chalk, their heads lying back on the pillow of the ocean. The terrible peace of them dreaming stirs something inside me and I know I must follow Mamie. Mamie will know where to go – she provides bread and honey like miracles, so finding New York will be easy-peasy. I won't upset Mam for all the peppermints in China or all the apple carts in America. I'll be the one to take the sadness from her. Above me is a plethora of white stars, and I call out to Da that there's entirely too many, and he shouts back from the darkness that one 'White Star' is one too many for a holy night such as this. His laughter comforts me.

And then I remember to feel inside my shirt for the white cloth with the blue ribbon. It's gone. And I'm barefoot too. For sure I'm going straight to hell.

9

SHIP TO SHORE

FINN – APRIL 15, 1912 – 12:20 A.M.

I'm from Ireland, so I know a thing or two about banshees and going straight to hell, and I was one of the first to die, so I saw the worst of it from high above Titanic. And now I know things I've no business knowing, what with me never going to school. And it's a grand thing to be a five-year-old boy with the language of a poet. I hear a thousand voices in my head – memories of past lives mixed with messages from future strangers, parts of a greater me, and not, because I'm only a fragment of them. I'm small as a child and deep as the ocean. I fill the sky.

Mam's stories come back to me. The ones meant to turn me into a resilient boy but left me awake in my bed, listening to the wind for the wails of banshees coming for the dead. A lot of banshees took people away from our village. Sure they took our Michael and tried to take Mam and me the night I was born.

To survive the dream, I turn what I see into a story to tell my new friends in America, but what I can't see is a full moon or a storm because the April ocean is a mirror without a breath of wind on a moonless midnight, and the gale I imagined was entirely in my head. But the iceberg is there right enough. Beautiful and cold. Looming like a castle over a black landscape of reflected stars.

I will tell my cousins a white lie. How a banshee sprang on Titanic's prow – a wild witch riding a dragon ship, stirring a calm sea into a boiling cauldron. Her face was terrifying, I'll say, and I'll make an expression to prove it. I'll describe a harpy with seaweed hair, green as a shamrock. And how she whipped around the funnels of the doomed ship and blew it into the icy peak of a blue mountain that shone like a diamond rising from the water. I will recount how she looked up at me, grinning, toothless hag that she was. I'd been fearless and shouted "Leave Bridie be," at her, but she cackled louder than ever. She moaned and whistled, circling the four smokestacks, and howled herself around the crows nest fogging the watch's eyes. I smelled burning coal. I'll lower my voice to a whisper, and the youngest cousins will whimper for their mothers. Surely Saint Michael will appear with his sword and kill the dragon hag, and lift us to the top of the blue mountain with his wings. That's what I'll say.

My older cousin's eyes will be round as saucers. They'll give me toffee and beg me for more. My story will capture them, so it will. How the banshee wailed a hellish lullaby that lured the infant liner into the iceberg. Hush-a-by-baby Titanic. And how the ship buckled in half in a frenzy of twisted steel, and the sea of glass turned frothy with the death throes of a kraken, roiling with the screams of the infants tossed into the water.

Like fallen angels, they were. And one of them was my Bridie. Truth is, even now I hear their cries, lost in the wind like the echoes of baby seagulls. There'd been a grey silence when they disappeared forever, lulled into the calm face of an ocean well-fed, now smooth as blackened silver.

But it's still glowing with the phosphorescence of a thousand souls... phosphorescence – such a grand word to know, that shows the powerful joy of the human spirit entirely leaving the body in a final blaze of glory. And I think I will write my Bridie a grand poem with the bright new words fizzing in my head like soda water so that I never forget how she kicked her fat legs and arms for the joy of me when I waved hello in the mornings, and the sparkles of light that flew from her eyes when she gurgled my name like a burst bubble, and most of all, her rosebud smile.

Will I wake now? Will Mam shake me into the morning? Surely we'll trundle off to breakfast in that clattering dining hall, rubbing elbows with our neighbors, vying for tea and sugar and sausages. Mamie will wave me over. She will have saved me a chair. I lick the blood from my lips. It tastes like a tarnished spoon. I feel in my pocket for the gifts Mamie gave me. They're still there. Mamie *did* happen. I *was* her darling boy. She was real. *I'm* real. I know I'm real because my bottom lip is bleeding and my head aches like the devil, same as the time Mam boxed my ears for saying a rude word about St. Michael. Surely he would never hold that against me, child that I am, and him being a sainted angel and all. He'd be full of the forgiveness.

Mam says saints only forgive us if we're truly repentant. So, I tell the sky I'm really and truly sorry-hope-to-die, and the pain in my head eases a little. But I'm haunted by promises too big to carry – and it's not fair that the holy relic of Ballymore was left in the keeping of a boy known for upsetting apple carts.

APRIL 15, 1912 – 2:20 A.M.

The black sky is singing with stars. And now I'm falling. Falling through a plethora of pride and sin. Falling through a cloud of prayers into a new life, but I don't feel at all like an angel.

There's not enough time to say goodbye to Mam or Da or Bridie, so I wish for the blue eyes and a tin whistle like my best friend Marky Doyle got for his Christmas, and I wake up howling fit to wake the dead. Sure, I'm no angel. Maybe I'm a banshee.

10

SALT OF THE EARTH

FINN – APRIL 15, 1912 – 2:40 a.m.

After the ocean stills, a phantom moon illuminates the darkness and a disembodied voice behind it speaks. "Time is an unspoiled stream of pure memories," it says. "Listen carefully. It runs deep beneath the River Styx, tracking the waters of forgetfulness bend for bend, winding towards rebirth." It shushes my childish questions and continues. "I promise you, all will be revealed... in time. Although the river of memories is bound by common banks and currents, nothing fished from this backwater of recorded dreams is erased or diluted. There's no ferry. No ferryman. No waiting. Finn, this is *your* river."

"Are you God?"

"I am your teacher."

"Is this school then? I'm mad for school."

He laughs to himself. "It is."

The voice is encouraging. It contains a smile. How strange it is that humans learn how to live *after* they're dead. Does it mean that the living spend their days perfecting the art of dying? I envision my teacher as the headmaster of an invisible school. I'm wary. I've heard the stories of masters caning their pupils when they answer back after making a show of themselves. Too big for their boots, Mam used to say about anyone who acted too grand.

"Master Finn," the man-in-the-moon says, "here is your first lesson. Fish your river but throw back any dreams that are too small. Look to heaven for your answers. But remember, what is lost inevitably lies at your feet."

For a moment the voice sounds like Da. But then comes the gentle laugh and it isn't him. What is this mockery? Here I am, an innocent. A dead child with questions. My anger overflows the banks of the River Finn. Surely Da is somewhere nearby and why isn't he here, showing me how to stand firm as a sailor with sea legs on an unsteady deck?

I may be bargaining with a changeling but I decide it's worth my while to be polite. "Please Sir, do I have the honor of keeping time with a saint?"

"You do not."

"Then who? Is it an angel or a water sprite that you are?"

The quiet laugh bathes me in a friendly chuckle. "You're a smart lad. You'll need your wits about you where you're going. And you're close – I'm a time-keeper but only a lowly fisherman such as yourself."

My faceless moon-clock without hands or ill-fated numbers gently tows me towards a spring morning in Nova Scotia. I surrender to its power and encounter no haunted wasteland of floating debris but wake disoriented, hovering like a seagull on an unfamiliar shore.

The leg irons of jealousy and guilt that I'd dragged with me fly from me like escaped birds. Worrisome doubts fly after them. Sunshine warms my back. I float golden and weightless without a care. I dive into my river of fearless questions with painless answers. A compassionate presence has my back. Love has my back. I'm happy. I'm in love with happy. I'm in love with joy. The sainted man-in-the-moon himself is my teacher, all will be revealed, and I can still go to New York.

I'm thrilled to be dead, finally on even ground with Michael. At last, Mam will love me for my terrible troubles. Sure as a rainy day she waits for me inside a wild memory beside a table laden with cream cakes, as near as the River of Finn. Death is promising.

And so I land in a library of fresh hours. After all, rebirth is the next chapter of my story. And a promise is a promise.

APRIL 15, 1912, 11:00 P.M.

It doesn't take long for a demon's pitchfork to pierce my bubble of joy. I beg my teacher for help even though I know the moment's lesson is to defend myself here in 'big school' where I must face down phantom schoolyard bullies, alone. I continue to fall. The bullies continue to prod. I'm beside myself with jealousy. I hate Michael. I hate Mam. I hate life; and now I hate death. But admitting these faults only increases their strength. Their monstrous teeth and appetites snap at my heels already raw from my new shoes. The salt of the Atlantic stings my eyes. I think of the Atlantic as an enormous pool of tears. Where had the happiness of being dead gone? Where had the happiness of my shoes gone? Think, Finn. Think.

A loving voice calls me, hugs me, and I cling to it as if I'm drowning all over again. It's Mamie. She's a shape of light in the darkness – a hand to pull me from the crowd of drooling leering bullies.

She and I, we'd got on like a house on fire, but that gives me little comfort because a burning house is hardly a place of refuge. I need to turn and fight demons. I need to run. Michael wouldn't run. He'd fight a demon sure as any true dragonslayer. I need to hide. Behind a mother's skirts is said to be a good place. Sometimes a boy needs his mother.

"I can be your new mother," Mamie whispers, so close I spin around expecting to see her.

It's only a matter of time before I land in the eternal fires of hell. But I'm not ready for hell. Hell can't possibly be ready for me. When Mam was determined she used to say 'come hell or high water.' There's no hope in either choice. St. Michael surely won't save me. I'm fairly certain there's no saint named Finnegan, and if there is he'll not be saving the boy who lost the holy relic of Ballymore and betrayed his own brother out of jealousy.

Even Mamie can't save me from the sin of hating Mam's darling Michael. I'm entirely unworthy of saving. But Mam taught me a lot about the act of penance so there may be a way. Sins burst in my head like soap bubbles.

A dark scene floats by of someone else's sin that I'm meant to see. Two men in shiny yellow coats are unloading a rowboat. Its mother boat rocks gently under the moonlight a fair amount of yards out to sea. One of them takes a silver spoon, a miniature jar of jam, and a blue baby's sock from a blue pocket. I can't for the life of me understand what's happening, so I wait. There's an entire alphabet of sins I've yet to understand. After hate and jealousy I only know two: being full of myself and breaking a promise.

I lick my lips and taste the salt of Ireland. From down the beach my voice shouts don't look back, find Mam. But Mam is with Michael and Da is with his Bridie princess. My river overflows. It's an ocean once again. I'm of two minds. Two places at once. Two places; one decision. I call on Saint Peppermint to ease the seasickness and clear my head. There's only silence where I tell myself Michael is a real saint. So what chance could I possibly have next to him with a false saint I've created to cheer up Mam? Maybe inventing saints is a fifth sin. There's a plethora of sins.

The bubble changes color. It's filling with light. "It's not right to rob the dead," the second man says. "Put them back."

"It's not like I'm going to sell them," the first man replies. "You've gone soft, you have."

"They'll haunt you for sure. *And* it's against the law."

The first man pushes a damp white bundle into his greatcoat. "It's only a child. How scary could that be? Unless you intend to tell." He sends his companion a threatening dagger from his eyes. The jam jar has a wide crack, and he lobs it well out into deep water. "Well? Cat got your tongue?"

"If you want to be a ghoul it's none of my business and it's no skin off my beak if you go to jail. But I'll hold my peace just the same. I'm not after a fight."

I watch the jar sink like a stone. The taste of strawberries lingers in my mouth. The smells of peppermint, shoe polish, and tobacco smoke wafts by. I call out for Saint Michael but he doesn't come. "Saint Peppermint," I shout, loud enough to upset the seagulls. There's an empty shoe filling with pink water in the bottom of the boat. I recognize the scratch across the toe as my last significant contact with Ireland, too tempting to resist. I'd put my full weight behind that kick after naming the stone Michael. Its mate dangles from a young ankle, twisted in a fracture. My ankle. A broken bone sticks out like a twig above a sodden grey sock.

I relive the time my boot slowly made contact with a long jagged rock the size of St. Michael's statue. I was kicking the old life behind. Shoving the last obstacle to happiness out of my way. And that's for you Michael Cleary, I'd said.

"These shoes'll be fine for my Tom," the first man says. He searches my breeches' pocket and unfolds a soggy note stained blue from melting letters. On one side is a photo of the princess liner Titanic cut in half by the fold. He discards it in the slimy muck gathering in the bottom of the boat but the second man retrieves it. His flashlight shines on the blurry ink.

"Cleary," he reads aloud. "We should keep this with the body. It's a name, that is. It could help identify this boy for his family. It's not right to..." but the second man takes the postcard, wads it into a ball and flicks into the tidewater.

"What note?"

"Are you going to leave the boy his shirt, then? It looks new."

"It's the wrong size." He makes a last minute search of all my pockets and pulls out a mat of blue wool. He unravels it. It's another baby's sock. He has a pair. It looks so familiar and dear. I remember there had been so many blue things.

The second man shakes his head. "Let's get these bodies loaded into the cart or the birds will have their eyes."

For a moment the two men grunt with the weight of several bodies in water-logged clothes. A pair of rough hands fill a sack with booty. In go my shoes. In go a pair of blue-knitted booties and a silver spoon with a star.

"Surely to God you're never going to let your Tom wear a dead kid's shoes. Are you crazy?"

The cart plods forward and the beached boat fades into a foggy low-ceilinged tavern of laughter and clinking glasses. The fog clears and I see a woman and a boy sitting at a table, laughing. The boy looks like me. The woman looks up and waves at me but the bubble bursts quickly and takes the memories with it. I know and I don't know why this is important and soon I forget even that. I hear the clop clop of horses' hooves moving off into the distance. I should follow my shoes but I'm down the beach a ways and can't leave the terrible drama unfolding below me. It's time to choose. Life and death hold hands and I'm that desperate I want to run and never decide another thing.

I can't go to heaven without my shoes. Sure Mam would kill me if I presented myself shoeless. I promised I'd be careful, and now Michael's shoes are lost at sea with a shipload of passengers and a cargo of eggs and jam. Sure I'm thinking I've been drowning in spilled milk my entire life. I've been drowning in spilled salt – in bad luck.

"Then let go," a voice says. "Take my hand."

The devil I know fades next to the one I've never met. But it's not a new devil it's an old friend.

11

GOING NOVA

FINN – APRIL 15, 1912, 11 p.m.
21 hours after the sinking

A bedraggled animal lies sprawled on its side. An outstretched arm clutches a lump of scarlet wool. A man in a gleaming yellow coat and a woman clad in grey wool hunch over it. The man turns the animal over, and underneath the fur there's a young pregnant woman in a French lace nightgown stained pink at the back. There are embroidered letters on the collar, joined together with swirls. I can make out the letter 'F' as it's the first letter of my name and the one I know best. But shouldn't it be an 'M'? I'm drawn to the glittering snake of black beads at her throat. Is she dead?

The grey woman asks "Ansel, is it a selkie?" even though it's plain she knows better. The animal is a passenger, arrived from the belly of a great ship that's been spitting up lost souls all the morning like a great whale harpooned by a dirty spell. It's been twenty-three hours since the mountain of blue ice slit its throat. Twenty-one hours since its tail rose, breaching the surface in a final death throe, and giving up the ghost, slid under the waves, entirely. I'd heard its soul hiss away, joining the flares bursting on the horizon.

There'd been a strange beauty to it but I was past the cares of a wee boy by then. I was a grand poet thinking how beautiful a dying ship is when it slides without a fuss, slipping without so much as a wake of moonlight, and how a halo of flares is fitting last rites for such a holy moment, fireworks being a celebration of farewell and all. I am free. If it weren't for losing my shoes I'd be with Mam and Bridie beside a table in heaven, groaning with peppermints and jars of strawberry jam and a mountain of scones with lashings of clotted cream. B is for...? B is for Bridie.

Ansel chides the woman in the shawl. "Don't be so daft, Rose." Ah, her name is Rose.

A few grains of sand cling to the monogram's needlework reflecting the first echo of Monday's moon like tiny sequins. It's long past fishermen's hours, as April 15th prepares to die. It's revelations I'm having. This knowing about needlework and the poetry of sequins.

The seal lady twitches in pain. The yellow man lifts her. She falls limp in his arms like a rag doll. He moves her away from the tide and lays her back in the sand. I see the red on his hands. I think I know her. M is for...?

Ansel and Rose skin her of the black coat and cover her legs in a felt horse blanket. She has no shoes and Rose wraps her feet and begins to massage her toes, all the while blathering on, one woman's nonsense to another. Would you care for another cuppa m'dear? Now you must try the scones with the sultana's from Spain, fresh-made not an hour ago, and will I get you the sugar? And will you take another spoon of the jam?

I return to the water's edge where a pool of pink seawater slowly fills the imprint of the woman's body. I've seen similar shapes before, dug by a wriggling seal, for all that I lived near enough to a wild coast. But that was a long time ago.

Ansel rescues the fur coat from washing out to sea. He

searches the pockets and finds a folded bit of paper and a grand bauble of a diamond ring. These he pushes into his vest. He shakes the ocean from the drowned foxes and carries the coat over his arm, holding it away from him like a valet, and goes to assist his wife.

I'm surprised I know such things. Valets and diamonds and the like. I'm the son of a crofter turned boatwright turned riveter from a village where potatoes are more useful than diamonds. But it seems, while I'm floating bodiless, I have access to the books I've never learned to read and a wealth of secrets from everyone else in the world. And my head isn't crowded at all. I'm filled with wonder at the vast memories of the dead and the language I have to describe what I know.

Perhaps the dead can hear my memories as well, for all that I've had only a few years to gather my own childish thoughts. A boy has a plethora of questions about simple things that matter as much as all the grand memories of lace and sequins, and butlers worried about tarnished silver, and valets desperate to find the master's best gold cufflinks. And I'm angry and sad that now I'll never go to school.

"She's young," Rose says. "She's strong enough to bear the pains. They're close together now."

The mother's skin is pale as frosted glass and her body flickers like a candle. "Acht, she's no more than a lass," Rose says, and she calls her 'child,' begging her to take a wee nip of the brandy. "Come child, will you no take a sip for the pains. Wake up child. Your babby's coming!"

I hear my own dear Mam's voice echoing the same words. 'Wake up child.' But Mam's back on the ship and I hope she's risen from it like me, and is floating somewhere knowing all the things there is to know.

Like I know the baby inside the poor lady is dying and that I'm going to take its place. And I now remember my

Bridie the day she was born, and although it pains me to think of being a helpless baby, I know it's better than being a corpse. I know this well enough because I can see how my body was freed from the wreck when it split in two, and so it came to the surface where men in a boat hauled me from the waves. I'm wearing my shoes but one of them catches on the edge of the lifeboat and my ankle shatters. I think my shoes will dry just grand, and I won't be getting another thick ear for the state they're in because Mam will be more worried about the state of my ankle. But my greater crime is yet to come, wrapped in white cloth tied with a blue ribbon.

I welcome another reason to stay. I have a promise to keep and surely Mam will be proud of a son who keeps his promises. Princess Mamie needs me. I hear her calling and I'm hungry for the honey and toffee she might be carrying. It's curious how I can be hungry and dead at the same time, yet be outside my body at the other end of the beach deciding between heaven or the chance to go to school.

Mamie wants me to choose school. She's talking to me the way she did back on the ship.

"It'll be all right," she says. "It's the next best thing. Don't be afraid. Darling boy, it's a way we can stay together... remember?... like a house on fire."

I'm amazed that in the space of a few days, Mamie is willing to save me. We'd been friends from the start. Her helping Mam with Bridie – Mam being sick from the motion of the ship and all. Da had been grateful to leave us for a pint, and Princess Mamie knew right away that we'd get on like a house on fire. And she held the secrets of the alphabet and peppermints.

Rose pries the lady's fingers from the handle of the red carpet bag. I know it's Mamie, but I don't want to think of her laughter drowned in this body on the beach and so I think of her as a lady I must have dreamed I passed on the decks of the promenade, for a lady with baubles this grand would never be strolling the likes of 'Scotland Road' in steerage. The crew let a few of us children play in Scotland Road – the long passage next to us, deep in the belly of Titanic. Urchins they called us but they said it with smiles and rumpled our hair. But then, my Mamie WAS in steerage for a day, before... before? I can't remember.

Losing the bag rouses the poor lady as if her life had depended on keeping it safe. And so it had. I worry that now she's let go of it she'll let go of her life as well.

Rose reassures her by lifting the bag high enough for her to see. "Your bag is safe Mistress."

The word mistress brings panic to the lady's eyes. Desperate they are with dark circles like bruises. Great wild eyes she has, in a wintery white face. But the light in her eyes is sinking like the ship. And I remember she was hired the day after we met. A maid to a mistress. 'The jewels belong to my mistress,' she's telling me. Make sure milady gets them. I saw her... milady... Izzie... in the lifeboat...' but her thoughts trail away like a puff of smoke, and once again she's Mamie and not Mamie, and I know she's going to die and so I hold her hand and tell her how much I loved the cheese and the apples and the chocolate biscuits, and the stories about spoons. She calms down inside where her baby decides to give up its spirit. "It's time," Mamie says to me. "Finn, listen to me. It will help me if you take her place." Her! I'm going to be a girl then. I don't fancy that but I want to help Mamie. Repay her for her kindness, and besides, I'm not keen on this floating business and I'm powerful hungry. Mamie smiles. "Promise me you won't leave her."

"I promise." Mamie's name slips away and comes back as Mam.

Rose rubs the woman's wrists. "What's your name my dear?"

The lady's fingers are covered in glittery rings. "Mam..." she starts to say. "Izzie."

"Is he what?" Ansel says, misunderstanding entirely. "Who are you on about, lass?"

Rose is sure. "I think she's asking if her husband is safe. Is your husband safe? Aye he is," she says for the sake of the birthing. But she shakes her head and sends her husband a look that says there's no hope. The lady's lost too much blood. And I see inside Rose's mind that she knows from her own miscarriages. She knows too well the limits a woman's body can take and no more.

"Mamie," the woman says clearly. "It's too soon."

"Och, she's calling for her ma," Rose says to her husband. She slides off the bracelets and a gold watch mindful of their value but for all their worth the pile they make looks useless as a hill of blighted potatoes. They fill the pockets of Ansel's yellow coat and their significance vanishes. "Rich ladies die as often as poor ones," he says.

Rose stops rubbing the lady's fingers and prods beneath Mamie's skirts, singing a Scottish song without real words that's barely a tune. She croons about high roads and low roads, and the baby's head crowns. I should look away but I can't. That thing is going to be me.

I hear the thing speak in my head. "No I'm not, Finn Cleary, I've a mind of my own, thank you very much."

I try to remember who I am. Who I was. Something about a ship and a lady. *This* lady.

"She's a nasty cut there on her forehead," Ansel says, and he fetches a clean rag from the depths of Rose's special bag she hauls out for emergencies. I read Rose's thoughts. She believes in emergencies. Out pours a river of smelling salts, evil-smelling ointments, gauze bandages, scissors, and another wee flask of brandy. Rose tips the bottle against the woman's lips but she turns her head and Rose has to dip a cloth in the brandy and moisten her mouth. Then the mouth opens like a baby bird, enough to take a tiny sip. She coughs up the brandy but I can't tell if it's blood or brandy or water because they're all the same color. Ansel pats a brandy-soaked cloth on the lady's cut. It must sting because the lady flinches away and tries to stop him with her hand. Gold rings flash and Rose says to take them off quick before her fingers swell and they kill her for sure.

Ansel is careful to count the rings and says "there's seven rings missus. Dinna fret, lass. They're all here in my pocket." But he turns away knowing there's no use. I see him place his huge hands on Rose's shoulders. He whispers "save the bairn. It's all we can do for her."

The lady tries again and manages to tell the whole of her name in a great long sigh. "My name is Mamie," she says. "There's jewels... I had a bag."

It's coming back to me again. I know this lady. This stranger. The name Mamie...? No. Is it Mam? And I remember another mother and another baby and a hill overlooking a cold harbor.

"Your babby's coming, Mamie, you must push m'dear," Rose says. "Your things are right here beside you. Think on your babby mistress."

Mamie is weak but she leans up on her elbows and declares a wild thing to a stranger birthing her baby. "I have to go now."

Rose shouts louder. "Hold on. Hold on to my hand Mamie."

But Mamie is swimming and I'm swimming with her, fighting against the current that's begging to take us. "I want to stay but I've got to go," she says. "It's so lovely and warm." Her words are in my head. Why is someone shouting the word Atlantic? But something's wrong; it means something different. What's right is that she's going to America. She's going home and I'm going to school. I hear a different voice call out, *hold on to my hand*. A woman screams and falls silent. Black hands grab Mamie and croon a lullaby, but the lullaby is for Mamie's new mother, an exhausted girl. I see her hair dark hair splayed against a white lace pillow. How can Mamie be a mother and a newborn at the same time? But I need to go and Mamie needs to come with me. She returns to the beach and the chill off the ocean brings her to her senses.

Rose is surprised by Mamie's sudden intake of breath. "I'm here Mamie. There's a good lass."

"You're all right," Ansel says, looking queasy. "You're on land, Mistress. Was your husband no on the ship?"

Ansel says he's going for help as Mamie squirms and fights with going or staying. She can't make up her mind and she panics. "I saw it. I saw it go down," she says. "The lifeboat... I saw it roll on its side. I waited for it to come right... someone... Finn... grabbed my hand. Where's Finn? Where's my ... mistress?"

"Mistress... aye, there now, was your husband no on the ship?" Ansel repeats.

The question is an echo now, breaking through waves of saltwater and panic. "What's your man's name mistress?"

I listen to Mamie's thoughts. Her name returns. Princess Mamie. She smiles. She's remembering the first night Master Carlyle pinned her in a heated embrace. He'd been gallant then, in his seductions.

I'm fighting to breathe. Who is Bridie? Hurry, the ship will leave without us. I look down at the lady on the sand.

"Come on Finn," she says without moving her lips. "Is this seat taken? Four spoons for everything."

The baby's shoulders are born and out it slips like a baby seal after all, on a wave of pink water. And this red thing follows that Rose cuts with her scissors and ties off with a ribbon of gauze. The newborn's cries fill the air like an angry seagull. And Ansel lifts the lady's shadow from the beach and tears off for help.

"It's a girl," Rose says, and I fall into the eyes of the newborn before it dies and jump back out although there's room for two. There is a rush of darker blood on the sand.

Rose covers the baby in another horse blanket but not before I see a dark bruise on what will soon be my very own leg. High up on the thigh it is, and I remember Mam saying she'd beat me black and blue if I ever gave her the lip like Brian Kennedy gave to his poor mother, but she would laugh and cuff my ear and kiss my cheek so it wasn't like I'd be worrying after the beatings that some boys got for their trouble.

"Quick, take her hand," Mamie shouts. "Finn you have to jump. Please. Promise me you won't abandon her. Save her for me. Promise me. You said you'd do anything for me."

"I promise again, crossing my heart, and say goodbye to Mamie and my own Mam before I jump, and say hello to my new Ma, Lilian-Rose Waters and my new Pa, Ansel, and a nameless wee baggage who's not best pleased to see me. But she's not long for this world and I'll have to be patient."

Mamie smiles at Rose Waters with that pale sadness I'd seen on Mam so many times when she didn't know I was looking. "Her father is ..." *shall she say the name?* Death says yes, it's now or never. "Her father is Master Carlyle Douglas, the son and heir to Lord Douglas of Fabersham Hall, Hertfordshire. His mother Lady Douglas knows."

"She's delirious," Pa says, back from down the shore where bodies are being piled. "There's nay doctors. Jimmy McPhee's away down the beach. He says they're all away to the makeshift morgue, in the ice arena up in Halifax. We'll have to shift for ourselves."

"No one knows she's given birth," Ma says quietly to herself as if she can't believe the truth of it. "If Mamie dies, we can keep the child safe enough, and look for her people when things calm down. There's no use while we can't get a sensible word from her poor wee mother."

But there's been sensible words aplenty, and now Mamie thins into nothing – a nightgown abandoned on a beach.

"Mamie!" Ma shouts, shaking her. "Come now. Dinna go. Your babby girl's here all safe and sound. So now then, let's be getting you to your bed and you can sleep a whiley all tucked up nice and dry."

But Mamie's fever races down the beach and I watch from somewhere above the scene of three people and a newborn at the ocean's edge as Mamie's ghost dives headlong into the wild surf, and swims back to the ship.

Ma gathers up her emergency fixings and another pink pool drains into the beach and for a moment the lady's shape is covered by the froth of in-coming high tide that pushes the bloody fluids aside with white foam, and carries it away as if nothing happened. The beach is washed clean as a new slate. And I know this from never being to school or seeing chalk because I learned how to make the letter 'F' for Finn on a bitty of paper with a pencil Da brought back with him from Belfast.

Ma covers the afterbirth and the carpet bag and the baby wrapped in a lace nightgown, with the wet fur coat that the woman... I once knew her name... no longer needs. The weight of the animal on top of me takes my breath. *Hurry the ship will leave without us.* I jump from the fur. I don't want to go back in there but the girl child is asleep. Ma wraps the lady in the horse blanket caked with red sand. The rescue workers, headed by Pa's drinking pal, Jimmy McPhee, come to take away the passenger lady on a stretcher. I see Pa give a nod to his friend and busy himself with his own business. Jimmy stares at the child but says nothing. "Is she dead?" he says. "I've room in the cart for one more but I have to go."

I jump back into the infant. It's lighter with the animal taken away. I can breathe. I need to sleep but I have to remember where I am. Where I was. And where they're taking me so I can find my way back to Mam. I hear Bridie crying. "Hush now ye're all right now, a voice says." Mam? But it's me that's crying as Mamie's child. I mustn't go to sleep. I have to remember. I float like a seagull and watch the procession below. I can go with Mamie or my new Ma. Mamie is beside me inside a seagull. We can fly away together but I've already promised her I'd stay. "Let's see your new life," Mamie says. "I have to go soon. You must stay. Please hurry, my daughter's spirit is slipping away."

12

KID BROTHER

FINN – APRIL 15, 1912, 7 p.m.

A line of twin tracks shuffle their way to the cottage in the dunes. Pa crosses himself and burns the afterbirth. He takes the jewels from his pockets and tips them into a bowl before hanging his yellow slicker on a hook. He sets the kettle to boiling and makes a brew of strong tea. Both cups are made sweet and topped up with brandy. I lie in the makeshift cradle between my new parents.

Rose keeps one hand on my clean blanket as she finishes her tea. Ansel reads the note. "It's a cleaning ticket," he says. "No name. A room number, I think. I can't make it out but there's a red flag and a white star, right enough."

Rose stands at a sink and rinses the blood from the nightgown with a strange look in her eyes, and the stain falls from the fabric like magic. She hangs it to dry... a silk flag in front of the hearth, looking for all the world like the ghost of the lady who left the white shell of her nightgown and a pocket full of gold rings on a beach. Was she a princess? My new Ma throws a handful of dried herbs on the flames, and calculates how many handkerchiefs she can make from the length of lace that dries instantly in the fierce heat. Maybe a dozen to sell to the ladies in Halifax.

The next day, Ma wraps me in the dead lady's nightgown to appease the spirit of the mother she imagines berating her for the notion of handkerchiefs. She stares like a dreamer, hungry for me to wake. "She looks like a rich babby," she says to the wallpaper.

"Ye ken it's the lace, mind," Ansel says, peering sideways, poking the nightgown aside with one calloused finger to check my face. "Bairns all look the same. Poor ones or no. But she's bonnie, I'll give ye that."

Ma fingers the fine silk. She traces the floral pattern of the lace border. It sends her into a trance and a lady's voice I once knew. "Save... the lace...," she whispers.

Rose hears too. "Lace," she announces loudly. "Lacey," she repeats, testing the strength of it, and shushes herself so as to not wake me. "Lacey Waters," she whispers. "Daughter of Lilian-Rose and Ansel Waters."

Ansel stirs himself and stretches. He tickles my hand with one of his fingers and I grasp it the way Mamie grasped the hand from the lifeboat. He smiles and shakes his head. I feel his thoughts as my own. We're both ravenous, and Ma's kitchen has been neglected for hours. There are no smells of cooking. No sounds of hissing steam. "Aye, well, call her what ye will," my new Pa says. "But leave the child be. Can ye no see she's sleeping? Lilian-Rose Waters, d'ye ken it's half-past-five? Will I go to the 'Mermaid' for my tea?" He's not happy.

My new Ma has two names. Pa says each of them in a different voice.

Lilian-Rose Waters doesn't hear. "You should be off now

to the 'Mermaid' for your tea," she says, speaking more to the fragile life that's me and not me, nestled in the cradle. Pa tells Lacey when she's older, how it was an old cod barrel cut lengthwise that Ma was intending for a garden of marigolds. "Be off with ye, and leave me to the wee lass," Ma says. "I'll no be clattering my pots and pans when it's quiet that's needed. Peace and quiet for her dead Ma as well. May she rest in peace."

Pa peels my fingers from his. I beg him to stay. He's my lifeboat, but he leaves, and Ma sits up, as if surprised. She pulls a box from under the bed. Her eyes are feverish. The box is full of baby clothes. She rummages to find something, and pulls out a banana-shaped glass bottle like the one Mamie gave Mam for Bridie. Ma fills it with warm milk and I don't know if I'm more hungry or sleepy.

I'm heavy with the milk inside me. I hear Ma humming as she folds the baby clothes.

Mamie leans over and kisses my cheek. "Thank you Finn," she says. "I have to go now, darling boy."

I sleep, curiously comforted by the scent of drying foxes and salted cod that settles over me in the cradle. I'm a fish in the sea and the storm is over.

It takes a week but the sodden black fur dries the reddish brown of a fox – the same color as my lost shoes. Shoes that used to be important. I know because when it's dark the moon tells me they are. But I'm forgetting myself, vying for position with the wee girl, Lacey, who hasn't died. I call Mamie to ask her if I can go now, but she doesn't come back. My promise is sealed.

The carpet bag is stuffed carelessly with small colored bags that spill with a hard glitter of sapphires and diamonds and pearls and jet and amber... brooches in the shape of birds and animals and flowers.

Curious twists of fine lingerie wrap ornaments and boxes, a silver hairbrush, and a change purse knitted with slivery chains and glass beads. "Was the Titanic a pirate ship?" Ma says, in awe. Pa says rich ships like that are always full of pirates. "This treasure belongs to Lacey," Ma says.

Pa agrees. "It's best to lie low," he says, "folk'll be asking questions if any baubles come to light. I've already heard it said the bodies are being guarded from pickpockets and souvenir hunters. Goulish it is."

"But we're saving Mamie's jewels for the child," Ma says. "That's no stealing."

"And will ye be telling *that* to a judge?" Pa replies. "It isna what it *is*, it's what it *looks* like, Lil. The wee babby won't be needing it for a long bitty. We'll see what comes, shall we. Nothing is certain.... except we'd be hanged for sure if we showed our heads. And not a farthing of it is ours. We'll keep it aside for the lassie and God will tell me what to do."

I guess Ma has more than two names.

I'm unceremoniously pushed out of the infant with the same force as the water that sucked me from the ship and propelled me to the surface, and I swirl away, caught in a stream of moonlight. Do I have somewhere to go? But where? In search of my mother? But which one? And who is this new force that takes my hand, pulling me into the cold? Is it the moon? Is it my shy teacher?

Mamie's daughter may not thrive and I intend to keep my promise and take her place or watch over her, although I don't see why Mamie can't be her guardian angel. Sure that must be a mother's first duty. Still, a promise is a promise, and I mourn the loss of my second mother. Mam used to say third time lucky.

In effect I'm a bodiless spirit who has been rejected-ejected from the body of an infant girl. It does nothing to lessen my sense of low self-esteem. I'm determined to leave the child in order to give her time to die in peace. Mamie had sensed her imminent death and who was I to argue with her. Mamie was perfect. The thought that I would be her special child and please her keeps me as happy as I have any right to be, all things considered. In the meantime, the voice belonging to the hand that dragged me, shushes me. "Finn, it's not too late. Mamie was wrong," and then the hand lets me go.

I must bide my time exploring what passes for heaven after I discover one doesn't just come and go. And besides, the gates of heaven are yet another set of bars denying me entrance. Gates with locks are ghastly things for exiting or entering. Am I to be forever denied a better life?

Mam's book with the terrifying rules had said yes. My heart isn't so sure. I listen to my heart and hope for the best. In other words, I cross my fingers against the evil eye and keep a clear head.

I am a lost boy, homeless and shoeless, left to play in a starry sky. It's that or play the ghoul, counting the hours waiting on a child's death for my opportunity to claim her body. I keep in mind it was an invitation from Mamie and no desperate scheme of my own. That seems to rest easy with me.

But my wish has been granted. I'm dead, so now Mam will love me. I'm glad we're all dead; there's no competing with a ghost who knows how to spell Cleary. I'll miss going to school and without my shoes my heels won't need to be as tough as Da's leather belt. Surely the hills of heaven won't require shoes that squeak like mice or feet that turn into shoes. And then a thought hits me a staggering blow. I won't *be* reaching heaven. Sure I've destroyed my chance of heaven with sins I can't even remember. But God will remember and so it's hopeless I am for the harps and the angels that Mam says sing all day long at the gates of heaven. For she saw them when she was there, and it was me who pulled her away, brought her back from being with Michael so she could never forgive me. And now I know why she didn't love me. Why she couldn't bear the sight of me in Michael's shoes.

I see Mam from a distance as I stand on my old rainy hill. She's smiling, singing to Bridie. There's no hint of sadness about her. I'm not missed. Mam is wholly content. I want to run to Mam and have her forgiveness but there's Michael looming over her like a guard dog baring his teeth, standing tall, wearing our blue sweater in its finer days. He holds out his hand to me and mine curls into a fist. I hate them both.

Michael looks fit as a fiddle. Heaven agrees with him. There's no hollowed eye sockets, grey from the consumption; no blue lips, no weakness at all. I can see he's full of himself. I don't need a big brother to teach me the alphabet. I have it safe in my pocket, and if I stay I can go to school and when I come back I'll have the big words to rub in his face the way his glorious holiness was rubbed in mine. But I'm a baby and I have no pockets. My alphabet is gone. I remember someone taking it, and then other interests consume me and I don't think about it anymore.

As if I hadn't seen Michael smirking in that corner my entire life, and how he turned away when I wore his shoes and glared at me until I fell, and laughed when Mam didn't catch me. And how Mam stared past me into the corner and left me crying on Michael's precious floor because I won't be falling anywhere again. I will rise and find New York. Mamie's daughter will find New York. These thoughts leave me feeling dizzy, choking down the hatred that's worse than cold turnip soup. As soon as I remember the soup, rain starts to pelt me like shards of ice. It tumbles into a blue curtain until I can't see the pair of them, Mam and Michael, hugging so close a communion wafer can't come between them.

A New York education will beat the bejesus out of Ballymore School. Michael will never write a book or meet a princess. Michael will never slay another dragon. Mam can lose herself in a book she can't read that rejoices over a useless word like goeth, and the God of her ceiling can praise her into heaven. I choose a world where there's a plethora of books and honey and peppermints. Sure, I already have a teacher.

I scream my hatred at them until I'm hoarse. I haven't the strength to shout how sorry I am but I'm not sorry anymore. Well, I am for my shoes but nothing more.

Michael is too strong for me, still guarding Mam like a bulldog. I want to punch his smile but he's twice my size. He turns his back to me, facing the wall of his blessed corner.

"Go to her.... it's *you* she wants," I shout at him. Mam doesn't startle at my voice. She refuses to hear me. "There's no need to tell her I was here. I only bring sinful news."

A grand entrance would be a wasted effort, and it's pointless to confess about the shoes if there's no-one to absolve me. It would only upset her. I can look after myself. My shoes can turn up like a bad penny if they so desire or disappear entirely. I don't care. I don't give a fiddler's fart. If she lives, Mamie's daughter will have shoes. I will have shoes.

I don't stay longer than the time it takes to impart my news. I'm towed back to earth as sure as lifeboat behind a ferry, and wake in a kitchen where a young girl is playing with a hideous doll. Her mother pours a glass of milk and suddenly I'm thirsty. The girl takes my sudden appearance as normal. "It took you long enough," she says in her head. "Where've you been this time?"

"This time?"

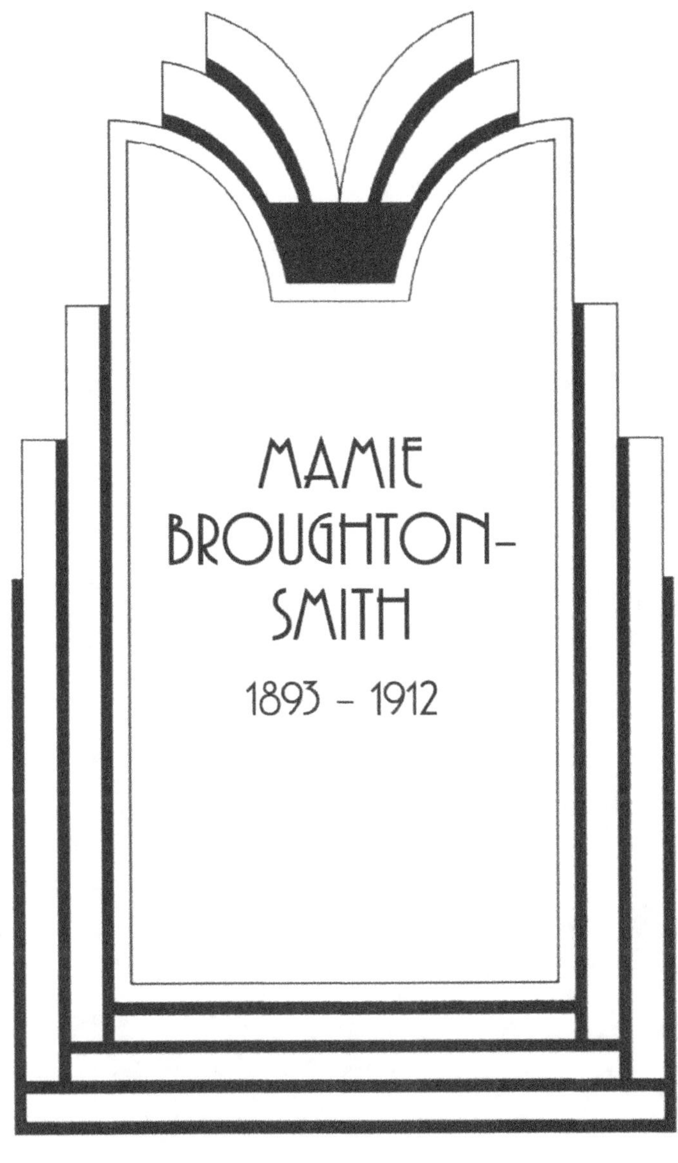

MAMIE
BROUGHTON-
SMITH
1893 – 1912

13

LITTLE RICH GIRL

The word excursion sounds like tremendous fun, but as the nanny of a spoiled child I'm hard put to consider it a holiday of any description. And when the trip is also a seaside birthday party for that child, it's a nightmare of transporting an over-excited miss already over the moon from five years of self-importance.

The return journey is an undertaking of a hundred untidy details. Packing up the remnants of exploded cake and parcels to get it all home again, shipshape, and then sort out the tired children, wind-burned from salty air, bathe them, and put them to bed.

Miss Millicent Douglas had been in a tizzy to be five. She and her older siblings were fair overwhelmed in the dither of comings and goings of secrets hidden inside bright wrapping paper, and possibly, at my wicked suggestion, the consequences of magic. The sort of faerie magic a nanny will use to best teach a child to mind their manners if they know what's good for them.

Baby Freddie stayed at home with my helper, so the seaside picnic included: Mistress Henrietta *'Hattie'* Douglas, and Master Carlyle Douglas, heir presumptive. These two represent the first generation of Douglases who act more like aunt and uncle to my charges.

The second Lady Douglas is young and fruitful, supplying three spare heirs and the daughter of the hour, *Princess* Millie. Her brothers, Masters William 7, and Theodore 11, attend too, both highly rambunctious and well-used to freedoms of infinite and loud expression where few reprimands can penetrate their privileged standing. Baby Freddie, not withstanding, my three older charges are impervious to any lasting effects of being told-off. There are no smacks or thick ears or clouts to be selectively administered in the shadows. Standing in a corner is as tough as it gets, and even that is relished as a badge of disobedience worth earning. Spare the rod and spoil the child is the unwritten law betwixt nanny and master.

The Douglas offspring may have been born a cut above the rules, but they suffer the adverse restrictions as dictated by their upper class. In many ways it's the children of the poor who have more joyous childhoods since they play unsupervised at all hours in unrestrictive clothing, free of nannies, and away from parents who know little of what to make of such small human beings, themselves being catered to by a succession of servants in starched uniforms.

The little-uns of the wealthy generally live in fear of their nanny's terrifying bedtime stories where make-believe children are punished in lieu of actual discipline which hopefully resonates and improves their character. Eventually, in addition to bonds of genuine affection, they respect nannies for their proximity to cream cakes as a reward after eating their dreary nursery meals of bread and butter and porridge and the endless bland ways a cook might contrive to serve eggs.

The moment the light dims in the nursery, I address the business of putting soiled clothes to rights. I set aside some for mending and match missing buttons from the button box. Last of all comes the sweeping of seashells sand dunes borne fifty miles from Brighton to London that pour from pockets and shoes like the cornucopias of plenty at a harvest festival.

The promise of soaking my burning feet in Epsom Salts and drinking a mug of cocoa spurs me on. I have to be up at dawn before baby Freddie wakes, fussy with his first tooth, not unlike his mother in a constant fret of what she should wear. I wouldn't be a lady's maid for all the tea in China.

Apart from my widowed mother, Alice Broughton, succumbing to toxemia, my own birth was uneventful. I was passed to the capable arms of Mrs. Smith the gamekeeper's wife, to be added to her brood of tough farm brats, and when I was nine it was my task to watch over the Smith's little-uns. I say task, but I took to it as a joy. And so, in time, when introduced to the big house as a scullery maid, I soon worked myself out of the kitchen and into the attic domains of the nursery and schoolroom as Nanny Simpson's assistant.

To my mind, Nanny Simpson was getting on for two-hundred-years-old, and so I waited until the first signs of palsy dictated her days of handling babies were no more. For the last ten years, Nanny Simpson had stayed 'in-situ' delegating any tasks that required her charges be dispatched downstairs, gliding regally on Monday mornings to hold court with milady to discuss all arrangements pertaining to the advancement and safety of her offspring. Most of the time 'milady's' head was too full of dressmakers and menus and gossip to worry over scraped knees and the loss or the arrival of an offspring's tooth.

Children are presented. Marched in and out with clean hair ribbons and scrubbed faces, to be looked over the way a general inspects his troops.

I liked that Nanny and I live at the top of the world in our own sanctuary where few visited due to the preponderance of steep winding stairs. Nanny Simpson reigned as Queen Servant, above the social bustlings below, with me as her chosen handmaiden. I was content to be the recipient of a parade of deliveries from tubs of hot water hauled up by the boy porters to the tea trays and meal trays ferried by the lowest kitchen maids (of whom I'd been liberated), and having them whisked away with soiled clothes carried off by the laundry girls, and tubs of cold water hauled down by the boy porters.

It was safe up high under the eaves where sloping roofs made the rooms round and friendly. Pigeons cooed us night and day, and our daily outings were usually restricted to idle walks in Regents Park and riding in open carriages for the fresh air. I intended to inherit that life of supreme authority, presiding like some great lady with underlings at my command, bouncing babes on my knee, and awarded all manner of perks that were the sole due of nannies everywhere. As it was, I was a new nanny. Nanny Smith, although my real name was Broughton.

How I loved bursting through the kitchens, wet as a salmon from the rain, and having a maid relieve me and my charges of our soaking coats and my umbrella, and another to wheel away the baby pram to be dried and kept covered until I called for it, and another to ask me if I wanted the tea tray straight away or should they wait until after my nap?

There's nothing cozier than a daytime nap when one's charges are asleep, other than cocoa in the night nursery, while wrapped in a shawl and slippers, ready for bed, sitting by a fire miraculously provided by a lackey.

I was a nanny with plenty to eat and clean clothes and a warm bed until Master Carlyle Douglas took the notion that I was his personal property. He professed his intentions gallantly. He was in love with me, he said. Declared it rather vehemently which teased my vanity. And it didn't take long before I forfeited my naps and reciprocated. We had a fine forbidden romance behind closed doors when the house was too busy to care.

Carlyle Douglas was ten years my senior, born to the first Lady Douglas, six years before his sister Hattie. He resented his four half-siblings, and met me when forced to spend Miss Millicent's birthday picnic with us. He'd seen me and paid me no mind, and me him, but we became acquainted quickly. From that day, Master Carlyle courted me. I felt like a princess. But the leap from handmaiden to princess was not that far as it turned out. And, as most princesses eventually discover, a prince can turn into a frog in the frenzy of a last kiss.

Deep down I must have realized that me being a princess was a silly dream. Me being rescued by the son of a lord who promised me the sun and the moon? It was all a lie. And the love I had for Master Carlyle dropped from me soon after I heard he was engaged to a young lady from a fine family. His gallantry stretched to the scurrilous invitation we can still meet in secret. He will send for me, he says.

So, I'm plain Nanny again with dreams of growing old at the top of the stairs with my own assistant, the way 'common garden-variety nannies' pass from service to retirement, and

I'm content enough with years of clean uniforms and plenty to eat stretching ahead of me until the afternoon of Master Carlyle's engagement party.

14

RULES OF ENGAGEMENT

MAMIE – OCTOBER 16, 1911

By the time I came to work in the kitchens of Fabersham Hall, Lady Isobel Forster, 'head house parlor maid Izzie Sparks that was', is a legend. She must have been born with an entire set of silver spoons in her mouth because she won the heart of a visiting lord's son while in service and he married her the moment his father died, and wasn't she just taken away in a bubble of golden adoration and made into a fine lady.

Her exploits are legend. Below stairs we call her Izzie, but when she visits to pay her respects to her cousin Jilly, our cook's assistant, she's Ma'am. We're all yes milady and no milady and will that be all milady? Because little pitchers have big ears.

But later, when I'm a new nanny and out of my depth with Master Carlyle, Lady 'Izzie' of Grailskeep Castle, gives me a private wink and a kind word as if we're kindred. She's never purely 'one of them' but forever one of us and proud of it. And I'm thrilled to be singled out.

She makes it known that she invents reasons to call on Miss Henrietta upstairs, so she can slip away to visit her old friends in the dungeon below. And not to gloat, either; she brings her best good cheer downstairs. She helps lay the table, and under protest, isn't above clearing away as well. She loves a nice cuppa with her feet up does Izzie.

'Below-stairs' we're one big family, trapped in service, born into it most like, happy enough when times are fat. But when times are lean, layoffs are frequent and new positions, few. We live 'underground' in an emotional rabbit warren where elbowing one's way through sibling rivalry is a matter of course. Hierarchy is formal so you learn to mind your P's and Q's. Rules are many and strictly enforced, and consequences can be harsh. Survival for us girls has its particular perils. If we present a pretty ankle and have a trim figure or a comely face it can be our undoing.

My foster mother, Mrs. Smith is a glass-half-empty sort of woman. She insists my downfall is written in the stars, blessed as I am with my mother's sweet face and disposition. Mrs. Drumm, the housekeeper, cautions me. 'Go about your business, my girl, but avert your eyes from the gentlemen,' she says. 'The eyes can say things that spark a pickle of trouble.'

As a scullery maid I learn to keep my eye on the nanny prize. Service isn't a stopgap measure for me; it's my future life.

Mrs. Clarkson, our cook, fits the pastry lid on top of an apple pie. Brisk motions without so much as a glance at her hands. She stares at me over her creation. "Lightning never strikes twice, my girl," she says, rotating the pie dish and tweaking the crust into even pleats. She means lightning in the same place, but more than that, she's referring to me and my mad fling with romantic fate. Izzie's myth lived on in all our young girls' hearts but never more so than in mine.

Mrs. Drumm cackles under her breath. She catches Mrs. Clarkson's eye and winks. "Flea in your ear, Mamie luv," she adds, wielding a soup ladle like a wand waved in my direction. "The road to heartache is paved with the likes of Master Carlyle's indiscretions, and no mistake." Cook sidles heavily around the kitchen table and approaches me, her still ladle poised, and stops. She points it at me, a fairy godmother on a mission. "Mark my words."

I've been cursed or perhaps blessed. Time will tell. My face is so serious that she breaks her own spell and pulls me into a rough hug.

At this, both she and Cook dissolve into fits of hilarity. Not at my expense but because of the cleverness of the joke they understand when the likes of me gaze vacantly as if they're a pair of nutters. When either of them begins a sentence with 'word to the wise, Mamie,' I duck out the room and busy myself with folding children's nappies. But the two older women look out for all us girls, and we love them in the way of underlings who find their betters inspiring and world-weary. They know things. We defer.

These two women are also my mothers. They teach my 'sisters' and I through a strange combination of fear and fairytale. But love is involved too. We girls are their daughters. One day we'll be old enough to understand the jokes they share and pass on the knowing to the new ones who arrive at the back door shy as deer and, if they're lucky, leave through the front, brazen as hussies.

The Sunday my life is rewritten dawns bright and clear. Church for us in service is held extra early so we can be back polishing and cleaning for the special luncheon to celebrate the engagement of Master Carlyle to Miss Beatrice Fawcett, a horsey girl with a handsome dowry.

I arrange a last vase of flowers for the centerpiece in the conservatory breakfast room and set the gold engraved place cards off-center on each Royal Derby dinner plate, mindful not to cover the family crest of a rampant boar and unicorn in the center. Cook always says it's 'a rampant bore more like' followed by more cackling and merriment. But that joke I *do* understand.

Three sides of glass give way to lawns that run on forever to the edge of a manmade lake. I see the hired tent being erected by a team of men, its blue striped canopy billowing like a sail as they tame it into a ceiling with curtains at the corners looking for all the world like a four-poster bed. It flaps away as the gilded chairs arrive. Musicians clatter their equipment across the grass, and a parade of white caps and aprons ferry glassware and candlesticks and flower arrangements in their wake. It's barely past dawn.

I hear a low wolf whistle from the ferns. Carlyle startles me by parting the fronds, and beckons me over. "One last kiss," he says, his lips puckering before I can reply. It isn't a request.

I shake my feather duster in his face, forgetful it's filthy and he gets the brunt of its dust, full in the eyes. At first he chokes and laughs but as his eyes water and he has to gasp for air, his expression changes to rage.

No longer trying to be coy, Carlyle grabs me, hurting my arm and kisses me with brute force. "Slut," he says, and he pulls me into an alcove where he proceeds to ravage me under my skirt. I'm stronger than I imagine and he's angrier. I grab the handle of something in the flowerbed and slash him across the mouth. Blood gushes. He grimaces with red teeth and rips my dress. We're now doing battle as if to the death. He punches me till I'm out of air, and then slinks away to the magic administrations of his valet to right himself for his bride-to-be and the soon-to-be in-laws, who cook says have been 'singed and plucked' like a golden goose, meticulously groomed for a 'right fleecing.'

I don't remember if I make my way to the kitchen or if the kitchen finds me, but I'm whisked away to Mrs. Drumm's sanctuary and given sweetened tea with brandy and plied with cold compresses for my face. Two people with cut and swollen lips are easy to connect, so I'm half-carried, half-dragged, up the servant's stairs and put to bed like a naughty child. One key turns in the lock and I hear the rest of the keys rattle away down the corridor on Mrs. Drumm's belt. I'm miffed even though I know she's locked me in for my safety, seeing's how locked doors keep out the wrong sort out as much as let the innocent in.

Hours later, I hear the hired band playing a waltz from far away that sounds as if they're warbling underneath the water of the Blue Danube itself.

The doorknob rattles louder than the keys. "Go away," I slur through a sore mouth. All I want is a bath, a ride to the train station, and a one way ticket to anywhere. No doubt, the lord and lady of the house wish this for me as well. Lady Isobel calls through the keyhole. "I'm getting the key. Don't be going anywhere, now."

I imagine her smiling at her jest. Lady Isobel, as often as not, is pure Izzie Sparks deep down – the insatiable cheeky sweetheart as often as the grand Lady Forster.

Izzie brings more than a key. Two scullery maids accompany her, loaded down with food and towels, and a porter ferries a jug of hot water inside an enameled basin, carrying a bucket of ice over his arm. Izzie carries a basket of bandages and ointments and other bottles, a batt of cotton wool, and a bottle of brandy. A third under-house parlor maid balances a tray of tea and a covered tureen, a bowl, napkins, and a spoon. These things I hear behind the door before they are displayed before me.

I hide my face behind the sheets as the key turns. Trays meet tables which is more than I can say regarding the averted eyes of the maids. Only the porter stares boldly until Izzie gives him a clout. Chairs are scraped into corners. Words are exchanged. Orders are given. Four sets of footsteps recede and the same key turns in the lock from the inside. I lower the sheet, glaring defiantly at milady Isobel, Lady Forster.

Her face is serious. "Can you stand?"

"Of course," I say. "I can *stand* anything. I'm a tough servant girl. Please milad..."

"Izzie," she corrects. "I mean, can you stand up? Let me look at you. Walk across the room. Are you dizzy? You've got a nasty gash on your forehead." Without waiting for me to answer, she gives my face a thorough inspection. "Jesus, Mary, and Joseph. What on earth did you say to him? Did you threaten him?" Lady Isobel Forster is being her usual self – a force to be reckoned with. I adore her but she wears me out.

I stay her hand from poking my inflamed cheekbones. "I hit him with a filthy duster. I think he got something in his eye. It made him upset."

"Upset!" she chuckles. "Livid's more like. Carlyle doesn't look so wonderful either, but he's got a tale at the ready. Did you know that he fell off his horse into a bramble hedge this morning? Everyone is treating him like a bally war hero, spoiled child that he is."

"I didn't mean to hurt him. He surprised me and then he... I haven't had my courses for eight weeks."

Izzie ignores my announcement and holds up her hand to silence me. "No need for details," she says. "I wasn't born yesterday. He's down there in his element – pampered by two mammas and a cosseted chubby princess, so vacant, she deserves him. Both fathers are leaving the women to it. They're trained from birth to be vaguely embarrassed by all emotional outbursts. The women will see that 'their boy' comes out smelling like a rose."

The pain is excruciating when Izzie wiggles my nose. "He always does. Is my nose broken?"

"It's straight enough," she says, "but it's blue and swollen, so I think, in time, you'll be beautiful again."

I smooth the hair from my face and straighten the bedclothes. "Maybe *after* the baby, then."

This time Izzie addresses my fears. She flops her full weight on the bed, crushing my feet, and lays a hand on my belly as if it was a stethoscope. "It's like that is it?"

My lips quiver as I get ready to cry. "What if I am?"

An exasperated Izzie-type-sigh issues from her. She stands to tower above me, pityingly. "Yes, it would be grim going for a while, but we'd get you through it." She plumps my pillow. "You can come and work for me if need be. My eldest son dispatches nannies on a regular basis. And he's only seven! What will you do? Will you keep it?"

I clutch her hand, terrified, as if she has the power of a saint. "Please... my mother died in childbirth." That says it all. "By all accounts it's a ghastly business all round. And I don't dare meddle with a witchy midwife and her dirty knives. I'm in for it either way. I've lost my position, and no character. I'm an idiot."

"Well, it's early days," Izzie says, "And it's not so bad. Fear makes things appear worse than they usually are. Besides, there are better jobs at sea. Over the sea, in fact. America has a short memory. Your posh-ified accent will open doors. High-society women think widows are safe, silly things, but men love a beautiful widow, and a child guarantees them safety, stupid dolts. I've had three babies and survived. You're young and healthy. You may be lucky. Violated isn't a happy situation but it's a timely warning to be more discreet in the future."

I can't help but blubber. "*What* glorious bloody future?"

"Most everyone learns their lessons the hard way."

"You're not like everyone else. You've got a fairy godmother."

Izzie sends me a knowing stare that shouts 'I take it back, you *are* an idiot.' "Good gracious child," she says. "You're *already* lucky. I *am* a fairy godmother."

Izzie's role as mother hen begins in earnest. She fusses over me, counting off the ingredients for an operation on her bejeweled fingers: hot water, witch hazel, lavender, towels, ice, and bandages. Then comes an assault of bathing and patting dry, and the application of cold compresses. Izzie plies me with tea spiked with brandy that's more like brandy spiked with a splash of tea.

Vegetable broth is administered every half-hour. Fresh compresses are dipped alternately in eucalyptus oil and dabs of cologne. Izzie brushes my hair, sticky with fight, pushes me into a flannel nightgown, and plumps my pillows for the umpteenth time. "He'll definitely get away with this," she says. "But so will you. He may have four parents in the dark, but I have your back, and the servants are in awe of me as your attending good fairy. I've put the fear of god into them if anyone breathes a word. No-one wants a scandal or to lose their job. Your errant Prince Valiant has already solicited my advice. How else do you think I knew? He expects me to smooth his grubby little footprints. In his eyes I'm low-life as in 'once a servant, always a servant.' Lucky for you he's right."

"I need a bath. He ... I need to wash him away." I rub my inner thighs. "From here."

Izzie looks bemused. "It's all right I'm not shocked. He told me what he did. And no, he was absolutely *not* contrite. He was smug. Proud as the cat who ate the canary. Sorry. He gave a rather impassive list of what he'd done. He left out the feather duster part, of course. He gave me the impression you hit him with a poker or something."

"A gardener's trowel, I think. Maybe a clay pot. Maybe a few clay pots. I heard the sound of smashing china. God! It was never the tea things?"

"By the look of the conservatory, a row of vases filled with lilacs were sacrificed. Nice crystal vases to be sure but no, Madame's Chinese cloisonné is safe. A dust pan removed the evidence and the lilacs were stuffed into new vases. Heavens, they have cupboards full of the things. I tweaked a few items on the table. You were lucky. If the tablecloth had been dragged a few inches further we'd be talking death penalty. You see, how lucky you've been?"

I close my eyes, relieved. "Who saw me? I remember a sea of faces."

"Everyone's busy outside. It was only a few scullery maids and some of the trainee porters, and Mrs. Drumm who sees all. She acted quickly to get you out of the way. Very efficient woman. Let me see your teeth."

"What?"

"Did the bastard loosen any of your teeth?"

I roll my tongue against the inside of my mouth and taste blood. "He might have. He punched me like a man in a brawl... I saw his face. He was deadly serious."

"Rinse your mouth with plain brandy," she instructs, "and spit it out. If it stings I'll get a dentist. If it's too red I'll fetch a doctor. You're going to come out of this lovely or I'll call my lawyers. I've told Carlyle as much. My god his face was a picture. The face of a young devil who knows better than to cross the bride of Satan. By tomorrow morning he'll be a gloating truant – a contrite fiancé cat on a boat to Europe for an innocent grand tour seeking new canaries. I doubt you'll have to see him again."

"I'd said my goodbyes to him weeks ago. It was terrible but I wanted to keep my job. He said all he wanted was one last kiss. But I wasn't obliging. It was as if time stopped and all the air was sucked from the room. He went out of focus. One of us snapped. It might have been me. I'm not keen on being attacked. Maybe it was inevitable."

Lady Isobel Forster stays my arm with her hand and squeezes it. "Maybe it's fate, little *canary*," she says.

NEW YEAR'S DAY, 1912

It turns out I wasn't completely lucky. I'm given my walking papers and a passage to America in my fourth month of maternity, and worse, when I present myself at Grailskeep, Lady Forster is in America on one of her harried crossings to and fro. Her housekeeper tells me, on the quiet, that milady is moving the family abroad at the request of Lord Forster who is investing heavily in the new world after making a muck of it in the old one. "Such comings and goings," she says. "You never saw the like."

There's nothing for it but to steam ahead into a new year towards a new life, swallow my fears for four months, and once it's April, meet New York. I have passage on HMS Titanic where steerage is like a palace – or so the rumors go.

15

STEERAGE FOR A DAY

MAMIE – APRIL 10, 1912
countdown – 5 days

Steerage isn't much different than 'below-stairs' other than there's no strict pecking order and no butler to control the chaos. It's every woman for herself. It's not a place to wait for the favors shown to a head nanny or a woman eight-months-pregnant. Chairs are offered for my comfort but food is a rare commodity to these folk. The niceties of waiting for one's turn is forgotten when there's a platter of sausages for the taking, delivered to a crowded table. It's like seagulls after breadcrumbs. Beaks pushing and shoving, and grabbing more than a fair share.

I fight my way to the sausages and eggs for Finn as much as myself. I met him moments earlier and it was love at first sight. I say a quick prayer that my own child will be as sweet. Finn's been left to fend for himself. His mother is seasick with a young baby, and his father is like most Irishmen I've met. Eager for the pint even before breakfast and to be away from crying babies and wives vomiting their fears into buckets.

I crave meat. I've no sea legs yet, but I'm more stable than some from what I hear. The sausages are gone and the jam is being passed hand-to-hand over my head so I dive to secure a couple of boiled eggs in china eggcups, a few slices of bread and butter, and three mugs of milk.

When I get back to Finn's bench his eyes are agog, as if *I'm* a fairy godmother. Down goes the tray and he consumes his first boiled egg, eyes first. I fall in love twice. He falls in love twice. Such a simple gift but for this lad it's Christmas morning. He asks about bread and butter soldiers, so I cut a slice of buttered bread into strips and lop the top off his egg. I dunk the first soldier for him and he eats it, dripping yolk down his chin. He wipes it with his finger and licks it. He's mindful of every morsel, and I leave my own bread for him to finish and sip my warm milk. Finn gulps his, and again the tongue comes out to lick his milk mustache. No food is wiped on the sleeves of his blue shirt. I ruffle his red hair and brush a crumb off his collar.

"It's my America shirt," he says. And then, most touching of all, he shows me his new shoes and his battle scars of blisters. "No-one has worn these but *me*," he says with pride.

"You'll have to wear them in," I say, thinking how I'd like to soak his heels in saltwater.

"No Missus," he replies, shaking his head solemnly. "These are outdoor shoes."

I nod and say of course they are, how silly of me.

Finn studies my shoes, buttoned three inches above my ankle. "You've got *green* shoes, Missus!" He looks as if they will bite but recovers his manners. "But sure you've lovely wee lady's feet," he says, making up for his blunder.

I look down too and wish I was wearing my bedroom slippers as my feet have swollen into flames and the pinching is unbearable. They were almost too big to fit into my boots when I dressed. I wonder if I'll have to wear them while I sleep from now on so that I'm shod when I touch American soil. It would never do to disembark in pink-feathered slippers.

The slippers were a parting gift to me from Lady Douglas when she said goodbye and turned me out, knowing her first grandchild was growing inside me. Of course, it never occurred to her that I knew the slippers were her old ones. Her eyes were stern, almost sympathetic, and they never left my face. She'd turned almost wistful when I took my leave. I believe she envied my freedom if not my circumstances. She handed me a character reference in an envelope that said I was clean. She wished me all the best in my next place. *America is it?* she said. As if an entire country was a job.

I stared boldly and rose to my full height, inches taller than she and replied *Yes madam* in a defiant voice.

The children wanted to give you a going away gift. A small token for a safe journey. She hands me a blue-enameled St. Christopher's medal on a silver chain. *I'm sure you will do well,* she said. *The children will miss you.* But I've known my replacement was already upstairs sorting her things in the vacated cupboards that had been mine and rearranging the children's photos I left on the mantelpiece. She'd already tidied the puzzles and toys in the nursery and ordered tea.

I've been lost in thought so it takes me a minute to understand what Finn is saying. He's still talking about his feet and his shoes.

"They're sore to be sure," Finn declares with an explanation. "But it's because they're not walking *with* my feet. One day soon they will and the blisters on my heels will be entirely tough as leather. Tough as Da's belt. One day these shoes will take me to school."

The word 'entirely' sums up his future. He imagines life unfolding, streets paved, if not with gold, then with boiled eggs and bottles of fresh milk and rows of new shoes. Shoes reaching to the horizon of his years to come. Shoes for Bridie when she begins to walk, and real slippers for his mother when she sits by the fire drinking American tea with her bread and jam.

Next morning after breakfast, I take Finn to my cabin where a white enamel bowl, a pitcher of warm water, a clean washcloth and towel, and a shaker of salt, await his blisters. He winces when he pries his feet from his shoes. The blood is congealed into the leather. Finn's socks are beyond repair, two scabs acts like darned heels. Before the water cools I dump in all the salt and swirl it until it dissolves into a cloud.

"Now then, put both your feet in there and soak. It may sting at first."

He smiles up at me, sweetly trusting. "Salt?" It will sting and he will smile through it.

"Salt cleans wounds," I say. "You seem like a brave chap to me. I had to do this all the time for my children." The words 'my children' fall to the floor like black beetles and scuttle away. They were someone else's brood and now I'm a broodmare and there's not enough salt in the ocean to cleanse what I've done.

The water turns pink. Finn smiles through his discomfort as I knew he would. Out come two red feet that pool a puddle of pink water onto the floor. I take great care to pat them dry, gently holding each swollen foot on my knee. The white towels are smudged with fresh bloodstains. I press the bleeding until it stops. His eyes never leave my face, and when I look back he bursts into a grin that would melt steel.

My medical bag contains salve and headache powders. A rummage produces gauze and a bottle of Mercurochrome. I tell him to think of something nice when I apply the red liquid.

"Cream scones and jam," he says.

"I'm going to paint your heels now. You're not to worry how red they'll be. It's red medicine."

His eyes widen at the first touch but he grips the arms of the chair and hums a song.

Finn leans on me and totters to the main hall on bandaged feet where I hang his rinsed socks over the radiators to dry.

The not unpleasant smell of wet wool steams up at us and I turn the socks from time to time as if I were cooking them. For the meantime, Finn can relax pain free and shoeless and drink a glass of warm milk and munch on buttered brack – the chewy fruit bread that accompanies tea better than any fancy cream cakes. Finn seems to read my mind.

"Have you ever had cream cakes?" he says, taking a bite.

"Many times."

I can't tell if he's shocked or impressed. "Many?"

I've come off smug and I didn't mean to. This boy has never been blessed with sugary buns and cream teas any more than the eggs he enjoyed yesterday morning when we met.

I leave Finn with his baby sister, playing with her toes to make her laugh, and return to the dining hall for a mug of tea. I plan to take my chances and soak my feet in Epsom Salts, and read with my feet up even if it means wearing slippers to dinner.

A surprise awaits me there when a hand taps my shoulder. I turn awkwardly, and it's Izzie. My friend, Lady Forster. The unstoppable force.

She's delighted to see me. "I'm glad I found you," she

says. "Come with me. We have business to discuss. Leave that tea, now. I'll order some from my cabin. Fine china cups and saucers, *and* lemon. Are you in pain? You're wincing. Good gracious girl, what's that on your feet? I've ordered cream cakes."

16
THE TOFFEE BROOCH

MAMIE

Izzie is delighted to see me. "You can save me," she says. "Please please be my nanny... well, of course you will."

"I'm pregnant," I say by way of reply, realizing it's a stupid thing to say the moment it's out of my mouth. I'm as big as a whale.

Izzie laughs and sends me an 'eyes to heaven' expression. I laugh too. "Yes, I can count up to nine," she says. "Or is it eight? Good Lord, Mamie, you should have written me." She fusses over me like a mother. "We're on our way to Atlanta. That's in Georgia. My dear husband has rather made a hash of business. Thank heavens he's still got interests in an American railroad. I'm afraid it's our last hurrah."

"You've never lost the castle?"

Izzie holds up a diamond ring for my inspection. "What do *you* think? Posh enough for a servant girl?"

She keeps up a steady chatter 'steering me from steerage.' When we reach the stairs she answers my question. "The castle has been rented for a year. No worries. I expect we'll return home as soon as Grailskeep's coffers are full of American dollars. Or I can always sell my jewels." The derisive sound she makes says there's no such chance in hell.

I take a last look behind me at the servant's hall. Izzie

takes my chin and turns it away. She points up the stairwell. "First lesson, Mamie luv. Never look back. Now we must hurry. Up in first class, no-one lets me forget that I came from 'below-stairs' even with my fancy title. Whatever happens my girl, you and I will never quite be accepted as gentry. True, I was like you, but I picked the right man. I was lucky he picked me, too. All you need, '*Miss Helen of Troy*,' is a little help and that face of yours will launch your own ship. You 'mark my words.'"

I stare at her disbelieving yet captivated. Mrs. Drumm's gloomy advice comes back to haunt me. I should run, except I have little choice but to *mark* Izzie's words.

Her gaze falls on my pink feathered feet. "On second thoughts," she says in a loud stage whisper, "we have plenty of time to change your footwear."

The Forster cabin is palatial. I get impressions of being surrounded with crystal and mahogany. I'm wrapped in gold and lavender wallpaper. I feel like a birthday gift. Everything white and metallic has disappeared behind the closed door. It's hotel quiet. No children quiet. Izzie's brood have been sent to a playroom in lieu of the nanny who jumped ship in France after having a nightmare about drowning. Sparks wink from a chandelier with ruby glass shades. Without asking permission I pull off my shoes and kick them aside. My toes are saved, luxuriating in thick red carpet with a border of white stars. "Oh dear God. I thought I'd never be free of these things," I say. "No-one told me my feet would be pregnant."

"I have big feet," Izzie says, as if we'd been comparing sizes. "Let's have a sherry."

Izzie's questions are more like statements. She pours me a sherry and continues where she left off, her own sherry in hand, now poised over a small leather trunk. When I accept my drink with mild surprise, she takes action. Up goes the lid in a flourish and she rifles through the contents in search of something she's sure is there. Finally, she lets out a 'there you are', and pulls out a pair of walking boots that will take my swollen feet with room to spare. "Pad those feet of yours in socks and get yourself into these after you've had a good stretch," she says. "A nanny with bad feet is no good to me." She winks. "Why I would have to *halve* your wages. The children need air, and after that cramped space in steerage, it couldn't do you any harm either, my girl."

"I need to fetch my things."

Izzie waves my concern away. "I'll send a nice man to carry them, later. The stairs are treacherous enough but in your condition they're slippery as eels in the damp sea air. Let's have tea first." She rings a buzzer and soon a steward dressed in immaculate whites appears to take her order for China Oolong tea and a Victoria sponge cake with jam and cream. And I'm emboldened enough to interrupt and ask for an extra pot of jam, and a salt spoon, if you please. The steward doesn't blink. Apparently it isn't bold of me to ask for unusual things. Neither does Izzie as she smiles benignly during the whole procedure. "Please bring that extra jam in a screw top jar," she says, "it's for the children."

The door closes and it's her turn to question me. "Jam? Eaten with a spoon? I craved pickled herring when I was pregnant with Imogen. Nothing so dainty as a salt spoon either."

I interrupt her with a mission of my own. "Is there a shop? I'd like to buy some toffee."

"No need. I believe Christopher's damn toffee is around here somewhere. He's got a stash of it. He hoards the stuff. He won't miss a bit as long as we don't tell him."

"It's for a young man I've fallen in love with," I say. "His name is Finn. He's five years-old but I'd swear he's an ancient sage. I have to say a proper goodbye. He'd love some toffee if you're sure Christopher won't mind."

"Not goodbye. We can keep your Finn well stocked with jam and chocolate," she says. "Of *course* Christopher *will* mind, IF he finds out. His father has spoiled him silly. We'll sniff out some sweeties for your boy tomorrow."

The tea arrives on a silver tray. Izzie plucks the salt spoon and jar of jam and hands them to me. "Now," she says. "Will you accept my offer?"

My new shoes say yes. I say yes, but Izzie has already heard the answer she wants before I open my mouth. She's already showing me where I will sleep. I have my own sink, and wonder of wonders, a porthole. I burst into grateful smiles. I say yes a few more times so I can believe it myself.

An opulent bed with a mauve silk coverlet to match the wallpaper teases me to test its springs. I'm to sleep in this lavish alcove adjoining the second bedroom which houses Izzie's three children: two boys, Christopher, seven; George, three; and her eighteen-month-old daughter, Imogen.

My little brass window opens to salty spray that calms my face to match my toes cooing and purring in soft heavenly freedom. But there's no time. Izzie is on a mission.

She checks her watch and chuckles with glee. "Goody, the children won't be brought back for at least an hour." She takes my teacup, sets it by my new bed, and takes my hand. "On with those giant boots, Nanny."

I wasn't finished my tea but since when do such details stop an immovable force. "Come on," Izzie says. "Time to promenade. We need fresh air. It's the deck chairs for us."

Two nursery maids bring the children. The boys are lined up to be introduced. Christopher eyes my swollen belly. His horror is plain. He ignores my handshake. "Servants aren't allowed husbands," he says to Izzie. "So they can't have babies."

So that's my running start. Georgie is a love, very shy; Imogen is a fussy infant, very pretty; and by the sneer on his face, Christopher is clearly going to be a handful. I award him a hollow peace offering. I give him the empty St. Christopher medal that Lady Douglas presented to me on behalf of her children for the sake of appearances. I was pally with Lady Douglas lady's maid, who knew the trinket well as it was kept in her sewing box, discarded from Miss Millicent's dress-up box.

"What's that supposed to be?" Christopher says, flipping it like a coin. "Heads I win; tails you lose." He roars with laughter. "Do you know why that's funny? It means I always win."

"Well, that's a fine joke," I say, "but I've no doubt that you're a very lucky boy to have such a lovely first class adventure on Titanic." I would gladly box Christopher's ears for no extra pay. He'll need my good luck charm if I'm not mistaken.

Finn is eating stew with his parents when I enter the dining hall. I'm no longer limping but waddling as all women do who are in the advanced stages of 'expectation'. Mr. Cleary introduces himself. James he says, and immediately changes it to Jimmy. He stands and tugs his forelock in lieu of doffing a cap, and I don't know where to look, I'm that ashamed.

"I'm a servant," I blurt out, embarrassed to be singled out as above his class. "I was a kitchen maid before I became a nanny. Please, can I sit with you a while? I could hold Bridie while your wife eats her dinner."

We sit and talk about the joys of America and I explain I've been hired as one of the passenger's nannies after their girl abandoned ship in Cherbourg. I have to move up to Lady Forster's cabin, and that I met her when she was a grand lady visiting Fabersham Hall where I worked. We spend a pleasant hour and then I turn to Finn who's been exceptionally silent. "Will you walk me to the gate?"

Finn's mother sits in perpetual panic, clutching her rosary and I understand why I call them worry beads. "I'll get Bridie a baby bottle for milk so you can rest a bit," I tell her. "You can rinse the bottle out each night and I'll see you get a new one each day. We'll be in New York soon enough so it's no bother."

Jimmy nudges his wife.

"Goodbye Molly," I say, offering my hand.

Mrs. Cleary looks up, her eyes vacant. She knows I'm there and that she should say something.

"Goodbye Mr. ..." I shake his hand... "James."

He blushes at the name and grins. "Goodbye Missus."

I turn quickly in case he doffs his invisible cap again. Finn pulls on his own cap and his chair scrapes across the floor with a loud squeak. "You'll not be saying goodbye for good?" he says.

For some reason the chair, Finn's lopsided cap, and the word goodbye lock together as a crystal memory and for a moment I want to decline Izzie's offer and eat stew with Finn for the rest of my life. "I have to go to work. It could mean a good position in America. Apparently I'm lucky. There's a boy near your age and his younger brother and a baby sister."

A cloud passes between us. I have done the unforgiveable. Finn is fragile when it comes to feeling special and I've spoiled things. His voice sounds strangled, but being Finn he forces a brave smile.

"What's his name? Is he taller than me?"

I tweak his nose. "You're a cheeky scamp. What are you?"

"A cheeky scamp."

"Well, if you must know, nosey clogs, Master Christopher Forster is a chubby sourpuss from morning til' night."

Finn's sadness changes to horror. "Master? Is he a schoolteacher?"

Finn looks too upset for me to laugh. "He's a boy, like you... well, *not* like you. Nannies are trained to address their charges as miss or master. Maybe I can arrange for you to visit him," I say, knowing it's something I would never attempt. The oil and water of class distinction is a demeaning recipe to destroy Finn's natural enthusiasm. Best leave his dreams and his chances for school and the American dream that can push the working class man into the occasional millionaire. According to Izzie, we're heading for a rainbow bridge where cats can not only look at a king they can eat out of his hand. Finn has as much chance as anyone, and if charm is a factor, more than most.

I reach for Finn's hand but he sidles past me to be in the lead. I throw another hasty goodbye to his parents and follow. He's already miles ahead of me.

When we reach the gate we're suddenly shy. The metal grid reminds me of an elevator cage. A place for ascending only. There's nothing for it, only a hug will seal the awkwardness. I enfold him and kiss the top of his head. His rigid body melts into mine and he sobs enough for both of us. Something has changed. Something unstoppable, and with me the adult, I feel I should stop the clock and... do what? I have lines and an exit and the next act is heaven knows what. Sentiment floods such abandoned moments – the sacred doorways on which life hinges.

I have to peel Finn from my skirts. He stares at me all tears without shame. He's showing me his true self and isn't the least bit embarrassed. I straighten his cap and wipe his tears with a "hush now," and straighten his collar. "Buck up lovey, we've got that alphabet to finish. We'll be friends in New York. Do you think I'd miss that?" I pass him the smuggled salt spoon with its engraved star, a miniature pot of strawberry jam, and a teacake, from out my purse. He's over the moon. But then I can read him clear as a bell. He realizes I'm leaving for another boy and his face crumples again.

"Thank you very much Missus," he says with the emphasis on the 'M'. "For the alphabet and the eggs." He pauses and looks in his hands. "And the wee spoon and the jam."

"Look, it's not goodbye. Darling boy, I'm not abandoning you. I'll bring you some nice things to eat whenever I get the chance. Meet me here in the afternoons. Ask someone when it's two o'clock. That's when my charges will be napping. Promise me you'll be here tomorrow. Will you do that?"

"I will."

"Master Finnegan. I shall expect you at two o'clock. Will you be here?"

"I will."

"Friends for life?"

"I promise."

FINN

I fall asleep with a smile on my face, thinking of Christopher with a sour gob on him. Someday I'll have a real teacher in a big school. He'll wear a black gown and cane the bejesus out of me after I've upset one of his apple carts. He'll keep me after school to praise me as being too brilliant for the class and I'll be thrilled to address him as Master.

MAMIE – APRIL 14, 1912, 2 P.M.
countdown – 10 hours

I forget that I'm wearing a daisy brooch of butter amber when I next see Finn's eager face pressed against the gate. Mamie found it in a box of what she calls trinkets and gave it to me. "It dresses up that plain shirt," she said.

I can't help but get the terrible impression that I'm visiting a zoo and feeding an animal through the bars. I shake off such a morbid thought and smile. Why do they have to keep it locked? Yesterday I lived down here. How is that possible? It reminds me of the entrance to the underworld and I shiver as if someone's walked on my grave. Finn grins when he sees me and waves his salt spoon.

I've brought a confiscated slab of Christopher's toffee broken into pieces with a hammer, a current bun, a green apple, and the baby bottle I promised. The bag is too big to pass through the bars and so I have to hand him everything one at a time. The apple needs to be cut in half so Finn has to run back to the dining room for a knife. I shout after him to walk after he has the knife but he hurries back without a care.

Finn asks if my brooch is made of toffee and will I eat it later? I tell him about amber and how it's millions of years old and that it used to be sap running from the trees like the honey we had that first day we met.

We each take a piece of toffee and spend the time in each other's company talking with it stuffed in our cheeks, and Finn tells me his Mam is feeling better but not grand. More than anything he's pleased I've remembered my promise to bring a bottle for Bridie's milk. He dotes on his baby sister. Another reason why he's so easy to love. I have a few last peppermints for his mother and tell him they will settle her insides. His eyes light up. I'm a fairy godmother full of miracles. He's forgotten about Christopher, the little horror who has already claimed me as his lowly servant.

I reach through the gate to tweak Finn's nose, his sweet face framed by the diamond latticework. "I'll see you tomorrow." I feel as if I've said this for a hundred years. I hear the echo of his chair squeaking on the dining hall floor and muffled conversation as if my ears are filled with cotton. I feel anxious. Restless for the promenade deck where I can breathe. But then this anxiety is the lot of pregnant women the world over. We're oversensitive and taken to strange notions. Suddenly the smell of peppermint makes me queasy. I notice my hands are trembling and that I've started biting my fingernails again.

Finn turns away, holding up the bag of booty like he's giving a toast. He blows me a kiss, and I make my way back to Izzie. Tonight she's dressing for a party and I'm to style her hair in a fancy chignon to suit a tiara. But first we have to decide on her gown and the jewels she will wear.

17

STAINED FOR LIFE

MAMIE – APRIL 14, 1912, 4 P.M
countdown – 8 hours

After tea in the nursery, Master Christopher wants to eat toffee and write letters on his mother's portable desk. I settle him on a sofa and open the lid of the inkwell, but he removes the bottle from its holder.

"That's asking for trouble," I say. "Objects tend to shift without notice on a moving ship."

He's sulky and belligerent. He blocks my hand. "Leave it. I want it where it is. I'm careful."

He's challenged my every request so far. Maybe that's why his other nanny abandoned ship; maybe it wasn't a portent of doom. "I'm not asking you. I'm telling you," I say. "Please put it back."

"Or what?"

I move closer to take charge but the ship lurches and Christopher leaps to his feet, sending the inkwell flying. I catch the full brunt of the ink on the side of my dress.

He bursts into laughter. "It wasn't my fault," he says, grinning. "It was the ship. If you'd stayed over there your stupid dress would be fine."

Apparently he finds the whole business hilarious. The thin taffeta fabric is saturated. Quite ruined. Blotting stops the flow from dripping onto the carpet, and I right the desk while holding my skirts away from my leg, but when I change into a dressing gown, I notice the blue-black ink has left a stain on my thigh that looks like an angry bruise. Soap doesn't remove it. It will take time to sluff it from my skin.

I show Christopher the ruined dress. "That's never going to come out. It was a favorite dress."

"If it's yours it's only a cheap rag," he says, and forgetting my place, I slap him. "A favorite dress of your *mother's*. She lent it to me."

It had been fortunate for me that Izzie had her old maternity clothes with her, for a friend in New York.

"You're not allowed to hit us. I'm telling Mamma."

Izzie stood in the doorway, holding up a flowing nightgown. "I heard you," she says. "Apologize to Mamie this instant."

"No. I don't have to apologize to servants." Christopher thrusts the desk aside and storms from the room. But the metal door is too heavy to slam which makes him angrier. "Stupid bloody ship!"

Izzie turns to me as if nothing happened. "I thought you could wear this. We can try soaking that stain." She pauses and smiles but it's not a happy smile. "When he's really mad he calls me a servant too," she says.

The slab of toffee is unscathed. I wrap it in a linen napkin to take to Finn. I see a vivid picture of him blowing me a kiss when I last said goodbye.

8 P.M.
countdown – 4 hours

Christopher's angry face follows me as I tuck George into bed. "It's only a stupid dress," he says. "Mamma will get you a nanny's uniform in New York. But you can't come with us to Atlanta. Papa says I'm to have a black mammy to look after me. She won't dare talk back to me. Papa says we're to have lots of slaves in Georgia, and I'll have my own pony. And my mother's name is *not* Izzie!"

"I won't *be* your nanny in New York. However, tonight I *will* be your nanny in the next room, helping your Mamma, and after she's left for the dinner I'll be reading my book. So, if you need anything it had better be now or wait until morning."

"You're a liar. You're going to take food to that *beggar boy*." He spies the toffee in my hand. I'm caught red-handed. "Here, that's mine. What else have you been pinching?"

"That BOY is asleep. And he minds his tongue. Come on piggy m'lad, it's way past your bedtime. Tomorrow is a new day."

"Where's your husband? My father says you're a whore!"

I leave the door ajar. The last thing I say to him is "I'll buy you some more toffee, piglet."

I can't model the dresses considering my present shape so I wear the lace nightgown and Izzie's jewelry and flaunt my hands full of rings and twist the diamond bracelets to catch the light.

Izzie turns her cheek to emphasize a daring low cut bodice that shows off a necklace to its best advantage. I parade, and Izzie chooses the emeralds. Her entire collection is housed in satin pouches matching their contents: green bags for emeralds, black for jet, red for rubies, blue for sapphires, and white for diamonds.

"Perhaps too décolleté for the Captain's table," I say. Izzie's just taught me the word and I've used it as many times as I can to make her laugh. For a moment we're two servants giggling over the gentry's obsession with fancy French words for ordinary things.

"Very 'day-coal-ate' oim sure," Izzie says in a vamped cockney accent.

I'm wearing my fluffy slippers with an elegant white fur stole which makes us laugh. "Do me shoes match me doimonds or me emeralds?"

"I predict you will wear jewels like these of your own someday," Izzie says. "I can introduce you to the right men, but they're ancient. We have wealthy friends in New York who would be pleased to show off a young beautiful..." *ahem*... "*widow* on their arms."

"Perhaps not quite yet," I say, posing in exaggerated profile.

"If I can do it so can you. You must never underestimate your feminine charm or the eyesight of a rich old man. It's the young men you need to stay away from. Carlyle was not a wise choice. The wiles to overpower rank don't last forever."

My face goes all droopy. I can feel my spine contract as my spirit actually deflates. "Carlyle chose me. It's not very romantic if they don't," I say.

"And living in a garret as a servant is, I suppose? Mamie, if I hadn't taken the bull by the horns, I'd be an old lady's maid mending clothes by a fire with my eyesight failing and chilblained hands, old before my time wearing hand-me-down clothes from the mistress's rag bag. Youth must will out. It's sad that beauty fades but on the bright side, courage grows, so now I am intimidating enough to wear too many emeralds. And who's going to say otherwise?"

The party's over. Izzie and I drink sherry while she describes the night. When the iceberg hits we're slightly tipsy, sorting piles of glittering jewels into colored bags. The porter who knocks on the door is in a panic which transfers directly into us. Suddenly we are empty-headed women in a crisis. I forget I'm bedecked in rings and bracelets and a necklace made of finely carved jet. We cram jewelry bags into a red carpet bag. But it's too late to go to the purser without an escort.

I stuff extra clothes for the children in a pillowcase along with a pair of Master Christopher's shoes for Finn. Izzie, suddenly focuses and collects a few portable valuables and wraps them in her finest lingerie: small silver ornaments, her watches, a French ivory box, and a matching fan. They fill the bag so it takes both of us to close it.

"I don't intend to lose my furs," Izzie says. "You'll have to wear one. Take the fox. That's another bit of your luck for you, Mamie. I've only just got it back from downstairs. It had to be properly dried. It was raining buckets the day we boarded, and I would stand on deck and wave farewell to everyone and no-one. It was like being a queen. Anyway, I nearly drowned the poor thing. It was soaked through."

I shout at Christopher to carry the pillowcase for me. "I'm not your servant," he shouts back.

I grab the baby, holding her on my hip. Izzie takes George and Christopher by the hand, but in the crush of leaving, the pillowcase is left behind. Damn Christopher. I carry the carpet bag in my spare hand. We are shoved and pushed into a lifeboat with several dithery women who are more concerned about losing their hats and getting their shoes wet. It's boat number five, one of the first away with only two sailors to row. Christopher moans about his damned toffee the entire time.

The two boys sit beside Izzie, and Imogen reaches for her

mother. I pass the fussy baby across the red carpet bag wedged between my feet, and realize I'm wearing my pink slippers. They're attracting odd looks from the other women. But in contrast, Mother Izzie and Imogen make a perfectly iconic religious painting. A frantic Madonna with a full moon for a halo, calming a child already pacified by her mother's arms.

I'm angry that the pair of shoes for Finn is back in the pillowcase. And there had been room enough to stash toffee in the carpet bag if only I'd thought. And then I hear a sailor relaying captain's orders that the poor bastards in steerage are not to be let out. "Bloody hell, we've only got an hour I reckon," he says. "We'll have to swim for it."

I scramble up the ship's side to reach Finn. Izzie's eyes are distraught. She pulls me back into the boat by the hem of her coat and shakes me, drawing my chin to face her. "My dearest girl, the gates will be locked. They won't let him out. If they opened the gate for you there would be a stampede. You would be trampled." And then she adds a terrible thought. "If steerage is flooded. All of them will be dead already. Just think you could have been down there."

I see Finn's cheery expression before me. Innocent eyes, lit with gratitude from the provisions he sees as miracles, and me, his angel of the jam and peppermints. "Izzie, he's only five-years-old."

A vision of Finn flashes before my eyes. He's triumphant holding up the salt spoon. "See you tomorrow," he says and blows me a kiss. My stomach lurches and I'm sick over the side. Christopher shows his disgust. I want to slap him for not being Finn.

Izzie is shouting at me, now. "You have your own baby to consider. The ship isn't going to sink. They're only saying that to get us into the boats. We'll be back on board by breakfast." But I remember what the sailors said, that they had an hour, and Titanic is lower in the water.

Our lifeboat splashes onto the ocean and we're frantically rowed away. But when the great liner breaks in half and sinks, a surge of water hits us and we're tipped into the ocean. I grab the nearest thing – the red carpet bag. Izzie has the baby. Georgie clings to her. I reach out to Christopher but he refuses to take my hand. Instead, he grabs onto George so that his brother and mother are torn apart. I meet Izzie's gaze. She screams "Georgie!" But he's vanished under the weight of Christopher, and she can't let go of Imogen.

Christopher is screaming, using George as a raft. I lose sight of them. I'm too far away, grimly attached to the carpet bag, now an anchor, and my hands are frozen to its handle. I can't let go. I must concentrate on saving my own child. I'm about to give up when Finn calls me. "Take my hand," he shouts and I reach for the only hand I can see. I'm dragged atop the capsized lifeboat, blood oozing from my legs, and face death. My luck has run out. My last thought is that a bag of precious jewels will be more than enough to bribe the ferryman over the River Styx. But the ferryman is wearing a cap with the insignia of the White Star Line, and nothing makes sense.

I never see Isobel or Christopher or George or baby Imogen again, but nothing upsets me like missing the two children who mean the world to me. Finn is gone but I see his shoes are in the boat with me, so he's not far, yet I'm helpless to save him. My own child might die. All I can do is follow Izzie's advice and survive to give birth. If it's a boy I will name him Finn.

I remember the last time I saw Finn on the ship when I'd said I'll see you tomorrow, and it breaks my heart when I don't see him on the other side with his mother and father and his baby sister... after the sinking is over, and yet I feel him as close to me as my unborn child had been. I see Finn's face whenever I think of my daughter, who is surely an orphan somewhere in America, although I'm not privy to where. I feel as if I have two children.

LACEY
WATERS
1912 – 1985

18

CHANGELINGS

I'm old now but Finn is with me still. Not all the time, but he visits on the days when one of the nurses takes me to visit the ocean. I know the exact direction to look for the smokestacks of the Titanic that could have... should have... lingered on the breast of the North Atlantic all those years ago. If I were an albatross I could drop down to circle her resting place and hover over her grave. If I was a sea-witch I could see through the foam and green depths and spy the great spill of her innards cast into an arc of treasure.

But I recall the year 1917 when I was five, when the only war that raged for me was the one in my head with the boy who'd taken lodging there.

My foster mother's name was Lilian-Rose Waters... Lil when my dad was hungry, fresh off the sea, Rose when he was worried, Wifey when he was angry or impatient or disobeyed, and Rosie when he'd had a few beers and was angling for an early tumble at 7:15. I learned the language of the names before I could write the alphabet. Whenever Pa called Ma, Lilian-Rose, I scarpered. I had hideouts amongst the rocks and seaweed where the wind drowned out their bickering and bullying. Seagulls cried louder than me or their arguing. When Pa was away at sea, Ma prayed he would drown. She prayed this so often she never noticed she prayed out loud. She'd have been horrified to know I heard her. But that's why I learned to keep my thoughts to myself.

Plenty of fishermen drowned on our shores. The Atlantic was a stern taskmaster but I also thought of the ocean as a living entity, and my true mother.

Ma said our wooden house with its sod roof was a barnacle because it was built on an outcrop of lichen-covered rock shaped like an overturned rowboat. How it didn't get blown clear away in the hurricanes was a miracle. The outside joins and seams in the decayed wooden siding were sandpapery, encrusted with salt, and the entire exterior blended seamlessly into the grey weather and mossy stone. Pa tried to keep it white with a blue trim but it wanted to be grey and so it sluffed its paint-skin every spring.

But inside it was cozy. Come spring, when Pa whitewashed, Ma cleaned with a vengeance. She took most everything outside and shook it until her bones rattled. Not so difficult a task considering she was a slight figure of a woman, forever stooped from hard work and the brunt of being badgered day and night.

Our kitchen reminded me of an illustration from 'Wind in the Willows' – of mole's snug little home deep in the earth, everything higgledy-piggledy but somehow in its place and glowing with domestic pride. A great Welsh dresser filled with mismatched blue and white crockery stood like a tall library shelf and covered an entire wall. The stove was forever pumping heat, and a pot always simmered on a back burner even if it was only to bleach Pa's handkerchiefs. Ma never sat if she could bustle.

Every third Saturday, Ma took me to the big library in Halifax where I was forced to borrow at least one book I didn't like because my choices were scrutinized by Pa who wanted me to read the bible and little else. Luckily, Ma had a large shopping basket, and any books that wouldn't pass Pa's judgement could be smuggled in under carrots and potatoes.

Pots and pans shone from the kitchen rafters. Jam jars of wildflowers and beach grass decorated each rotting windowsill and the center of an oak table that took two men to budge. The big copper for baths and heavy laundry days hung outside, scoured from the seawater driven by the wind and then rinsed by the rain that forever shadowed our door – the door that remained navy-blue as it was easier to paint on a regular basis.

Ma grew flowers in fish barrels cut lengthwise that created islands of brilliant color dotted amongst the thatch grass. Daffodils bloomed in May if the weather permitted and pansies and snapdragons reigned in the summer. Sweetpeas and Clematis clung to the furthest side of the house with the tomato plants, away from the ocean, so when one approached our house from the road it looked cheery enough. Lavender and verbena grew wild under my bedroom window and turned my room into a perfumed bower. Geraniums in terracotta pots adorned the rickety stairs that ran topsy-turvy to the beach. If I had to describe our humble dwelling as a stranger might, I'd have said we lived under a 'Merlin's hill' covered in a wild sprawling roof garden.

The sandy soil rejected potatoes and cabbage and lettuce seeds but the local market was only a short bus-ride away. Ma and I considered it a vacation when the two of us took ourselves away from Pa and his constant need to be pandered.

Ma said in a former life he must have been a king. He sure enough knew how to give orders and heaven help us if we took too long to answer his call.

I didn't believe in heaven in those days. However, I *did* believe in lost souls. I had one as a best friend. Ma called him my invisible friend and warned me to keep his existence a secret. Pa would have declared I was possessed of a devil and called for an exorcism from his church-elder cronies to banish him.

Finn was an angel. He still is. I never saw him for my first five years, although he was in my head on and off and I could see the results of his presence. Things moved in my room when there was just the two of us and he liked to close the window. He was away a great deal, more than Pa, and I would never ever have wished him drowned because he'd had that terrible misfortune already.

Supper on the table was sacrosanct at 5 p.m. There was hell to pay if it was 5:01. Pa was gone come 5 a.m., and I was adopted five minutes after I was born. I guess that's some kind of record.

FINN – APRIL 15, 1917

Mamie appears to me unsummoned. She doesn't smile, but launches into her mission as if the hourglass of the world is running out of sand. "You can change your mind," she says, "but once you're visible to Lacey there's no going back."

"I'm tired of wandering."

"You're not tired of wandering you're sick of postponing. It's been five years since Titanic sank. I make no veiled threats so it will do you good to consider that anniversaries contain power. I'm here to tell you that you have to decide today, your birthday, and that your teacher is worried about you."

"Then why didn't *he* come?"

She finally smiles and I'm more at ease. I know she's trying her best to help me. "He's never left your side. But some things you must learn on your own, the hard way. Finn, please pay attention. I was wrong. Do you understand? I thought my baby was dying. That's why I urged you to change places with her. I took unfair advantage of you and for that I'm deeply sorry. You wanted me to be your mother. You might even say it was your death wish. In the heat of the moment I thought it was best for all three of us. And now, Lacey is alive and well, but she isn't yet under your skin or rather you aren't under hers. But if you decide to stay with her, you will fall under a different spell. Life on earth will exact its price."

I tilt my head, and focus on the amber brooch she's wearing, hair in my eyes, all innocent. "Why should I listen to you? You were more concerned about saving your daughter than protecting me."

"I *had* to save her."

"Exactly. Saving me was useful to you. Some of us are better off without mothers."

It shocks me how fast Mamie's tortured expression turns to resignation and then indifference.

It's her turn to shrug. "Think, Finn. It's time to grow up. I can only suggest."

"What happens if I can't decide?"

"More wandering than you could possibly imagine. It would be pure folly."

"I can't go back without my shoes. You know I'll be in for a clout if I do. Sure Mam will disown me entirely."

"Your Mam is beyond clouting anyone, least of all a child she loves. She exists in the great silence it takes to hear the worst truths. I've visited her and she's changed. She listens. And a clout never stopped you before."

"Says you. And where's Michael?"

"Some days he's with her still. Others, he's off gallivanting like you, somewhere exploring his latest options. Michael hasn't decided where he wants to land. He's been circling similar ground to yours. You're two of a kind, but you refuse to see him, and he has all the time in the world because he was smarter than you. He refused to materialize for your Mam. She and you imagined what you wanted to see. You're a powerful danger to yourself. But you don't have to be. Let me help you. Let Michael help you."

"Chance would be a fine thing."

"Jealousy is a nasty business. If you stay, don't be surprised if your fears grow teeth. You can stay or come with me and I'll take you home. I can't promise anything but...."

"Promises are trouble."

"So are some decisions."

"Lacey might go to New York someday, or go to school. That would suit me. I can wait."

"You're already in school. But you act as if you're the class dunce in a corner."

"Please spare me the image of a boy stuck in a corner. That's cruel. I never pegged you for being cruel."

"Remember, I was a nanny. I had to be strict with my charges for their own good. I'm a dreamer not an angel. I make mistakes."

"You mean sins."

"I can't foresee the future but I can assess the past and I can save you an alphabet of grief, here in the present. 'C'mon. I'll take you home. Don't be so bullheaded. You're acting foolish."

"Foolish is it? Bullheaded am I? I was your darling boy when you needed me to be your daughter. What do you want from me this time?"

Mamie reaches out to me with open arms the way she had when she'd said her last goodbye, and I turn from her to hide my eyes. "Take my hand. It's that easy," she says.

I hear Mam in my head going on about my last boyish kick on the wharf. An involuntary cat scratch of a scuffmark made in the excitement of the moment, and one she won't let me forget in a hurry. *Finn Cleary, you're always lollygagging. Too clever for your own boots. Michael wouldn't have scuffed HIS new shoes.*

I peek at Mamie over my shoulder. She's still there, open arms and all smiles again. "I have work to do here," I tell her. I guess I've decided because she shakes her head and her smile freezes. She isn't moving. She looks like a painting and I look the other way, knowing I'm banishing her in a spell I've no business using. Her signal blinks out. I'm bereft, once again a lost boy facing a vast ocean of bitterness.

Teacher's voice swoops in to take Mamie's place but it does nothing to take the chill from me. Have I broken a promise or kept two? "Can you not see that sibling rivalry is a waste of breath," he says. "Pettiness is next to foolishness. If you can't see it, then for goodness sake, *feel* it. Will you fight to the death over a pair of shoes?"

"I will."

"Michael wants to help you."

"Then why did he break his promise? Why did he leave

Mam? I needed a big brother to teach me the alphabet and how to spell Cleary. Where was Michael when I needed him?"

"I'm a *time*keeper not your *brother's* keeper. Feeling sorry for yourself is a small dream. Throw it back."

19

FINNISH-ING SCHOOL

I wake on my fifth birthday to a new doll, a bouquet of red balloons, and pancakes for breakfast. I name my doll, Daisy Paisley after a Presbyterian preacher my Pa always quotes – a man 'back hame' in auld Scotland. We live in *new* Scotland, Nova Scotia, where my parents settled on the eastern shore, near enough to the industrious harbor of Halifax and far enough away to feel the pull of the open sea. Pa is a fisherman. He follows the cod off the grand banks for weeks at a time. And sometimes his crew stays over in Newfoundland to wait out bad weather.

Ma is content with her hardships because she has me. After all her years of childless grief I'd come along on the tide of the ocean and she never looked back. I was a gift from out of the blue and she was a mother. That was enough. Her dour husband existed to bring in the catch and provide for us but nothing more.

Pa spends his spare time away from us down at the Blue Mermaid with his fishing cronies, drinking and telling stories. And even though he believes liquor is the devil incarnate and that he's jeopardizing his good standing with God, he drinks himself into a stupor at least once a week. But he never leaves his deepest Presbyterian sensitivities behind. His sense of right and wrong outside 'The Mermaid' never wavers. His law isn't to be questioned. He's king. But always, Mamie's jewels weigh heavy on his soul. Still, he keeps his innermost darkest secrets, confident he'll be returned to God's favor. I'm his ticket to heaven.

Daisy is a baby doll but you'd never know it from her sticky-out eyelashes like the bristles of a toothbrush and her painted lips the color of birthday balloons. Her eyes are blue marbles that alarm me because they click when they open and close. Plastic windows clunk down and Daisy cries *maaaa maaaah* like a goat when I bend her backwards, something I know instinctively never to do with real babies. I remember babies. Lots of them. My own babies from another place and another time in my dreams – my pretend children who live down the road inside my mind. I don't remember exactly where, somewhere nearby, but I do remember that none of their eyelids clicked.

"Finish your milk," Ma says. "You've a surprise waiting." The word finish hits me like a wet Monday. Fin – Fin...ish.

"What?" I call out, but I'm not talking about the surprise. "I'm Finn," I say.

"You'll have to wait and see. Unless you FIN-ish that milk."

"My name's Finn." I repeat.

Ma laughs and wipes the syrup from my face and fingers. "Finish as in drink all your milk, not Finish as in Finland. Run along you silly girl. It's in the sitting room."

"My friend's name is Finn. He says hello."

"I'm Irish," Finn says.

"And he's Irish."

"Well that's very nice but don't be letting your Pa hear

such nonsense," Ma says. She goes back to her stirring and humming –a little grey bee in a world of abstract busyness.

For a long minute Finn doesn't know where here is or who I am because he's returned after a long journey again, and it takes him a while to adjust. Ma turns her back to her cake batter as if our lives haven't changed because she doesn't know there's no Lacey without Finn anymore. At least not in my head. I've asked Finn to show himself for a while now, but it's only me who leaves footprints in the sand. It's only me who has a shadow that flutters against the cliffs. Sometimes he thinks he's still at sea... on the Titanic as well as meaning confused.

But today is different. Here he stands before me, as real as the table and the pitcher of milk – a boy in short trousers and a blue shirt, waving cheekily from behind Ma. He doffs his wool cap and twirls it on the end of a finger, mocking me. He's better than any surprise.

"What're you laughing at?" Ma says.

I can't wipe my smile away fast enough. "I was daydreaming about a picture I like in 'The Wind in the Willows,'" I say. "That book we borrowed from the library about ratty and mole."

She makes a sound like *wsssht*. "You're a funny wee child. Away with ye now. And take your dolly off the table."

Finn's hair is almost red. Lighter. Not quite ginger. But he has reddish skin and freckles, and when he smiles it's like the sun itself has warmed the room. He scoots past Ma who can't see him, and tugs at her apron strings, but she pays him no mind. He frowns and the sun goes behind a cloud. "I'm still invisible," he says.

Ma's apron slips to the floor. "Lacey, fasten my apron lass, my hands are all batter. I'm all sixes and sevens this morning."

Finn speaks as if he's puzzling something out. "I was a passenger in a ship," he says. "It's my birthday... but... I died today. And then... and then I promised Mamie, and I was born."

"Quiet, you. It's *my* birthday."

"But it isn't raining."

"It's my special day. Let's go and see what my surprise is."

He frowns. "It's a special day for me too," he says. He's gone behind a cloud again because all the colors drain from him. He's all grey, and I shiver. "Something happened," he says, "but I can't remember."

"Couldn'ta been very special then," I reply, as cruel as any five-year-old can be.

The colors return to his skin and clothes. "Sure, but that wee doll is ugly as sin," he says. "Maybe it's a tin whistle!"

"What?"

"Your surprise."

My surprise is a crib for Daisy Paisley with pink blankets and a lace pillow.

"Lace," Finn snorts.

"What?"

"Lacy pillows are all scratchy on the face."

"Well, that's all *you* know, stupid boy. My *name* is Lacey. Don't you remember anything? And I'm *not* scratchy."

"My name's Finn. You brought...," he hesitated. "Brought on...? Broughton."

"I don't understand."

He shakes his head. "You *brought* me jam and peppermints and chocolate biscuits... and a green apple. You had to cut it to get it through the bars. And something else..."

"Was it a tin whistle?" I prompt.

Finn walks around me and peers into my face. "It's you, Missus. It's Mamie. Sure ye look enough alike about the eyes."

My insides tangle with fear. He's mistaken me for my dead mother again, and I turn cold as seaweed. "What bars?"

Finn mumbles something about a gate. He glances about the kitchen and I know he's lost his bearings again. Soon he'll remember the gate and I will feel the ship as if I'd been there. I don't want to see it again. Please Finn, not the ship.

Finn reads my thoughts and immediately remembers the Titanic. "The gate!" he shouts in panic, and I feel an accordion latticework of cold steel bars under my fists that I try to shake open. "They're not letting us out. PLEASE. Mam! St. Michael, save us. Mamie!" His screams hit the wind and float up into the sound of seagulls shrieking after bread and bits of green apple.

Finn settles down, and my heartbeat slows to normal. "It was locked," he says, looking mystified. "They locked it."

"Was that the surprise?"

His words become slurred. "I can smell the juice from the apple," he says. "It was sweet. And the cheese, so yellow it made my mouth water."

I feel hands covering my mouth. "My name is watery, too," I say, snapping out of his dream. "Remember? Lacey Waters. I can write it. Wanna see?"

"Cleary," he says. "M is for... Mamie, is that you?"

"I'm not your mammy. Ma always says to speak *clear-ly*."

"My name is Finn Cleary. Do I have the blue eyes?"

"We're going on a birthday expedition," I say. "Wanna come?"

"And my eyes?"

"Blue as blue can be," I tell him.

The expedition is a family tradition for Ma and me – a trip to the Titanic plot in the Fairview Cemetery. We wander down the outer paths but Finn hangs back. He doesn't want to go near the marker for the unknown child. The one with all the toys. They're soaked in rain and dust so they don't interest me but visitors have left them for Finn. I go on without him and he calls from a long way off to come back or he'll give me a smack so he will. I pick up a teddy bear for the unidentified child and tuck it under my arm to give to Finn.

"You've had enough for your birthday, my girl," Ma says. "Besides, it's bad luck. Childy childy... that's grave robbing, that is."

She takes the bear from me and sets it down but it won't sit up straight and I bend down and pick it up again, all the while telling her it's for the boy in the ground who's standing right over there, so it's not stealing. "He won't come and get it himself," I say, but she's not listening. She's far away, standing with her bare feet in the Atlantic tide, and it's the fifteenth-day of April, 1912, all over again.

The cemetery is a place where apologies are expected. People still come here to cry. Ma goes all quiet and remembers the day I was born. She stares long and hard at me, squinting, turning my chin to the light. "Some days I'd swear your eyes are blue," she says. "It's a trick of the light." But the rest of the day she checks my eyes and shakes her head. "No. Definitely grey as granite. Grey as a bleached boat." My eyes reflect the colors of driftwood we collect on our beach. Our backyard is the Atlantic Ocean as far as the gull flies, as far as the masts of the old tall ships could sail before disappearing below the horizon.

Finn is a poet. To me the Fairview Cemetery is a treed park where everyone whispers, even the birds. Finn calls it a sacred grove lost in an acre of bereavement. He talks funny like that but I love to listen. He's a teller of stories that scare me half to death.

"This is as close to going home as I'm likely to get," he says.

"But you can live with us." I've asked him before. I've begged. He's my best friend, and now that I can see him, he's my magic brother. My twin brother, invisible to everyone else.

Finn shrugs like he always does when I call him my brother and stares at his bare feet. But this time he launches into a speech inspired by the surroundings. His words send me into a daydream. Somewhere I know what they mean.

"This place is a Flanders Field of regret," he announces in a lofty voice, and drifts off into a trance. It's like him to be moody but this large voice of his isn't my brother. It's like a grandfather who knows everything from long ago. And once started, he's bound to reminisce for hours. "I'm put in mind of a patch of hallowed ground on a different western shore," he says. "The western side of the Nile that belongs to the dead – a valley of lost kings and queens and princes and princesses." He points to the ground. "Your mother was a princess. She's buried here in this unmarked grave."

I take a step back and stare at the grass as if it may bite. "What are you talking about?"

Finn gestures to his left. "My Mam and Bridie are over there. Da must have stayed in the ship. None of us are really here. At least the others have moved on. But not me. I can see the Egyptian sun setting on 'Thebes, Nova Scotia,' sure as seagulls." He walks off and leaves a pool of water in his wake.

I can't follow Finn's words, but then I'm five, and all I know is I'm an orphan and that this plot of land was once a farm and now it's a garden of stone that's got some hold on Finn and Ma that I don't fully understand. I wouldn't want to linger where I was buried any more than I want to remain at my birthmother's graveside, now. I should place a flower there but Ma will think I've gone soft in the head, and she won't want to waste the expensive store-bought roses for the monument. I only hope Pa never finds out what we're spending today. He'd skin us alive, and have us on our knees praying for his forgiveness as if he was God himself.

Finn smiles crookedly. He looks shy for once. "I've decided to stay," he says. "Happy Birthday."

"Oh Finn, not here!"

"No. I mean I won't be going on journeys anymore. Well, perhaps a few. I'm going to live with you. Is that alright?"

Ma will think I'm crazy if she sees me hugging the air. "Of course you can stay." I'm thrilled to have my brother home. As always, he reads my mind.

"In a way, we *are* twins," he says. "Our mother's name was Mamie, and now your Ma will be my new mother. I'm used to being ignored. Mamie's bones may be here but *she* isn't. Sometimes I see her on your beach, so if you want to offer her a flower, we can leave one of your homegrown tulips on the shore together. She'll like that. Tonight. I'll show you where. And you should know, sometimes, in the moonlight, it may look as if I'm talking to myself because I have an invisible teacher. But because I met him under a full moon I think of him as the man-in-the-moon."

The three of us stand in front of a painted sign. "But it belongs to FINN," I say, to Ma, offering the bear to the shape of a boy shorter than me. I wave it at him, but he won't take it, and his eyes are all round and he backs off and runs away into the trees. I put it back gently, leaning it against the white gravestone, slipping it half-underneath a toy ship that even I'm old enough to realize is a strange gift to give a boy who died at sea.

Ma's face makes me stop. Is she gawping at a ghost? Maybe she can see Finn. But no, it's me. Her jaw drops open like a ventriloquist's dummy. "Ye can read that?" she says, dumfounded. "About Finland and the wee boy?"

"Yes," I lie. "It's about the big ship that sank and a lost boy."

Ever since I can remember I've heard tales of a fearful ocean liner's four black chimneys and its white star. It's still big news up in Halifax every April, and we trudge along with other well-wishers to trek the rows of eternal remembrance to honor the memory of Titanic's victims.

I only hope Finn doesn't leave puddles in the house that I can't explain.

LACEY – April 16, 1917

The Atlantic is having a greasy day. Grey waves roll like oil slicks on the water. I sniff up great lungsful of heavenly air scented with dead crabs and seaweed and toss the table scraps from our breakfast to the gulls. Some days I'm more Finn, and on those days I hate the Atlantic, nor can I be sweet-talked into putting my toes into it, even on the calmest day. But I love the ocean when I'm plain Lacey, and could never leave it. It's my mother, and Pa says its brine I have for blood. We breathe the same rhythms. We heave our oxygen in and out in chilly gulps, and the seagulls cry the same way I did when I was born. Finn is curious about the blue birthmark on my leg. "Sure it looks like spilled paint," he says. "Were you painting the front door?"

I've been talking to Finn in my dreams for a long time now. Mam thinks it's funny for me to have an imaginary friend. Pa thinks it's foolish, so we never mention it in his presence after that first slip when he looks surprised and says *whssht* several times followed by a more serious *'away with ye te the fairies now.'* But my fifth birthday is the first time Finn appears in the daylight. He says he wants to grow up, and next year he wants to go to school with me. I hope he means what he says, that he's decided to stay.

"Lacey's reading is coming on lovely," Ma says to Pa over our supper of fish chowder and cornbread. "She read about a Finnish boy yesterday at the memorial."

Pa grumps back, "Lil, did ye no make that apple pie?"

"Aye, that I did. So's you wouldna fuss."

I wink at Finn. "It was green apples," I say. "I saw them."

Ma takes yet another opportunity to kiss my cheek. This time she pauses. "Look at me child," she says. "Your eyes are quite blue again. Or am I going mad." She covers her eyes for a few seconds and stares again. "Ansel will you look at Lacey's eyes. What color are they?"

"Grey, like always," he says, without looking up from his newspaper. "Lil, will I need to pay for eyeglasses now?"

Ma has known for some time that my eyes change from grey to blue but not that it reflects which one of us in control. She suspects. But that's the part she daren't share with Pa.

Pa grins at me and ruffles my curls. "Green apples were they? Aye, Granny Smiths they're called, and they're as sour as your mother's tongue when she's a gripe on her. But that's why we have sugar, ye ken. Will you be away fetching that pie for your poor old Pa, now. And rub my feet, Lace, there's a good lass." He takes my chin in his hands and examines my eyes. "Your mother's off with the fairies," he says. "Your eyes are as grey as a thunderstorm."

FINN

While Lacey wades into the tide looking for seashells I spend another Saturday afternoon on my back, arms behind my head, staring at the clouds. I'm top of my class in daydreaming. I read them like a kid with a storybook. I search for signs. Where are my shoes? Shapes come and go but I see no pirate ships or dragons, and no flares darken the sky.

Lacey squeals somewhere to my left. "I found a baby crab," she shouts, her hands cupped together holding a miracle. "Throw it back, it's too small," I shout.

"Grand advice Master Finnegan," Teacher's voice says out of the blue. "You're a teacher."

I point to Lacey's leg. "What's that? Did you fall?"

Lacey stamps her foot. "It's always been there. And no, I wasn't painting the front door. You should mind your manners Finn Cleary. Do you want to build a sandcastle or not? *Pleeeeeze.* C'mon Finn. I'm *borrrrrrred.*"

She's got a touch of the sun and is out of sorts. I can see a black headache forming around her head.

Teacher is unimpressed. "That little miss could do with a lesson in the silent art of beachcombing," he says. "It's meant to be soul-searching, so it is."

"Lace, come and read a few clouds with me," I shout back.

Teacher sighs. "You're going to spoil that girl. Is that the time? I've got to run."

Wind and sunshine wear Lacey out. We trudge home, hungry and sunburned and leached by salty winds, towards shepherd's pie and carrots. Lacey almost falls asleep at the table. Ansel wolfs his food and puts his coat on before swallowing the last bite. "I'm away to 'The Mermaid,' don't wait up," he says.

As if. Ma sighs, relieved to be alone. "Away with you too, Lacey," she says. "You look all in. Straight to your bed, my girl. I'll handle the supper dishes."

Lacey unwinds in the dark, tucked into bed. She's that exhausted her eyes have almost disappeared. She's overtired. Feverish. "I can't sleep. I'm itchy with sand and grit," she says. She staggers to the bathroom and returns with toothpaste on her chin.

It's early days. We're still getting to know each other although Lacey guesses a lot about me that's dead on. We've been circling the truth. I'm her invisible companion. She doesn't know if I'm really shy because she's used to being what Ma wants at any given time. I have no such guile.

"Be my radio," she says, mid-yawn. "I'll close my eyes and you can tell me one of your ghost stories. Nothing about drowning or the Titanic. But, I mean, really scare me, okay?"

"I will. Did I ever tell you about the banshees? Like the ones that are outside right now?"

The wind shrieks around the house, rattling the windows and the handle of the bedroom door. Lacey dives under the covers. I can't tell if the sound she lets out is a shriek or giggle. Girls are hard to decipher. But it's only Ma at the door. She studies the hill in the bed that's her daughter and watches Lacey pretend to be asleep. That girl is a wee actress. Ma is satisfied. She can't help herself from tidying a little. She throws Lacey's clothes over me, sitting in the chair. Books to bookcase. Drapes pulled to close out the moon.

I hear Ma's thought. She's brought her grand traditions from the old country and is fair wrapped in superstition. I hear her ward off the dark. "Moonlight on the bed is bad luck," she says to herself. Moonlight almost anywhere is bad luck to Ma. When she leaves I'll release the man-in-the-moon again.

Ma says it's bad luck to pour boiling water into the teapot if the lid is too far away from the pot. Ideally, the left hand holds the lid at the same time the right hand pours. If you can count to three before clamping the lid down, it bodes ill for something. Shoes must be laid side-by-side facing the door in the correct left-beside-right, order. I wonder what kind of a fit she'd have if she knew that an invisible boy in her daughter's room is looking for two shoes that might be miles apart from each other. Sure she'd be banging pots together to clear the air of the badness.

I sit there and think of banshees. Long after Ma's gone to bed, the curtains remain drawn. It feels safe to be out of the moon's power.

20
SCHOOL DAZE

On the first day of school I squint at Miss Robbins' name on the blackboard. I'm tall so I sit near the back of the grade-one rows. But Finn's shorter and puts up my hand and says he can't see the letters.

Immediately he, that is I, am moved to a front seat. Miss sends home a slip of paper with me that says I need an eye exam. Finn laughs and says glasses will make me appear that much smarter. But I don't need glasses. Finn needs them. And he fusses enough to get me an appointment with 'auld' Dr. Mullen and his eye chart.

My file says blue eyes and lists their dysfunctions, and I'm fitted with a pair of plain glasses although I tease Finn that I want a pair of pink frames with sparkles. He believes me, but frames like this are only in my imagination and Finn thinks I settle for wire frames to be nice. I didn't.

I refuse to wear spectacles on my grey-eye days, and Miss Robbins is astounded how I can read the small print on a poster at the front of the room on Monday but not on Wednesday. I tell her it's the blinding headaches which lands me back at Dr. Mullen's where he examines my eyes and pronounces them grey. He doesn't even notice he's got two different colors on my file. I dismiss him as a quack and Finn wears my eyeglasses when I let him or when he insists and convinces me he's more interested in Shakespeare and books than I am, which is true. So Finn wears my glasses during English Literature and I remove them when its math. It's Finn who loves to read poetry and fairy tales of lands across the sea. We compromise. He tells me the stories in that special way he has, and soon the ballet of the eyeglasses is more or less ignored. They're his.

I'm sure Miss Robbins has me down as a troublemaker. Ma has already told her I'm sensitive which is almost always Finn playing the hooligan, or so he likes to think. Ma accepts by now I have an invisible friend. She pretends it's a lark but Finn says she's not amused. Finn says she prays over it which is so unlike Ma that I think Finn is telling fibs.

Then one night I hear her. "Please God, send Lacey a real friend so she won't be hobnobbing with sprites and fairies. I hear her talking to a boy named Finn. I'm sure it's only because she's so beyond the other children in her class that she needs to find a playmate who is clever and bright. She's a sensitive girl, takes after her mother no doubt. A strange lassie but nevertheless, I'd feel better if there was no wee boy to lead her astray even in her imagination."

And with that she thanks Pa's god and turns down the lamp, saying out loud that she wishes Ansel would fall into a ditch on the way home from The Mermaid, and then she has to start her reluctant prayers all over again and say she's sorry and she didn't mean such a terrible thing but she DID mean what she'd said about the wee boy. And to bless him if he was a pookie sprite, and tell him to be on his way. "I promise to leave out some bread and milk for him if he will leave my Lacey alone," she prays.

The next morning, sure enough, there's a bowl of milk and some crusts on the step and Ma says it's for the birds. "There's a robin's nest in the eaves and baby robins deserve a better start in life than a few old worms," she says.

At bedtime, Ma is quiet. She tucks me in and kisses my forehead. When she does, she looks me in the eye. "You tell that pookie to take his blue eyes and skedaddle," she says.

Finn is confused about Miss Robbins and the robins and says his head hurts and so it can be off with the spectacles and it's fine with him. And as it's fish stew for supper, he won't be coming home until it's time for cocoa and digestive biscuits.

FINN – September, 1917

I can do no wrong. It's winter. Lacey and I have snowball fights in her head. I'm crazy for the words and she loves the math. We argue over which homework should be done first. I need my specs and she is mad to have them off her face when it's math. Miss Robbins doesn't know what to make of us. She calls Ma in for a showdown.

Lacey sits in the hall with my latest selection of half-a-dozen library books while Ma and Mrs. Robbins battle it out in the teacher's lounge, painted yellow and orange so it feels warm. It doesn't work. In fact, it's a room full of headaches. I want to leave but I stay and listen to everything so I can report back.

There sits Ma, clutching her empty handbag, scanning the room for something domestic. I can see into her mind. She feels out of her depth. She wants to put a kettle on and offer Miss Robbins tea, but of course here, Miss is the one to play 'mother.' But after the ritual of pouring and adding the right amount of sugar and milk, the time comes for business. They're here to discuss Lacey and when a parent is called in it's never entirely good.

Miss Robbins sets down her cup and folds her hands in her lap. "Mrs. Waters," she begins. "Lacey has a vivid imagination." It sounds like an accusation.

Ma smiles. "She's a clever lass. Takes after her..." She pauses and looks like a cornered rabbit. "Her father. And you might think I'm old-fashioned, but I've had to clean her room with lavender more than once to rid it of... ah, well, never mind. I'm steeped in the old ways to deal with unwelcome guests, if you mind my meaning. Lacey is an oversensitive child. She sees things."

Miss Robbins clears her throat. "*Um*... I have to ask... is she prone to telling fibs?"

Ma's eyes go cold. I refuse to wait in the corner as if I'd been sent there to mind my manners. Who does Ma think she is? She's not my Mam and I'm not her Michael.

Ma clucks like a hen and draws herself up in her chair. "My Lacey is no a liar."

Miss Robbins looks equally shocked. "No, no, please don't misunderstand me. I meant does she tell stories... tall tales and such?"

Ma relaxes. "Aye, she loves to make-believe. She's always reading. She even has a wee invisible friend." She looks shocked at this admission. "My husband nay approves, mind, but Lacey tells me some of the things they get up to and such. Is that what ye meant? That's no harmful is it?"

"Not at all. But it explains a lot. I think Lacey brings him to class."

Ma is horrified. "Oh, Miss Robbins, surely not."

My teacher smiles. "I had an imaginary pig when I was

her age. Took him everywhere and nearly drove my mother crazy. These things pass." She pats Ma's hand. "It doesn't do to discourage creative thoughts in our girls. They'll have enough challenges when they're older."

Out comes Ma's anchor. A lace handkerchief made from the torn hem of Mamie's nightgown. In times of stress I've seen her pulling it from her sleeve where it's kept just in case. She takes a deep breath from it and I remember my old Mam with her nose in Michael's sweater. It grounds her. She's been gifted a child and it has been her loving duty to do her best by Lacey. Those in authority: Ansel, God, Dr. Mullen, and Miss Robbins... all of them knew better. But Ma knows her kitchen and her child. No-one cares more about Lacey than Ma, and it feels as if she's warming to me. If I'm good she'll eventually care about me as well in order to please her wee princess daughter.

Ma never gives Lacey a clout although we've given her plenty of occasions to tempt any mother. I've the 'devil' in me I tell Lacey, but that's the last thing Ma will want to hear.

"I'm so glad we had this little chat," Miss Robbins, is saying. "Lacey isn't playing up she's playing out."

"Her father reads Keats," Ma says by way of explanation. She has no way of knowing what that means or how unlikely it is. I put Keat's name in her head. Poets fair bring out the devil in me.

Miss Robbins nods with gracious enthusiasm. "Lacey is ahead of her age. I think it's wise to give her more to do. Clearly, she's bored with ...."

"Aye... she can't get enough of books," Ma says.

I know this is true. Most of the books Lacey chooses are for me. In essence, I have two bodies. One feels solid as a table, the other, so Lacey says, is misty. She sees through me in every way. I've looked in the mirror and I see a me who is perfectly sound. It's a good partnership. Brother and sister, each older than the other in years or in wisdom. I began as her twin. She's growing into my big sister, and I, her ageless kid brother willow-the-wisp, know as much as a professor. I am her guardian. But like all girls she's naïve.

"She loves her poetry," Ma says.

Miss Robbins' eyebrows lift. "Poetry. Goodness. Which poets other than Keats?"

Ma is crestfallen. She's already forgotten Keats. "Oh. Well, I'm no sure. I mean I don't look at her books, ye ken. I've too much to do." I send her some help and she suddenly brightens. "I remember the name Yeats. Are they two different poets?"

Miss Robins smiles politely. "No worries, Mrs. Waters. I'll have a word with her. Can she stay after school once a week?"

"If her chores don't suffer. It's her dad ye ken. He believes in the rod. It's me who spoils her."

Miss Robbins nods knowingly but she has no idea. My Pa, Ansel Waters, is a bully when it comes to God, but the rest of the time, when Ma's out of earshot, he's a teddy bear in Lacey's hands. Ma offers to wash the tea things. I run ahead and tell Lacey to open the works of T.S. Eliot from the pile.

Mrs. Robbins declines Ma's offer, and when they find Lacey, she's deep into 'The Love Song of J Alfred Prufrock.' Miss Robbins glances at the title and shares another smile with Ma. Ma beams at Lacey. Lacey seems bathed in a spotlight from two women who share a singular vision of a double-edged girl.

We leave the school. Ma carries some of our books. It's a silent walk home. Lacey and I chatter in mind-speak as usual, lost in our own language. I make her laugh out loud. "Two heads are better than one," I say.

"What's so funny," Ma says.

Ma sends Lacey to bed with instructions. "One hour to read and no more before it's lights out." She is duly pampered with warm milk, cookies, and a hot water bottle.

"That Miss Robbins is a lovely teacher," Ma says. "Don't be forgetting her in your prayers, now."

That jogs a memory of the man-in-the-moon. My Teacher. "I'm here, Pookie," his voice says in my head. "Biding your time."

When the door closes, Ma misses a sight that would surely unhinge her. I sit in a chair, legs outstretched with my feet resting on the foot of Lacey's bed next to a pile of books. She sits against plumped pillows, sipping milk. Being the observer fills me with envy. We share the cookies. Lacey eats one and gives the rest to me. If Ma had Lacey's second sight she would see a transparent boy reading poetry. Sure, it would kill her. But I slam the book closed and hold it on my lap so all she sees is a book on the chair.

We're lucky to have such a devoted Ma but something bothers me. I'm still as invisible as I was in Michael's shadow with Mam, and yet *he* was the one who wasn't there. Rose Waters dotes on Lacy as is proper, but just once I'd like to be given the center of attention. I remember when Da said I was full of myself. Still it would be grand to be a best boy. It's Lacey's birthday every day. If I study hard and find my shoes, Mam will be proud of me. I can teach her and 'Himself,' our Michael, how to appreciate Keats.

An hour goes by quickly. Ma puts her head around the door. I cringe by force of habit as if she can see me. "Night darling girl," she whispers as usual. And then she says a thing that surprises me entirely. "Night night Finn," she says. I'm that shocked I drop my book. It crashes to the floor. Ma assumes it's Lacey kicking it from the bed. She picks up 'The Water Babies' and places it on the chair. Pats it like a cat, and I'm left in the moonlight feeling loved. I remember a precious book with a lock of Michael's hair.

I'm speechless for once.

Lacey uses our shorthand code. "Bedbugs," she says all muffled in blankets.

I'm that choked it takes me a moment to respond. "Bedbugs."

I wait until Lacey is asleep before wandering outside to savor what happened. Tonight the air is crisp with the smell of new snow. Warm air has melted the surface and turned it into a violet crust that glows in the dark. My bare feet feel as warm as Lacey's resting on the hot water bottle but I leave no footprints nor do I melt the snow.

I run into one of the raccoons that ravage our rubbish tip. He's up to his ears in our table leavings meant for the gulls. He rears up and swears at me, swipes the air, and slinks away from a hoard of juicy potato rinds in the compost barrel.

Years go by like sailing ships. There's debris floating in the water. I know it's not really there. It's things long gone from Titanic but I see them right enough. I pull what I can from the icy water: a folded postcard, a cloth cap, and a pot of jam. I leave them on the beach and return to the raccoon, back gorging itself on potato peelings.

I let it be. It watches me and leaves me alone until it

grows light. The clouds glow red as if a fire burns behind them. I remember a thing Pa says: *red skies at night, sailors delight; red skies at morning, sailors warning.* The chirping voice of the raccoon lulls me to sleep and it's the seagulls that wake me. The raccoon has left me empty eggshells. The scraps of green apple peel are gone.

Ma doesn't hear it but Lacey cries in her dreams like a seagull. Like my Bridie. I've had three mothers... two who can't see me.

LACEY

There's a new girl in class – an older girl with pretty red hair. She makes a cheeky face at me that tells me how much she hates math. It's as if she's passed me a note. I smile and concentrate on Miss Robbins, writing sums on the blackboard. I love math.

"Meet me at the Five and Dime," the girl whispers. She points at the clock. "When the little hand is on the three and the big hand is on the six." Message delivered, I expect her to look away but she nods her head and promptly vanishes. I've seen her before. But where? In her place is Finn, staring at me with rapt attention, sniffling. He removes his spectacles, wipes the corner of his eye and spends a long time polishing each lens with a handkerchief. When he looks up, his eyes are red. "I miss her too," he says.

21

A CHRISTMAS MIRACLE

Some days... most days, my eyes are grey. And some mornings... most mornings, I wake from an internal clock set for school. But the first day of December, my room is exceptionally cold and I brush aside a wake-up shake from Finn as if he's an annoying fly. I have an overriding desire to be warm and left alone. "Go away. One more minute." But wait. Finn's not here. He's been playing truant for a few days. I fling aside my covers. "Finn are you back? Is that you?"

"It is."

Finn is across the room grinning like the Cheshire Cat. "I thought you'd never wake up," he says."

How lovely to see him filling my armchair. "You're really back!"

"I am."

I'm that thrilled to see him, I forget how to get out of bed. I sit there exposed to the chill. The times Finn returns after one of his jaunts always feels like a Christmas morning.

The only way to get out of bed during a Nova Scotia December is to plunge into the day. It's not that different from diving into deep water. It must be done fast and accompanied by immediate flapping of the arms and legs. But first I put my slippers on under the covers where they've been toasting beside me all night. My dressing gown is similarly warmed, pinned under the length of me like Peter Pan's shadow. There's no glorious unfolding of rise and shine. It's slippers – leap – robe – commence to flapping, and head for the kitchen.

"What have I missed at school," he says.

My answer is swift. "Me. You've missed me."

"I have."

"And Mrs. Robbins is reading us 'Treasure Island.'"

"That's grand." He goes quiet. "Lace, we have to talk."

I've let my robe get cold. "I'm listening," I say, putting my arms into cold sleeves. "Gosh why couldn't *we* live where there's palm trees and talking parrots."

"I mean, it's something serious. Life or death serious."

It's hard to feel serious. Finn is back, and I grab his hands and dance him in a circle and sing the Finnegan song that always coaxes a smile. *There was an old man named Mr. Finnegan he had whiskers on his chinnegan the wind came out and blew them innegan poor old Mr. Finnegan beginnegan.* "All right all right, I'm that wild to see you too," he says. "I'll race you to the kitchen. I've missed Ma's breakfasts as well."

A snowy morning is one of the best times to appreciate a mother like Rose Waters. Pa seems impervious to the cold so he stirs the fire at dawn, throws on an entire scuttle of coal, and gives it a good rattling with the poker. Bang goes the door when he goes to refill the scuttle. Bang goes the door when he's back inside. It's Pa who fills the first kettle of the day. He helps himself to the night soup and bangs the back door when he leaves for work. That's him gone for the day or a week. And that's the signal for Ma to enter her kitchen – an actor waiting in the wings for her cue. The first thing she does is take in her empty kitchen with a satisfying sigh. No husband. Her smile dances a jig. Next it's cocoa for me. That's when I skip in, flapping and waving my arms.

We perform our mother daughter ritual. I give her a peck on the cheek and ask, "why are you singing, Ma? And she gives me a peck on the cheek and answers. "I sing to the porridge because it's for you." This varies if Ma's stirring scrambled eggs, flipping pancakes or frying bacon. I'm adored. Because of me, Ma sings to bacon and hot chocolate and pancakes.

When Pa is home, we say grace solemnly, monks over a silent breakfast. Ma and I eat methodically, go easy on the jam, and maintain eye contact with our cutlery. If Pa isn't working he's away as soon as he's drained his tea, off to meet his pals to wait out the bad weather in the 'Mermaid.' Smiling confuses him and will invoke the inevitable question. What's wrong wi ye? Are ye tapped? Roughly translated it means have you gone 'round the bend'?

I pad after Finn, to the kitchen where my clothes have been stewing and then baking to a gentle crisp by the potbellied stove. As usual he takes the head start. His words trail back to me. "Come on onion, get yourself dressed and warm, sure I'm remembering the damp Irish mornings just watching you shiver."

"It's easy for you," I say, pushing past him, "you don't feel the weather." He lets me win again.

The kitchen heat blasts me like a summer day. I stop and absorb it, happy as a lark that my brother is home.

Finn is truly home now, basking in the glow of belonging. "It's easy for *you,*" he says. Rose cooks you a hot breakfast. In Ireland, it was my job to tend the fires, and my mam was no good to anyone without her tea." He sighs. "I always made her that first cup of tea." Finn is in awe of Ma and me. I thinks he's even jealous because I see him look away when we hug and tease each other. "Most mornings all we had was turnip soup," he says.

All my clothes are grey at the start and greyer as the soot dyes them a little darker each night. But they are delightfully toasty. Soon my feet are cozy inside grey socks inside house-boots made of grey felt that fit snug inside my winter overshoes, and I've donned a flannel undershirt and two grey sweaters. Ma laughs at me and calls me an onion but she's the one who taught me that layers of clothes keep the winter away. I pull on a pair of fingerless gloves and wrap my hands around a mug of cocoa and take a long sniff of chocolaty steam. Only then is it possible to consider breakfast or to listen to Finn blathering in that Irish way of his.

Pa has risen early for the catch and is gone while it's dark. Ma is bustling in another room but she's made porridge and I help myself with Finn still rabbiting on about how nice it would be to have boiled eggs and soldiers some morning and couldn't I put in an order just once on a school day. I try again to explain the ins and outs of timing a boiled egg between getting dressed and leaving for school. He refuses to accept that boiled eggs are weekend things and therefore a treat he can look forward to, if he put his mind to it.

Frosty mornings mean hot cereal. This is Ma's law. Some days it's cornmeal and others rolled oats, but it's always hot with a dab of butter and brown sugar. I add a dollop of strawberry jam to keep Finn quiet. "You're a good sister," he says, and takes a huge spoonful.

But today is urgent. "I've a message more important than school," he says. "It's why I came home so soon."

"Go on then, blather away, but you'll have to tell me on the way."

After my snow pants, I yank on my winter boots over the felt liners. Last comes a parka. Ma ties a scarf over my mouth and nose and pulls the drawstrings of the hood nice and tight over everything so I can't turn my head without my face disappearing. A maritime child simply faces the appropriate direction and plods forward as the crow flies.

I am as December-proof as a Nova Scotian child can be. Luckily, the wind off the Atlantic is at my back and pushes me towards the school. Ma pulls back the scarf, kisses my nose one last time, covers it again, and hands me my school bag. "Ham sandwiches and a hard-boiled egg," she says. "And chocolate chip cookies."

The door opens and out we go, hand-in-hand into the white world, me, a bundle of red snowsuit and Finn barefoot in short pants, blue shirt, and a cloth cap. The wind never ruffles his curls but I have to squint my eyes against it. I feel Ma smiling, watching me till I'm out of sight. No matter how cold, it's only then that she closes the door.

The red schoolhouse has two floors. One downstairs classroom with the indispensable potbellied stove and a kitchen alcove with a gas cooker. Its whitewash interior makes it cool in summer and extra freezing in winter. Miss Robbins lives upstairs. Eighteen wet coats dry on the row of coat hooks, eighteen pairs of mittens steam on the radiator, thirty-six boots ooze puddles on the wood floors. We can only hope that our sad coats will be released from the lion's share of melted snow by the end of the day. All we need to do is head from home to school and back again, from one potbellied stove to another. Beeline journeys for hungry children in damp coats.

Recess is abandoned in winter. It isn't worth the carryings-on dealing with wet coats and taking up the time for at least an hour's worth of reading. Besides, if we get dressed in time to play for twenty minutes, we will cover ourselves in snow, and our coats will have no chance to almost dry for the trek home.

Miss Robbins gives us a rest instead. She calls it a respite. Recess is story-time and we fall into a dreamy space to listen to ourselves write stories in the air. In the meantime, the snow howls and the windows become encrusted with frost. The building fairly roasts tucked inside a garden of snow like a bright candle in a window.

If it grows stormy there are mattresses piled ready for the kids who live a long distance away or if their fathers don't arrive to take them home. Some of them have town friends they stay with. At most, in a whiteout, there are a dozen of us who are pressed into a few domestic chores, but it's no hardship. Our only chores are to wipe the blackboard and release clouds of dry snow to the great outdoors, from the chalk on the erasers. The chalk dust mingles with our white breath and we clap the erasers together for exercise like windup monkeys playing cymbals.

Miss Robbins and the girls retreat to her kitchen and add extra potatoes and carrots and onions to the soup that simmers all day long, to make it stretch. The boys stoke the stove with wood and tidy the books. We sit at our desks, with the radiators clanking like ghosts, eating hot soup and dumplings while we tell stories of our own. Well, it's one story really. Each of us makes up a new line that is passed around like a game of musical chairs, trying to outdo each other and impress Miss Robbins who opens the story with a great big what-if. I have to be careful. Oftentimes, when it's my turn, Finn blurts out something disturbing about the Titanic – a sore subject for an uplifting tale meant to inspire and comfort us, alone there in a red cube of wood blasted by freezing snow.

But the school stands at the end of Shackleton's main street, so we are within help of the townsfolk if the weather gets truly stuck-in. Cabin fever is a real thing whether caught in the schoolhouse or at home, but for us only-child families, it's more fun at school with each other for company surrounded by books and art paper and crayons, than alone, left to ourselves for inspiration. It's like summer camp with snowmen and icicles.

My boots begin a fresh trail, crunching in foot-deep snow. Finn likes to hear it. We usually walk in silence most of the way, content in each other's companionship. His dreams of walking to school in his new shoes are strong and the sound of the snow reminds him of squeaking leather. But today he's anxious to speak and for me to listen. It's just as well; talking is hard inside a cocoon of wool.

"I know something," he says. "It's a terrible secret and I may tell you some of it but no more because that's all I know, and you'll have to promise not to tell anyone else, so will you?"

I speak to Finn in our special way since my scarf is stuck to my face with ice crystals. "What's wrong?"

"Do you promise? It's a being-dead-thing."

"But you're alive, inside my head. And I'm *not* dead, in case you hadn't noticed."

"I'm almost alive, but it's not enough. And I think I made a big mistake," Finn says.

I'm that alarmed I pull down my scarf and expose my face. "But I don't want you to go. We're brother and sister. You said, together forever and three's a crowd, right?"

Finn replaces my scarf like a good brother. "I'm alive and not alive if you can understand that," he says. "When I go away for a while I suppose I'm more dead. Then I come back because it seems only you can save me. Together we can find my shoes and then I can find Mam."

"And after that are you going to desert me?"

"We can work that out later. Sure, desertion is a terror of a word. As of a few days ago, I've had an inkling of a disaster that involves you. Now don't be scared. If you do what I say you'll be fine. I guess it's a perk of being dead but it seems I *can* warn someone I love. That appears to be the rule. Not just anyone, but someone close."

"And we're close as peas in a pod, aren't we?"

He nods enthusiastically. "That's the truth of us."

That cheers me. I bumble my plans without thinking. "You can take me with you when you find your shoes and I can meet your Mam and Bridie. And maybe my mother will come and..."

He frowns. "It's for you to listen and *not* interrupt. Forget my leaving. I know it's hard for you but you must pay attention."

"I *am* listening," I say in a bit of a huff.

"Ma is planning a trip to Halifax for the Christmas shopping. She's going to do something she'll live to regret...*erm*... possibly live is the wrong word. Look, it doesn't matter right now. It's something dangerous."

"And I must save her from financial ruin. Is that it?"

"No. It's yourself you'll be saving and Ma along with you. You're to stay home that day. You must keep quiet and let her surprise you. She's planning an expedition. She thinks December sixth is going to be a treat – a 'princess for a day' lark. Promise me you'll find a way to beg off. Coz if you don't I'll be throwing a fit and land you in the madhouse sure as apples."

"You wouldn't dare."

"I would. I will."

"Then you would be in the loony bin too."

"Of course I wouldn't, I can come and go as I please. I'd be leaving you there, alone."

I work the wool from my mouth and nose, again, furious that Finn can be so selfish. "Then you can kiss your shoes goodbye for good," I say. "Find em yourself."

"Sometimes you act like a wee baggage," he says. "And I know what that means now. Look, all you have to do is pretend to have a fever. Fevers are the worst, so they are. They fair turn mothers into *eedjits*. Make sure it's a good un. No time for the doctor. Just Ma who is quick to panic with you the apple of both her eyes. She will stop and fuss but you must be nothing less than delirious. Let me do the thinking. I can put the fear of god into Ma. My memories can take her onboard Titanic, and you'll not be wanting that. She knows of your invisible friend and that frightens her more than you know. But we'll use it as it suits us, as often as need be."

Now his storytelling has me worried. "What on earth is going to happen?"

"I know and I don't know. I know something horrific about a white mountain and a ship. That's all I've heard. That's the truth, and it will be so whether the likes of you and me understand it or not. It's a given that we *will* understand when it's too late."

"There are no real mountains in Nova Scotia, Finn. You know that."

"I do but it's a real mountain not a local molehill. I've heard it whispered and then everyone's silent no matter who I ask. Truly, I've begged shamelessly but no-one will say. Maybe that's all they know. People can do nothing but stand by and hope to survive. But it's not an iceberg. It's something as fierce as the ice but different. I see a black pall over Halifax and no mistake. You and Ma have to be here at home that day. Promise me."

I'm hooked, terrified. "I promise. Can I do anything to stop it?"

"You're a wee girl. And the likes of grand disasters are the sins of men. I don't understand why but they are. I think it's some sort of grand reckoning that balances history, but even that makes no sense. I know things in the spirit world but no-one explains anything. It's a mass of feelings without words and those who have 'passed-over' from a marine disaster know the signs. It's in the wind and the waves. It's in the absentminded inklings of sailors dwelling on other things. It's hidden in their mistakes."

"And this will save Ma and me?"

"I'm saving myself too," he says. "Don't ask me how. I just know. Mamie knows too. She's shouting at me to keep safe and to keep you safe. It's one in the same thing. If Mamie shows herself it's got to be important. She's not able to *do* much as she's already in another body. She has to dream her way into my life, and even then she isn't completely sure of what she's saying. It's not her words I hear, it's her fear. Her fear for you and me. It's a powerful fear there is between a mother and child. My old Da told me so."

"Now you're scaring me."

"Surprise and fear look the same," he says. "To be sure, sometimes you giggle when you're afraid. When we were nearing the end on Titanic you should have seen the glory on Mam's face. She was full of the joy of seeing Michael. Death was nothing. She worked her beads under the water smiling fit to burst. And wee Bridie was given to the water to float away. The cold took Bridie. She didn't drown like the rest of us."

I agree just to stop him sending me his memories that I can feel. "Okay, I absolutely double-dog promise."

"Well, that's grand because I swear I'll deliver the fears of Mamie into Ma, so she won't know what she's about other than locking you in a closet for the rest of your natural life."

22

THE WHITE MOUNTAIN

For three days Ma's smile beams out the top of her hat. She winks at me a few times, giggles a great deal, and calls me a gooseberry more than usual. She chucks me under the chin. She pinches my cheek. "This is going to be a fine Christmas," she says. "I have a surprise." She pats her purse. "And we won't breathe a word of it to your Pa. It's our secret. Just you and me, mother and daughter."

That tells me everything. Her purse means it has to do with money and that if Pa were to know it would be cancelled as a holy sin. It is either extravagant or too pleasurable to bear or both, flying against the judgement of God. Pa's God is vengeful for reasons past my understanding. He punishes frivolity in all its forms. And according to Pa's strict Presbyterian ways, we must be dour and serious in order to be worthy of heaven. I once asked him if his drinking was a frivolity and I didn't half get a licking. Between Pa's dreary expectations and Finn's locked gates, heaven doesn't sound like a hospitable place. I have no intention of going there because Finn's not going. He told me heaven's gates are like Titanic's, except they won't let him *in*.

For the same three days, Finn is fixated to the point of irritation. On the fifth of December he's pretty crazy even though I assure him I'm willing and ready to rain on Ma's fun. His threat of taking over my body and throwing some kind of fit convinces me to agree to his wishes several times a day.

I'm stamping the snow from the top of my boots, holding a warm hand over my frozen nose when Finn barks a command in my red ears.

"Come now. It's urgent. Do you know what tomorrow is?"

As if I could forget the date.

Last night, Finn made a giant number six in my dreams, surrounded by a wreath of holly for good measure, and it exploded like a bomb that made me sit up in a cold sweat. Good, Ma will see the nightmare sweat and I won't have to act so hard. I can toss and turn and moan and let Finn say things to send Ma diving into her special bag for emergencies.

When I wake proper, I feel the fear of standing in a destroyed city. Wreckage is all around me. It's the end of the world. But there is no mountain.

"It's the sixth," I say wearily. The clock reads 4 a.m. two hours earlier than school hours and today is a holiday. What is Ma thinking?

I soon find out. Ma crashes around the kitchen. She puts her head in my door. "I'm making your favorite," she says. "I've been telling you today's a special day. We have to leave extra early on the workers' bus. We're going to Halifax. We have to be there early so I can do some... some business and then the day's ours."

What business was Ma likely to have?

"I've made a list," she says. "We're going to be rich for a

day and spoil ourselves silly. I've made you soft-boiled eggs and soldiers. So let's be having you. The kitchen's lovely and warm. The eggs'l be ready in the shake of a lamb's tail so don't be late or they'll go all hard."

Finn groans a long wail, upset at missing his boiled eggs because as hungry as I am, I have to miss breakfast in order to feign an illness worthy of staying home. And forgo lunch and supper too. There's no choice. I can't miraculously heal in twenty-four hours, but I needn't have worried. The events of December 6th, 1917, shatter the worries of me recuperating from an unusually cool fever.

Mid-morning, Ma is mumbling over the state of my forehead being perfectly fine, when we hear a distant blast of thunder and feel a soft tremor. A whuff of wind blows the curtains inwards and flutters the greased paper that seals the cracks around the windows before tearing it into strips. A great draught blasts under the front door and blows it open. It flaps wildly in the disturbed snow. Is there a blizzard? But the sky is clear. The drifting snow resettles and it's calm over the expanse of blue landscape from the house to the shore. But before the wind retreats it reaches down the chimney and releases the catch on the stove, covering the kitchen in soot. The breakfast table, still laid with abandoned boiled eggs and soldiers, is destroyed. Finn is wretched that he couldn't scarf them without causing a fuss. The 'invisible friends with sticky fingers', lecture.

To make it worse, Finn vanishes the moment the stove explodes, and I worry about him all the time Ma and I scrub every inch of the kitchen. For the rest of the day we empty buckets of grey water outside until one side of our house has frozen into a grimy ski hill.

FINN

The Titanic's dead startle, dreaming about the collision of a ship and an icy mountain. I'm drawn into their collective and a few of us assess the damage. All I can think about is that the devastation in Halifax would surely have taken Lacey and Ma or inflicted them with terrible injuries. For a moment I wonder if it wouldn't so bad if Lacey died. She could meet Teacher and go to school with me. Possibly have her own teacher. It's a stupid childish thought, and Teacher shows up to chastise me.

"It wasn't stupid," he says. "It was a completely *selfish* thought. Finn it's not your job to recruit spirits. Do you know why you were alerted?"

"I don't"

There was no sympathy. No ounce of teacher compassion. No mothering of any kind. "Find out. It's important. Pay attention to any forebodings. They're always big messages. It's something particularly relevant to you or you'd never have known. And don't go thinking it was cleverness. It was pure happenstance."

"So, Lacey might have died?"

"Correct. Tell her from me she's a lucky girl."

But I can hear Lacey's thoughts, and all she's thinking is how *unlucky* she is because a rogue wind attacked the front door, nearly blew the stove sky high, and possibly delivered a bout of pneumonia to her feet.

I show up outside her bedroom. She's coughing, and Ma has her ear to the door, opened ajar, shell-shocked in the hallway. I watch her close Lacey's door softly with extra care as if it's breakable. As I flatten myself against the wall to let her pass, her head lifts proudly. "I know you're there, Pookie. I canna stop you from coming but if you've any affection for my lass you'll leave her be tonight. She thinks you're a wee angel and she's a bright judge of a soul, so I'll be givin' you the benefit of the doubt, for once. She's abed with a fever and her lungs are sore with the coal dust. She needs to rest. So I'll say goodnight to ye."

I touch Ma's arm and sent her a blast of love that bounces back through me, leaving me momentarily breathless with joy. She smiles. "Guard her well, then. And thank her wee mother for me." For tonight, at least, Ma accepts me for an angel.

Lacey is waiting for me in the 'candle-in-the-window' sense. All wide-eyed, her face flushed and glowing with fever, bundled in a plaid shawl. She looks truly ill and I feel guilty for my part in it. I've learned a thing about telling lies. An honest person never quite gets away with it. Events contrive to make the lie true, and now Lacy has a real fever. I can see the heat of it surrounding her.

She shifts her legs to make room for me on the bed. "I must have caught a stupid chill. Ma and I had our hands in water all day. It was blowing a gale inside here with freezing water and soot everywhere. And Pa didn't come home, so it was only the two of us. I thought you were supposed to *save* us." She gestures to a tray near the fire. "Anyway, I saved *you* some soup." Her hands were raw with dirt embedded around her fingernails. "And there's not a turnip within a mile of it. I told Ma they make me sick."

"I'm sorry you don't feel well, but I *did* save you, if you're up to hearing about it."

"Maybe I'm still seeing things and you're not real. What happened? Did you see a mountain?"

"I did."

She shuts her eyes and turns over, dismissing me. "Yeah right. Was there a banshee as well?"

I bounce the bed a few times, forgetting it might not be the best thing for someone feeling ill. "Come on Lace. You love spooky stories, so you'll want to hear this."

"Finn, I'm not in the mood," she says from beneath the covers. "Ma's going to hear you."

I tell her anyway. Lacey comes round when there's a good story started. "There WAS a mountain but it was a French freighter called the 'Mont Blanc.' And here's the spooky part. In English it means the White Mountain. And wouldn't you know, it was carrying dangerous munitions for the war."

She peeps her nose out. "What're mun...?"

"Ammunition for the soldier's guns and cannons. Things that explode. Things that did explode when they collided with another ship headed for New York. No wonder my attention was piqued."

"Okay smarty pants, what is piqued?"

"That I was more curious than usual... Wait... you were *seeing* things?"

She emerges reluctantly and smooths the bedspread. "It was bad stuff. Bits of my nightmare from yesterday, kinda flashing at me every so often. I guess I was rambling, coz Ma went sort of crazy. Fussing about, all guilty about not believing I was sick and then more guilty that she'd made me clean the kitchen. She may never plan a surprise again. Why does Ma think everything bad in the world is her fault?"

I rub Lacey's hands to make her feel better. Her headache thumps inside my head. "My mam was like that with Michael. As if she'd invited the consumption in by the front door and could send it away again with a brisk 'now out you go but thanks for stopping by.' That's how powerful mothers think they are. They're so 'should or shouldn't' about everything that when something goes wrong they can't help but believe it's something *they* could have prevented."

Lacey closes her eyes and slumps deeper into her shawl. "Tell me a happy story."

"I can't. Except, well, you may not believe me yet, but you're better off with that fever than blown to bits. Lace, your visions were real. There was a terrible explosion in Halifax. A lot of people were killed."

She came fully awake, then. "People screaming and fire everywhere was real?"

"It was."

"So you did save Ma and me?"

"I did."

Teacher's guffaw breezes through the room and cuffs me behind an ear.

"Well, I sort of did. Maybe."

"I didn't believe you. I was pretty mad, too," she says.

I sit up straight in my best storyteller pose. "It was kinda the weirdest thing."

"Tell. Tell. What was weird?"

Teacher's voice is sharp enough to make my headache worse. "Kinda sort of maybe?" he says. "Tell her the truth, Finnegan. It won't set you free entirely but it'll put you on the 'high' road."

When Lacey settles down, I tell her the weirdest thing. "Remember I said it was no wonder that I was piqued? Well, Teacher told me to find out why..." I sigh and take her hand. "It was partly a Titanic connection, you know a maritime tragedy with hundreds of innocent casualties, but that wasn't what alerted me, as it turns out it was more my *personal*

Titanic thing because the ship carrying munitions was also carrying a cargo of *shoes*. Army boots for the troops overseas. It was the shoes. Lacey, those shoes were like a beacon to me. I'd like to think I had a hand in your escape, but the truth is, it was those shoes that saved you. Those shoes saved your life."

The newspapers ran late but slowly the truth trickles into print and they carry the unfolding tragedy of how two ships that should have passed uneventfully in the light of day, destroy the heart of Halifax and take many lives. Pa has us gather around him the way we rally around the radio to listen to overseas broadcasts with news bulletins of the war.

Pa reads out loud in his best fire and brimstone voice. He sounds like a preacher admonishing us personally from a pulpit:

"As World War I continues to rage in Europe, the port of Halifax is busier than ever. On the morning of December 6, 1917, the Norwegian vessel 'Imo,' bound for New York City, left its mooring in Halifax harbor at the same time, the French freighter 'Mont Blanc,' its cargo hold packed with relief supplies and highly-explosive munitions for the troops overseas, was forging through the harbor's narrows to join a military convoy waiting to escort it across the Atlantic...."

Ma squirms in her chair, her lips trembling from remorse. Lacey holds her hand, fully-recovered but worried about Ma who imagines her child has only been spared by a coincidence. She has practically engineered her daughter's death. The injuries that could have occurred haunt her day and night. Probably, the pookie had its hand in it.

I whisper in Ma's ear mimicking Mamie's voice. "It's not your fault, Rose. Things happen at sea. Things happen in war. Thank you, Rose. You're doing a splendid job taking care of my daughter."

The massive Halifax explosion killed more than 1,800 people. It killed Pa's friend, Jimmy McPhee. Another 9,000 are injured in the chain of fires that snaked through the city, jumping and leaping in the wind tunnels of densely-packed buildings. It out-disaster's the human losses of the Titanic. The resulting shock waves shattered windows fifty miles away. Folk carried the echoes of that horrific thunder into their dreams.

But the worst terrible-awful thing – the aftermath of the first premonition, is another presentment that I must keep out of Lacey's head at all costs. Somehow the factory that manufactured the army boots on the 'White Mountain' will one day bring Lilian-Rose Waters closer to her death.

LACEY

Ma is contrite. Much too quiet to be healthy, but all the while praying how I had been saved from sure death as if her life is nothing. The items of jewelry in her bag lay inside her handkerchief and she makes a solemn confession to Pa. He sees immediately she's sincere and so he praises God instead of blaming her which is a miracle in itself. But he takes evasive action. It's winter and the ground is too hard for digging. But he tells Ma, that come spring, the jewelry will rest out of harm's way until it's given to me when I reach twenty-one, and then the matter will be sealed in God's eyes, the Waters will be redeemed, and that will be an end to it. Amen.

Ma's Halifax 'business' was to sell two insignificant jewels from Mamie's red bag to finance an outing fit for a princess. Pa says Ma is daft. That she's been reprieved from the gallows right enough, for by selling missing jewels belonging to a first class passenger on the Titanic, whose husband had surely claimed them for the insurance, was tantamount to committing the crime of murder, for wouldn't there be an enquiry to deal with the death of a woman who survived the sinking but succumbed when safely ashore?

The worst of it is that Mamie's body had been tagged with a number, and Jimmy McPhee had given Pa's name to an official bit of paper. Pa calls Ma Lillian-Rose for weeks and I stay out of his way.

Ma is shaken. My fever that saved us passes into religious mythology where Pa says God had inflicted me to save the family, otherwise there was no accounting how I recovered the same afternoon as the explosion. I almost believe it myself.

That Christmas there are no presents for me other than a skimpy stocking. Pa makes it clear he doesn't approve by placing a piece of coal in the toe. We go without butter and jam and Christmas delicacies, and Pa never takes sugar in his tea again. But I make sure to ask Ma privately for a tin whistle. She doesn't let me down. It's there under the tangerine and a striped candy cane. Of course, it's for Finn. He loves it and thanks me over and over, and whenever he looks sad, I blow it at the seagulls to make him fall about laughing.

But he's distracted when I eat the candy cane. "Peppermint," he says after a taste, and goes all quiet. Then he scares me. "Don't look back, Mam." He points out my bedroom window. "Look. That's where we'll sleep. Beneath the gold line."

23

SEPARATED AT BIRTH

LACEY – 1918

Pa forces Ma and me to pray through January and February, skimping on anything slightly luxurious.

Finn disappears a week after March roars in like a lion, announcing he'll be back in plenty of time for our April birthday and the groundbreaking ceremony to bury my treasure. But the ground is still frozen on the fifteenth.

We have barely survived a humiliating Christmas so I know there'll be no birthday fuss. No Titanic cemetery and no birthday cake, as Pa's still chafing from the fiasco of Ma dipping into my dodgy inheritance. Ma's face is grim. "You may as well have these," she says, handing me something wrapped in a man's handkerchief. Out drops a brown brooch in the shape of a daisy and a necklace made of black glass. Nothing for a child to wear. "Keep them out of Pa's sight. They're not toys. And sure enough he'll call them sins. Someday you might be glad of them. Who knows."

The necklace drips from my fingers. "Are these.... the Christmas jewels?"

"The very same. Your Pa's going to hide the rest. God knows where."

She means exactly that. It was Pa and God's secret now.

"He hasn't destroyed them," Ma says. "I thought he

might, but he said that would have been wrong considering they're your property. He thinks I put these two bitties back. I chose them because they were the least of the glittery things that could raise questions. I'm not too simple to understand that the likes of me sporting emeralds would be a situation for the police. I think the necklace is glass. Still it's a delicate thing the way it's woven together. It's a bit like black lace isn't it? The brooch is costume jewelry. But you never know if they're old or maybe they have sentimental value. They might have belonged to your grandmother for all we know. Anyway, such as it is, happy birthday, child. We must hope for better days and that your Pa's memory will fade. He's that cross with me."

Her voice trails off.

Finn looks down in the mouth too. "That brooch has bittersweet memories for me," he says. "May I hold it? No, wait, I can't. That is, I daren't. Boys aren't supposed to cry."

For a double-special day it wasn't proving to be happy or momentous. Nothing like the way it had felt only one year ago on the fifth-anniversary of Titanic's sinking when Finn decided to stay.

"Cheer up," Finn says at last. "Pa's away for a few more days. We don't have to be gloomy. He'll never know if we laugh."

I have to agree. "I think that's exactly right."

"You're a year older than me now," Finn says. "You must remember this day, and never allow anyone to reduce you to a servant. That's not the life Mamie wants for you. She thinks of you and I on this day even if she can't quite remember why she's so melancholy. You can bet she's not going to let a man bully her. And I won't let one bully you."

"Thanks little brother," I say, thinking he'll laugh, but the beginnings of his smile evaporates. His eyes narrow into a demonic squint. I know I'm in for it – about to be punished, Finn style.

"How about a scary story for your birthday?" he says. "One that I *promise* will freak you out."

I face him square in the eye. "You can't scare me, I'm six."

He settles into my bedroom chair and I get comfy on the bed. The story begins innocently enough as any fairy tale, set up as a 'once upon a time.' "It's time I told you about your father," Finn says.

But then he launches into page two. "Your father's name was Carlyle. He was an arrogant, violent, vain man. He beat Mamie and sent her away."

"What!"

"Mamie was a servant girl in trouble, leaving for America, pregnant with you."

"Ma said she was a passenger in first class."

"Ma *assumed* Mamie was a rich lady from first class, but she wasn't. She was in steerage with me."

"But the jewels?"

Finn seems to realize the dreams he's crushed, and tries to end the story quickly on a happier note. "Mamie was alone and scared but she made time for me and Mam, and she always made us feel better. She loved me in her way, but she loves you more."

I actually feel sorry for him but I let him stew. Clearly, he's mortified. But now I'm worried about the jewels. Were they stolen? It doesn't bear thinking about. Ma could have gone to prison.

"Lace, I'm sorry. I'm that wretched I don't know what to say. I wasn't thinking. I was angry off my head. But I'm not a *kid.* Don't call me a kid. Promise? Oh my god, Teacher's going to have my guts for garters."

I roll off the bed and pace back and forth. Every now and then I give Finn a pathetically sad face to teach him a lesson. "It's okay," I say, holding back fake tears. "I'm a big girl now... *sniff* ... You didn't destroy my dreams, Finn, and I'm not going to destroy Ma's. But how did Mamie get the jewels?... *gasp* You don't think she stole them do you?"

My poor brother is devastated, but I'm not done. I continue to punish him, Lacey style.

"Mamie would never do that. Please don't ever think that. She was wonderful. Look, I *do* know what happened but I think I've already said too much for one day. Just believe me the jewels were hers and now they belong to you."

I sit down rather too heavily on the bed. My spine jolts but I pay it no mind. "My father was a monster?" I put my head in my hands so it looks like I'm sobbing. Serves Finn right. He's that contrite he forgets I'm an actress.

Finn crawls over and hugs my legs for a long time. "Buck up Lace. It's as if Mamie gave birth to twins," he says. "She tells me that when she's dreaming, and I see her on the beach some afternoons out the corner of my eye. It's night where she is and she's dreaming. So I bet she's here today. Let's go down and talk to her."

"I feel her around me sometimes," I say.

Finn lets go of my legs and pulls me to my feet. "Somehow, having one foot in heaven gives me strength and the wisdom of the ages," he says. "I'm five. I will always be five, and yet I'm grown so big that some nights what I know fills the sky. There's something sad about that but nothing really bad. You have a brother who fills the sky and two mothers to watch over you. Pa loves you too, in his way. He's keeping Mamie's legacy safe for you."

"What's a legacy?"

"You see? How do I know these words? A legacy is something you deserve. A gift handed down when someone dies. Now let's have a picnic in the spot where you and I were born. I know the exact place. There's magic in that sand."

I lean across and kiss Finn's cheek. "I promise never to call you a kid. Happy birthday big brother."

"Happy birthday little sister. Now let me tell you about that brooch of yours. Bring it with you. I first saw it on your mother when she brought me bread and cheese for fear I was too puny and shy to compete in the dining hall for a proper share of anything other than gruel. I thought it was made of toffee. Mamie said it was butter amber a million years old. And then didn't she just bring me some toffee the very same color. Mamie saved the finest things I've ever tasted from her first class meals. Grander delicacies than could ever have landed in my sad begging bowl. She said they arrived on a silver tray kept warm under a silver hat. She wrapped meat and fruit in miniature white sheets embroidered with a white star that she called napkins. Mam loved them. Each one was smoothed and folded." He stops, misty-eyed. "She was going to wash them when we got to New York."

Finn looks about ready to break, so I look the other way and nearly choke trying to suppress a laugh.

"What? Are you laughing, you wee baggage?"

"Ma thinks you're a leprechaun."

He looks relieved. "She's right. Leprechauns are devilish cunning. I never know what will show up in my mouth. These words and grand meanings, now that I'm dead I know what a legacy is and a million other things. I'm a great know it all, but I still lash out when I'm cross. I don't like being called a kid."

It was a great conversation for changing horses in

midstream. "Ma said Mamie was dressed as a fine lady. I've seen the lace nightgown and the fur, and now these baubles. They may not have been hers but still. They're my... leg..."

"Legacy."

"They mean something special."

"Better than that ghastly doll you got last year."

I tickle his ribs until he begs me to stop or so help him he'll skin me alive. "Better than a penny tin whistle?" I release him and he stands up to adjust his shirt. Suddenly I'm aware of our disparate heights. He does look like a little kid.

"Well now, there you might be wrong," Finn replies. "Because as you well know, a person who's never heard the terrible din a tin whistle makes hasn't lived. My friend Markey said it was fit to wake the dead."

Ma would say, 'out of the mouths of babes.'

We traipse to the shore, following the sounds of the loons, and sit on an old horse blanket that Finn says played a part in our birth. We drink ginger beer and eat bread and butter and yellow cheese and two of the green apples that Ma was saving for a pie. The loons swim in close and laugh at us, and the seagulls dive around us for the leavings.

We pretend Mamie is one of the gulls. Sailors often said they were the ghosts of drowned travelers. I hold out a crust and a young gull comes close and eats from my hand. Daintily for a ravenous bird, and when I feel the tug of the bread leave my hand I hear a voice call out happy birthday darling girl.

Finn hears it too. But his face darkens. He jumps to his feet and heaves our apple cores onto the rocks in a fit of temper. They splatter one-by-one, causing a frenzy of interest. He kicks the last crusts for the birds in a rough spray of sand, and stumbles away.

"What's wrong?" I call after him.

He answers without turning. "Mamie never said happy birthday to me and I was her darling *boy*!"

Before I can comfort him he vanishes and pops up much further away. He's left me to tidy up. I fold the blanket and pour the last of the ginger beer onto the sand. Finn rants at the waves from far off down the beach. I catch the word teacher but the rest drifts out to sea.

24

THE BOY KING

age eleven

"I'm king of the dirty rascals," Finn shouts, playing about, arms raised in victory, claiming my bed for a mountaintop, but it's another boy king who takes me to the height of my imagination.

I've been stung by an ancient bee. The newspapers burst with the story of a boy who lived thousands of years ago. The world has been focused on the Valley of the Kings ever since King Tutankhamen was discovered by Howard Carter last year. But now the tomb is revealing its treasures. It's magic time. The world has Tut fever but I have it more. I've become a library girl and pore over books too big to bring home. I want to know everything about Egypt. Pictures of the Sphinx, the Great Pyramid of Giza, and Tut's golden death mask adorn my walls like movie star pinups.

After lights out, Finn and I sneak down to the water's edge with a flashlight. I take my library book and head for the seashore so I can amaze Finn with the facts without garnering attention. "It's a place so hot that it never rains and there's no such thing as shoes," I say. The loons laugh over the water. I often wonder why their wobbly call breaks my heart. But it does.

Finn listens intently as I read. "Get away with you," he says almost after every sentence.

I show him the image of a dead sandal. "Look, Tut's shoes were only a sole held on with string.

One minute we're having a riveting discussion. The next, I'm alone and terrified. Finn disappears before my eyes. I count to ten. No Finn. When I feel tears forming he reappears. He's been crying. It's Finn's sadness that's surfacing within me. How can I help him? We face each other, too upset to speak.

My anger shocks me. "What made you do a thing like that! You scared me to death." It's an unfortunate turn of phrase to shout at a dead friend. My best friend.

"I've been that smitten with school I've forgotten Mam entirely," he says. "What manner of a boy would do a thing like that?"

"I'm sorry. I didn't mean to remind you or upset you. I hoped you'd forget about your stupid shoes and stay here with me instead. What manner of a girl would do a thing like *that*?"

At this he rallies with an ear-to-ear grin. "You *want* me to stay?"

It's not up to me. "Do you want to stay?"

"More than anything," he says.

The loons laugh with us as we walk back to the house hand-in-hand. Tonight the loon's laughter sounds sad. It's the loneliest sound in Nova Scotia.

FINN – 1923

And don't I just feel like a *soul* held together with a bit of string.

But Lacey WANTS me to stay! I'm her 'boy in the moon.' The news fair shatters me into an explosion of rose petals and sunshine. I feel the sun inside me. My cheeks are burning in the dark. I need nothing more than to belong here where I'm *wanted*. My past boyish crimes are reduced to a flattened bump under the carpet. I've exorcised the ghosts of every shoe I ever knew.

"It's easy to do," a voice says.

"Jesus, Mary and Joseph! Teacher? Is that you?"

"It is. Did I scare you to death?"

I'm too excited to be angry. The man-in-the-moon has deserted me these last five years. But I suffer from the affliction of remembering and forgetting in equal measure. Lacey has put the notion of Egypt into my head, and now here are my dead shoes come to plague me. I suppose my sad confession awakened him. Nothing less would stir his stumps.

"It's time we had a little chat," he says.

His lack of apology fills Lacey's room. His lesson can wait. He doesn't care that he's abandoned me, but it no longer matters because Lacey wants me.

"I'm that busy at the moment," I say. "It'll have to wait."

"Will it now?"

But I'm curious. "Did you come here to tell something? Well, what is it that's easy to do?"

"Fall in love."

"I'd like to see Egypt," I say.

"Oh would you now."

"I would."

"And what could Egypt teach you that I can't?"

"A boy can thrive there without shoes. Even a king can rule without shoes."

Lacey's room fades. "Timing is what you call a big deal," Teacher says. "Come with me."

I'm taken to a library where two chairs are pulled up all cozy to a fireplace. A moon-faced clock hangs above the mantelpiece but this one has hands and numbers, and the hearth is ablaze with a single blue flame. I remember this place. The rows of gold embossed spines shimmer around me and flatten into wallpaper. The clock strikes twelve inside my head, so loud that I clamp my hands over my ears and beg it to stop. If I can reach the clock I can smash it to bits but it's too high. It's as high as the real moon. The flame flares high and freezes into the shape of an iceberg. THE iceberg. Now I'm livid. My bones are vibrating with the echoes of the ringing. People are screaming. I hate this Teacher, Time-keeper, whoever he is. "You abandoned me!"

"And how does it feel?" Teacher says. "You abandoned your mother. You abandoned your shoes! Sure you abandoned yourself."

Someone in a white coat is running down a corridor pulsating with alarm bells. They're frantically pounding on doors shouting abandon ship!

"If you're here why won't you show yourself?"

"Perhaps I am," he says. "Sure I could be the chair."

"You're plain daft. I don't need a daft teacher. I have a new teacher. Miss Robbins, in a real school."

"Only crazy people tell the truth. Perhaps I'm the clock."

I must be suffering from moon madness. The ringing is making my heels bleed. "Make it stop!"

Teacher's voice takes on a threatening tone. "What if I

brought you glad tidings from your shoes? Wouldn't all the shoes you ever knew throw a party in heaven?"

Lacey is restless. She stirs in her sleep and cries out, no doubt sharing my anguish in a nightmare of her own. I'm on my knees for the ringing. I'll die from the ringing, but I'm that insane I'll fight this demon of a teacher I can't see. "If demon chairs talk and demon shoes send tidings and have parties in heaven then I don't want to go there," I shout. I'm touched by the moon. The loons are splitting their sides laughing at me.

"Is it a demon I am?" Teacher says. "There's many a way of speaking without a mouth. Ask any angel."

I hear a voice screaming, do *you* have a mouth? How would I know? The scream is mine. The bells are going to kill me. I try to stand but I'm slipping in the blood.

"I do."

I don't care about anything but silencing the wretched bells. An invisible hand reaches out and pulls me up. I remember how to stand like a sailor with my legs apart. The blood is rushing in my ears trying to drown the bells. It's flowing towards me down a corridor. It's over my ankles. It's a torrent of a river. There's red water up to my knees. It's the River Finn. My teacher stands behind me and whispers. "What if your shoes could make the ringing stop?"

He has my attention. The red water drains away but I'm left standing in a pool of blood. There's blood on my knees and hands and my ears.

"All you have to do is stop your blathering and listen. Can you do that?"

"I can."

"Then listen."

The library disappears. I'm clean as snow, sitting cross-legged on the tip of an icy peak, marooned alone on a blue island. The horizon stretches in a ring. I am in the center. The world is topsy-turvy. There should be stars but the sky is a slick of greasy waves and the island is surrounded by a pattern of stars. The silence hurts almost as much as the bells.

"Your shoes are moving towards you. It's only a matter of time. Watch for the signs. Listen to the silence. I will be there with you," Teacher says. "Only love can save you."

I definitely feel like a soul held together with a bit of string.

LACEY – 1923

It's late. Yesterday's nightmare is fading. Finn and I linger as long as we can on the beach. Soon Ma will call out that it's past my bedtime. The sunset lies crimson over the water. It turns gold, and winks out in a blue flash on the horizon. The voices of the loons call down the moon. Finn is under a spell. I click my fingers in Finn's face. "Hey there. Where did you go?"

He smiles. "There's nowhere else I'd rather be than with you. I guess I was in Egypt for a minute. Sorry, what were you saying?"

I continue to describe the Sakkara plain as we stroll back to the house hand-in-hand. Finn has a goofy smile pasted on his face. I guess he's fascinated. "No rain?" How can things grow? Are there trees in Egypt?"

"There's water," I tell him. "The River Nile floods and either side of it, flowers grow and grasses and palm trees."

Finn snickers. "But there's no puddles for the splashing, and no catching raindrops on the tongue. Still it'd be grand to be dry, and the sandals would never bite your heels."

I'm over the moon with plans for growing up. "I think I'm going to be an archaeologist," I say.

Finn squeezes my fingers. "Will I be going with you?"

"It depends on your stupid shoes I suppose."

Finn sighs. "It depends on my stupid shoes, entirely," he says. "But I'd like to visit a while and hear what a dead Egyptian boy thinks of my shoes. I bet he's still there in his wee chamber. He wouldn't be leaving all that gold behind, now would he?"

"Maybe he's been trapped under all those sarcophaguses and now, thanks to Howard Carter, he can fly."

"Tut is an empty shell of a boy, dry as a wasp's nest," Finn says, "but if he's a walking spirit I can talk with him right enough. I can tell him what it's like to live on an island green as an emerald and to be drenched in rain for months and tell him all about bread and butter soldiers."

I love Finn best when his wisdom falls down a rabbit hole and he's my kid brother with 'Christmas Eve eyes' and a grin that lights up his face. My little Christmas-tree-brother, wild about tin whistles and honey.

25

TUT TUT TUT

Sounds filter down from above. We pause to listen on the first floor landing of the building that houses an 'almost museum.' The laughter of a family get-together carries me away and fills me with longing. Two flights up, I hesitate at the door, afraid to intrude upon a private party. Silence. Have they heard us approach? Have they stifled their merriment hoping we'll go away?

"Open it," Finn says. "Go on with you. He won't bite." Finn's words are bravely uttered but I can tell he's upset from the happy sounds that have now dissipated into the creaking of the rough wooden planks beneath our feet. The door we're looking for has a paper sign tacked to it that reads Room 301 – Moon's Maritime Museum. It's unlocked.

Inside there's a stark room that smells of sawdust. Boxes on boxes crowd shabby office furniture.

Finn can't disguise his anguished expression but his anger is apparent when he lashes out and kicks the door shut behind us. He sends me a sorrowful scowl. "We're here now," he says. "Spilled milk is spilled milk."

"I don't understand. Is this about the sounds we heard?"

"Things done in the past sour the future forever," Finn says.

"Behind this door is your *new* future."

"Is it now? Well, if it's not, then my shoes are wee liars."

The slamming door alerts a voice that calls out 'can I help you' from another room, and there's Mr. Moon, entering our lives, smiling and wiping his hands down his lab coat, sidestepping boxes, and offering to shake hands with me.

Professor P.V. Moon is a scientist, wholly besotted by Titanic. He's set up a lab that wants to be a museum, housed in a cramped storeroom on the third floor of a shop in the warehouse district. I like him at first sight. I've already decided to call him Mooney.

So far, Mooney's 'museum' is little more than a haven for a motley archive of donated loot packed in cotton wool. As in *looted* artifacts with grandiose ideas because Finn tells me that objects have souls. That's how we found Mooney in the first place. Finn's shoes told him. Finn had been talking with his shoes, and Mooney is the key. That's all the shoes would divulge other than the address and that it's early days and patience is required.

Finn's high expectations return. There are unopened boxes piled shoulder high, leaning like an Italian tower. Packed wooden crates snake across the floor with straw poking through the slats, and sealed cardboard cartons are stacked flat against the walls. Yards of cotton batting is folded like clean laundry. A sea of tea chests contains heaven knows what. The enterprise appears promising. But I'm rooting for failure because Finn will leave when his shoes appear.

His derogative *arragh* is followed by a deep breath. "Promising is it?"

"Are they in one of those boxes?"

"If they are, they're asleep."

"Very funny."

Finn stares through me as if I'm an idiot and shakes his head. "Jaysus, only heaven knows what to say to a girl," he says. Once again he makes me feel cold inside and special at the same time. I asked him once if it was deliberate and he'd answered with a lift of his eyebrows and a smile. His expression for wouldn't *you* like to know.

Finn fidgets and refuses to look directly at Mr. Moon. I nudge him in the ribs with my mind. Our little conversation continues while Mooney makes hot chocolate. He's making a terrible clatter in his improvised kitchen, still mumbling, "I don't know *how* you found me. Do your parents know where you are? It's not the safest of neighborhoods for a young girl." He pokes his head around the door. "How old did you say you were?"

"Eleven."

He bustles away. "I have something to show you," he calls out, lost behind a wall of cardboard. The sound of heaving and hefting ensues before... "Ah, *there* you are." He emerges with a shoebox under his arm and a tin whistle. He barely breathes as he addresses it. "Now who did you belong to, eh?" His eyes are wet when he looks back at me. "It's little things like this that can move a body to tears. It was found with one of Titanic's children."

He places the toy in my hand. I'm ashamed. I've been going on about gold masks and precious jewels. "There was a pair of Tut's sandals in his tomb," I say to redeem myself. "Just a few beads and some straw matting. *Um*... I was... moved."

"So, dear girl, you *do* understand." He lifts the shoebox high. These objects are fragile. Sacred."

Mooney takes the whistle from me, tenderly wraps it in

white cloth, and replaces it in the shoebox. Before he closes the lid he speaks to it again. It sounds like a prayer. "One day, I promise you the world will marvel at you under glass." He looks at me which is more like through me or behind me to some invisible audience. "We are guardians," he says solemnly. "We have been entrusted."

It's not as if Finn can make eye-contact with Mooney but I feel there's more. Finn's body fades from color to black and white when he's distressed. And he's flickering like a lantern on a windy night. A sure sign of anxiety.

As always, I hound him when he's upset. "What's the matter with you?"

Finn has picked up my slang. "The guy can't see me, so it's no big deal."

"Well I can, so what's up?"

"I may know this guy."

And off he goes to listen to boxes, walking backwards, singing to me, *I'm just wild about Egypt and Egypt's wild about me.*

I slurp hot chocolate and pick Mooney's brain about Egypt. "Artifacts are artifacts," he says, "whatever the country. They're the crystallized hours of someone's heart." And so I wander off during his lecture to traipse across a dry landscape of burning sand for signs of Tut while Finn swims in a sea of boxes, looking for his shoes. We're twin explorers. I may be able to convince him to stay. If he loves grade school he'll be over the moon for university.

Mooney taps my forehead with his finger and I startle, surprised to be in Halifax. "You're off on an adventure in there," he says.

While my new friend shuffles away to refill our mugs, Finn sneaks up behind me and touches my shoulder. He turns me around to face him but averts his eyes and stares down at his feet. "I think he may be my Teacher," he says. "I recognize his voice."

I tip back my head, squinting at the blue sky. I wish I could fly. I'm determined to reach the pyramids. I'm that captured by the newspapers I'm walking in a heat mirage with the pyramids of Giza on the horizon. I describe it to Finn and he says maybe I'm dead. Cute.

There's a boy king, thousands of years old, buried in gold and mysteries. I eat and sleep King Tut who never had sausages for breakfast or hot chocolate at bedtime. I am stunned by such insights. It's lucky I have little enthusiasm for school right now because I drag my feet even from the delightful weight of math and social studies. My head is in the clouds. If it wasn't for Finn's desperate need for education I would spin off into space. I'm all for geography except we're studying about the North Pole. Now I'm all for truancy.

One thing we're sure of, if Mooney is the missing key, Finn's shoes will make their way here.

There are pictures every day of Tut's sandals and his jewelry and his childhood toys, all shelved in carved boxes for his afterlife and I can't help but be reminded of the toys left on Finn's grave. Nothing that interested him at five, and I wonder if Tut is the same. Tutankhamen is eighteen. Unlike girls who treasure their old dolls and teddies, teenage boys don't care a fig for childish things.

Mooney's Emporium holds no gold masks nor mummies wrapped in linens but I feel the need to wander in halls dedicated to the past... as far back as Halifax can go. Our aboriginal natives wore beaded moccasins and feathered headdresses. The first nations of North America are our 'Egyptians'. Mooney's museum has a few more recent references to pirate ships and the hint of buried treasure on nearby Oak Island, a dream that has plummeted a few men into bankruptcy but fueled the fire for boyish adventures. For that's who the men are who search the island. Boys with dreams of Robinson Crusoe and Long John Silver. Nary one of them denied their chance to dig and be as excited by buckets of mud as I am for shards of clay bricks bearing the hieroglyphic names of eternal royalty that emerge from the Valley of the Kings.

"I am going to be an archaeologist," I announce to the calm smiles of Ma who doesn't know it means that I will be traveling clean across the world and to the scorn of Pa who says digging up graves is bad business, and by the time I'm old enough, I'll see the error of my ways.

So like most wise children, I bury my dreams in the sand and keep my biggest hopes under my pillow lest they be doused with water. But I let them out at night so they won't smother. After lights out, a child has a place to breathe. The end of my bed is where my future begins. I will have to study harder. I will go to university.

But Finn understands me. He shares my new enthusiasm. He wants to travel halfway around the world with me. Finn, my 'twinned' brother who adores school. He is my internal alarm clock on school mornings, so the prospect of me going to bigger and greater schools is taken as a wonderful promise.

And promises to Finn are as permanent as Egyptian names chiseled in stone.

MARCH, 1924

Six months pass before Finn and I enter 'Moon's Maritime Emporium,' relocated to a less-seedy address. Finn is beside himself to acquire his shoes. He leaves ghostly imprints in each room, moving too fast, hot on their trail. I follow to catch up. I like to think his shadow clings to me in order to join its master. Finn gives bittersweet hints too. He will be sad to leave me but his eyes glow round with excitement until he remembers his promise to Mamie.

I pine for the hush of sacred space that I've seen in magazines about the British Museum with its orderly rows of display cases and the small tags that evoke an entire mystery in the letters B.C. Finn runs up the staircases calling his shoes. "Where are you?" Last night it had been a more anguished plea of *what do you want from me?*

<u>His</u> shoes aren't here and neither is Mooney. We make do with a room full of ships models and newspaper clippings of the great explosion, and another room dedicated to the local first-nations' Mi'kmag artifacts.

I am impressed with the dignity of the museum as quiet as library. Mooney has cast a spell over his four spacious rooms where ordinary objects become things of significance: clothes and jewelry worn by long-dead strangers, arrowheads, and bones of strange creatures. But each one pales to invisibility compared to the golden hoard of an Egyptian pharaoh. I will have to practice the art of conservation on items like these to be ready for my own lost-boy-pharaoh, waiting for me, hidden deep in the sandy desert of Sakkara. And then it occurs to me. I already have a lost boy, standing in the next room, calling his shoes.

Finn remains intrigued by Egypt's lack of rain and constant-sunshiny climate where it's so hot a body has to wear sandals in order to walk on the sand. The saving grace for not finding his shoes is the prospect of university and the chance to wear 'half-shoes' in Egypt, and never be cold or wet again.

Together we pore over encyclopedias and my scrapbooks and plan where we will go and how Finn will be an English Literature professor and I will be the first woman Egyptologist.

Finn takes solace from studying every locked door as if staring at it will open it wide and that one of the doors will yield his shoes, languishing on a velvet cushion, carefully preserved.

The only door that's unlocked is filled with mops and brooms, shelves of soap, and a large bearded man.

"You gave me a fright miss," the janitor says, doffing his cap as if I was a grand lady, and here's me, only a poor girl from Shackleton. His eyes twinkle. "My name's Joe... Joe Burt, what be yours?"

"I was looking for mummies," I say apologetically.

"Is it lost you are? Well your mummy can't be far. Let's go find her, eh."

"No. *Egyptians*," I say. "Dead people wrapped in bandages. I describe the gold coffins shaped like a man for burying the dead with carvings inlaid with turquoise and glass.

"Oh, lordy, he says, we've got pictures of the like but they ain't a fit sight for children. Not gold, just plain wood coffins.

Plenty of linen though." He puts his hand over my head. "Bales of it stacked this high. You're a strange one to be sure wanting to see things like that."

"I'm not a child; I'll be twelve next month," I say, and I must have been dignified because Joe is so impressed he says "right this way but don't be telling your mummy who showed you, eh." He grumbles his way to the hall of murals and brushes flecks of dust from the wall with his duster.

We're shown a wall filled top to bottom with a single enlarged brown photograph of a dock with horses and carts loaded with coffins, and men wrapping bodies in linen. Several bodies are already laid in a row, wrapped like mummies. If I stare at it long enough I'm sure I'll be able to walk into the picture and feel the sun on my face and smell the reek of embalming fluid. It's hard to look away but the reporter in me has a job to do.

"These is Titanic victims," Joe says. "Poor folk. Some of em had to be buried at sea. But I remember it well. I helped with the gruesome goings on. You never forget such a thing. It was as bad after 'the explosion' except there were less bodies on account of them burning to ashes in their houses."

Finn reminds me about shoes. I give Joe my best reporter face. "What happened to the people's clothes?"

"Everything was burned that wasn't buried," Joe says. "Although some people took souvenirs."

Finn gasps like I've stepped on his toes. I gasp too and put my hands over my mouth rather than shout at Finn.

"No need to be shocked," Joe says. "Burning's the proper thing to do."

I stand there hoping to look meek. "I'm interested in shoes. Ever seen any of those around here?"

Joe ignores me. He scratches his head. "Mind you, some things were numbered and shipped to New York and such.

Professor Moon's off on a trip collecting more stuff. It's all stored under lock and key." He points to the door. "Crates of the stuff back there. Every day something new arrives."

Finn *promises* me, all he wants is to find more doors and more possible places to hide a pair of shoes.

"Professor? Mr. Moon is my friend. When will he be back?"

"It's all DOCTOR Moon around here, now. Best part of six months I shouldn't wonder. Gone halfway round the world to Egypt, he has."

I'm stunned. "You mean those crates you mentioned are full of Egyptian artifacts?"

I'm thrilled. I know someone in Egypt! I'm the friend of a professor of Egyptology. Each newspaper headline about gold and mummies and curses is better than the movies. I'm inspired, more determined than ever to be an Egyptologist when I grow up. Finn says I'll never grow up which is the pot calling the kettle black considering he's been five since forever.

Pa says I'm getting to be a regular scholar but not to get my hopes up because a woman belongs in the kitchen, *hint*, he glances at Ma reading a book with her glasses at the end of her nose. She's so taken with a love story where a man treats a woman like a queen all the days of her life that she doesn't hear him.

Pa scoffs at her. "Novels," he says with great disdain. He pours me a cup of tea in my favorite blue and white cup with the pagodas and birds. Ma calls it her 'Blue Willow days' when she uses it, but Pa doesn't know it's for special occasions. Nothing is special enough to account for different crockery in his opinion. He spends more time down at The Mermaid than ever and the house is quieter for it.

Ma and I like to feel peaceful walls around us, and when Pa's gone we pick wildflowers and armfuls of pretty grasses, and refill old jam jars with life from the sand dunes. Ma reads her love story and I nurse a love story with a country named Egypt.

26

APRIL FOOLS

My thirteenth birthday almost comes and goes with little significance. Ma makes an extra fuss over me as she always does, serving my favorite breakfast of boiled eggs and soldiers. She looks lighter. For once she isn't reliving the day I was born with the shadow of Mamie lurking in the corner. Corner ghosts are another thing Finn and I have in common.

"Mamie's definitely *not* in the corner," Finn says, sulking. "She's never there. Other than the beach, I've only seen the hem of her dress and her buttoned shoes when we walk to school. Did I mention her shoes were green?"

"Happy birthday darling girl," Ma says, depositing a vase of spring daffodils in front of me. A present wrapped in white tissue paper and blue ribbon follows. "You can open this now."

"Shouldn't I wait for Pa?"

Finn's stares at the box and chews his lip. He's scowling. It isn't like him to not brighten at the sight of egg cups.

"What's wrong?" I ask him.

He leaves the table to stare out the window. "Blue ribbon," he mutters. "Everything had to be blue."

Ma sits down, nursing a cup of tea and beams at me. "I hope you like it. Go on then. Open it."

Ma has more fun than me as I'm being over-careful to unwrap the box methodically, the way she likes. Her ritual hides every trace of extravagance in case Pa gives her one of his lectures on thrift. The paper and ribbon are conserved for next year. She gathers up the ribbon and winds it into a loop, irons the paper with her hands, and folds it neatly, all the while intent on my expression. The shoe box waits unopened. I savor the moment before I lift the lid. "I hope you like it," she repeats. "You're so grown up. A teenager."

It's an expensive silver hand-mirror, hairbrush, and comb set for my dressing table. The initials 'L' and 'W' are engraved in a monogram on each piece. I've never had anything so beautiful. "Oh Ma. It's like a real lady's." I run around the table and give her a kiss. "Thank you, thank you."

She sips her tea, content. "You *are* a real lady."

I look in the mirror and scoop my long hair away from my face. "You promised you'd tie it up with pins when I was old enough. Can we?"

Finn appears in the mirror, looking over my shoulder. "I like your hair loose," he says. "Let's go. I'll race you to the beach."

Finn watches Ma twist my hair into a soft Gibson Girl knot. The transformation is amazing. Ma and I giggle using the new mirror to check it from every angle. "You look lovely," Ma says. "Now you run along, I've got a birthday cake to make."

I give Ma another hug. "Thanks Ma."

"I love you Lacey."

The cemetery excursions are a thing of the past. Even Mooney's Museum is closed. Mooney is gone again, but only after I bend his ear about Egypt. It was wonderful to see him but he returned empty-handed of jewels and gold. The department of Egyptian Antiquities jealously guards their golden treasures.

Finn and I hold our own vigil for Mamie and his family on the beach. We build a ship made of sand and make the ocean out of seashells. I'm about to place the white star flag I made, when suddenly, Finn screams NO. He stomps on the sand-ship in a rage, kicks the shells, and runs down the beach screaming fit to terrify every seagull from here to Newfoundland.

Melodrama is beginning to be a regular occurrence on our birthdays. "Hey. Come back here," I shout. "Stop acting like a baby."

At the end of the day, Pa pulls me aside when Ma is fussing over the table, setting my birthday tea with her good china. "Close your eyes," he says, keeping his own eyes averted to the floor. He pushes a wooden box into my hand. "I made you a wee gift."

I'm stunned. Pa doesn't believe in gifts and what he calls folderol. The top of the box has a picture of a woman's face. She's hiding something.

"I made it," he says. "It's for a lady's 'gewgaws.' One day if I'm no mistaken," he winks, "you'll have a few." He taps the picture. "That's a famous painting, that is. I pasted it onto the lid and varnished it a hundred times so it's good and tight under there." He smooths the picture with calloused fingers. "Do you know who she is?"

Finn knows. "It's the 'Mona Lisa'," he blurts out. I shush him as if Pa can hear him, and answer "It's a painting in the Louvre Museum."

"It's the 'Mona Lisa,'" Pa says, proudly. "Leonardo da Vinci painted that five-hundred-years ago. It holds a special message for you. Today is Leonardo's birthday. Same as yours. April 15, 1452. So in a way you're famous." I can see he's gone to some trouble to glean a fact to impress me. He knows how I'm mad for art and history and museums.

"Thank you Pa. I love it."

"They say she's mysterious," he says, "because her expression changes and no-one can decide what she's thinking. As if she's in two different places at the same time. I saw her in the newspaper the year before you were born. She'd been stolen and there was one helluva row. And when you came to us, something in your eyes reminded me of her. You were always a puzzle. I'm not sure your Ma and I did the right thing, keeping you, Lace. We never saw eye-to-eye about finding your family. You were from another world. You were meant to be somewhere else. But your Ma insisted you were sent to us. I prayed over it until it was too late."

I'm in shock. Pa, chuffed as a peacock surprises me. Pa near to tears astounds me. But Pa reaching into my heart and finding a profound truth without mentioning his God astonishes me.

I shift the box to catch the light. When Mona Lisa looks deep into my eyes her mood shifts from happy to wistful. I know how she feels. I'm moody. One minute I'm sunny, and the next day I'm downcast and homesick, as out of sorts as Finn on the beach. I know we're not where we're supposed to be. I miss tall skyscrapers and the Statue of Liberty. In my dreams, I climb flights of wooden stairs to an apartment crowded with familiar loving faces. At night, the sky is too bright to see the stars. And when it's hot, I sit on a fire-escape holding hands with Finn. "She does look as if she's hiding a secret," I say. "Thank you Pa. I'll treasure it forever." How does Pa know I don't belong here?

Pa's expression darkens. "You must keep it close to ye. D'ye ken? He grabs my hands and searches my face. What is it lass? What are ye missing? Now, I can see that ye want to be away. And don't think I don't notice you talking to yourself. Who can you see? Where is it you want to be?"

"1452 is the year Columbus sailed for America," Finn interrupts. "We learned that in school."

"No." I said. "That was 1492."

Finn scowls at me.

Our scowls fight a pointless duel. "Hey, dates are numbers and numbers are math, so I should know," I say. "I'm the math expert, remember?"

Finn crosses his arms. "But *I'm* the historian."

"Well, I can't help that time is measured in years or that you can't change history."

This doesn't placate him. As usual, Finn's temper rises when he's corrected. "Just because you're eight years older than me and Ma's precious *darling*, there's no need to lord it over me."

I reassure him, "I don't know what's brought this on but you're wrong."

"Four-hundred and seventy-three."

"Scuze me?"

"Years," he says. "Since that Leonardo feller. I wonder who he is now."

Our inner spat takes place during the few seconds it takes to kiss Pa on the cheek and thank him mightily for the surprise.

Pa's words sting behind my eyes. This person he's showing me is a stranger. He's been a lonely man. "Maybe one day, if ye listen hard enough," he says, "Mona Lisa will tell you her secret. Promise me you'll keep her safe by you to remember me by."

"I promise. I'll never forget you," I tell him, but truth be told I'm so used to dismissing him for my own peace of mind I've already forgotten he's there. I've already broken my promise.

Pa rumples my hair. "I hope ye find your place in the world," he says, and tells me to be away with the fairies and help Ma with his tea. He's already forgotten tonight is *my* special birthday tea.

Finn is headed for one of his grey sulks. "Daddy's wee girl now is it," he says, dismissing the box with a sneer. "For gewgaws is it? Sure they're going to do you a world of good."

His antics infuriate me. "Stop acting like – a – baby."

Finn loses it. He attacks an innocent library book – a reference book that I managed, at great length, to pry from the cold clutches of the head librarian in Halifax on pain of death. "Hey," I shout. "I promised to keep that safe."

Finn acts like an escapee from a loony bin. He's gone wild. His hair is a scruffy red halo. "Well you should never make a promise you won't move heaven and earth to keep," he shouts, pushing past me and out into the night. I rub my bruised shoulder and follow him. I know where to look.

As usual I find him at the water's edge. This time he's hurling fistfuls of pebbles into the surf that pepper the water, scattered like the harmless breadcrumbs we toss to the ducks. Crazy laughter warbles in the moonbeams playing over the water. The loons are in good form. Tonight they seem extra close. Extra-moonstruck.

FINN – APRIL 12, 1925

It makes me wild that Lacey and I aren't where we're supposed to be. And it's getting worse now that Lacey is becoming a holy terror of a dreamer. But when she's awake, I may as well be part of the furniture for all she cares. I'm trapped in a dirty half-life while she's posing in her mirrors and growing up towards a plethora of gewgaws. Ma and Lacey fuss and bother all lovey-dovey with their heads together. They're the same as Mam and Michael in another life – two against the rest of the world. And here's me, the outsider, forever looking in. I'm disgusted with promises and blue ribbons, and precious sons and daughters. I hate what Titanic exacted from me. I hate that I'm love-struck. The loons are going to have a field day.

I've the devil inside me and I'm glad. I want to out-hooligan the worst boys in Ballymore. I dance around Ma like a tornado and lift a spoon from the table when I know she'll see. I'm even amused at her fright.

Ma flops into a chair and stares at the cutlery, now tamed on the table. "Is that you Mamie?" she says.

I rearrange the knives and forks into a circle and whisper in Mamie's voice. "It is mistress. What have you done with my jewels? Do you know Lacey is down at the water's edge wading into the surf at this very hour in the dark with a pookie? Is that how you look after my girl!"

"Oh, Mamie. She's never in the water? I've always told her to stay in after dark."

"Can you not manage that husband of yours?"

"Ansel is punishing *me*, not Lacey. And he has a secret map to give her on her coming of age."

"Well, isn't that just grand. And why can't *you* see it? Can you not be trusted?"

"Sharing is no the way of things between a husband and wife. Were you no married?"

Perfect. Ma is a lamb led to the slaughter. "How dare you imply I wasn't married," I say. "Lillian Rose Waters get that map or I'll turn your life upside-down and find it myself." At that, I sweep the cutlery to the floor in a clatter.

The racket jolts Ansel from his nap on the sofa. "What're ye doing in there woman?" he calls out. His voice is like a raised fist. "Can ye no take more bloody care when a man's sleeping!"

I levitate the teaspoon again and drop it in Ma's lap. "You've gone white as a ghost," I whisper in her ear. It's then that the torn pages from Lacey's book blow into the kitchen on a wind of my own creation and land on the subdued cutlery. I single out a page with a picture of a mummy's desiccated face and place it on the table under Ma's nose. "The jewels of the dead never rest Mrs. Waters," I say in my coldest whisper.

Ma pushes herself away from the table and creeps into the parlor where Pa is already snoozing under a newspaper. He's snoring and her loathing is plain. I hear her thoughts. *I wish you were dead. I hate you, bully that you are. You ruined my life. I'll be glad to see the back of you and your spiteful God.*

She tears the newspaper from Pa's face and kicks his foot. Pa snorts and rearranges himself without waking. It's the shrill accusation that follows that fully wakes him.

"You're a nasty small-minded bugger," Ma shouts inches from his face.

Ma takes the newspaper and rustles it in Pa's face. He raises his eyelids, dazed. What's hap...?"

"I said, you're a nasty small-minded bugger, Ansel Waters. Tell me where Lacey's jewels are. If you don't tell me right now I'm going to the police. No doubt they'll want to know of your Titanic pilfering. And don't pretend you don't know what I'm talking about. I heard you. I heard you and McPhee when the pair of you were in your cups. Neither of you could keep your gobs shut. Do you think Jimmy gives a tinker about saving you?"

Pa's head clears quickly but for an innocent man he hedges defensively. "Woman. I'll ask you to keep a civil tongue in your head."

"Ask! Since when have *you* ever asked *me* anything?"

"You'll hold your tongue in my house!"

"This is MY house too. Tell me where Mamie's jewels are. Tell me or I'll tell everyone what you and Jimmy were about that night. D'ye think your God wasn't watching you? D'ye think I didn't hear the two of you yammering? Always prattling on about your daring deeds. You and Jimmy McPhee bragging, a couple of filthy thieves. What have you done with them? Did you give Mamie's jewels to him? Are they gone? Do you ken I've got the ghost of Mamie in my kitchen waiting on you."

"Ye're touched woman."

"Did you no think to ask me before hiding Mamie's jewels?"

"WITCH. Harpy!"

"That obscene God you're always shoving down our throats. He knows what you've done. Or was that all blather too? You and your wee elders lying all the while. If you've stolen from that girl..."

"I'm no a thief. God knows I've made a map for Lacey,

but you're too witless to keep a map about you. You'll use it to start the bloody fire some evening."

"You consort with thieves. I heard you and your drunken mates, robbing the dead. And now you've robbed our Lacey of the life she was born to have."

For all his indignation, Pa remains seated. He even takes up his newspaper as if to resume reading. He dismisses Ma from behind the crumpled pages. "A life with you? Aye, you robbed her right enough, you barren auld bitch."

Ma flinches. She glances at the poker with blood in her eyes.

I want to stop what I'd begun as a wild tantrum. Mam and Da were at odds but never like this. My old mam carried an aura of disappointment about her. It was a tiresome restlessness my old da had that provoked her. Their gentle bickering only scored a few harsh words glancing off each other's burdens. Nothing like this room filled with visions of murder and bludgeoning.

Ma's demons are out, wriggling their dirty red tails over her clean floor. But I'd been right to do it. The dancing cutlery was sheer genius. Ma needed the wind up her to have her big say. Floating spoons gave her the courage.

I'm standing on Titanic, once again, screaming obscenities at Michael. Tiny black demons leap from my mouth into the sea, leaving me free to meet a princess. I'm purged fresh and clean after the rains to be rewarded with the best breakfast of my entire life served up with an alphabet and an understanding of maternal bliss. Mamie was my angel of mercy. After Mamie, the punishments made no sense. I was forgiven and sent an angel with an unblotted copybook. Our breakfast had been my 'last supper.' Mamie freed me from guilt by offering to sponsor my rebirth. Well, now we are even.

Not more than an hour ago, Mamie was the recipient of a ship made of sand. Ma was icing a birthday cake and Pa was dreaming under his newspaper. Lacey was growing up in her mirror, and I'd run down the beach shrieking like a banshee released from hell. But it was more like running *towards* hell. Lacey is a teenager and I'm a child of five. She thinks I'm a wee nuisance of a brother. She'll never understand how I think of her as a beacon. I'm cast off – left behind to play in the sand like a wee boy. Lacey is Mamie's darling one. Mamie ignores me. She's forgotten our house-on-fire friendship. She's forgotten to be my mother.

And now Ma is unrecognizable. "Mamie is no best pleased with you Ansel," Ma says, baring her teeth. "She knows everything. You've gone too far. You've gone and disturbed the dead."

Pa rises from his chair. He carefully folds and smooths his newspaper with chilling precision in the identical painstaking manner as Ma with the birthday paper. I sense he's summoning his true nature. Ugliness stalks the two of them.

I whisper in Ma's ear. "Rose. Come away now. The kettle's boiling dry." I need to get her from the room. "I'm sorry for frightening you. You've told him, now. You're free. I know where the jewels are."

But Ma ignores me. When she speaks next her voice is different. Deeper. "The devil with you. Barren is it? I thank that God of yours I never had a bairn off ye. I wish you the joy of Mamie's company."

Pa is up now, his eyes narrowed. He stands his ground. His fists are clenched and his jaw is all twitchy and white. Hatred spews from his mouth. "You dirty auld besom."

Ma is unstoppable. "Why don't you mince off to your

spineless mermen and buy that malicious narrow-minded God of yours, a pint."

I was never so relieved as when Lacey enters the room. She melts Pa into a beaten man with a single word, almost a whisper. "Pa?"

"I'll no be spoken to by a harpy in my own house. I'm off to The Mermaid and heading for the banks in the morning. You'll no see me for a week."

The door slams on Ma's parting words. "I don't care if you're off to Davey Jones Locker," she shouts.

This is the worst birthday I've ever had. Worse than the turnip soup day when I was sure of cream cakes and jam. I feel the wrath of the elementals getting up my nose. I bat them away like flies. *Away with you!* But they stay, and tonight Ma's right. The soul of a poltergeist is unleashed from my entrails. It spins about the room bashing into walls, rifling papers, and blowing the curtains into a tizzy. I'm restless as a cat before a thunderstorm. I need to run wild.

I hightail it to the beach and run feral under the stars, trailing venom, and come to a full stop. A zigzag of bloody footprints behind me bears witness to my anger. They end with me standing in a clear pool of saltwater shaped like a heart. I tear at the sand on my knees but the heart reforms. I feel as beaten as Pa. I've had dealings with a harpy before. But Ma was terrifying.

I remember something I *can* do. "Teacher?" I shout over the water. "Help me!"

Nothing. The word teacher echoes as an insult and drops like a stone. Only the loons call back with a sad lament to mock me. The moon is a thin crescent. No room for a teacher but I know he's watching me. I can feel him. "Coward," I shout. "Show yourself!"

I wait there until sunrise. Teacher's voice hisses past me

and sends the seagulls patrolling the shore into a frenzy. "You wee poltroon. You should have said please."

I'm not impressed with afterlife school. The thirteenth year of my half-life stretches ahead. Yesterday, Lacey was a cruel princess. Today she's a pretty teenager with fancy hair and a silver mirror, and I'm her kid brother – a wee poltroon.

27
REVERSAL OF FORTUNE

FINN – APRIL 17, 1925

Two of Pa's drinking mates, arrive at our door, caps in hand, breathless with news. Pa is dead. Lost off the Grand Banks, fishing for cod. But he didn't drown. He hit his head, slipping on cod guts and fell hard on the anchor, and they couldn't wake him. So the boat hadn't floundered and none were lost at sea. Just my Pa, Ansel Waters, leaving us destitute and mapless because by the end of that day it was apparent to Ma and Lacey that Mamie's jewels would be as dead and buried as Pa.

LACEY

Ma's first comment when we are alone makes no sense. "God. I'll be having two ghosts in my kitchen now."

She stands at the kitchen window for the longest time like a wife on a widow's walk, staring out to sea for her husband's ship, but in her case, happy he's never coming home. I wonder what she can see amongst the daffodils with their long stalks bent from the wind. Then she rallies. "Lacey. Get out the good china. Let's have a cup of tea and a think."

I rattle around the kitchen table where Ma had been polishing the silver while she straps on her apron and sets the kettle on the hob with extra force. "Damn that old bugger to hell," she shouts. "Damn him. Damn damn damn!"

I hover at her side, stricken. "Ma. Calm yourself. Pa's gone. There's no need to be mad at him anymore."

"Is there not?"

Finn slides into a chair and puts his head in his hands. I'm the man of the house now," he says.

I nudge his elbow. "Is Pa here? Can you see him?"

Finn takes a cursory scan of the room. "Pa is long gone. He wandered through the house once, and then... *whoosht*... he was out the door."

Ma sits next to Finn who eases his chair away slightly. She never notices it move. Her voice wavers high and shrill "Oh, Lace, your beautiful jewels. Gone!"

Finn ducks his head, looking guilty.

Ma's face is haggard. Her body seems to have shrunk. "We'll find them," I say. "The map's bound to be around here somewhere."

Ma's fingers twitch on the table and she toys with what Finn calls the haunted teaspoons. "There's no fool like an old fool," she says, her eyes dry. "I don't know if I'm furious or happy. Mostly, I'm terrified. These spoons are possessed. Mamie was here. Oh Lace, your mother was here."

The salt shaker does a jig out the corner of my eye.

I can't believe Finn is playing games at a time like this. "Stop that," I say to him. "Can't you see Ma's already in a state. What did you do to her?"

Finn looks straight at me and tips over the salt so it spills into a tiny mound. "If Ma was a lady she'd know that rich people have fairy spoons for this stuff?" he says. "It should be in a silver bowl with wee legs."

Ma airs her thoughts. It looks for all the world as if she's talking to the spoon she's singled out. "Men need to feel in charge. They're great bullies. They want all the power and they take it at a woman's expense." Ma waves the spoon at me. "Don't ever let that happen to you, Lacey Waters. Jesus, dying is the easy way out. And isn't that just like a selfish bloody man. He's gone and destroyed us."

The kettle whistles and Finn freezes. "Don't worry it's not the Titanic," I say, grabbing his hand. "It's only the hot water boiling." Loud cracks of thunder and flashes of lightning send him quivering into memories of ship's flares. I have to hold his hand tight during the New Year's Eve fireworks while he cowers, covering his ears until dawn.

Ma sweeps the salt into her hand and throws it over her shoulder. "Lacey, be more careful. D'ye ken it's bad luck to spill salt? *Acht*. What can it matter now." She lines up the spoons from smallest to tablespoons and the forks and knives in rows– a common army of shiny pawns on one end of a battlefield facing down the invisible ranks of powerful kings and warrior knights forever gathering against her. She looks like a great Titan commander preparing her earthly pawns on a kitchen table battlefield. Soon she will wave her hand over them and they will animate to do her bidding and the other gods will laugh and wager on another human game. It's hard not to think we're all sitting targets for their pleasure. There's Finn, the innocent victim, and me his ally against the world of constant dangers.

Ma keeps the best tea for special occasions. She always says the good china deserves Earl Grey. In any case, Pa wouldn't drink from it. He said it was going against God's laws to act high and mighty and that tea smelling of cheap scent was an abomination above one's station. Plain tea should be served in plain mugs. Putting on airs was asking for trouble.

The heady scent of bergamot wafts from the hot tealeaves. We drink our first cups quickly as if we're parched. And there, suspended in our desert island of a kitchen, we pour seconds and thirds in silence, and eat thick cuts of brown bread and butter spread with marmalade. I have the uncanny feeling that if we leave the table, time will resume and all the responsibilities that come with it will crash down and flatten our barnacle of a house on its 'Merlin's hill.' That once we're up and about, life will careen off a cliff.

"Lacey," Finn says. "You'd better stop promising such fierce things. It's tempting fate, you are."

I ignore him and shatter the sanctuary. "Ma, I'll get a job."

Ma starts to protest and stops. She pats my hand. "Oh hen, we both will darling girl."

"That's torn *our* dreams then, *darling girl*," Finn snarls in my ear, and I have to agree. University is out of the question and I'm a penniless heiress, three years short of the doors to a higher education. Eight years shy of the keys to archaeology.

On the way to the sink Ma drops a cup. It shatters on the tiles. She sighs but still no tears come. She just walks around the mess muttering "What did I tell you... bad luck," and off she goes to her bed.

I'm left to dispatch the remains of luck lying dead on the floor. It strikes me as I picked up the largest pieces of Blue Willow china, that archaeologists do this with shards of pottery. I lay the pieces together on the floor as if they're precious. As if they will be glued together and placed in a museum.

"Ma's going to need you right away," Finn says, taking up

the dustpan and brush. He waves me away without looking up. "Go. I'll finish this."

I don't know how he knows, but a low wail comes from down the hall that chills me. It's Ma.

Finn concentrates on the floor. "It's not grief," he says, busy sweeping my careful pattern into the pan. "It's fear."

"I'll no lie. I'm no sorry he's dead," Ma whimpers. "I thought I'd live in my own house forever but I can't wait to see the back of this place. It's haunted by the dreams of your poor dead mother and now your Pa and heaven knows what manner of sorcery. Your invisible friend's still here too. Did you think I wouldn't feel him?"

Finn inclines his head from me to Ma. "Go on. Tell her." He makes the sign of wiping tears from his eyes and nods again. "Tell her."

"Oh, Ma. It's all right to have a cry," I say. "It'll do you good."

Ma stops sniveling. "All I know is that love withered and died here. I died here. I was drowning in hate here, old before my time and you saved me, darling girl."

"Ma, my invisible friend is a *darling boy*. If only you could see him. Know him as I know him."

"Enough now. Let's have no more talk of mischievous fairies. I ken enough of him to know what's meant by mean-spirited."

"He'll come with us. He'll follow me. You know he has a name."

"Don't be saying it out loud, child. I've put it away out of my mind."

"Finn."

Ma gasps. For a moment I think she's going to slap me.

Finn heads for the door. "Leave it alone, Lacey. I'm nothing to her but a threat to her darling girl."

I run in front of him, block the door, and beg. "Please Ma, give him a chance."

"I'll no forgive your Pa. May he be punished in hell for his thieving ways."

"Hating Pa will make you sick. I know a boy who hates his brother so much he would rather turn his back on heaven."

"That invisible boy?"

"Finn."

The anger leaves Ma's eyes. "And he's Irish you say?"

"He was ..."

"No. Stop. Stop! I don't want to know any more about him. He's a ghost now, is he? A wee trickster poltergeist."

For the first time it hits me that Finn *is* a ghost. Why didn't I see it before? To me he was an invisible friend, a persistent acquaintance who became my brother. A companion, but never a ghost.

Finn sends me a pitying look. "I'm dead but I'm not a ghost. Sure by now you should know *that*."

I hardly know where to look. I wish he wasn't so cavalier with the inside of my head. "It's all good," I tell him. "Well, except I'd like to have some privacy. Sure by know *you* should know *that*."

Facing down Ma's superstition is never easy, but now it borders on an intervention. It's no good pretending. I'm not a kid.

Finn expels a sarcastic "Are you not? Fancy."

But I can't be a kid anymore; my Pa is dead. Ma is no breadwinner. Time has to speed me into a grownup. "I admit Finn's got a temper on him lately, but it *will* pass," I say to console Ma. "He's upset. He needs his mam."

Ma blanches. "For the love of heaven child, have you gone daft? It's a wee poltergeist you've let loose in the house. Can you no see he's telling ye tales. He's no after his mam; he's after you."

FINN

The tiny mound of salt on the kitchen tabletop means something. I shrink to the point of view of a grain of salt – the mound is a mountain of white stars. An iceberg of crystallized bad luck.

Lacey browses the titles of books piled on the mantelpiece. I topple them over before she selects one just because I can. She says nothing. She bends down and picks them up, ignoring me.

I'm feeling sorry for myself but underneath it is pure anger. "For you it's the end of school," I whine to Lacey. "For me it's the end of the world." Sure my whinging is even getting to myself. I flail about. I'm a restless spirit, after all.

But Lacy fakes an upbeat slant of the truth for my sake. I'm her *wee* kid brother, a lost *wee* soul, a *wee* simpleton child in need of coddling. More like handling. "Of course it's not," she says. "It'll be different that's all. It'll take longer. We'll make it an adventure." Sure she must think I'm tapped. She calls me a kid. Is it a baby goat that I am?

Ma had said it all when she painted me with tar and feathers. I blame Mamie. "I'm NOT a trickster; I'm the victim of a trick. It was your mother, my fairy godmother or angel or whoever she was, who tricked ME. Mamie caught me out with a promise. There was me, a helpless wee boy, and Mamie a mother who swept me aside for you. For all I know, I could have been lording it in heaven stuffing myself full of cakes and sausages for the last thirteen years." But if I'm honest, I can see the past in new colors. I see a different corner but now it houses a beloved sister. The more she makes me crazy, the more I love her. It's the monkey in me who wants to tease her. Maybe I *am* a wee poltergeist after all. These are childish pranks, and here's me, a poet and a world traveler who can see into forever.

Lacey's protests are perfectly reasonable. "I'm not *doing* anything. Ma can't see you."

"So what. Sure I don't give a shiny shoe!"

Teacher arrives for a heartbeat and leaves like a wind whipped by a cane. He's particularly harsh. He shouts the word betrayal as if it's some sort of greeting. The night echoes with his farewell. "For the love of heaven, make up your bloody mind."

This time I feel worse because I *know* Lacey; I never *met* Michael. But is Lacey another version of Michael? Am I cursed to have brothers and sisters who tower over me with their precocious visibility? Even my Bridie knew the happier side of attracting attention.

Lacey's tired. Her voice is at breaking point. "Look Finn. I've gotta go help Ma."

I recall something Lacy read to me from one of her library books. It was a quote from the Egyptologist Howard Carter, Tut's master-savior. *Things ... wonderful things*, he'd said when he glimpsed the hint of gold the day he opened the door to a boy king's nursery.

It had been our dream to open such a door. And now

doors are slamming shut in our faces with dirty great padlocks. It's time to make do and making do is going to be an enormous task.

Lacey echoes my thoughts. She does that when I let her in. I guess I have a broken padlock on the door in my head. "It's going to take an enormous amount of work," she says. "But together, we can do anything."

"Enormous is a grand thing," I say, trying to be helpful. "I remember when it was everything in the world."

Lacey leans over and kisses my cheek. "We shouldn't fight. We need each other." She rubs out her kiss with her hand. It chokes me up. I've seen mothers do this to make boys feel less embarrassed. As if the wipe of a mother's hand can undo the feeling of being a perpetual child. I remember Mamie's first kiss. I wanted it to stay planted. I wanted Mam to see it.

Lacey's kiss and her words inspire me. Shame on me; I'm her guardian. "I've thought of an enormous door," I say. "Come with me. It's not far."

28

ELECTRIC STREET

FINN

Lacey and I stroll into Mooney's museum on Electric Street as the first drops of rain patter dark spots on the grey pavement. Joe will know what to do.

Only the night before, we had read about a museum with a glass cabinet displaying a plate of petrified bread with ears. I remembered a lifetime ago when Mam told me that ears could see, and now Lacey has created a bridge by sharing the news about Egyptian loaves trapped in a tomb for thousands of years with their dough pinched into ears to enable the prayers of the dead to be heard forever.

"Just think," she says, "No rain. No rain boots or cold yellow slickers. No snow. Beach everywhere."

I close my eyes and listen but I can't resist a wee dig. "Actually, you can't have a beach unless there's water." Like a smart teacher, she ignores me. But I love to forget my troubles and curl up in her armchair wrapped in a wool blanket while she plays teacher. *Class – today we're going to learn about magic bread and sandals*. Every now and then she passes me the book to look at the pictures of palm trees and pyramids. The Valley of the Kings in 1923 shows crowds of sepia bystanders wearing straw hats, standing under the unforgiveable sun for the glimpse of a shrouded tray of treasure, literally a tourist hot spot.

"Carter sure put Tut on the map," I say.

Lacey gives me a dirty look and I go to the bottom of the class. "I'd like to forget about maps for a while if you don't mind," she says.

Tut's servants had archived his childish toys and clothes in a museum cave for his afterlife. Soon they would be the center of attention behind thick glass cabinets padlocked like transparent doors.

A pair of mummified babies remind me of Rose's two miscarriages and Titanic's lost infants, and of course, my Bridie. It's good to remember that Tut's wife, Queen Ankhesenamun, was once large with child. Like Mamie.

Tut's tomb gives up his thin linen tunics fallen into transparent disrepair. I think they were shifts for sleeping. Again I see transposed images of Mamie's lace nightdress and Michael's blue sweater full of holes. Michael's Irish sweater from a cold wet land, ironically *laced* with holes. His *holy* sweater, and Tut's disintegrating royal robes and beaded sandals against Irish shoes, mine and Michael's for a shabby afterlife.

The last thing I see are the sleeves of Mamie's nightgown, Michael's sweater, and Tutankahmen's shirt holding invisible hands across time. Once again I'm excluded. Then I'm back in the warehouse looking for Joe so Lacey and Ma can eat, and I can go to school.

LACEY

I see Joe before Finn or perhaps he sees me. I hear my name shouted across a sparse room furnished with a few tables. I wave, too frozen too move. Luckily, I don't have to. Joe shoulders his broom like a soldier and crosses to where I stand.

Suddenly I'm tongue-tied. Finn kicks my shin. "Ask him!"

"Miss Lacey, well look at you all growed up," Joe says.

"Enough to get a job tell him," Finn shouts in my face.

"I'm thirteen," I say stupidly.

"S'pect you're looking for shoes."

I grin.

Joe taps the side of his head. "You see I remembered."

What a nice man. "Always," I say, "but today I'm looking for a job."

"Here you mean?"

"That would be my first choice. My real mother died on the Titanic you know. I never knew my father. And last week my adopted father died. Now I need paid work to help my stepmother. We're moving here, so I need to find a place to live as well, if you know of anything."

"She needs a job too, don't forget," Finn whispers.

I almost see the humor in it. Some job interview with a ghost for a reference.

Joe scratches the growth of beard on his chin. "You know me, ears to the ground. Happens I know of a room for rent. Now I *can* hire one cleaner. But there's the shoe factory down the road. They always need workers. Not as glamorous as a museum though."

Finn screams at Joe as if he can hear. "Shoes! Is it kidding me you are?"

Only Joe would see that cleaning floors was glamorous.

He scratches his chin, again. "You'll find plenty of shoes there." He grins at his joke.

I grin back at Finn, amused by his anguished expression, as Joe draws directions to the factory on a bit of paper.

"Well, now you have a bloody map," Finn says, "And don't be looking at me like that. I'm deadly serious."

Both of us fall about laughing. We're on the same side. Our cage door is open.

Joe laughs too, no doubt thinking he was funnier than he'd imagined. "One of you can start tomorrow," he says. "I'm thinking that should be you Lacey. You've a strong back. Factory jobs are, you know, mostly sitting down things."

FINN

Workday one, reporting for duty. Unfortunately, with Mooney away, the archive room is still out of bounds. Heaven only knows what's stored in Mooney's cave of Titanic/Egyptian delights.

Lacey gives me one of her disgusted looks. "I thought ghosts could walk through walls," she says.

I hate to lecture but her odd notions irk me. "Some doors are forbidden. Matter is finicky. And by the way, just so you know, I'd be a girl if it wasn't for you."

She points a finger so close to my nose I have to take a step back. Her arm remains poised. It's all I can do not to slap it away.

Now the finger wags at me. "What brought all that on? Are you saying I should have died?"

It galls me when anyone waves a finger in my face. "Of course not. I don't want to be a girl. I'm saying that sometimes you don't appreciate how much I sacrificed for you. I could have found my real family but I promised Mamie I would look after you. And don't be poking that thing in my face or I'll..."

Lacey lowers her arm, waggles all her fingers at once, and jams them into her pockets. "Better? "Sometimes I think you dwell on our birth far too much."

"I did what Mamie wanted. She thought you were going to die. I was your replacement. But you survived and I became your guardian. Your companion. That's not what I was promised."

Lacey crosses her arms in defiance. "Are you saying you're stuck here?"

I have to say something to uncross those arms, but it's time I stopped telling half-truths. It's a rock and a hard place question, so the answer is yes. "We're both flies caught in flypaper."

Her arms tighten, and now, so does her jaw. "And you want to leave? To be somewhere else?"

"I want to be someONE else. I don't want to be five-years-old. Inside, I'm older than you. Can you understand how humiliating that feels? And why I want to kick a ship made of sand to the moon."

The wind howls and clatters the shutters. "I don't understand. We're family," Lacey says, her bottom lip quivering.

I pull Lacey down to my level on the sofa. "It's not an insult. I don't want to be your invisible friend. I don't want to be your kid brother. I'm you and not you. I'm me and not me. I was put upon, tricked into Nova Scotia. Given a taste of the better life, yes, but with no spoon of my own; estranged from my family and invisible in yours. Surely even a half-life should be better than that."

"Could you not take a new pair of shoes to your mother? Ma can get castoffs any day of the week. They go to charities otherwise, so employees get first choice. And then, after you've said hello and made amends, you can come back."

I think of Da and his reaction to charity shoes for New York. Nova means new. Charity shoes for New Scotland is an insult to the Clearys. I hold my head high to honor Da. I have my pride. I have his fierce pride. Pride isn't an entirely sinful thing in my opinion. And mine isn't about to goeth before a fall if I have any say in the matter. But who am I to be so grand as to look a new pair of shoes in the face and turn away?

LACEY

Joe delivers his news while rearranging his brooms and mops, counting the handles from shortest to longest. "The professor sent me a letter. He expects big changes, he's already hired an assistant. I wrote back to him about you. He remembers you. Says I can give you a raise if your work is coming along. How's your ma?"

I'm delighted to spend more hours in the museum. I pretend it's the Louvre and around the corner the 'Mona Lisa' waits to grace me with her smile and tell me her secret. Or it's the Cairo museum and the display cases I dust full of ship models are filled with ancient mummies and gold statues. Wherever I imagine, it's more glamorous than here.

Finn hangs around the back loading dock trying to pry into any boxes not nailed shut. He pokes his nose into every box that arrives. I'm jealous of his leisure time and dream of the years beyond my broom.

Finn remembers more details from the Titanic and I become almost as interested in the great ship as Egypt. At times he still creeps off to a secret cave to growl.

"You spoke of your brother the other day without bending my teaspoon," I say. "That means you're in control of your temper."

The extra money means a dry room with a decent kitchen and a back garden where Ma and I can grow tomatoes and potatoes and, much to Finn's distress, turnips.

Finn admits that while I'm in crisis he will never leave even if he finds a dozen pairs of talking shoes. I remind him there are always stray pairs lying about with no owners in Ma's factory. Army boots are the mainstay, and no-one would miss a pair of small boots that are made in between the consignments for the war. Children still need shoes and they're easier and faster to make.

All the color drains from Finn's body. Kid gloves are in order. "Are you upset?"

"I am," he says. "Because you won't stop asking me. It has to be my Queenstown shoes destined for America. Now, let that be an end to it."

There will be an eventual way into Mooney's storehouse, of that we have no doubt. We will have to work hard for it. But both of us are too clever by half to be dissuaded by a few locks. Together we are a force of nature. But we have no idea it will take three years to penetrate that 'holy of holies'.

29

MOON IN JUNE

FINN – JUNE 13, 1925

I'm late for Heaven School. I think it's pure convenience to meet Teacher on the beach. But I finally figure it out. The signal is clearer there on the birthing beach. The place where boy met girl, where life once hovered between going and staying. It's a crystallized classroom. I lean back on my elbows and study the face of my sage. Whether he's a sliver or full moon, my silvery-blue teacher is always there but never around. And I, the naughty truant boy, learn at his feet only after being ignored out of my mind. The trick of contact is to look away so my teacher can approach. He makes surprise entrances to impress me.

The loons sing down the moon. I dig my bare heels into the sand and create two channels. I'm just a kid under the stars. It's late after a day of play but no mother is going to call me in for supper. I'm alone.

I refuse to look up at that shining face. I keep the moon in peripheral vision to gain its trust. It's something about how the eye is designed. To see more by looking less.

"I'm feeling mighty sorry for myself," I say out loud.

"Wallowing is an art," Teacher replies.

"I thought you'd come. Sure, I'm that over the moon to finally hear you," I say.

"You're a cheeky little beggar, I'll say that for you."

"I'm learning this is where you are. This is where WE are. This one patch of sand is us, isn't it?"

"Calling down the moon is an old magic," he says.

He's trying to remain the aloof 'old school' authoritarian. "But we're friends too."

"It's about time," he scoffs.

It's nice to sit and not have to talk. In a way, all I want is companionship from a familiar voice who identifies with my situation. I let the sand absorb my residual anger. When I speak it's purely conversational, not a whine in the entire thing. It's the rare core of me who doesn't flap about trying to keep warm. "Death isn't fair. I was too young to make such a decision," I say, to tempt him.

"As your personal time-keeper, I can assure you it's not only long past your bedtime, it's time you DECIDED to make peace with Mamie and Michael. Give them a chance to explain."

"That ship has sailed, don't you think?"

"Finn, Finn. Is it always going to be like this?"

"This is the real me," I say.

"Is it?"

"It is."

"You're a bright lad. Sarcasm is so... well, unworthy." He stops and chuckles in that endearing way of his. "You were so... oh, I don't know... PROMISING."

"Okay, I concede. I *promised* Mamie. But it wasn't my fault that Mam had a bee in her bonnet about promises. I was doing as I was told. Being obedient. She was my first teacher."

"You were scoring points, Mr. Doasyou-wouldbedoneby or is it Mr. Bedonebyasyoudid?"

"That's Lacey's favorite book."

"That's because 'The Water Babies' is about you and her. Did you not notice? Who do you think put that book in her path?"

"Ma picked it out because she liked the title."

"Mamie," he says. "It was *Mamie*."

"Mamie?"

"YES. MAMIE!"

I feel a small hackle of irritation tingle the back of my neck. "Michael broke *his* promise, which by the way, was an enormous whopper. Is he relegated to eternally writing *I shall not make a promise I won't move heaven to keep* in some limbo school of detention? Has he been sent to the corner for being a bad son? Is that where he gets his corner complex?"

"If it's droll you want, I can play," Teacher says. "I can out-guff even the likes of you, Finnegan Cleary. And, *by the way*, Mamie is a now a young girl the same age as you and Lacey. An 'instant return,' same as you. Don't you think *she* might have a little unfinished business of her own?"

I keep the conversation casual and change the subject. "Did you go to man-in-the-moon school?"

"I had to learn the alphabet too. 'B' is my personal favorite. B for blarney, Blether, and Beguile were my teachers. Sure a wee boy requires a working knowledge of flanneling."

"Did you have a brother?"

"Did you ever stop to consider that I may be like you?"

"That we're both dead as doorknobs?"

"For a canny little devil you don't twig much on the first go," he says.

"I've become a philosopher. I'm a great one for the thinking. It's only you that thinks I'm in the dark."

We both fall silent so I can practice some of that grand thinking. I'm Peter Pan's shadow sewn onto the heels of Lacey's life. I remember my blistered heels, red with blood. Lacey is my Wendy to a lost boy who never grows up. Left behind like Toodle's marbles.

"I want to be real; to get older," I announce, as if Teacher can wave a magic wand.

"Being dead isn't being immortal," he says. "You can still die. Didn't you know? And Mamie sends her love. She's sorry for the mix up."

"Well, as long as *she* feels better."

"There's a deal of the snark in you Finnegan Cleary."

"There is, sir."

"You think you were hard done by. Duped by a pretty face. But perhaps you were just stupid."

"And there's me, believing I've made a grand impression. Maybe even advanced to the head of the class and earned a chocolate button or two."

30

THE GRAVEYARD SHIFT

LACEY – AGE 15, 1927

It amuses me that the museum staff refers to the midnight-to-dawn cleaning hours as the graveyard shift. There are three cleaners when I start, but not long after, the other two quit in a frenzy to be rid of the strange goings on in the Titanic galleries. How apropos that I stay, considering it's Finn's presence through me that heralds a variety of apparitions, and Finn who encourages them to stay.

Some are brought by Finn. Others are sent by other invisible agents, and yet others, encouraged by the work of the living who document all things Titanic. They arrive with their own agendas, both insightful and inquiring, with my ears the only living ones open to receiving them. In truth, I want to meet Mamie.

Sleepless nights come with the job but I rarely take a break until the work is done. Only then can I bask in the aura of times gone by and think of Mamie and the members of Finn's family. It's not as if Finn and I are joined at the hip. He spends time bobbing about heaven knows where, showing up in odd presentments so often that he no longer surprises me with a tap on the shoulder. In fact, I often feel him approaching moments before his arrival and love to flummox him by waiting with arms outstretched for an anticipatory hug.

But it pleases him. His affectionate nature retreats when he's moody but it's quick to return. He tells me that love has been his prime motive for living and dying and living again. I don't doubt it.

My favorite exhibit is the Titanic deckchair – the jewel in our crown and our most popular draw, one of six surviving chairs from the six-hundred once set in orderly rows on two promenade decks. The security guard has to be vigilant for treasure hounds with sharp penknives, either taking a sliver or leaving their initials. Mamie had reclined in such a chair and who was I to say it wasn't this very one.

We cleaners have a routine. First we attack the dust and then clean the glass, including the insides of the windows. Next, lemon polish is applied to the wood cabinets and doors. Every second week the brass plaques, light fixtures, and doorknobs are cleaned. But the nightly backbreaking work of hardwood-floor-duty is next to last.

Halifax rain and mud is tramped up the stairs and in the aisles most opening hours. Joe jokes that it must be like swabbing Titanic's decks. The three of us sing songs and have our own areas mapped out to coordinate our efforts until we arrive together at the bottom of two staircases. We work ourselves to the back door where we store our mops and brooms in one of two cloakrooms. I stay on until the floors dry and steal upstairs in stockinged feet for my final ritual.

I'd been quick to accept the unique perks of being a cleaner in a museum, and after my two colleagues leave, I save the best for last. Of course, it takes no effort to breach the silk rope barriers installed to separate the thrill seekers from the vulnerable archive.

Back on the second floor, I take a deep breath and stretch my back, and as always, I steal a satisfying moment to admire the freshly-waxed floor, before claiming Titanic's deckchair as my personal domain.

Polishing with intent is one of the most perfect ways to unwind. I savor our time together and know every battle scar from its war in the saltwater of the Atlantic. I let the work take my imagination where time no longer cares. I am an archaeologist excavating a tomb of gold or a grand lady with servants or a blissful bride on her wedding day. All these adventures and more are engaged as I lovingly apply fragrant beeswax to every inch of the chair's surface.

After I close the tin of wax, I need to rest. The thought of sleep feels heavy as lead. I wiggle myself comfy into the chair's shiny contours and run my fingers over the surface of its arms. But it's only after I close my eyes that I hear violins playing the 'Blue Danube', and the rustle of silk skirts and the clicking of heels on the promenade. I hear a dog bark too, and a male voice that says, "will that be all Madam?"

"Yes," I answer, lightheaded but lucid.

"Splendid day for reading a nice book," the young man says without the slightest edge of sarcasm.

I feel a book in my hand, and smile. Images and words swirl in my head, and I'm that tired I follow where they lead. It's a pleasant enough daydream. I check my watch. It's almost time to meet Finn. The packet of treats I've gathered waits in a cloth knitting bag next to me. He will be delighted with the toffee. My legs are snug under a wool rug, and the sun, warm on my face, takes me into a flight of fancy. I'm going to be a grand lady. This deckchair is a throne. The contrite Master Carlyle Douglas has doubtless realized his blunder, and even as I lie here, is chasing after me on another ship to beg for my hand. I imagine myself married with jewels of my own. Carlyle tells me every day that I'm more beautiful than Helen of Troy whose face launched a thousand ships. In the meantime, I'm a happy-ever-after princess on the White Star line's luxury liner, Titanic. Any moment now Carlyle will arrive with love in his eyes and kiss me like a prince in a fairy tale.

His shadow falls across my face and I look up.

It's Finn standing and grinning beside the chair. Barefoot as usual. I'm surprised. Finn isn't allowed in first class.

"How did you get up here? Did anyone see you?" I pat the end of the chair for him to sit and then my bag. "I've got some more peppermints for your mother and a new bottle for Bridie."

He beams his magic smile at me, looking suspicious, but says nothing which is odd. My Finn is an exuberant child always breathless with a question that bubbles up before he can even say hello.

He stretches his legs from his new perch and wriggles his toes. I can't believe my eyes when brown boots manifest over his bare feet. Finn blinks into the sun. A breeze ruffles his unruly hair. "Look," he says. "This is what my shoes look like." Up he stands, parading in a circle, staring self-consciously at his shoes, bouncing on his toes and heels, trying them out – the way a child does, delighted with new shoes for the first time. Clearly, he's proud of them. He holds up one foot for my closer inspection as if to remind me once more to take notice. "Keep your eyes peeled," he says. "This is what we're looking for."

I don't want to look too hard. I want him to stay. But he mustn't stay here or his parents will be in trouble.

Finn shifts his weight from foot to foot and I think he's going to dance a jig but instead he sobers and I see a dark stain above his left heel soaking up into his sock. His shoes fade into nothing. His socks fade next, and the red sores form scabs, and finally white scars in the shape of five-pointed stars.

I look for the steward, somewhat anxiously. Steerage passengers are not permitted above that terrible demarcation line of locked bars. I half-expect a white sleeve with gold buttons to appear, grab Finn's collar, and haul him off. But Finn smiles in that lopsided way of his, and he must have heard something behind him because he looks over his shoulder and says "uh oh, Lacey's here. I've got to go."

"Lacey? LACEY."

I startle awake with Finn poking me. "Sorry, what?"

Finn has a strange look about him. Wasn't I just dreaming he was here on Titanic? I sit up in a panic.

"You're all right," he says. "You're back in the museum."

"BACK? I never left."

"Aye, well I may have taken you on a wee excursion. I didn't like to wake you. Was it a good book?"

"What book?"

"*The Water Babies*. Was it good? Was it as good as you remember?"

I search my memory. "*Um*... I think Tom was being thrown out of Ellie's house... No. Wait. It was you. A steward was... I was reading. And yes, it *was* 'The Water Babies.' Remember how Ma always called it the Waters Baby."

"You can't loll about here all night. It'll be morning soon. Ma will be setting off for her work in half an hour."

"I was dreaming I was a princess."

"We should go. You know how Ma loves to see you safe home before she leaves."

Half an hour. There's only time enough to store the polish and grab my coat. "You're a good son to Ma. What would I do without you?"

Finn blushes. "No worries Your Majesty. Sure, I won't be going anywhere without you." He bows, "Princess Lacey."

Once a month or so, the tea dream reoccurs. Yet I never *see* Mamie. I *become* Mamie for a brief moment, and I never truly think of her as my real mother. I know her as an ethereal lady who Finn regards as someone between a princess and a wicked witch. Rose Waters is my Ma in every sense of the word and she still treats me like a princess no matter how poor we are.

FINN

One passenger in particular unnerves me. I think it may be that Christopher creature Mamie was looking after. He shadows me everywhere. I'm not keen on his constant amused expression – ironically, the ghost of a smile better known to me as an overconfident smirk. He leans casually against the staircase banister, arms folded, assessing me as I walk towards him. But I have an equal opportunity to assess him. His clothes aren't nearly as fancy as I imagined. Clearly he knows I have a bead on him as he straightens slightly in anticipation of my arrival.

I offer my hand to shake. "Finnegan Cleary. Have we met?"

"We haven't. Well, not officially. But I know who you are."

"You're Mamie's... *um*... friend."

"I am," he says. He looks around, his smile unfaltering.

"Mamie isn't here," I say. "I mean, she was but she left. Do you still carry a grudge about your toffee?"

"Grudges are for fools."

He doesn't sound as bad as the spoiled brat Mamie described, but he's arrogant, right enough. I'm relieved he isn't more hostile. I grab his hand again and pump it with enthusiasm. "Friends then?"

His smile changes to a straight line. I'm not sure what it means. Is he lying or genuine? He nods. "Yes. Friends. So, are you the main man here?"

"I am."

He glances around the room as if he owns the place. "Well it's a fine job you're doing. So many of us are in search of something we don't understand. Maybe I should ask that girl over there. Or does she follow your orders."

"Lacey doesn't know anything. I'm in charge."

"Only, some of the passengers are saying she has a list," he says.

"Who is it you're looking for?"

"I think I'll be letting *them* find *me*. Say hello to Mamie for me."

Lacey drifts over to us, not unlike a ghost herself. "Miss Waters," Christopher says, grandly with a formal bow. "I've heard so much about you. Any friend of Mamie's is a friend of mine." And with that, he tips his cap and melts into the stairwell.

"Who on earth...?"

"Christopher Forster esquire or some such nonsense. He was a couple of years older than me. Not exactly in my league. That sort never travel steerage. Mamie looked after him and his brother and sister. Nasty piece of work by her accounts."

Lacey taps the top of my nose. I hate it when she does that. "Well, he's a polite piece of work. I'm heading out. Are you coming? Of course everyone can stay as long as they like."

I draw myself up to my full height. Christopher is a fop. Had he lived he would have been insufferable, of that I'm sure. "They aren't here for the fun of it, you know. They're lost. They've lost their spouses and children. They've lost their bearings. These are the real ghosts. They're haunting their dreams of New York."

Lacey bristles at that. "Hark who's talking. See you at home then." She reaches out to tousle my hair but I duck her hand and back away a few feet. "I'm *not* a kid."

"I know, but sweetie, you look like one," she says, moving forward too fast for me and taps the tip of my nose again. "And you're very cute."

"Arragh!"

LACEY

Finn and I compare notes. Possession is not an altogether pleasant experience for me; I welcome my mother as a dutiful daughter should.

One night I have a different experience as an unfamiliar Mamie, wholly enamored of being served tea, having been a servant herself once, but now dressed in her friend's finery. She relishes the sun on her face.

"Who are you?" I ask.

She starts to say Mamie but hesitates and then stops abruptly, speaking in a breathless accent. "I'm on my way to England, and I wish I hadn't promised."

She's nervous. I have no idea why. Nor why she thinks she's headed in the wrong direction on the Atlantic. Her deepest thoughts are shielded from me, as is proper.

Only her hand reaches out from under the travel rug. All tucked up in a soft blanket, she is, charming the socks off the steward by daintily accepting the fine teacup poured for her. He brings the cup close to her hand to minimize its exposure to the brisk wind.

The teenage steward, no doubt younger than herself by at least four years, then stands back and turns to stone. He reminds me of a cuckoo in a clock waiting for the hour to strike. He stares politely out to sea as if oblivious of Mamie's presence while 'madam' drains her cup. As soon as he hears the slight click of porcelain against porcelain, he stands to attention, manifesting at her elbow, ready to refill the teacup with military precision.

Suddenly I'm outraged. I swallow the urge to cry, deeply ashamed. The old Mamie I'd come to know, returns. "But for an off-chance," she says to me. "I would be bending and scraping in a starched cap, yes madam no madam, three bags full madam. I'm a terrible fraud."

Mamie declines a second cup of tea although she wants it, just so the steward will be spared further discomfort in his thin white jacket whipped cruelly from the winds off the North Atlantic. I am fiercely proud of her.

Each night I anticipate learning more about Titanic's last moments from its victims. Some are still searching for their loved ones. Others are keen to visit and catch up on events. I keep a ledger of all the passengers' names and their status to guide them home. On these vision quests, Finn mingles with the crowd, smiling and shaking hands of those semi-visible to me. I see him listening intently to a passenger. He takes their arm, only to disappear. I always wait until Finn reappears, alone. Often his eyes are red as if he's been crying. I never push him for a reason, but sometimes I hear his thoughts as if they're my own. He's been hoping for a glimpse of his mother and father and Bridie, wanting to thank his father for his compassionate act moments before his drowning. He understands the bravery of it.

Finn shrugs off his sad mood. "My Da must have loved me," he says. "I saw him crying."

"Did you see your mother?"

"Mam must be having tea with Michael and the angels," he says. "It's just as well. She'll be happy, and Bridie will be with her. I'll see them all soon enough when it's my turn." But he sees Mamie many times, and it's *almost* her in the deckchair, when she's the grandiose servant of the guilty tea.

But Mamie can't feel *me*. Finn tells me as much. We we're close in proximity but far away in spirit for reasons no-one knows because she never fails to ask about me and Finn relays her love to me. Mamie says she's been reborn and is the same age as me, living the American dream, She won't say her name or can't. There are strange rules between the living and the dead and arguing with any of them is plain useless.

Tonight, Finn wears his ghost shoes. He unlaces one of them and places it in my hands. "There," he says, "feel the weight of them. Notice the color. How they're almost red where the firelight hits just there."

There's no fire, but I agree how they shine.

It becomes obvious that connections happen when they do for the good of all and not before. So an anxious survivor is never overwhelmed by a loved one until they're in a state of acceptance.

Frightened victims are accompanied around the exhibits with a passenger who has made his or her peace with April 15th. They're led to each object and photograph until they melt away into their own memories, a little stronger for camaraderie. The atmosphere in the rooms is neither sinister nor celebratory. However, objects shift about and frighten the other cleaners, so much so, that it's left to me alone, to oversee the night shift. The graveyard shift. And I come to be known as a young girl with uncanny affiliations with the disaster who's in touch with its crew and passengers.

I become the object of much teasing. But the truth of it is that every time a man or woman dares work the night-shift they damn near faint from what they see, leave the employ of the museum, and refrain from telling tales to reporters in case they're 'followed.' That's what I lead them to understand, and they believe me. They are frantic to pretend nothing has happened. Their eyes say I have no idea what you're talking about when captured on film.

I feel their scorn for me as a curse but Finn says no, it's fame or infamy, and to bide my time. Besides, there's nothing else I can do but comply.

My old friend, Joe, sometimes waits up and brings me a cup of tea in the predawn hours to see for himself, but although he sees nothing untoward, he reports feeling strange in his 'waters'. That makes us laugh. "Your name being Waters," he says, "your insides are the only place *for* you to feel things." And it isn't Joe's imagination, for he's had many sightings of heavy objects beyond my lifting after they've moved clear across the rooms.

Before I go home, the first line of duty for the morning shift is to call in a few burly men to put things to rights. They joke, brave as lions in the daylight, but hightail it out of the galleries as soon as they can to cups of black coffee, and move on to outdoor tasks, competing with each other's ever-increasing displays of false bravado. But work is scarce so they stay on, refusing to discuss anything related to Titanic at midnight and drink themselves senseless.

I'm becoming a bit of a celebrity. And soon that notoriety proves to be a godsend rather than a curse.

31
INNER SANCTUM

If I may be so bold as to use an odd word to describe the passenger spirits of the Titanic, they continue to 'thrive' in Moon's Maritime Museum. They drift in on spring nights even during the frequent thunderstorms. Some were never on the ship but are the loved ones who have passed on hoping to reunite with the victims.

Teacher shows up after a perplexing night that propels me to our meeting place. I'm plagued by a flagging sense of hopelessness. Again, we meet beneath a full moon. The damp sand at the water's edge is like a school slate. I sit cross-legged writing the alphabet with a branch. After all, this IS my classroom. I smooth out the letters and like all schoolboys, carve my initials in my 'desk'. But I don't have their childish innocence of having my whole life ahead of me, instead I have several entire lifetimes *behind* me. Why does this beach always reduce me to maudlin thoughts? I think of Lacey and how she *did* have her life ahead of her and that I have more or less been assigned to her. I am her servant. In many ways I've been her nanny, and now I'm her lifeguard. Mamie is playing a joke on me. I'm trapped in service and in trouble.

My toes touch the compacted wet sand sculptured into parallel wavy lines. So beautiful.

As has become our custom of late, neither Teacher nor I say hello. We just wait for a conversation to present itself naturally. We require time between our thoughts. And I'm beginning to see the appeal of timekeeping.

Teacher's voice breaks first. "Lulls before storms are grand things," he says. "More or less."

I didn't even startle. Underneath the moon is the precise place for him to show up unannounced and uncalled for. "And you call yourself a timekeeper," I reply. "Is that the best you can come up with?"

"It is. Because there's nothing better to clear the way for buried treasure," he says.

"So, all I got from *that*, is there's going to be an almighty storm."

"Sure, I never involve the almighty," he says.

I concentrate on the surge of the tide. Its swooshing sound as it swoons over broken shells and miniature crabs is the kind of lull I understand. Its dance of swell and retreat leaves those beautiful lines of ripples hard-etched into the sand. I haven't the heart to destroy them with my branch.

"Your shoes are stirring for the big move," Teacher says.

That's when my stick decides to disrupt at will. I gouge an angry channel through the wavy lines, cutting them in half. Battle lines. Somewhere an ocean liner breaks in two.

The air crackles with static. Teacher's voice rises in an oratory tone. "I bring you these... *tidings*..." He pauses to chuckle at his own joke, "To let you in on a secret."

Silence.

"Suit yourself then. You know Finn, it's rude to dismiss

the art of lulling. I've come all the way from the moon to teach your sorry wee self as a courtesy. To you."

I plant the branch in the wet sand and draw a circle around it with my finger. "I claim this sacred stick for Ballymore," I say. "Consider it an olive branch, taken from the wreckage of Titanic, the greatest ark of all. Noah may have boarded his passengers in twos but Titanic did one better. She loaded doomed pairs of every kind of shoe, including mine."

"Do you enjoy destroying magic?"

"I don't."

Teacher performs a slow auditory clap directly in front of me and whoops and hollers like a schoolboy.

"Very funny," I say.

"Now then Master Cleary, did you ever stop to think that these meetings of ours are your exams? That you're being assessed? Do you even want to know the score? And I mean that in every sense of the word."

"I'm discontent where I am, thanks," I say. "Why don't you just expel me from your wretched school to save time."

"Ah, Finnegan Finn," Teacher says, "You've gone and asked the impossible for a time-keeper. You may expect a miracle... or not. But the choice is always yours, son. Even through the limbo years of waiting that come to us all."

I wasn't to be placated with a lie. "Well, you've delivered your message, and I've chosen to doubt the abundance of miracles."

"Don't be so greedy. Sure one miracle is enough for a lifetime."

"It would take a plethora of miracles to sort out *this* lifetime," I say.

Teacher's sigh blows through me like a bitter wind. "I hate to be the one to tell you, but you haven't sorted out your *last* one. Think, Finn. What was it you truly wanted in your last life? Were you careful of what you wished for? Was it new shoes? Was it a chance to lord it over your brother? Did you want to impress your mother? Or was it the chance to go to school?"

He'd caught me out. I'd been lying through my teeth. I miss Mam and Da and my Bridie. Perhaps it's time for Lacey to miss *me*. It would be hard to leave her behind, but one day she will die sure enough, and there I'll be at the gates of heaven, having been redeemed for my reckless behavior befitting a lad with spirit, to welcome her in. The thought so entirely beguiles me that I suddenly crave heaven. I'm willing to sacrifice and accept my punishments.

The beach echoes with my pain. "But I can't break the spell!" My anguish settles on the water and floats there like a layer of grease. I'm cursed. Did I enjoy destroying magic? Maybe I did.

It's then I discover Teacher has gone without an answer, taking his secret with him. He's left me to agitate over the past. School had been my powerful overriding desire to negate the other things he listed. School would top Michael's education. School would enable me to read to Mam. Sure I would look grand strolling into a New York school in new shoes. After Titanic, I'd been granted the only school open to me. In a sick way it's perfect. Did the universe have a sense of humor?

I howl at the moon and curse my apologies without shame. In my perverse little way I'm thanking Teacher the best way I know how. I feel vindicated. Purged. I close my eyes, and dare a miracle to surprise me.

The moment we step into the main entrance I know. A vision of my shoes in a glass box floats ahead of me like the Holy Grail. "It's today!"

Lacey is still peeling off her wet coat but I run ahead of her, disrupting the loose pamphlets on the ticket desk. I leave them flapping like wounded birds. Lacey collects them and shuffles them into a tidy pile. "Finn. Wait up!"

I know they're here. I can feel them. "This way," I shout.

Lacey catches up to me outside the door with a small brass plaque.

S.A. TOMKINS
Office of the Curator
Department of Archives

PRIVATE

Do not Disturb

"Hang on," she says. "Stay calm. I don't want to lose my job. One step at a time."

I'm tingling with excitement. Lacey is bemused but distant, on the lookout for Joe. She's brought him a fresh bannock for his breakfast, but my hand rattles the brass doorknob of the archive department. I can't wait.

Lacey hangs back. "There are ways to do this properly," she says. "You're making enough noise to wake the dead."

I send her an incredulous look.

"Sorry," she says. "I wasn't thinking."

She's lucky my fists aren't pounding the door. "Not at all. Death is so very amusing," I reply.

We create a considerable racket, and the bespectacled curator appears abruptly from the other side of the door. His expression of annoyance fades when he spies Lacey. "How may I help you little lady?"

Beneath his benign face is a perfectly knotted tie under a spotless white coat. Lacey reaches to shake his white-gloved hand. The man wipes his right hand on his coat, and thinking better of it, he peels off both gloves and tosses them into a wire wastebasket overflowing with white cotton gloves.

I push Lacey forward, foot-in-the-door style. To her credit she doesn't say Dr. Tomkins I presume. "I work here at night as a cleaner," she says. "My boss, Joe Burt, says you know what the real kit and kaboodle is. He means your office. I've come to ask questions whose answers lie behind your door. This very door."

"Does he indeed. Well, Joe should know." He peers down the hall. "Is he with you?"

"No it's only me and...," but she catches herself in time. "I don't know what a kaboodle is," she says in a nice segue. "Is it Egyptian by any chance? I'd like to see some mummies, and I figure if Mooney, I mean Professor Moon, has sent any in those crates that arrive so often, they'll be locked away... *um*..." she points to the open space behind him, "in there." She raises her eyebrows hopefully.

"Not as such," Tomkins says, turning away, leaving the door wide open. We take his absentmindedness as an invitation to enter. "Not as such. Not as such," he repeats. This admission seems to require repeating several more times, each time more quietly. It sounds like an invocation that trails after him. We follow his voice into the center of the room. Lacey stands there like a lost kitten in search of a home.

The inner-sanctum's radiators rattle with heat to stave off the usual damp. The walls are lined with shelves painted with ghastly shiny-blue paint. A radio crackles music on one of the countertops. Most contain a hodgepodge of items with labels. Nothing is tidy. I'm appalled. Mooney's rooms were immaculate. His respect for donations bordered on the obsessive.

My second impression is a jumble of boxes and papers and a floor littered with packing material. Some objects peep from beds of straw, mostly innocuous pieces of carved wood. Lacey takes a closer look at a feathered headdress and moves on to a splintered chunk of oak paneling. She studies the molding, as close as her nose will allow and sniffs.

"Wood floats," Tomkins says, by way of preoccupied explanation and bumbles away muttering something about teapots.

Lacey stays respectfully up-close with her hands behind her back. "It smells like history," she says. "May I touch it?"

Tomkins reacts with surprise. "No-one has ever asked my permission to touch anything before. Grab a pair of gloves from that box over there. One can't be too careful. Germs don't you know."

Tomkins has it all wrong. The contaminator would have been Lacey.

Lacey pulls on a loose pair of archive gloves. "That's why it needs to be away from sticky fingers." She means thieves as much as dirt and grime.

I draw Lacey's attention to an object I recognize as a slashed and stained lifejacket. "Kind of misnamed don't you think?" she calls over her shoulder.

Tomkins raises his head and mutters. "Yes. Quite... What?"

"These things didn't save many lives did they?"

"Cold was the real killer," I shout in Tomkins's ear.

Lacey calls out again. "Have you got a file cabinet?"

Tomkins waves his arm in the direction of the window. "Somewhere."

"Who keeps a record of all this... this stuff? We're custodians you know."

"It's a damned tricky business. It must be done by a trained technician. There's no secretary who can make heads or tails of these documents. I'm the only one qualified."

Lacey makes her boldest move. "I could learn how if you need some help. I can stay after my shift. I happen to know that artifacts have to be logged and catalogued for later authentication. Mr. Moon told me so himself. And these counters couldn't half do with a proper clean. Ah, germs don't you know. A good scrub down is more like."

The seed is planted.

LACEY

Cleaning another scientist's conservation lab is as close to archaeology as most women can hope to get. Life has given me a way to remain close to my dreams. Finn isn't so fortunate.

Finn points to a new door, left ajar. "In there," he mouths. "The inner-inner-sanctum."

"You do remember he can't hear you, right?"

But Tomkins looks at me as if he *does* hear. Or rather he hears but doesn't much care. For some reason the man's benevolent eyes make me think of the 'Mona Lisa' on my trinket box. He's present yet somewhere else.

Finn is nearly spinning on the spot although there's certainly a space large enough for him to slip through. "Go on

Princess. Dazzle him then," he says. "I've waited this long. I can wait to hear what he has to say."

I deliver my most innocent smile. I stare at the buttons on Tomkins' lab coat with unfocused eyes. "I'm also interested in shoes," I say. I must have looked odd. I locate my best adult voice and try a different tack to button-watching. "You know.... shoes from Egypt... shoes from the Titanic. Shoes throughout the ages."

"Indian shoes," Finn prompts.

"Or native moccasins," I add. "Any shoes really. My mother died on Titanic." *Pause*.

Finn knocks me off balance. "Is it mad that you are? You're blathering, girl."

I stand up straight, and start again. "So, I was reading about Tutankhamun and I was wondering about how the Egyptians saved everything for their afterlife, including old clothes and sandals. I study them, you see. But what did those entrusted to preserve the memory of Titanic's passengers, do? With their shoes, I mean."

Finn isn't amused. He smacks his forehead and pushes me again. "Are you trying to lose your job?"

Once again I attempt to sound more grown up. *Ahem*. "I should say, what happened to the passenger's shoes?"

Tomkins smiles. "That's quite a question," he says. "I'm about to make a pot of tea. I've got a tin of chocolate biscuits somewhere if you'd care to join." He extends his hand. "I'm Seamus Ashe-Tomkins, assistant to Professor Moon while he's away."

"Say yes," Finn blurts in my ear, and I counter it with a *yes please* that would be lovely. "My name is Lacey Waters."

I telegraph Finn. "Shut up you. I can't hear myself think."

"S.O.S." he replies, his voice dripping with sarcasm.

"Regarding the biscuits, I don't care for the dark chocolate ones." Finn is as infuriatingly single-minded as Tomkins.

I send Seamus whoever he is another captivating smile. "Mr. Tom? May I call you that?"

He nods yes, dreamily. "I put a tin around here somewhere," he mutters.

Finn elbows me and points to a square silver tin labeled Peak Freens. "I wonder, might they possibly be the promised biscuits do you think?"

"I see them Mr. Tom," I call out.

"I believe they were burned," he shouts back.

"The biscuits?"

Tomkins clears papers from two chairs and brushes aside clutter to make way for the tea tray. He indicates where I should sit. "The shoes and clothes. Anything not actually on the bodies. Anything lying about loose."

Finn edges towards the inner-inner-sanctum, too excited to care. "Hey, there's more shelves in here," he shouts from inside. "But it's all papers."

"I hope you don't mind me repeating this, Mr. Tom, but you could use a proper cleaner in here," I say. "Someone like me. These things require a delicate touch. A woman's touch."

Finn is back on the scrounge for milk chocolate. "You don't think you're being a bit obvious?" he says.

I ignore Finn and focus on my main mission to work inside the archive room. "Well, how else do you think it's done?" I say. "We could wait another month of Sundays and never see the comings and goings inside this room. And besides, Mooney would have kittens if he saw his lab in this state. Wouldn't it be brilliant if we were the first ones to sort through this mess? There's no telling what's in here. And, by the way, it was you who taught me the old 'flea in the ear' trick."

"It's called the power of suggestion, in higher circles," Finn says.

My arms encompass the room when Tomkins isn't looking. "Be my guest," I say to Finn. "Sort through every crevice and corner. Eyes only for now. No poking into boxes. All we need is for Tomkins to see levitating straw. Just pretty please don't further disrupt my conversations or topple a shelf. I know my lines."

I needn't have bothered. Finn's attention settles on an aisle between two high shelves. If his shoes are here they have to be down there a-space. "Brilliant," he says, grinning with chocolaty teeth. Even I can detect a faint glow of phosphorescence that seeps from a large crate in the corner like mist over a bog. I hope it isn't Michael. The crate is nailed shut.

The day comes a week later when Joe gives me a wink and announces as formally as a butler "Mr. Seamus Ashe-Tomkins, wants to see you, Miss."

Joe unnerves me even though I know Mr. Tom for a scatterbrain. "He's not a bad chap," Joe says. "And he's been cornering me about cleaning the inner-sanctum. That's highfalutin talk for the archive lab. I always managed that when Professor Moon was here. We were a good team. But Tomkins keeps a locked door policy. I imagine it's pretty bad in there for him to notice."

"I've seen it," I say. "It's a pigsty. Mooney would have a fit."

Joe gives me a stern look. "*Professor* Moon, if you don't mind."

"Professor Moon is a perfectionist. Tomkins is more of a ... tinkerer."

Joe bends low and whispers. "He wants to hear about the ghosties. I think he wants to join you some night. Anyway, he's a believer. He understands things. Told me flat out that goings-on with the dead are sacred and are to be respected. Timing is important he said. And now it's time. I think he wants an invitation delivered by you, considering the Titanic passengers have made you their queen. Oh, and Professor Moon's coming back. Won't that be nice, eh."

"I'm hardly their queen," I say, to Mr. Tom. "And they don't speak directly to me."

Mr. Tom nods. "Fascinating. So you can't formally request anything?"

"No sir. I'm only a listener but there's the spirit of a boy who directs them to the list of survivors and victims. They pretty much help each other and I happen to catch some of their memories when I'm sitting in the deckchair. It's not as if the gallery is swarming with ghosts, sir. I've see one maybe two and no more at a time. Different ones each night. It's as if they're waiting their turn. And they're shy if anything. A bit afraid to learn the whole truth and so they only stay as long as is comfortable. A few minutes is all, for most of them. They don't see me, at least they don't make eye contact with me. If they do see me, all I can say is they're respectful of my feelings. The boy says they're in awe of the magnitude of the sinking. Some seem almost proud of it. People gravitate to the photographs and the news clippings. I'm given to understand that the fixtures move of their own accord due to a form of magnetism. Opposite polarity and no more. This boy's privy to a lot of information. One of Titanic's engineers was on board. He was especially pointed out to me."

Entranced, Mr. Tom slowly stirs his tea during our entire conversation and lets it get cold.

"Opposite polarity," he repeats. "Quite remarkable. Well-done."

"The apparitions have a blue glow about them," I say. "It looks like energy to me."

He nods vigorously. "Incandescence. Yes, yes. Of course." He jots something down in a notebook.

That's when my white lies begin in earnest. Grey lies became darker. "I'm able to speak with the boy who wishes to remain anonymous. He refuses to tell me his name. I won't take the liberty to ask if you don't mind. The situation is already a bit fraught as I'm sure you can understand. It's bit of a fragile miracle. We need to proceed slowly."

"Quite right. The lad should be humored until he wants to join the light."

"Sorry?"

"Yes. I'll bring in my spiritualist group and we can free them."

"No! I mean, they *need* to be there. I told you. It's a fragile situation. We don't want to scare them off, sir. They have to free *themselves*. That's what the boy said."

"I quite understand. It's unprecedented. Can't afford to bungle it. However..."

His 'however' caused my fear to kick in and I act as his superior without thinking. "No no no. NO intervention! The boy said it was a sensitive transition that required patience and time. He may not even sanction your visit. He might send them all away."

To my astonishment, Mr. Tom's eagerness reverses without a fight. "Interfering with unhappy spirits in opposition is ill-advised," he says. "But I *will* inform my group and put them on standby. This is a unique opportunity. Let the boy stay in charge, for now."

"Mr. Tom," I say, with all the power of authority I invested in myself and Finn, "You must not tell a soul. Absolutely *no* spiritualists. The passengers will know. The boy himself is in this room, listening, right this minute."

A slow smile creeps over Tomkin's face. "How marvelous. Where?"

"He fades in and out, but he's not happy with you. I think he's okay for now, but you need to trust me on this one. He's clever but jumpy. This is *his* show. Yes?"

"I'll be right back. I need to make a call," Tomkins says.

Finn has watched the proceedings with growing disgust, acting the child, poking his tongue out in Tomkins' face. I thought to placate him. "I had no idea a man who calls himself a scientist could be so stupid. He's a spiritualist for heaven's sake. Join the light indeed."

"Stupid is it?" Finn says. "Perhaps, like you said, I'm *not* happy. And what do *you* think my fellow passengers want? They're in search of light as much as I'm in search of my shoes. But it's true enough, that Tom fella has to be watched. He could spoil everything." He thumps his feet on Tomkin's desk. "Like you say, for the sake of heaven."

32

MENTOR-SHIP

FINN – DECEMBER, 1929

Lacey's hero returned to make her a princess. First Mooney is a Christmas present and then her New Year's Day future.

She's inundated with attention and praise, even for the things I've done, promoted to inner sanctum officialdom, and given her own set of master keys.

Ma and Lacey move on opposite clocks. For the last four years they've rarely seen each other, working opposite shifts – Lacey's nights to Ma's days. Ma used to say that she and Lacy were like ships that passed in the night. The thought of ships colliding in Halifax harbor still makes me shudder. I wonder if unsettling memories are the ghostly equivalent to human nightmares.

Lacey races forward into each dawn while I float around her like a retrograde moon. Speaking of moons, Teacher has waned into silence. The longest yet. These must be the limbo years of waiting he mentioned in passing. He certainly has a weird sense of the profound.

LACEY – JANUARY 2, 1930

I'm closer to being an archaeologist than I ever thought I'd be. Being Mooney's assistant requires diplomacy. I have to remind myself to address him formally in front of the other staff, dignitaries, and visitors. But between him and me and the sanctuary of the lab, he's chuffed to have a nickname. From this, I sense he's been a lonely man, dedicated to his life's work. I don't know if I could be so selfless.

My job is evolving into a career, shifting literally, from night to day. The second week Mooney is back in power, Mr. Tom fades away like one of the museum's ghosts.

My training begins in earnest. The arts of preservation come first. I learn how to dust for fingerprints in the world of white glove protocol. Nova Scotia and Egypt are polar opposites –the wet climate of the Maritimes versus the dry landscape of Egypt. Mummies were embalmed using great quantities of natron, whereas Titanic's treasures have to be purged of as much salt damage as possible.

Almost immediately upon Mooney's arrival, he moves our deckchair into a gigantic glass aquarium and orders several replicas made to satisfy the sightseers. They're placed at several locations throughout the second-floor gallery and it's amusing to see the passenger ghosts using them, considering they'd never touched the authentic chair when it was available. Too many memories, I guess.

If shoes can talk, then surely a chair can remember. But new deck chairs absorb nothing of the holy saltwater terrors of those using them as rafts. I've reclined in every one of our replicated chairs and only the true article delivers shock waves to overwhelm even the least sensitive. I swooned myself from a feeling of overwhelming panic. Titanic's wood is imbued with vivid impressions from floating amongst the dead and dying. I never know if I will revisit one of Mamie's tea rituals, or experience the desperation of hands reaching for it – hands clawing and clinging and finally dropping away to sink into the sea.

LACEY – APRIL 15, 1931
age nineteen

Mamie approaches the end of my bed. "You're not dreaming, child," she says. "Our cycles have reached a crossroads today. I died the moment you were born, when I was nineteen, and your life is about to begin a new chapter.

33

THE GHOST
OF A CHANCE

FINN – 1933
age twenty-one

Could Lacey be getting too big for *my* boots? The question is not as odd as it sounds. We rarely discuss the pursuit of my lost shoes anymore. She's too busy. It's as if my life is an insignificant shadow of hers. Lacey goes to work and advances even if it's often 'snakes and ladders' progress, and I follow along to placate the passengers in the museum who still believe they've landed in America. I inevitably stay the same, more Lacey's Peter Pan playmate than ever, forever five-years-old on the outside and a hundred-and-five on the inside. The fountain of eternal youth is overrated.

Lacey's twenty-one. She has the key to the door in every sense, and she's taller for it.

Delusions of grandeur are a trap. Lacey's meteoric rise as Mooney's right-hand-girl is perhaps a tad heady for the thirteen year-old-girl once weighted down with a plethora of mops and brooms. The good old days when we were equals in age and appearance are long gone.

These are the thoughts that trouble my thinking place. I sit tonight with my cloth cap squashed down over my eyes. I like

265

to feel as if it hides me. Protects me, somehow. Wearing my cap is my ostrich-in-the-sand-approach. I can't see the moon and it can't see me. But even that's another misconception. The moon floats in front of me, shining in the water. In effect I remain eye-level with the man-in-the-moon's mirror. I shatter the reflected moon with a few well-aimed stones. I wonder if that means seven years bad luck? My gloom deepens. I wish I could share Lacey's optimism. I'm wiser but she's older.

Lacey rarely joins me at this latest drop-off at the edge of the world where land ends and the ocean begins. Halifax's inner harbor hasn't the same magic as our birthplace, and she has girly things to do. She sets her hair in pin curls and times her beauty sleep. Lacey is no longer a teenager but a young woman grown into a deal of overconfidence. But I have ways of keeping her honest. It never fails, when she shows me an artifact that she's painstakingly cleaned ready for display, I throw stones into her reflection and burst her bubble with five chosen words: it's not *archaeology*, is it? I rub it in of course. It's more *archiveology*, I say.

The moon stirs into wide concentric ripples. "Don't begrudge the girl her dreams."

"What?"

My thinking place is suddenly invaded by the trickster-philosopher who leads me by a celestial ring in my nose. It's painful to follow but more painful when I stop.

"Dear Teacher. Do you always eavesdrop on my private thoughts?"

"Now there's a lad who's grown too big for his own boots," he says. "And if I'm not mistaken, if anyone has abandoned their quest, it's you."

Hang on a minute. He's wrong. He's *dead* wrong. I speak directly into the water as if he's under the surface looking out.

"The miracle you predicted, nay *promised*, was too small to notice."

The water moves like the wash behind a ferry boat. "I promised nothing. Remember what I said about dreams that were too small?"

"Throw them back."

"Small fish grow into large miracles. Have you never heard of the fairy fish that offers a silly bumpkin three wishes? If you're canny that's three miracles by my reckoning."

"Your saying I'm a bumpkin?"

"I'm saying you mam's book with the miracle of the fishes was once a fleeting thought. Aye, all books begin as an alphabet. A single word is sand to the oyster, Finn. Did you know you're a speck of sand on this planet? Sure you're irritating enough to make a pearl."

"Were you this obnoxious when you were alive, then?"

"I was."

"Your notion of a miracle left something to be desired."

He bursts into splutters of laughter. "Ah Finn, it's priceless, you are. What else could a miracle be but a desire?"

"Shoes are not miraculous."

"Are they not?"

"Mine are too careless to pass for miraculous," I say. "Sure, they're off gallivanting heaven knows where."

"Heaven DOES know where," Teacher says. "But when the lack of shoes sends a wee boy to the depths of despair, he may want to reconsider his priorities. Something to be desired. Is it being a tall strapping lad that you desire? Or is it the attention from Lacey you crave? Attention is big with you. Now I can see you've powerful feelings for the lass but, excuse the irony, you've missed the boat on that one now, haven't you?"

The water stills. Maybe he's gone. He was forever leaving without so much as a goodbye. I shout into the place where the moon's reflection had vanished. "Did I say obnoxious? I meant insufferable."

Teacher's voice grows smaller as if he's walking away, into the wind. "I'm saying miracles grow when you allow them to think the unthinkable."

"You can't know what it was like. You weren't there. Sure and what happens when we overthink them?"

"They grow teeth and scales and a tail," he shouts back.

"But isn't a dragon of a miracle grander than no miracle at all?"

His voice echoes in side my head. "It isn't."

LACEY – April 15, 1933

I'm twenty-one. It's the year of my majority and no treasure map. But I have one treasure. Mooney brings back a scoop of Egyptian sand from between the paws of the Great Sphinx, and he allots me a teaspoon of it in a glass bottle. I can hold Egypt in my hand. I've tasted it on my tongue. Much to Finn's horror, I eat a few grains of sand. "It's far less than I'd gather on my teeth if I grinned at the pyramids," I say.

"Right then," he replies, as if all is explained. "You've no argument from me on that score."

If I'm ever able to attend the prerequisite university classes in ancient history and classical studies, I'm all set. I've read every textbook in advance, and even have a reasonable understanding of hieroglyphics. No-one can deny me Egyptology as a hobby. I pester Mooney for his memories and make notes. What did Giza smell like? Is the sand really pink at twilight? Did you see movements you couldn't explain in the corners of the tombs? Did you miss the rain?

"Sure you could be teaching those classes," Finn says to cheer me. "If Mooney could give you a diploma he would."

Finn's right. I'm Mooney's protégé. He's divulged his secrets of preserving artifacts both in-situ and under the precise scrutiny of laboratory conditions. Every technique of delicate examination with sable brushes and puffs of air without intrusive damage is second nature to me. With each passing year I've progressed to become head-assistant to the curator, and as much as my boss wants to keep me, he wants me to advance and leave him. He says the student has become the teacher and he's as proud of me as any father could be.

Ma's anger at Pa has grown into a steady drip of unhealthy preoccupation since he passed. Eight years has only sharpened her tongue. Finn is critical. "Ma has a powerful anger on her. It's unhealthy for someone to keep the fires of hate burning, so. It'll be the death of her, sure as eggs."

Professor Moon is true to his word. He writes persuasive letters to his colleagues in London. There is to be a conference and I am to go in his place. Me. Me attending a conference at the British Museum, home of Egyptian rooms second only to the Cairo collection. Even the Metropolitan Museum in New York has fewer prizes.

Finn takes the news stoically. "I'll go with you mind, but I'm not so keen to travel the Atlantic in either direction."

"You can't die twice," I say.

"I've already drowned three times Miss Clever Clogs."

"You can't keep pulling that metaphorically-speaking-game. I'm on to you sweet pea."

Finn grimaces. He loathes childish references to pecking order.

Ma says she's happy for me. "Your English roots are calling you child," she says. She smiles and touches me at every opportunity. She squeezes my hand, pinches my cheek, and smooths my hair, so much so, I unconsciously avoid her.

Finn notices all. "I don't understand why you're steering clear of Ma. I would have died to have such attention from my mam."

"You should talk. From what you told me you've been avoiding your mam since before the Titanic. By all accounts you missed your chance to face her when you chose me. I can't remember the last time you were intent on finding your shoes."

I catch Ma staring at me with a woeful expression when she thinks I can't see her. The worst thing is when she grabs my hand at odd moments as if to save herself from drowning.

Today is no exception. She pins up my hair with her fingers grown crippled from the constant handling of leather shoes. "This might be the last time I get to do this," she says, with a brave smile.

I counter with a lame "Don't be silly. I won't be gone long."

Finn watches us from his usual throne-like armchair near the fire. "Listen to her," he says. "Ma means she's losing the ability to *dress your hair*. She's losing the use of her fingers. Can you not feel that?"

I'm momentarily ashamed. I had felt Ma's fingers less energetic and been ignoring how many hairpins she dropped, and how I had to pick them from the floor because she couldn't manage it. "Oh Finn. I thought she was droning on about some morbid fixation with her death. It's been getting on my nerves."

Finn gives me an intense look, momentarily stumped at my lack of psychic insight, or so I glean from his thoughts. Ma finishes my hair with a weak flourish of my silver hand-mirror. "Lovely," she says, tucking in a loose curl.

Finn's a compassionate son. Ma's hands look tortured. "You do know I'm coming back," I say to Ma.

"Don't tempt fate," she says, wagging a gnarled finger in the mirror. "Remember they said Titanic was unsinkable."

Finn makes a derogatory snort from across the room. "That's right Ma, sure there's no discernible difference between motherhood and martyrdom."

Ma is sounding more like a senile woman these days, and if her arthritis isn't punishment enough for a life of servitude, the chemicals in the factory have bequeathed her a tormented cough.

I raise my eyebrows to agree with Finn. Ma's Titanic remark is unusually insensitive.

"That's what they call a *nagging* cough," Finn says, laughing at his own joke.

I take up Ma's hands and look into her eyes. "Now it's your turn for some pampering," I say. "I bought the latest salve for sore hands. I work with chemicals too, mind." I massage the ointment in and feel her finger joints crackle.

"It's hot," she says.

"That's the eucalyptus."

"It smells like cough medicine." The word cough seems to remind her and sets her off, hacking again. I fetch her bottle of foul viscous medicine and a tablespoon.

Ma swallows it down like an obedient child. "Your

father... your *real* father... will be delighted to... see you," Ma says, gasping to catch her breath. "How could he... not be... with such a... daughter."

"I doubt anyone will remember my mother or want to see me," I say. Ma looks hurt. I must think before I speak. "You know that I meant Mamie."

Finn waves his arm to get my attention. "As long as *you remember* that, princess."

It's not the first time Finn has warned me off my parentage. I think I know the score. I'm not going to be welcomed in with open arms. It's the British Museum I want to do that.

My birth father is Lord Carlyle Douglas. Mamie was never his wife nor his intended. Finn had announced these nuggets, shortly after the treasure map fiasco.

"Mamie was thrown out like a pair of old shoes," Finn adds, "and given a ticket to America, steerage class to belabor a not so subtle point. Them and us. Masters and servants. First class and as low as one can go before they're at the bottom of the sea. Titanic's gold line separated the rich from the poor. Even if all the cabins were below that line, we poor immigrants descended into the living hell where a floor separated us from the coal bunkers and the fiery furnaces."

Ma unpacks Mamie's fur coat. The new way of dry cleaning has refreshed it like new. A bit of professional attention has brought a lovely sheen to the red fox pelts. We air it in the kitchen to rid it of the chemical smell and it sets Ma to coughing again. So close are the dry-cleaning solvents to the tanneries, it's a wonder anyone survives into old age if they wear clothes saturated in poisonous fumes or spend their days making shoes.

Ma's anxiety increases when I slip into the coat. She turns away in a fit of coughing. "The trip's off," I say. "I won't leave you in this sorry state."

Ma coughs over the coat's mustiness but she refuses to have it set aside. "It's Mamie's grand legacy," she says, deliberately avoiding the mention of jewels. The smell of mothballs fills the room. "Lacey, give it a good shake outside in case Mamie's ghost is trapped in there," Ma says.

"It isn't haunted," I reply. "It's just a coat." I stare down a sleeve and shout hello to make her laugh.

But Ma looks more serious than ever. She crosses her fingers against the evil eye. "Ye do ken it's a Titanic coat? Your poor mother *died* wearing that coat."

Finn snickers. "To be sure it's a fine coat, Lacey. Sure there's plenty of room for at least *two* people in there." He's joking yet serious. He likes to chide me about our first meeting when we were once two peas in a pod, vying for sole residence inside Mamie's baby.

"Soul residence," he corrects, tugging his cap to acknowledge his remark.

"Well, then that makes three of us counting you," I say. "When did you become such a sarcastic romantic?"

Finn bounds over and bows formally. He kisses the back of my hand. "Hello missus, I'm a leprechaun. Have we met? Finnegan Cleary, at your service."

Twenty-four hours later, like the winding down of a clock, with the fox fur all sweet and empty of camphor and ghosts, Ma apologizes for the missing jewels and falls asleep never to waken.

The cemetery has a fine view overlooking the ocean but the

salt-blown grass is brown, still bitter from the driest winter on record.

"A body can die whenever they've a mind to," Finn says. "This time I had no warning. I didn't see Ma go. She just decided." He snaps his fingers. "Just like that."

"Do you think that's what Ma did? Died on purpose so I would be free to go?"

Finn sprinkles rose petals on the grave. "She knew you would forgo your one chance for advancement to stay with her. She knew you were a caring daughter who would repay her love in kind. Besides, I have it on good authority that mothers are born to sacrifice themselves for their children." He looks out to sea. "Sometimes."

Finn scatters loose wildflowers where a headstone should be; where a low cairn of rocks marks Ma's place. I'm sad and relieved. I want the conference but I could care less about Lord Carlyle Bigwig and all his rotten family who would discard a human being they knew to be helpless. They, with their titles and money, and it didn't matter a fig to me if I never laid eyes on any of them.

Finn shakes my shoulders. "You promised Ma you'd go."

"You and your promises. There's such a thing as a white lie."

"Is there?" he says. "Well I never heard of such a terrible thing."

34

UNCLEAR SAILING

FINN – MAY, 1933

Teacher is adamant. "You have no choice, Finn. It's time to face your demons," he says. It's the start of my worst day. A waste of a glorious day that any human would store forever as one filled to overflowing with energy. Even the wind is golden. I'm happy. No visiting moon-man is going to destroy my peace of mind, as unsettled as I am with Lacey's impending journey.

That was my first mistake.

Teacher is a spoilsport. I point to the blue horizon where the Atlantic meets the sky. "You mean her?"

"I mean Ballymore."

"You mean Michael."

"You demonized Michael to avoid your real foe. Yourself."

"It's strange to be with you under the sun. We belong in the moonlight."

"The moon is always there, Finn. Sure you don't think it disappears during the day?"

"Why now?"

"I'm a timekeeper," he says. "Trust me. I know these things. It's time."

These days, when I walk alone, I take myself off to the birthing beach and crunch through the crush of stones away from the water where I have to be mindful where I step. The stench of sea slime chokes me. The claws of dead crabs and great tubes of rotting seaweed grab at my ankles. It's slow going with every unsteady step sinking into loose pebbles, but as always, I grab a pine 'sword' along the way for balance. Just carrying a branch to swing at my side lifts my mood. I strip away the needles and swish it ahead of me. I swat flies and I scrape it across the crumbling banks. Every now and then I poke the end of it into a hole to rabbit out anything of interest. Not much as it happens. I pretend I'm a brave explorer trudging a foreign shore, free of docks and rat-infested ships. Out here the seabirds scream inside my head.

A man and his two dogs walk towards me. The dogs see me and investigate a boy on his own. One of them comes close enough to be petted. The other runs around me in a circle until I throw my sword for him. Off he bounds. His master calls him back with a whistle but not before he drops the retrieved stick at my feet. "Good dog." He's that happy, his tail is likely to fall off with the wagging.

I should be eager for a new adventure, bounding like that dog, panting for a run. I needn't go but I promised Mamie I would look after Lacey.

Teacher's voice trails after me. "The secret you've been keeping nigh on these eight years was never yours to keep. Sure it's too big to keep. I think your wee demons have caused enough damage don't you?"

"Lacey's fine."

"I mean you, you great poltroon. They're eating you into a shade. Every time I see you, you're thinner. You begged for school and here I am, but you refuse to learn. Soon I may not be able to help and...."

He catches me doodling Lacey's initials inside a heart in the sand. "Damn it Finn! Do you want to wander this earth for all eternity like a spent shadow, reduced to poking at hornet's nests like a wee boy? Do you not want an Irish heaven? Fresh starts await you. You have a chance to live a new life of your own. And Lacey's *not* fine. You know she isn't. She copes. You could learn something from that girl."

"She's *not* a girl."

"Well now we have the truth of it. An honest wish."

"I have two wishes left then."

"Hark to the cheek of it," he says. "You as good as put Rose in the workhouse."

"I never did. It was her destiny."

"Oh, was it now?"

An invisible hand wipes my drawing from the blackboard sand. "You're being unfair to Lacey. You do know, don't you, that it's yourself you're harming. You know where hell is?" He points to the ground. "It's not a fiery pit down there." His arms gesture to include the airs surrounding us. "It's being insubstantial and alone. Right here. Friendless and teacherless where you're some small bitter vapor. A hopeless wind drifting over other people's love and happiness. Do you want to be trapped here forever?"

A cloying stench of coastal death hits me full in the face that says it's time for recess. "Holy Mother," I shout. "Can you smell that? Did you throw that just now?"

"Buck up m'lad. That smell's an unholy mixture of love and fear with a fair helping of jealousy. Only you could sense the likes of that. My task is to tell you there's still time. But only a wee sliver of it. You've a dragon to slay. It's grown from a harmless wee wretch the size of a mouse into the snarling three-headed beastie you can feel breathing down your neck at midnight. This depression of yours. This pettiness for revenge and your insistence of jealousy and hate is an anchor the size of Titanic's. It's no bloody wonder that your heels don't heal."

"You're laughing at me."

Teacher's sigh makes the treetops sway. "Poor simpleton. You hard-done-by waif. Your sad whingings are no longer the protestations of an innocent boy but the melancholy ravings of a baby coward. You're not the only boy to be smitten by a pretty girl. You know more than anyone that wisdom is never how old you are, yet you persist in blaming an eleven-year-old boy for your troubles. Fear keeps you close to the earth. It's haunting you're about, and now a girl has turned your empty wee head."

"Fear didn't keep me away from heaven; my mother did. She's a temper on her when it comes to my brother's shoes. It's not my fault."

The silence between us lasts so long I'd thought he'd gone but he's still there and I'm in for it. "Lacey was an excuse," he says. "Promising a dying woman is hardly an act of compassion. You would have taken any path to avoid your mother. SHOES MY ARSE! You promised Mamie in order to save yourself. She tried to redress her mistake, but you would have none of it."

I prod myself in the chest three times for effect. "So you think all this is my own fault?"

"Fault is a terror of a word. It's your own doing."

I take a deep breath and wait for the axe to fall. I didn't wait long.

"Well, Finn, your green-eyed dragon is here. Bigger than Titanic, he is – a green-eyed monster you've called from the depths of your self-pity. And there's no St. Michael to help you. It's your big battle. If that throw-stick is your idea of a sword, then the best of luck to you. The boy you were had a flimsy excuse but you've the mind of a sage. I'm not your enemy. I'm not here to shame you. No-one but you can do that. You've made a conscious choice to separate yourself from your due."

"I never asked to be born."

"One day you'll be thanking me, so you will."

This venomous lecture is reeled off under an incongruously bright day. The sun is let loose, touching and hugging and kissing everything into liquid gold. Even the putrid smells on the beach burn away, paling into the robust scent of salty air and pinecones.

Teacher's next six words are meant to seal a new sanity. "I love you. You know that?"

I'm gobsmacked by an emotion that bursts through me. For now the sun is inside me, beaming out through my skin. My new fate is etched into a soft clay tablet, left to bake under the god Sol.

"Tick tock," Teacher says. "Remember this – soldiering on isn't the same as being a warrior."

LACEY – JULY 4, 1933

The size of the ship that's taking me to mummies and my estranged father is big enough to me, even when Finn scoffs at its insignificance. "It's a wee rowboat," he says, digging me in the ribs. "Sure you'd better secure your lifejacket, first thing."

I make a big deal out of pretending to be scared. I cover my mouth with a stifled scream and roll my eyes. "Quick. Send an S.O.S. Save our souls."

"I'm only after having a wee bit of fun with you. You're surely not deny me that," he says.

"I doubt it would make any difference if I tried."

"Let's be clear of one thing, here and now," Finn says. "I'm on your side."

"Gotcha. Good to know because sometimes it's unclear where your loyalties lie." I reach out to shake on it. "Together, thick or thin," I say.

"What!" He shakes my hand but won't let go. He pulls me towards him with a wild look in his eye. "Who told you to say that?"

I shake him off. He's not going to spoil the joy of being underway.

Finn hears my thoughts. "Aye well, missus, you're best not to look back."

I'm delighted with the compact space: a stark hospital bed, a small bedside shelf, and a wall lamp. I'm a nun in a cell. The bed is raised high enough to store a fair-sized trunk underneath. I hang the fur in the closet where I find an extra blanket and a bowl.

"That'll be your puke bucket," Finn says.

I stare him down without blinking. "I have no intention of being seasick."

When I close the door we find a lifejacket hanging on a hook. Finn takes one look at it and turns away. "I don't remember our quarters being so cramped," he says, examining the head of a nail in the wooden headboard. "It's entirely math," he says after a bit. "Survival is a powerful equation. It's the balance of passengers to lifeboats. That wee jacket there will only keep your dead body afloat."

"Thanks. Can we focus on something, oh, I don't know, positive?"

I lay out a pair of long white evening gloves and my jet

necklace together with my biggest splurge – a red evening dress with a matching shawl and crimson shoes. I model my shoes for Finn by tapping the heels together like Dorothy and say there's no place like home.

Now, I know perfectly well that Finn shares my love for 'The Wizard of Oz.' I have my own copy, dog-eared and sticky from reading it during meals and at the beach and in the bath. But now he turns up his nose at my reference.

"There's no place anyone can really call home," he says.

It seems I've made a bit of a conquest. I receive several invitations for the Captain's ball from admirers. Finn lets me know he's unimpressed in that usual way of his. "Permission to abandon ship Captain," he says, scowling. "A nun in a cell, is it?" he shouts before making a dramatic exit through the lifejacket on the back of my cabin door.

35

DIGGING FOR HAPPINESS

When Lacey uses the words thick or thin I remember Teacher telling me I was fading into a thin phantom for lack of fortitude. Fat lot of good *that* did me. I was also thick-headed. I hadn't acted the loving brother because I didn't want to *be* Lacey's brother. My secret suddenly feels like poison that's slowly working its way through my system. I guess that's all guilt is. A slow poison that eventually kills or cures. There is no antidote for loving Lacey. Timing is tricky. Besides, I've built up a resistance to the truth. Yet harboring a crush on Lacey is nothing to my terrible festering secret. One day it will come out and I will have to tell a heap of white lies. In the meantime, and it will be meaner when Teacher shows up, I must bide my time and await the moon for further instructions.

I keep two things in mind to sustain me. Lacey is family, and family forgives the thickest mistakes and the thinnest of white lies. Maybe even the grey ones.

LACEY

Finn wastes no time in delivering what feels like an ultimatum. "Mamie wishes you to confront your father for her sake."

"I know I promised Ma I'd go, but not Mamie. Why would she want me to feel the same rejection she did?"

"Mamie had a problem with telling me all the details," he says. "But when it comes to your welfare she's on your side. I'd bet my life on it." He stops and sighs. "I'd bet my tin whistle on it. It's what's best for you."

"She said *her* sake."

"*Arragh.* That's just her talking like a mother. What's best for you is best for her. I think that's what she means."

From the first time Fabersham Hall comes into view it gives me the heebie-jeebies. I have second thoughts but Finn more or less hypnotizes me as we plod our way to the grand doorstep.

"It's only the jitters," he says. "Look the lot of them in the eye and pretend you're talking to Mr. Tom. Sure, they'll be eating out of your hand like seagulls."

"Nope. It's creepy. And yes, I'm nervous. It's this place. It's sinister."

I swear the gargoyles preen their feathers as we approach. Even the lion's-head knocker at the service entrance has a grim expression. Its rust-filled eye sockets look demonic. Finn has to rap it a few time as I'm reluctant to touch it.

"Whatever you do, don't hem and haw," Finn says. "Shoulders back. Look em in the eye but keep your foot in the door. Right? Good. On you go, now."

It takes an age before we hear sounds of footsteps. "I'm looking for work," I say to a scruffy maid wearing a lopsided cap over a tangle of wild hair. She squints at me, shows me in without question after looking my fur coat up and down, and points to a small dining hall "Wait in there," she says. "What's the name? Mrs. Drumm likes to have a proper name, miss."

"Don't give her your real name," Finn says. "Go on."

"Who shall I say is calling, miss?"

"Mamie Broughton's daughter," I say.

Finn chuckles. "Good. Very good. Go to the head of the class, darlin'."

Mrs. Drumm, the housekeeper, bustles in like a wet hen and takes both my hands in hers. "Well I never was," she says. She turns my head sideways, beaming a red-faced smile. "And don't you just look like your mother. We heard about the Titanic. Terrible business but that's all over now."

There's gasps and a surprise round of hugs. She turns to a trim young servant girl and barks brisk instructions. "Janet. Kettle. Dundee cake. There's a good girl."

The disheveled maid who ushered us in sits discreetly at the far end of the table with another girl, heads together, excited over a stranger who has provided them with a diversion from their duties.

I look askance at Finn. "Tell her," he says. "Tell her it *isn't* over. I can see into her. Mamie was one of her favorites. She'll at least hear you out. People like Mrs. Drumm have more ways to skin a lord than you can imagine."

Janet Seeley, the head parlor maid, is a darling. She offers me a plate of freshly-cut sandwiches supplied by Mrs. Finch, the cook. It isn't long before I confess. "I'm not looking for a position. I want to meet my father and I have no idea what to do next. I expect you know who I mean."

Mrs. Drumm slurps the last dregs of her tea and slams the cup into its saucer. "That'd be ill-advised, luvvy."

I sip my own tea daintily and peer at her over the rim of my cup. I drain it, settle it gently onto its saucer, and focus on a pattern of tealeaves stuck to the sides. "I made a promise to my mother. And I've crossed the ocean to see him. As you might imagine, that wasn't lightly done."

"No, of course not."

Finn motions to me from across the table, where he's been keenly examining the sandwiches. "Tell her the truth. Give her head a good shake. Don't be shy. Trust me."

I stare into my tea leaves trying to read them, hoping they might offer a clue. Nothing is there, of course, but my voice speaks of its own accord and startles me. "Mrs. Drumm, I promised the ghost of my mother. Mamie told me to come. She wants my father to see me."

Janet looks over her shoulder, her eyes wide. I squeeze her arm. "It's all right. She isn't here."

Mrs. Drumm rubs her hands together. "It's like that is it? Well, we'd better have a good think."

A sandwich triangle disappears from the plate without anyone noticing. I have their attention. Finn checks their faces and takes two more.

"Janet, you'd better fetch Mrs. Smith. Tell her that her granddaughter is here, there's a good lass." She turns to me with a matter of fact sigh. "Mrs. Smith, is the widow of our old gamekeeper. She was Mamie's foster mother. She'll have a few things to say and no mistake."

But Janet remains seated and brashly pours herself more

tea. She has a plan. "There's a grand reception in a few weeks to introduce Lord Carlyle's new bride," she says. "Another pretty lady won't look amiss."

"Hang on, they're not even engaged," Mrs. Finch says.

Janet snickers into her tea and surfaces to dry her face on her apron. "No woman's going to turn *him* down."

Mrs. Drumm winks at me. "She might. And it won't be the first time, neither."

"Stir your stumps girls," Mrs. Finch says to her girls. "Time to get on. Janet you're excused to fetch Mrs. Smith. Be back quick, mind. Prue, Kitty, you're with me. Those potatoes won't peel themselves."

"I've got to get back too," I say. "I think we've caused enough trouble for one day. But I'll stay to meet my... *um*... grandmother."

Mrs. Drumm missed the word 'we,' takes her cue from Cook, and pushes back her chair. "It's a crying shame Mrs. Clarkson isn't here to see this day. She was cook when Mamie was here. Loved her like a daughter, she did."

Janet looks sideways and takes two slices of cake. One drops stealthily into her lap where Finn pinches it. "You come back on the quiet, Lacey," she says. "My big sister is the best seamstress around here for miles. Our Cissy knows how to dress a lady. Let me have a quiet word. We'll sort you out."

Finn returns to the far end of the table waiting for his turn at another helping of cake when no-one is looking. "Talk about the luck of the Irish, and you're not even. Some of us come by it naturally," he says with his mouth full.

Janet looks into her apron for the extra slice of cake, and then at the floor. I smile at her, all innocent. "Did you lose something?"

"No, no. I'm all a muddle today. I had some cake to give Mrs. Smith. I swore it was in my apron."

"It's that ghost," Kitty says. "She took that cake. I saw her."

It's decided, I must return to Fabersham, stroll in casual as I please, and mingle upstairs until fate takes my hand and either presents me with a chance introduction or simply affords me a look at a despicable man who'd lent me his bloodline long enough to ruin my mother.

In the meantime I will visit on weekends and stay with my grandmother and meet my cousins who seem endlessly sprouted throughout the estate and sprinkled from Hertfordshire to Surrey.

Janet removes the cake to the larder and Finn follows it there to eat at his leisure.

Mrs. Finch claps her hands. "No dawdling, Janet. Straight to Mrs. Smith now, and back to me, sharp-like. We've got dinner for ten tonight."

I will have plenty of chances to collaborate with my female conspirators to find a suitable dress culled from the ladies' 'poor box.' My red one may be too conspicuous.

"A few bits and bobs and they'd never know their own gowns," Janet says. "There's more than a few they've grown too stout to wear. I'm sure something special can be turned out between our Cissy and Lipton. She's Miss Millicent's lady's maid. Lipton has a way with the latest hairstyles. Yours will look grand all tied up in a big swirl."

I feel a stab of sadness remembering Ma and her poor fingers, bravely gripping hairpins, taming my long hair, and me impatient to dismiss her.

"By the way," Janet says, "Lipton is your second cousin."

It 'turns out' that my red dress is too flouncy, a bit out of date and provincial. Janet is true to her word. My debut takes on the magnitude of an epic adventure. Cissy and Lipton outdo themselves so even Finn has nothing cheeky to say when he sees me, jewels and all.

36

VICTORY DANCE

The grand hall is lit with a thousand candles, but it feels dark. I sense resistance within. Ladies in bright colors swan by me in their slinky fashions. It is the age of elegance. Long form-fitting dresses accentuate the attributes of being tall and slender. They all wear long gloves. Some have ornaments in their hair: small feathers, solitaire gems, and satin flowers. Tiaras have been replaced with wide headbands embroidered with seed pearls and fancies. I am a stone pillar, frozen in fear, clad in a sheath of lavender silk.

Nonsense, I tell myself. They're only people in a room.

"You look like a princess," Finn says. "Just like your mother. And sure I never saw her in a dress like that. You can walk over and say hello, and be downstairs and out the door in the shake of a lamb's tail."

No-one knows I'm an intruder... yet. Folds of clinging fabric slink diagonally across my torso and gather into a hip clasp of art deco silver inlaid with matching jet. But the fluid movement of the black glass necklace gives me away. Liquid coal woven into a lace collar, moves like a heartbeat on the surface of my skin. I'm sure the candlelight is glittering from it, sending sparks with my every breath. Soon everyone will notice and stare. I will be weeded out. Escorted out on a footman's arm and the world will go on inside this grand room without me.

I may have turned to salt because I can't move.

"In for a penny, in for a pound," Finn says. "Do it for Mamie. Make Ma proud."

I suck in my stomach. "Finn, sweetie, give me a push, will you. I believe I'm stuck to the floor."

To my horror, Finn is no longer beside me. I've been abandoned. The little rat has deserted me at the critical hour, just like a mischievous kid. But I notice him across the room, standing on a chair, next to a stunning blonde woman in a red strapless dress. He's whispering in her ear while she backs away from a man I instinctively know is my father. Finn confirms this by pointing to the man's head and then at me. The lady must have heard him because she looks over to the doorway where I stand like a terrified doe carved from marble, and sends me a ravishing smile.

My first thought is that I'm glad I'm not wearing my red flouncy dress which looks almost identical to the lady's. Her gown has the only full skirt in the room and she looks gorgeous. The second is that she's not English, her smile is too ready. A gentle light from the candelabra catches the diamond comb in her hair, making it look like a crown. And she isn't much older than me; she's just used to sophisticated finery. I like her immediately. She detaches herself from the drooling man at her side and floats off, reaching her hand towards me from several feet away. Her arm is draped in diamonds to match the ones at her throat. I wondered if there is an engagement ring underneath her gloves.

"I'm May Carter Wilding," she says in a warm southern drawl, "from Atlanta, Georgia."

Her eyes captivate me. I feel embraced by an old friend. When I touch her hand there's a definite spark. "Hi. Lacey Waters, from Nova Scotia, that's in Canada."

"Lacey Waters," she repeats. "Why honey, that's so romantic. Now, I'll just bet there's a story to go with that name of yours." She lifts her eyebrows in a question. It's my turn.

A footman drifts by and offers me champagne from a tray. I'm not sure if I should drink alcohol. If I'm even the slightest bit tipsy I could make a royal fool of myself.

Finn is hot on May's trail. "Did she say she Atlantic?"

"Atlanta. It's in the United States," I reply, "somewhere in the south."

Finn snickers. "Yeah, I was making a wee joke to ease the tension. You're about ready to burst into flames, girl. But otherwise, you're doing just fine. Take it slow, Lace. Only fools rush in."

May takes a glass and puts it in my hand. "Some stories need fortification," she says. "I'm thinkin' y'all could use a few of these."

I feel strangely calm, as if I've known this woman all my life. She is so confident. A hothouse flower but spicy as a red pepper. This world of privilege is not alien to her. But anyone outside the English aristocracy knows what it's like to be labeled an outsider even if they are smarter or richer or more compassionate.

"She's a kindred spirit," Finn says. "But she's hiding something. I'm going to find out what if it kills me." His eyes twinkle. He's enjoying himself. "Sorry, I couldn't help myself."

There's a quality in the air that makes me feel like a complete failure, but I forge on.

"It's May Day, mayday," Finn says. "Trust me. You need to tell this lady everything."

"But you said she's hiding something."

"Well, it's devilish complicated to know what any girl's thinking. Sure, you're the very same."

And I'm off and I'm running towards May and away from Carlyle. "Then you're going to love this," I say to May. "My mother was on the Titanic."

May fans herself with exaggerated attention. "Oh lordy, your mama drowned! Why that's just pure awful. I've been afraid of water ever since I was little. My mammy had to bribe me with honey-drops to give me a bath, I was that scared of the bathwater."

I thought I'd misheard her. "Mammy?"

"She looked after all us children, except I was an only child on account of my brother dyin' before I was born. I gave that poor woman such a time over nightmares. I still have em. I do some powerful dreamin'. I swear it seems as if I'm right there. It's always me, adrift in a small rowboat on a black sea. Now here's me goin' on about myself and your poor mama *died* at sea."

It's my luck that Finn is at my side playing bodyguard and able to translate. "She means a *nanny*," he says. "Kind of like Mamie."

May's fan freezes. "Sorry, did y'all say something?"

I drain my champagne glass. "I was saying that my mother gave birth to me on the shores of Nova Scotia, half-immersed in water, so she didn't exactly drown. And I'm here to upset that man over there. The one who was draped all over you. He doesn't know he's my father. It's a coincidence that my stepparents were named Waters. My real mother was a servant here in this house. Her name was Mamie. Your darling beau got her in the family way... but without the family, if you know what I mean. And here I am, pushing in to confirm what a cad he is or be won over by a reinvented man with a heart of gold, which by the way, I sincerely doubt."

Breathless, I grab May's champagne and down it.

Finn touches my arm. "Well, perhaps a wee bit slower," he says.

May does the perfect thing. She laughs, and motions to the waiter for a replacement glass. She tips her head to assess me. "Well damn girl. That's some kind of a howdy-do. I like you, Lacey Waters from Canada. And that old fossil ain't my beau. I've been wantin' to throw a drink in his face ever since we met, but I promised my daddy I'd be civil."

I stand there holding two empty champagne glasses, all wild-eyed, flushed, and tipsy. "I'm going to be a professional fossil-digger one day," I say, and started to giggle.

May giggles louder. "Oh honey, now you're pullin' my leg. You, an undertaker?"

"No," I hiccup. "I'm working at the British Museum studying dead Egyptian kings."

"Well honey, they don't come much colder than old King Carl."

We giggle behind May's fan like a couple of sisters catching up after a long separation, and soon, much to Finn's chagrin, we naturally drift into a corner, the better to spill secrets that would topple the English gentry in the room. He hisses in my ear and tries to steer me into the room. "You know how I hate corners," he says.

"So, you're here to upset Carl's itty-bitty applecart?" May says.

"I don't know why I'm here. Well, I do. I promised someone and it seemed like the right thing to do, until now."

May nods her ringlets. "Promises can cause a heap of

trouble. Maybe I can help. Let's kill two birds with one little ole secret, shall we? I was wonderin' how to rid myself of old Carl. His estate is in trouble. He's cash poor, and I'm the fatted calf who's supposed to be all delighted with a title. No surprise. The English think we Americans succumb to girlish dreams of marrying a prince. I'm already a princess to my daddy. I live in a house not much smaller than this but it's happier. Carlyle insists on calling me Mabel. My name's Maybelle, but sakes alive, the way he says it is downright humiliatin', so I call him Carl as a punishment. Lordy how he hates that. He's not partial to lordy either."

"Then why are you...?"

"Even here? Same as you, honey. I keep my promises when I can. Oh, wait he's comin' over."

Lord Carlyle Douglas smiles as he makes his way through his guests. He's charming in an unsettling way. More of an emotionless statue than I'd been in his doorway. He takes hold of May's elbow and inclines his head for an introduction.

"Darling Mabel, are you going to introduce me to your new friend?" He's definitely chilling.

"Carl honey, this is Miss Lacey Waters. She's from Canada, and I have to tell y'all this gal has me hypnotized. Why we're just gettin' along like a house on fire. Her mother, Mamie, well, *she* was on the *Titanic*. Now, imagine that. This little lady's earned the name Waters and then some."

Finn's loud intake of breath startles me but he disappears without explanation. I think it might be the sight of a miniature wedding cake being wheeled into the room. Cake easily distracts him.

"No need to tell *me*," Carlyle says, still smiling. "I recognize her necklace."

I raise my eyebrows. "You have a keen eye but surely

these glass beads are common enough. After all, here I am, a country girl from Nova Scotia. It's a little bitty old thing of my mother's."

Finn returns and continues to stare at May as if she's sprouted wings. "Steady on Lace," he says.

Carlyle sizes up my elegant dress.

"Nova Scotia be damned," Finn says. "He's thinking you're higher than a common girl but less than a lady. What a cheek. Shall I be kicking him for ye?"

"Not funny," I say. "Behave yourself. This is for Mamie."

"Madam," Carlyle says, "it's not glass; it's Whitby jet, hand-carved by the finest craftsmen in Yorkshire. They're famous for it, which is why I commissioned this *particular* piece with the letters 'C and I' worked into the central medallion... but here on the underside." He reaches over to my neck. "If you will allow me."

He doesn't wait for my response but his eyes bore into mine as he turns over the jet teardrop with his icy fingers. It's impossible for me to see, but he shows May.

May addresses Carlyle in a patronizing tone. "Why, so it is." She elbows him gently in the ribs. "Why, you sly ole thing, I had no idea you were such a dark horse." She taps her fan on his nose. "You naughty boy. What else are you hidin' darlin'?"

I keep my head held high, mortified. May takes the jet from him and replaces it on my neck. "He's one dark horse's *behind*," she whispers to me behind her fan. She pats the jewel and winks at me. "Why Carl honey, she says over her shoulder, "I do declare there's a juicy story hidden in you yet, you stuffy ole fox. Pray tell darlin.' We're all ears." Her fan closes with a dramatic snap. "Why Honeybunch, I do believe your blushin.'"

The name Carl rankles. It's easy to see I'm not the only

one uncomfortable. But, like the aristocrat he is, Carlyle ignores the jab and smiles valiantly with an arrogance only an imperious blueblood can produce under pressure. "It was a romantic gift," he says. "If you see what I mean. Private. A matter of some... delicacy." He smiles, pretending to be shamefaced. "I was young and foolish. A bit of a Jack-the-lad, I'm afraid." He shrugs. "I favored several women with such trinkets. This one I recall especially. The lady was the wife of a cousin. I fancied her and she fancied jewels. But it was not to be. Lady Isobel Forster and I were not well-matched. And by the way, SHE was on board Titanic as well. That must be how your mother came by your necklace, Miss Waters. No matter, it's yours now and it suits you." He looks away. "A sad business, the Titanic. But how appropriate, Miss Waters. Jet is famous for its association with death and mourning."

"It's also mighty pretty," May says, overdoing the emptyheaded rich girl. "Landsakes, Carl. I see black beads everywhere. Why back home they're the rage. You can't tell me every lady wearin' black beads is celebratin' some kind of tragic love affair."

Carlyle stares at May as if she's a bad odor, but never loses a moment of patronizing control. "You know best about fashion, my dear," he says, and he steers her back towards his original trysting place.

"By the way Carl, my mother's name was Mamie Smith," I say while he's still in earshot. "My foster mother had a chance to speak with her before she died. By Mamie's account she worked for your mother as a nanny."

Carlyle keeps walking, but he stops and faces me. His eyes glint with pleasure for an unfair fight. My superior, comes in for the kill. "You're mistaken again, Miss... Waters? Mamie worked in this house for my STEPmother, as nanny to my younger half-siblings but you know this or you wouldn't be here. I take it you want money?"

"I was hoping for a kind word and a goodbye."

"Goodbye then," he says, and he turns and leaves me, never losing his smile, dragging May with him like a hunter bringing home the kill.

I stun myself and the room by calling out. "I'm sorry for your loss. Lady Isobel, I mean."

My father turns to me, still charming. I catch his glint of battle. "Isobel didn't die. She lives a few miles from here, mad as a frog, with her son, Christopher." He points to an overweight man in the corner, "He's over there. Would you care to meet him?"

"That can't be Christopher," Finn says. "He's an impostor. We met Christopher in the museum. That man is far too short. And Christopher is dead."

May acts thrilled. "Only if I can come too," she gushes. "This *is* excitin,' and here I was thinkin' this party was going to be one of your stuffy ole English... *affairs*."

"Goodbye Carl. You're always were a bastard!" I shout, and leave the room. I used the word bastard in its greater sense of rude behaviour.

The silence behind me pushes me on. May says "Well now, how d'ya like them apples?" in a shrill stage whisper.

But those words I'd said, that voice, had not been mine.

37
DECLARATION
OF INDEPENDENCE

LACEY

Downstairs the servant's hall is a nervous beehive stirred with a sharp stick. It's the middle of a long work-night for the staff. I wave to Janet. "I'll get this dress back to you," I call over the din. She stops midstride and comes over, her eyes excited for her part in a daring uprising. "How did it go?"

"Well," I say. "I made an exit that was pretty spectacular."

Finn weaves through the crush of servants like a delighted child, grabbing food off platters without care.

A maid bursts in the room with an empty tray. "You'll never guess what's happened upstairs," she says.

Janet puts a hand over her mouth afraid to upset me from grinning. Her eyes are bright as well as sympathetic. "I'm sorry, are you all right? I don't mean to belittle your adventure. You aren't half-brave."

"Well that's torn it," another voice says. "Lord D has lost his heiress. Some of us will be let go."

Mrs. Drumm claps her hands over a traffic jam of gossip. "That's it busybodies. Let's get back to work. You can hear all the news at breakfast." But she spares a wink for me and guides me to a large decanter of brandy and a snifter destined for upstairs. She grabs them in stride, and pushes me into a room lined with oak panels. Her domain.

I break down into a confession before I can change my mind. "Mrs. Drumm, I heard my voice shouting something upstairs." I took a deep breath. "It was Mamie."

Mrs. Drumm steps back, afraid to touch me, but she smiles. "Settle yourself here then... Mamie?"

"No, it's me, Lacey, Mrs. Drumm. You're all right."

Mrs. Drumm nods, clearly relieved but she looks behind her.

"She's not here," I say.

"Righty-oh I'll bring you some food. But you won't be able to swallow a bite in a dress like that. Did Janet sew you into that thing? There's no room in that dress for nowt but a drink."

I try to pour the brandy but my hands shake so badly, I have to set it down.

"There, there, lass. No-one's died."

She looks so horrified at her words I have to laugh. And that starts Mrs. Drumm giggling. For the second time that night a welcome glass of spirits is placed in my hand. This time Mrs. Drumm wraps both her hands around mine and waits while I take a sip.

Finn pops in. "I'm proud of you," he says, "but I'm going back up to be a fly on the wall. Something's wrong. It's May. She bothers me. She's devilish good with a secret. See you soon." He too, has a devilish look in his eye. I can only hope he isn't going to push Lord Douglas down the stairs or at least give him reason to believe a bruise on his leg might be from unconsciously encountering the leg of a rogue chair.

"Your old clothes are in Janet's room," Mrs. Drumm says,

"I'll get a girl to fetch them. You can change in here. No-one will bother you. They're all worried about losing their jobs. Miss Harding was a ray of hope for the house but that's not to be. The time's coming for letting a few servants go. Still worse things happen at sea, don't they." She freezes mid-speech. "Oh child, I didn't think. Forgive me." She pats my cheek with a long look of sympathy but recovers quickly, ever the practical matron. She pours another shot of brandy. "Come now drink this down. Upstairs is not above a bit of drama on the best of days. His lordship's got a temper on him. Only Chase, his valet, is privy to the breakages. He's copped a few bruises an' all in his time. Goes with the job. Some men are born a tad too sure of themselves. It goes hard on them if bettered by a lass."

At no time do I feel like crying. I even hope May will come downstairs looking for me if Finn isn't delaying her. If she does, I have no doubt of her performance playing the innocent or the fool to prevail within unfamiliar society. I comfort myself knowing that loyalty below stairs is a formidable thing. Lady Isobel and Mamie are legends here. And I'm the latest chapter in a fairy tale they know by heart.

Janet can only spare me a moment downstairs the next morning. "The master takes breakfast in the conservatory," she says, balancing a loaded tray.... "If you're interested." She gives me directions, but Finn leads me there. I'm so nervous I couldn't have found my face in a mirror.

Mr. Stiles, the butler, is in the conservatory, turning a centerpiece of roses on the breakfast table to its best advantage. He tweaks the cutlery and delivers his standard greeting without a shred of his downstairs familiarity. "Good morning Miss." It puts me off. But then I realize. He's a professional and being formal is his job. The more formal he is, the more important his master will feel. And the master needs to feel like royalty all the time but especially after last night. And a butler can never let his guard down in case there are spies waiting for him to make a mistake. A moment later, my suspicions are confirmed.

"The Master can't see you today," Stiles says. But we both know the opposite is true because at that very moment Lord Carlyle Douglas is hiding behind a large display of ferns, watching every move I make.

I have a strange déjà vu feeling about the ferns. A voice says *"you be careful now"* in my head, but it *isn't* Finn. "That's fine," I say, drawing out one of the chairs, and seat myself. "I take my coffee black, Stiles. And I'd like some toast, buttered while it's hot. That's the Canadian way. And marmalade if you have it. Thank you Stiles."

Stiles pauses and glances over at the ferns without moving his head. I gather from what happens next that he's been given the nod to comply.

"Very well, Miss." He leaves without a hint of tension but his eyes widened for my benefit when his back is to the ferns, and he exhales melodramatically, visibly relieved.

I face the ferns, address my father as casually as if he's seated comfortably opposite me behind a newspaper. "Well, what have you got planned for today?"

38

TEARS IN AMBER

Lord Carlyle Douglas slips out from behind the ferns as if he's been there at my invitation. "You can't possibly imagine you're the only bastard I have," he says. "I don't hide from them as a rule."

"I asked you a question... *Daddy*."

He emerges with amazing dignity, as if he always takes a stroll through the ferns in his conservatory before breakfast. I wait for him to blink but his gaze remains steely jet beads. He's still playing the statue, hands in the pockets of a wine-velvet jacket. His eyelashes remain immobile. "For a start, Christopher is keen to meet you. You left in rather a hurry." He brushes off his jacket as if nothing is amiss. How does he not have to blink?

I glance down at my leather belt and hang on to the buckle for life support. For the moment I feel protected with both of my hands clasped over my stomach. In the moments he scrutinizes me I taste bile in my throat and concentrate on shallow breathing. I rehearse my words, afraid to release them.

Finn stands with me. Facing me. He solemnly places his hands over mine. "Breathe from here," he says, and stands aside.

I'm wearing a white blouse with a mandarin collar over a brown hiking skirt and boots. The amber brooch at my throat looks like globules of stone honey, and echoes the colors of the leathers. I'd been pleased with my reflection in the mirror. Mrs. Drumm remarked on the brooch. It makes your eyes shine like gold, she'd said.

"Will I do like this or do I need to change my clothes? I'm only a country girl, after all."

Carlyle's shoulders rise in a soundless chuckle. "He's only interested in what you wore last night."

"Sorry, that dress wasn't mine."

"I was referring to the necklace," he says browsing the array of silver chafing dishes on the sideboard. I count them out loud. There are seven.

My coffee, toast, and marmalade decanted into a crystal jar, arrives with a poker-faced Stiles. "Will there be anything else, sir?" he says, as if Carlyle had ordered them.

"Thank you Stiles, we have absolutely everything we need."

My father opens the lids of several dishes and returns to the table with a plate of fried tomatoes, kidneys, and several rashers of rubbery bacon. "Help yourself," he says, without making eye contact. "I believe there's Atlantic *cod* in the kedgeree."

"Steady," Finn says as I spoon a large portion of fish and rice onto my plate. "I can feel your upset tummy burbling. This meal is all show. Stay calm. He's baiting you. I'll eat whatever you leave. Besides, I'd like to see his face if I levitate a sausage in his face."

"Don't you dare. I still want to meet Isobel."

Carlyle remains unruffled At least on the outside. "Isobel is quite mad, so you needn't meet *her*," he says, "but

Christopher runs her estate. I can let you have the farm cart. One of your *cousins* can drive."

"Actually, I'd love to meet her. I'd like to know more about my mother."

Carlyle pauses after loading his fork with a ridiculously tiny piece of hot slippery tomato.

Finn sniffs over Carlyle's shoulder. "That's not the way these fops eat when they're on their own, I can tell you. You're observing a well-rehearsed act of aristocratic affectation. They can gobble with the rest of us." I half-expect Finn to stir the contents of Carlyle's plate with his finger.

The overcooked tomato refuses to behave. It slides down the convex tines of Carlyle's poised fork. "Isobel won't be able to tell you her own name, let alone remember your mother," he says.

I deliberately scoop a decent-sized mouthful of fish and rice, Canadian style, using my right hand with the fork's tines concave. But before I put it in my mouth I lift my loaded fork towards him in a toast. "But YOU can."

He observes my lack of etiquette, horrified. "It's lucky there's no peas," I say, scooping another bite of kedgeree. "I eat those with a knife." I want to shovel food into my mouth to shock him but I take normal bites and wonder how he can possibly eat so frugally when there's food for an army behind him.

Finn sits in the chair beside Carlyle, puts his feet on the table, and chuckles. "I told you. It's all an act."

My father puts down his own utensils and studies me. "I honestly don't remember her. Servants come and go so often."

The kedgeree tastes of nothing. I feel as if I might choke. Calmly, with precise movements, I make room in the center of my plate, exposing the Douglas crest, and place my knife and fork together as I was taught. I'm done. I wipe my mouth daintily, fold my napkin, and scrape back my chair. "No surprises there," I say.

May sweeps in, eclipsing my exit, all pink chiffon and bows, frantically waving her ivory fan, stirring the room into a party. She makes a beeline for Carlyle's cheek, gives it a peck and takes a stance behind him massaging his shoulders where she winks at me with audacious charm, and whacks the top of Carlyle's head with her closed fan. She's a loveable hussy. I have to stop myself from smiling too loud.

He's plainly uncomfortable and squirms out of her attentions by reaching up and capturing her hand. He leads her away to his side, and I get the distinct impression that he's sorry his arm isn't long enough to seat her as far away from himself as possible. "Mornin' Honeybunch," she says. Her magnolia perfume overpowers the vase of roses.

"Perhaps you'd care to join us for afternoon tea," Carlyle says, addressing me through the roses. "If you're back in time. Summer tea is served in the rose garden, promptly at four." He looks aghast at May applying her bright pink lipstick. It's the only time he and I share a personal moment. "May has been telling us all about iced-tea. You might care to try it."

May winks at me and stage-whispers behind her splayed fan "I can't think why y'all persist in drinkin' that hot ole tea in August. Carl is such an old fuddy-duddy. I'll soon have him on a little ole leash, just beggin' for a mint julep. Won't I precious?" She reaches over, pinches Carlyle's chin, puckers her newly painted lips, and sends him an air kiss even though her mouth is only a few inches from his face, dismissing him to the status of a distant acquaintance. She speaks to me. "But honey, I simply *can't* go with you this mornin'. I had an awful night and I'm goin' to take a little ole nap after breakfast if Carl can spare me."

Finn and I arrive at Grailskeep in blistering heat. I insist being dropped at the main entrance, and to my surprise, Christopher answers the door before I can ring the bell. He is expecting me. I think he's laid on a special tour for me as a magnificent gesture of friendship which goes to show how one's intuition can be so blatantly wrong.

He joins me outside. "Let's go in another way," he says. "It's around the back. Mamma's in the morning room. She likes to be near her flowers."

We file past topiaries and manicured flowerbeds. The overnight rain has boiled away to dust and left the oak trees steaming with heat. Even the birds are too hot to fly. A few listless robins flap aimlessly in a dry birdbath. The drowsy scent of peonies permeates the garden and clings listlessly to the hem of my skirt. I trail it into the house through the French doors. Indeed, the elegant figure on the sofa lifts her head and sniffs the air as we enter. I am to be presented. I stand exposed, only too aware of Christopher's disparaging search of me from head to toe, dismissing me as a peasant. I am humiliated, sweltering in my boots, and wish I'd worn a cotton dress.

Christopher announces me curtly as if he's a butler whose employer is deaf. "Mamma, this is Lacey. She's come to see you about that Mamie woman." It's an insulting introduction. He gives the nurse dressed in the guise of a lady's maid, a curt nod. "I'll see *you* after," he says to me on his way out, and then, under his breath, maintaining deliberate eye contact, "dirty little by-blow thief."

He leaves through a heavy door that leads into the house.

Finn resists the urge to run after him. "I'll give that fat poltroon a good kicking, so I will," he says.

I give Finn a 'mother's' stern: *remember what we talked about and how you promised to be on your best behavior* look. "You're not my mam," he says, "and I never promised." He sulks like a kid and goes off to examine a sleeping wolfhound languishing by an unnecessary fire. I have to wonder if it hasn't expired from the heat.

I get the impression Christopher has stayed listening at the door. I cough to catch Finn's attention and incline my head towards the door. "Can you check the other side of the door," I say.

Finn evaporates and returns within seconds. "He's gone." He looks best pleased.

I guess my intuition is not to be trusted today. "You kicked him didn't you?"

"I did."

The sofa surrounds, rather than contains, a stylish lady wrapped in the scent of violets and a paisley shawl. Startling white hair, softly piled in a chignon, frames her lovely blank face. She sits solitaire with pillows propped either side of her. The scene is reminiscent of an invalid queen sitting on her throne. Vases of roses flank her dais on low tables. But as I watch her stir to life, it seems more like Isobel Forster is trapped in a wide wheelchair – an ancient child-woman plied with rugs over her knees on a perfectly warm day by an insensitive nursemaid. The fire blazes even as the sunlight drenches the room.

Carlyle was wrong. Isobel reacts to me as if she's been given a whiff of smelling salts.

Isobel's stoic lady's maid manages to curtsy without

actually moving and retreats to her knitting, discreetly out of earshot. The calming click of her plastic knitting needles joins the rhythmic ticking of the mantle clock, creating an elegant room suffused with sedating peace where time feels suspended.

Isobel reaches out towards me like a blind woman and speaks to my amber brooch. "Mamie, it's been a long time. Did you get to America?"

I take Isobel's hand. Her tiny wrist is weightless and dry. Bones like a bird. But she wears a large emerald on her right hand. It's hard to imagine the heavy stone being comfortable as it keeps slipping sideways. Perhaps Christopher had decreed she wear it for my benefit.

Too right," Finn says. And then something unexpected happens. Finn speaks to Isobel using my vocal chords as if he's Mamie.

"Izzie. It's me, Mamie. I'm so sorry about George and Imogen. But they're with me. You're not to worry. Heaven is a real place and they're waiting for you."

"This is wonderful. Two visits in one week," Isobel says. "I see you saved the brooch. I remember we... we were... what was it?"

"You were trying on clothes," Finn says, "for Captain Smith's dinner party. You couldn't decide what to wear. We had gowns and jewels laid out everywhere, and you finally chose the emeralds. They're your favorite. And we matched them to a dark green dress. That one with the daring décolleté neckline."

Isobel tilts her head to one side like a bird. She's listening. She's remembering. "Very 'day-coal-ate' I'm sure," she says.

"You always said your shoulders were your best feature. You were lovely," Finn continues.

Isobel touches her throat. "And the necklace too? But

no... something..." Her anguish is plain. Her hands drop and clutch at the blanket. "Something terrible happened."

Finn was quick to distract her. "Christopher spilled ink on me and you gave me a lace nightgown to wear, and by the time you came back from your party, a bell rang, and a porter banged on the door telling us to get to the lifeboats. There was only time to throw your valuables in a bag and to dress the children."

Isobel holds up her ring, looking lost. "My emeralds. Like this one. It was part of a set but I left this ring home by mistake. I wear it all the time to remind me." Her face clouds. "But I don't want to remember."

Finn calms her. "You threw your jewelry into a bag while I dressed Imogen. Christopher helped you. I saw him put several rings in his pocket and I took them so they would be safe. You'd closed the bag so I put the rings on my fingers. Christopher swore like blue blazes at me, but a porter burst in the room and grabbed your arm. I carried Imogen. You held Master George's hand, and in the end, Christopher followed you."

"Actually Mamma, I followed *both* of you," Christopher says from the doorway. "Mamie had your jewels and she lost us in the crowd. She took your jewels Mamma. Just like the food she always stole for that boy. This girl is Lacey, her daughter. She has your jewels."

Finn glares at me. "Sneaky bugger," he says. "I swear he *was* gone."

"I gave her this brooch to keep," Isobel says, rubbing it. "We wore my best coats. You didn't want to wear one of them at first, and I said never mind Mamie I have no intention of losing two furs... TWO!" Her hand with the emerald ring flies to her mouth. "Oh God, I lost *two* babies." She grows agitated, twisting the ring, her eyes frantically searching the ocean only she and Finn can see. I'm worried she'll collapse but Finn holds her hand and Isobel looks into my eyes with lucid recognition. "Mamie had a daughter?"

"Mamie stole your jewels, Mamma. We need to inform the police," Christopher says.

"That's enough Christopher," Isobel says. "Mind your manners or I'll tell your father." She pats my hand. "Thank you, Mamie dear. Don't worry. I'll sort out Christopher, and meet you in New York."

Finn curls up beside Isobel and thanks her for the toffee. "Finn?" she says, "I'm sorry I took Mamie away from you. I never thought there wouldn't be a New York – no afterwards."

A sweet breeze blows stray wisps of Isobel's hair and Finn tucks them into place like Ma used to do with my mine. Isobel lifts one of her pillows and caresses it like a baby, soothing it, kissing its face. Finn looks up at me with tears in his eyes. "Her children are still in the lifeboat with her," he says.

Christopher's presence continues to corrupt the room. He strides over to the sherry tray and pours two glasses. He doesn't ask if I want any. I'm not a guest. He pushes a drink in my hand and says "There's no reason we can't be civilized, is there?"

The dog whines in the back of its throat. Miss 'Nursey's' knitting needles pause as if waiting for a sherry of her own.

Christopher bulldozes ahead. "By last night's count that's at least two pieces you've still got from my mother's collection. Where's the rest? I have photographs of her wearing them, and of course the ones documented for the insurance policy. Would you care to explain how they came into your possession?"

"Let me do the talking," Finn argues which is fine because I'm speechless at Christopher's rudeness.

Thankfully, Isobel retreats into herself. Her nurse covers her in another blanket and gives me a look that says it's time to go or it's time for her nap. I can't tell, such is her lack of expression. I rise and head for the door without asking permission and Christopher has no alternative but to pad after me from the room. He dismisses his mother in the hallway. "Mamma thinks everyone is Mamie," he says.

The scent of peonies calls me back in the room to say goodbye to my mother's old friend. Isobel Forster, the former Izzie Sparks that was, languishing in her bower of flowers, stares into her past, smiling like a girl, twisting a great emerald on her finger. The ghost of a young boy sails a toy ship over the carpet, and his baby sister's spirit toddles over to the dog and tries to place a daisy chain around its neck.

39

PANNING FOR DIAMONDS

LACEY – 1934

Finn and I follow Christopher the length of the carpeted hall. It's hospitable enough but midway up a flight of stairs we cross into a hostile dimension, worlds apart from Isobel's heavenly sanctuary. The house sways. I lose my balance and have to grab onto the banister for support.

Finn takes my hand. "Call her," he says. But before I can ask who, the smell of the ocean wafts up the stairwell. My skirts swirl against my legs. For a moment I'm on-board Titanic with Mamie's memories inside me. The top step reminds me of the absolute demarcation line where Titanic's steerage passengers defer to first class – the point where only angels dare to tread. I sense a gate closing after us at the bottom. Finn grips my hand tighter. This can't be good.

I've heard about the mysterious California Santa Anas bearing moon madness, and out of season Chinooks blowing unseasonably hot over Canada's winter prairies, and other superstitious winds that breeze mischievous sprites into innocent lives. Ansel used to relate eerie accounts of salty gales at sea that lasted fast and furious for only a minute. It occurs to me that strange winds such as these may be swarms of malcontent ghosts who have bones to pick with the living. In any case, Finn takes my arm and we muddle along to a darkened library. Are all the rooms closed up like an abandoned house?

I love libraries, so other than the darkness, I'm at a loss how Grailskeep's library feels so sinister. Finn throws open the tall mullioned windows, inviting in a blast of hot sunbeams for sheer shock value to unnerve Christopher. Net curtains billow around Finn. He glows like a light bulb inside a tent.

Christopher sees him for a heartbeat before the reptilian part of his brain shuts Finn out.

Christopher is fuming, but Finn is a boy tornado. He whips the heavier damask curtains into angry flags. Downstairs, Isobel basks in a garden of flowers with her lost children. And all the while Christopher's childish jealousy of Finn and his loathing for Mamie, incubates into an irrational hatred of me.

I have a metallic taste in my throat. I imagine it's from the terrible words I'm choking down that I want to scream at Christopher, the White Star Line, and a blue iceberg that has surely melted without a trace.

Christopher is so focused on interrogating me he ignores the curtain's strange behavior, and wastes no time in staking his claim. "You've got my mother's jewels," he says in a low even tone. "However you managed it, you're in possession of stolen property."

"Let me do the talking for you," Finn says. "I know his dirty little secret."

Thoughts of Mr. Tom's spiritualist connections and Christopher's continual reference of possession repulse me. "Absolutely not," I say. "I can fight my own battles."

"Lace. Be reasonable," Finn says. "I know things you don't. Listen to me."

"I'm *not* listening," I reply, much louder than I intended.

Christopher squares his shoulders. His smile changes from condescending to threatening. "Well you'd better *start* listening."

Obviously Christopher heard me. So much for brother and sister privacy. Finn grins innocently. Ice wouldn't melt in his mouth. "Sorry," he says. "I needed to start a fight and you were right there."

Christopher's expression softens. "Look, all I want is my mother's jewels, and there's no *earthly* reason why we can't keep this out of the courts. We like to keep things private in this country. I run mamma's estate so everything can remain civilized, behind closed doors."

I used to have that sort of connection with my KID brother. Finn uses me as his conduit anyway. "Well, I have an earthly reason," my voice says, "and a few *unearthly* ones as well. So, why don't we just ring your insurance company? Right this minute. Because you've already accepted a settlement, haven't you? I say we blow the hinges off those closed doors."

"Your mind games may fool a sick woman but I'm not so easy to intimidate," Christopher says.

"Are you not?"

"Are you threatening me?"

The curtains still. The light that had been Finn blinks out. "I am," Finn says.

Finn is too energized for me to suppress. I relax into the mellow scent of leather bindings and polished wood, and I wait for him to reveal his secret weapon. Christopher Forster is about to be punished, Finn style.

In the meantime I prep Christopher hoping to diffuse a

catastrophic bomb. "We didn't come all the way here for a fight," I say.

"Who's we?"

Finn materializes, and positions himself as sentry. "The Irish peasant who ate some of your precious toffee and the nanny whose dress you ruined," he says.

A small boy with his arms crossed might have been laughable but Finn is transparent. And as he stares down Christopher I experience a vicarious shiver of being on the wrong side of an angry spirit.

Finn locks the door. "Is it mind games you're after?" he says. "Because I can help you out a wee bit, there."

After that introduction, Mamie appears wearing an ink-stained dress. She too, faces Christopher who has considerably paled. "You were always a greedy little piggy," she says.

Christopher's gaze shifts from Mamie to Finn, and to me. "Who's put you up to this? It's Carlyle isn't it?"

Mamie steps towards Christopher, close enough to whisper. "I know everything he knows and so much more."

Christopher stands his ground and addresses me. "I'll not be had by a dirty little thief."

"Neither will the White Star Line or Lloyds of London," Mamie says.

How ironic," Christopher says. "My mother, leaps from a kitchen maid to a lady and survives. But her jewels somehow pass into the hands of a servant who doesn't survive. Now, how did you manage that?"

Finn uncrosses his arms and walks towards Christopher. "If it's a touch of the irony you're wanting, you disparaged the Saint Christopher medal Mamie gave you, and him your namesake and the patron saint of travelers. And yet, you survived Titanic. Although to be fair, your bread *was* buttered on both sides. You were a silver spoon child. Sure, I can only imagine the shenanigans you'd have pulled to get in a lifeboat had you been an adult. "First-class boy my arse! But you *were* a first class poltroon. I'll give you that."

A scene of bizarre theatre unfolds as two powerful life-forces pin Christopher to the wall with fear.

He turns his attention to me, clearly desperate. "You came here playing the innocent. What did you hope to achieve? Did you expect a reward? Are you seeking a rich husband?"

"I asked her to come," Mamie, says. "Sometimes a reward is just a comeuppance. Sometimes happenstance kills two little piggies with one stone. Your mother was a very great friend of mine. I didn't know she was alive until last night. I came to Fabersham to rescue May Wilding because Carlyle Douglas is fleecing her for her dowry, but now it seems *you've* given me a reason to stay."

Mamie and Finn circle Christopher, tightening their net. "So you want the jewels in addition to your settlement?" Finn says. "Do you not see a wee problem with that?"

Christopher swats feebly at Finn. "That settlement was a pittance to what they're worth."

"You thought they were at the bottom of the Atlantic," Mamie says. "So it was better than nothing."

Mamie catches Christopher's hand as it swipes the air. "Spoiled little piggy." He doubles over as if to be sick.

"You were a disgusting knocked-up little whore," Christopher says, shaking her off.

Finn releases my tongue in a white lie. "Well, the best of British luck to you," I say, because I don't have any jewels. The two pieces that caused all this fuss are the only ones I've ever seen. The day my mother died was a little bit out of the ordinary. As I understood it from my parents, my mother's body was taken."

Christopher is too arrogant or too stupid to keep his mouth shut. "No doubt stripped of my mother's jewels," he says. "There's nothing so keen as the lower classes where there's prime salvage for the taking."

Now I'm angry. I raise my voice to that of a peasant with a rifle to Christopher's pitchfork. "Delivered of a child. Me."

"I saw Mamie with the bag," Christopher says. "She was a light-fingered little chancer. My mother just couldn't leave her servant roots well enough alone, could she?" He glances at Mamie. "She took pity on you. But you were nothing but a contemptible fortune hunter who used her."

"I quite liked children until I met you," Mamie says. "You were always a jealous little boy."

"What?"

I pull the brooch from my shirt, jump out of my chair, walk through Finn, and thrust the brooch in Christopher's face. "Mamie was half-dead when my stepfather found her. She was wearing the jet necklace, barely able to give Carlyle's name before she died. And your mother just told us this amber brooch was a gift. No crime was committed."

Mamie makes a great display of nestling luxuriously in a plush armchair to assess the room. She looks ready to claim it as home. She utters a contented sigh and rubs her hand over the leather. "I rather like this house, Piglet."

Finn sends an expensive vase crashing to the floor. "Aye, tis a lovely place for playing childish games," he says.

40

MAY FLOWERS

LACEY

Christopher chokes on his comeback and is violently sick. He looks horrified at defiling a valuable Turkish carpet. Mamie glances over at me and silences me with a finger to her lips. "We'll talk later," she says in my head. "This will be over in the shake of a lamb's tail."

"How those lambs' tails do love to shake," I reply.

Christopher is visibly shaken, and wipes his mouth on his sleeve. He forgets about me, wholly preoccupied with two ghosts edging closer to him, one soundless step at a time. I watch, incredulous, as he regains his composure enough to laugh hysterically. He's beaten.

But in case he still credits Carlyle with some truly amazing feats of trickery, Mamie lifts her skirt to expose an irregular blue blotch on her thigh, the shape of Ireland. "Would you like to see my birthmark? I'm not at all shy," she says. "Ink can make a nasty stain."

"Oh, no," Finn says. "That's *never* going to come out."

"You're like all bullies," Mamie says to Christopher, "a little coward grown into a big coward. But you're not stupid. What do you want to do? What *can* you do, I wonder?"

It was at that moment that Christopher risks walking through them and makes it to the door.

"Run little piggy," Finn shouts after him.

We hear Christopher clattering down the stairs and out the back door. He doesn't stop until he reaches the lawn where Mamie and Finn materialize either side of him. I wave to them from the open library window.

Christopher sinks to his knees. Mamie's words float up from the lawn. "You have a decision to make, don't you, Piglet?"

"By the way, neither of us are ghosts," Mamie says to me after the fun settles down. "Finn and I are as alive as you are. We've just got one foot in the grave, so to speak."

I wrinkle my forehead in disgust. "That's a terrible thing to say."

"WHY? Finn has been your friend ever since you were born and he's not so terrible. He was never a spirit rattling his chains, and believe me, Finn Cleary *has* chains. He's bound to earth as a lost boy more than even *he* knows." She draws Finn into the conversation. "Isn't that right, Finn? You're attached to Lacey more than you're willing to admit. Tell her. Go on."

Finn sends me a look of desperation. His body fades into the wallpaper and out again.

Mamie places her hands on my shoulders, so that we face each other. "And it's not as if I'm a spectre dripping seaweed on the floor. I'm dreaming, Lacey. The new me is asleep, barely a mile away at Fabersham. "I'd like you to meet her although you met her yesterday and I believe you got on like a house on fire."

"May?"

She smiles and becomes more solid. "Precisely. I'm May now. May is me.... Mamie. But I'm still your mother. Why else do you suppose I felt so familiar to you?"

Finn cries out "Holy Mother of God!" and zaps out. Gone. May is a surprise to him too.

"Finn's being melodramatic," Mamie says. "I'm just an *ordinary* mother."

Mamie waits, staring at Finn's vanishing point. "He'll come back once the shock has subsided," she says. She guides me to the sofa and motions me to sit. Both of us keep silent vigil, but Mamie sighs several times, her hands clasping and unclasping in her lap.

I check my watch. It's been over ten minutes.

"He needs time," Mamie says. "He hasn't gone far. I can feel him close by."

The room warms and Mamie's hands relax. Finn materializes slowly, his determined chin emerging first. Next his sweet face, and his arms crossed in defiance. His bare feet are the last to appear in a wide stance. He's making a defensive statement.

I attempt to go to him but Mamie stays my arm. "Names carry over through lifetimes, gaining power," she says. "The key word is *times* – as in more than one. You already know this, don't you Finnegan?"

It's Finn's turn to sigh, but he nods yes, keeping his gaze averted from mine. It's rare to see him this helpless. For once he truly needs me.

Mamie glances at the grandfather clock and inclines her head. "Time observes us and waits. Time times us. It sounds as if we're helpless but of course we aren't. We're counted, not in hours or years, but in promises. And take note, we keep time with devices called watches. Time bends into itself and delivers new events that are the same but different. It's how we remember to change."

Finn's face is impossible to read, for once. "My teacher never explained it that well," he says.

Mamie beams at her favorite student. "Finn. I want you to pay close attention because what I'm about to say could change your death."

"But his death is over," I say. "That's what death is. An ending."

"Lacey you need to hear this too. Nothing ends; life is a continuing spiral. But Finn is in danger."

Mamie seems to fill the room. "Anniversaries hold extraordinary significance," she says. "Humans celebrate birthdays but they also place flowers on graves to honor the dates of death." She pauses, smiling at some pleasant memory. "Some even leave toys. A calendar cycle of one-hundred-years is especially momentous. Finn... please listen carefully. Pay particular attention. A centenary marks a point of entry and exit. If you're willing, the year 2012 will set your promises free."

Finn has never looked younger. My kid brother, meek and trembling, holds a terrible gift in his hands. He's incredulous. "We aren't free?" he says.

"You're nearly home," Mamie says. "But we made a pact, you and I. I've done all I can to redress the wrong I caused in haste. I've forgiven myself, and Lacey has never blamed me." She favors me with a dazzling smile. "Now you must find it in your heart to do the same, Finnegan Cleary. It's up to you now."

Finn looks as if he might blink out again. I rush to his side and grab his shoulders, standing defensively at Mamie. "But Finn didn't know what he was agreeing to," I say. "He was only a child."

Mamie's eyes unfocused, her face is ashen, even for a spectre. Clearly she's tired. "Was he? Are you so sure?"

The ticking of the clock increases, filling the room the way blood fills one's ears in the heat of a moment.

"A mother's love is forever," Mamie says. "My darling children, I've always watched over you. Finn, my darling boy, never forget you were significantly blessed with three mothers: Your mam, me, and Rose. Four, if you count Lacey who is protecting you right now. But that's what big sisters are for. She loves you."

Mamie heads for the door and brushes past Finn. "Are you over the MOON yet?" she says without turning back.

Finn's expression indicates he's heard. He sends his response to Mamie in his thoughts but the echo resonates inside my head. "Which moon I wonder? There are so many. I'm guessing it's the blue one. And, by the way, I forgave you a long time ago, and I'm *not* a kid!"

Mamie reaches the door and leans her back against it. "Who said it was me you need to forgive? Think child."

Silence.

Mamie's form suffuses in a flare of white light that dissipates to reveal May Wilding. May has brought her fan with her. When she speaks again it's in May's southern drawl. "Lacy? Honeybunch? It's me, May. Well, now isn't this cozy. We're sure enough havin' ourselves a fine little dream together. Now don't you fret, sugar, we'll be just peachy as soon as I figure out where we are. What are all these books doin' in my bedroom?"

She approaches Finn, moving unsteadily like a weary woman heavy with child, her feet planted apart for balance, and one hand supporting her arched back.

"Don't I know you little boy?" she says, examining his eyes. "Now, where on earth did we meet?"

"I – – am – – NOT – – a – – little – – boy!" Finn shouts.

"Well of course you aren't, sugar. But gracious child, if

you ain't just about the sweetest little sprout I ever did see, with that red hair and all. Gosh honey, don't y'all have any shoes?"

Finn is dangerously miffed. Enough to punish her, Finn style. His eyes lock onto hers with brutal force.

"No Finn, don't," I shout. But he isn't listening.

"It was *on Titanic*," he says. "We met in the steerage dining hall on Titanic a few days before it sank in the North Atlantic. Now do you remember? You – were – on – the Titanic. You died!"

May becomes agitated. She appears to be pushing aside people in her way, fighting through a commotion I can only imagine. "Where is that little rascal?" she calls out. She swings around, overwrought, searching an invisible crowd, one hand protecting her belly. She sways unsteadily and grabs hold of an imagined guardrail. Her other arm appears weighted down. I can almost see the red carpet bag. She peers over the railings of the ship that Mamie remembers. "No. I can't go; I have to find Finn. He's just a little boy." She claws at someone's arm. "Now you go tell those lily-livered cowards that they have to open the gates or my daddy's goin' to raise hell." She clutches the handles of a red bag but has to let go in a spasm of pain. Her knuckles whiten as she hangs onto the railing.

I grab May's hand. "May, you're safe in England, remember? It's okay to let go of the bag. I have it safe. Take my hand and follow me. We'll go back to that lovely bedroom of yours, shall we?"

I glare at Finn. "Why on earth did you have to do that?"

"I couldn't help it," Finn says. "She upset my apple cart."

May covers her face with her hands and sobs. "I just can't be here. I won't."

I pull her hands away and lift her chin. "May, look at me.

You can trust me. You're just having a bad dream. Nothing is real. Okay? Nothing can hurt you. And when you're awake you won't remember any of this."

"I swear on my daddy's life, after I get home I'm never settin' foot on a ship again. Not any boat at all. Oh my God, the water's freezin'. Help me get home. Please Lacey, we can't stay here. It's too dangerous. It's so cold. Finn needs me. She turns towards Finn. "That's you, isn't it honey?"

"Tis."

May's panic changes to relief. "Well, you look just fine, sweet pea."

"It's okay, May. I'm Lacey's..." he sighs deeply, "I'm Lacey's little brother, now. You saved me."

May walks towards the door, speaking with Mamie's voice. "My darling children, I love you both. But I have to go. May's afternoon beauty sleep is over."

It's Mamie who leans back and melts through the door. Her outstretched hand is the last to disappear. Her voice comes from far away. "Let go Finn. Take my hand."

Incredulous, Finn and I make our way back to the garden, alone. "By the way," he says. "Try not to walk through me again."

I embrace the scent of the flowers as a tonic, and envelop Finn in a bear hug. I sound out the syllables in his ear, excitedly: "May... me = Mamie. Finn, she never deserted us."

Before we leave, May presents me with a lace handkerchief steeped in her magnolia perfume. "Lace for Lacey," she says. "We must keep in touch Missy. I feel as if I came all this way just to meet you. And I am *not* lookin' forward to that damn ship. I'm goin' to kiss the ground of Atlanta as soon as I get home. I have seen jolly old England, thank you very much, and once is enough."

I can't resist a test. "Once?"

"Why you sly little minx. It's true I did dream of England more times than I care to recall. Dreams that were so damn real, that when I wake up I swear I've been here before. Dreams strong enough to pull me onto a Goddamn steamship. But there's a handsome beau waitin' for me back home. I can feel it. I'm a great one for dreamin.' Last week I dreamed I had old Carl backed against a wall, terrified. I think it was him. Well, it felt like it was him. Anyway, it did me a heap of good, I can tell you."

M is for Mint juleps and Magnolias and my new friend, May.

41

CROSSING APRIL

As for my new fate that Teacher once inscribed in stone, the word hero is carved too shallow to be legible from a worthy distance. I plan to make a full heroic confession when we reach the longitude and latitude of Titanic's encounter. I plan to tell Lacey Waters that I'm in love with her.

I sit in her tiny cabin when she has lifeboat drill and I scan the horizon for icebergs when she sleeps. I count the lifeboats at least three times a day. But I'm also privy to the way men's heads turn when she sashays by.

My temper becomes shorter than short. I'm barely civil, deliberately sabotaging any plan to unburden my feelings. And then I experience a breakdown. I snap. Maybe it's simply the tension of approaching the coordinates of my death. The ship is a monster and I huddle deep inside its entrails, hiding in my lower bunk, terrified of drowning.

I revisit scenes of my life in Ballymore. I revisit scenes on Titanic. I relive my one 'salad day' with Mamie and how we got on like a house on fire. I love her. I obsess about Lacey. I hate both of them. I rage against being a man inside a boy. And I call for Mam.

Teacher shows up after I've moaned myself into a gibbering *eedjit* and gives me a shake. "Okay," he says, "it's time. The mirror is right here in front of you. Sometimes you have to sit with an open mind and listen. You've dug yourself into the perfect place. I'm going to lead you to a door by asking a single question. You let go of my hand this minute and open that door. Now, what can you tell me of similarities?"

I'm too listless to be bored, and drone by rote. "They're the same but different."

"And why do you not find that realization exciting?"

"You're the teacher. You tell me."

"Have I not penetrated that thick skull of yours with logic yet?"

"You haven't."

"Finn, wake up. Your voice is yawning. Say the first thing that comes into your mind."

"I'm the same as Mam but different."

"Because?"

"Mam obsessed about Michael and I obsess about Lacey. We're both clinging to the impossible. We can't let go."

"More. Who else is in that room? Listen."

"I'm the same as Michael but different."

"Get it out. Sure, hasn't it festered long enough?"

"And both of us... Oh! Neither Michael nor I can grow up. We're both stuck in death."

"Halleluiah. Keep going."

"I'm afraid of being abandoned by Mam."

"And?"

"I abandoned Mam."

"One more."

"Mam is afraid of being... abandoned by me?"

"Finally."

I have a lot to digest. Teacher tells me to sleep on it, that events are snowballing, and I need to brace myself. And then he says something entirely true but brutal. "It's time to sink or swim," he says.

LACEY

I leave England more determined than ever to be an Egyptologist, a goal I consider to be one step above a regular archaeologist. If Tutankhamen's curse is real, I'm a victim. He controls me. An Egyptian teenager, dead thousands of years, speaks to me in my dreams and whispers secrets during the day. In a strange way, I pretend he wants me to know him. He wants to tell me his story. The hidden stories we all have that history overlooks as smaller than life. He has singled me out as his biographer. And I want details. I want to walk the century of his short perfumed life in privileged sandals.

Had a childhood deformity sealed his fate or had he been murdered? Weeks spent with the British mummies pose unanswerable questions: the gaps in hieroglyphic translation, the lost personas, and the foggy, albeit lofty status of Pharaoh's first wife. The matriarchal chain of royal succession leaves the English aristocracy in the dust. If Finn survived Titanic to live with me, then why not the ghosts of these ancient vital women: wives, sisters, mothers, aunts, and daughters?

"I don't see any spirits in the rooms," Finn had said, "but I feel an energy that doesn't match the excitement of the visitors. It's thin, and it comes and goes. I believe the spirits have moved on but the mumbo-jumbo of the priesthoods have retained some control."

A new thought blows into my head. "The Egyptians believed if their names were destroyed their souls were destined for a void worse than death where no reincarnation was possible. It was the reason for a new regime to literally deface royal statues and hack out their cartouches. So, in some way, is not knowing who the mummies are, still a curse?"

"Let me put it this way," Finn says. "If you do hit upon their identities, their energy will leave. I doubt most tourists would notice. But you would. And it would lift a layer of murky curtain from their afterlife."

Finn is Titanic's celebrated unknown child. Apart from me and a few ghosts, his name has been obliterated.

Finn answers my thought. "My name was last seen on a postcard but ..."

He pauses, refusing to tell me the rest.

Sometimes he's one stubborn little kid.

The crossing is rough which means Finn is calm. "I only worry when it's calm," he says. "Banshees love the element of surprise."

"Maybe I should have bought you a St. Christopher medal."

I got the drop dead expression. "Very droll. But I'll tell you this... the wreck of Titanic is almost underneath us. I can feel it." He points above the horizon. "I can see the flares. It's sending out an S.O.S. as if it's still sinking. Down there it's yesterday. Up here, I have something urgent to tell you."

I miss his hint. "Radio signals are like any other flotsam, I suppose. Ghost messages in a bottle, adrift in time and space."

We are aboard a relatively small Cunard ship, 'The Franconia,' and it's an unpleasant task to walk even a few feet as the lurching in my stomach matches the side-to-side swinging of an unstable world. I'm a good swimmer but I find it difficult to process the possibility of swimming in choppy water filled with ice cubes. "I think it's bread and cheese for supper," I say. "I'm not about to bruise myself black and blue finding the dining room."

"My favorite," Finn says. "You take the top bunk so you can feel what it's like up there in the sky."

I eat for Finn's sake. He finishes my endless parade of room service plates. Picnic food had been his normal fare as a child: bread when you can get it, rarely meat or cheese or eggs, a few cold potatoes, slabs of cold porridge, fish head soup, and chunks of turnip, eaten like apples. "What is that urgent thing you wanted to talk to me about?" I ask, sipping hot milk.

"I forget."

He's in a mood.

I clamber up the ladder with my vanity case, and manage to smooth a dab of cold cream on my cheeks and brush my hair. I steal a moment to savor the jet necklace stashed in the 'Mona Lisa' box before I close it. Her mystic smile can mean anything. Who are you? What are you hiding? Are you happy or sad? The varnish flashes when the ship heaves and it seems as if she winks at me.

"Sleep tight," Finn calls out.

"Bedbugs."

I peek over the bunk. It's always a pleasant surprise to catch Finn off guard. I think of him as my age and sometimes it's a shock to see him as a five-year-old boy. My older brother and baby brother. My best friend. An odd guardian angel. Sometimes he speaks like a worldly scholar, oftentimes a poet, and yet on other occasions he's a poor boy who has grown up in Nova Scotia which is also his truth.

The ship lunges sideways and I catch the edge of my suitcase sledding over the blankets. But moving to catch it means the trinket box falls from my knee and plunges to the floor. It hits with a sound that can only mean breakage. Splintered wood rolls across the floor. Finn puts his head out and sends me a sly look. "Oh dearie me, that *will* be hard to repair." He's grinning.

I jump down as my jet beads slither away under Finn's bunk. I reach for them and come back with the lid from the box. Mona Lisa is intact. The box isn't entirely destroyed. But the underside of the lid has split. I gather my hair combs, a pearl hatpin, and a garnet bracelet wrapped in a lace handkerchief that May gave me when we said goodbye. The smell of magnolias fills the room from the handkerchief. I had decided to keep it in the box so the scent would last. I wanted to be able to retreat to it like smelling salts whenever I got depressed. May cheers me. Not as the memory of my mother but as her own unique self. This helps me understand Finn. He's more aware than May, but he's two boys. My 'twin brother Finn' is a separate boy from "Titanic Finn.' I hope the magnolias will bring back the power of that strange Grailskeep night and give me strength for the years that stretch ahead.

"Nothing a little glue won't fix," I say.

Finn watches me with some amusement. He swivels to a sitting position on the edge of his bunk and crosses his arms.

"Geez Finn, you look as mysterious as the Mona Lisa." I face the ladder again and decide against it. "If you don't mind, I've had enough of 'upstairs.' It's safer down here.

Besides, 'below-stairs' is in my blood." I pull the suitcase down to join me and slip my trinkets and the pieces of wood into it.

"I'd check that lid if I was you," Finn says.

"It's split. I really don't think now..."

"You know you can be a pain in the arse."

"That's what sisters are for," I say. And then I remember Bridie. "Except for Bridie." I examine the lid. "Hey there's a bit of paper under here."

"Oh really? What a surprise," Finn says. "I wonder if it's a *map*?"

"It's a birthday card. From Pa. Pa's left me a message."

Happy birthday lass.
May God tell you what to do with this gift from your
poor dead mother. You'll be twenty-one now. I swore
I'd reveal the box's secret on this day. I feared your
Ma-Rose would be tempted by now, so she's been in
the dark with you. I will probably get cold soup for my
tea tonight. I just wanted you to know that it was
worth all the bother to have had you in our lives.
– Love, your Pa.

The card is a typical store-bought greeting card folded into four from a single sheet of paper. There's an ink arrow pointing to the right lower corner with the letters PTO, please turn over. When I unfold it flat, I find a map of Oak Island, just off Nova Scotia's western shore – the infamous local magnet for amateur treasure hunters, not more than half a day from Halifax by bus.

I'd have known it for its familiar shape but Pa had written

'Oak Island' underneath it. To dispel any doubts, the title at the top reads 'Mamie's Treasure.' Somewhere, legend said, pirate treasure lays buried beneath its sands. It's the perfect hiding place – a privately owned island, sealed off from the mainland and well-guarded. A classic X marks the original mineshaft, and in the curve of a small cove is Mamie's 'X' – a large 'M' placed in a circle.

"What a perfect place to hide a secret. Behind Mona Lisa's smile. Pa said she was hiding a secret."

"We don't actually need the map," Finn says slyly. "I watched Pa bury it."

Earth stops revolving around the sun. I feel like smacking him. Finn edges towards the wall when Ma's words to Pa spring from my lips. "You self-centered small-minded little bugger! You might have spared Ma the suffering," I yell.

"It wasn't until now it was safe to tell you. You know, after Christopher signed that letter releasing you from any further Forster claims. Could you not shriek like a banshee?"

"Liar! You didn't know about Christopher's scam until a few days ago. Pa died eight years ago."

"Do you think I didn't want to stop Ma worrying? I couldn't tell her. What would you have said? Oh my invisible pookie friend told me where the map is?"

"I could have dropped the box on purpose."

"And Ma could have *dropped* into jail and no jewels for Lacey. No money for the University and no Egypt. Now you're free. And you know, I'm that keen on university myself. I've a notion to study the poets. No-one will see me, and the two faculties are on opposite ends of the campus. I've had a look."

FINN

I scarper. A woman in a rage is no match for any fella. Lacey is having a go at me with good reason, and it irks me because she isn't far wrong with her scathing description of me in a university class. She says I will be like a plaster saint that sits in a niche and eavesdrops on dirty secrets, and I can stare up at heaven all day long, as far as she cares.

And then, don't I just go and fall headlong into her trap. "I'll not be put in a corner like my brother," I say. "We'll fetch your treasure and I'll be on my way." To my everlasting embarrassment my lips tremble and I burst into tears, but Lacey never sees me, I spirit myself away to the seashore where I have a good howl and frighten the seagulls."

"Never underestimate the power of tears," Teacher says. "You should have stayed. Women can't resist them."

I keep my tear-stained face hidden in the crook of my arm, and send him a muffled, "I don't give a shiny shoe."

To his credit, he doesn't laugh. "What about those revelations? Have you had time to think about the consequences? In higher circles?"

"I'm not a timekeeper."

"If you hadn't died on Titanic I'd say you had the luck of the Irish on your side. You slip out of the trouble you create like a pig in a poke. But you can't fool your teacher, laddie buck. You orchestrated that broken box because you were too scared to tell Lacey how you feel about her. You wanted her to need you."

I lift my head and give the sky a dirty look.

"I have to take my hat off to you. There you were, caught in a sin, and you fought like a cornered rat. Sorry. Corners are everywhere when there are secrets and plots and treasure maps."

"It was a white lie."

"And you wiggled free of it blubbing like a wee baby. Well-done. That's a master stroke, that is."

"Well, it'll all be over in the shake of a lamb's tail. Lacey will get her jewels and I can go to hell in an applecart. How would that be?"

There's a long stony silence. The ocean surges a little in my imagination. "Sorry, Finn," Teacher says, "there's hell to pay before that can happen."

LACEY

Mooney embraces my enthusiasm the moment I breeze into his office. Cleopatra entering Rome in triumph. "I guess that's it for Nova Scotia and the Titanic," he says. "A few desperate relics can't possibly match golden masks and pyramids."

I hem and haw while he studies my face. He gives me a hug. "Don't listen to me Lacey. I'm proud of you. You made some real conquests over there. Not an easy task. The English are a closed book when it comes to sharing information. But all reports say they'll be pleased to add their recommendations to your grant application."

I stand grinning on a mountaintop, basking in his praise.

Mooney winks at me. "Although, I think you might be interested in something that came in the day you left. A pair of boy's shoes..."

"WHAT! ... WHERE?"

"Keep your shirt on. I'm cleaning them now. I want to

keep as much of the original sediment on them as possible, so it's an 'easy does it' sort of task. No-one wants to see a pair of polished boots in a museum."

He leads me to a box in a tray and tenderly opens the lid an inch as if the contents might fly out. I guess they're asleep because he takes the lid off completely. I half-expect to hear the Titanic's orchestra playing as if it's a music box.

"A kid wore these," he says, his voice barely above a whisper. "For all we know he died in them. He may even have survived Titanic. The person who took them failed to document them with a number. They were whisked away. Pure contraband on many levels, but it's wonderful that he did. I have to say their provenance is sound. They've been in a lawyer's safe and then in an attic and moved around to several homes. One of the addresses actually blew up in the big explosion of '17' so we're lucky to have them at all. They were finally deposited in a bank under lock and key. We have no idea if they're from first class or steerage. They're as anonymous as the child out there in the cemetery. Our task is to document their history and strip away twenty-two years of time without destroying the shoes' soul." He laughs. "Or should I say soles."

There they are. The shoes that began a grail quest for Finn, lying on an examination table – an emergency patient under hot lights with archive brushes, Petrie dishes, and chemicals. Cotton buds, tweezers, and knives are laid out beside them in rows like instruments on a surgeon's tray.

I'm captivated and appalled. Captivated by brown leather with traces of red, encrusted with salt, one lace missing, water stained and twisted with heat. Perhaps they'd been stored under a heavy object because they both tilt to the left. Strange that in that moment Finn is elsewhere. I'm appalled that they herald an end to Finn's companionship. The thought of losing him makes me dizzy.

Mooney grins at me when I start to cry and hands me a pair of archive gloves. "I thought they would surprise you. I guess we're not an also-ran outfit after all, eh?"

I hold one shoe as if it could break, tears streaming down my face, and I put it down gently. "Oh my God. Oh my God. Oh my God."

"Yes," Mooney says, patting my back. "They did that to me, too."

Finn must have felt me sobbing my heart out and he returns. "You were happy as a sand boy when I left," he says. "What on earth?"

I have to make him look. "I know they're here," he says. "I've been feeling that strange in my waters, for days. I almost don't want to see them." I feel his reaction and understand. He is happy but subdued-happy. "Yes, that's them. Sure, they're a sorry sight. I bet you were expecting a grand pair of respectable shoes, weren't you? I wore them the day I stepped onto Titanic and the day I floated free of it."

"I was expecting a whoop of joy and you smashing one or two objects in wild abandon," I say. "I'm a tad disappointed."

"I'm a big boy now," he says. "Sure they're just shoes."

A secretary calls Mooney from the room. "A special delivery needs your signature," she says.

I receive another wink from Mooney. "Maybe someone's found a gold mask in their basement. I expect it's a bill. I'll be right back. Don't cry on those things, there's enough salt on them as it is."

After he's gone I slip off the gloves and touch the shoes, tracing my bare fingers over the leather, around the lace holes, and over the stitching. The soles are starting to separate. A small gap is wider at the toe of the right shoe. Technically, they're boots. Schoolboy's boots that look like they're for kicking footballs. A black stain discolors the inside of both heels. I know it's blood. Bad blood.

"It's rather appropriate that one of the laces is gone," Finn says. "I guess it represents you."

I'm quick to pull on the white gloves when I hear Mooney's returning footsteps clacking down the hall.

"Amazing," he says, waving an envelope. "Make a wish and stand back. The other lace was just delivered to the front desk. I think the owner is a relative who wants them out of his hands in case there's an enquiry. This used to be contraband. You've got to wonder how he wound up with them and who took them in the first place."

Finn gets all wistful and drifts off into a body mist, but he doesn't stay misty for long. He returns with a thunderous look. "I recall a small boat," he says. "Then Mamie came to collect me. Dragged me off, she did. It was a man in a yellow slicker. Like the one Pa had."

We stare at each other, twin style, not wanting to give voice to what we we're both thinking, and then I shine the dirty spotlight on the elephant in the room. "Do you think it was Pa?"

Finn gives me that 'I'll be back later' look, and disappears. Mamie materializes almost immediately to tell me who'd taken Finn's shoes. "It was a friend of Ansel's, name of McPhee," she says. "Jimmy McPhee took a lot of things that day. What's worse, he destroyed the only document that would have identified Finn's body. I saw him crumple the postcard I gave him with his name on it. He tossed it away like it was nothing. And Ansel knew too. Look in his toolbox."

Right on cue, Finn returns. The two of them can't help but be ships that pass in time.

Mooney snaps his fingers in my face. "Did you go to Egypt again?"

I smile. "I'm sort of always there. But this is *your* dream come true," I say. "It's as good as the deckchair."

I clap my hands as if breaking a spell to get Finn's attention. "Hey, do you know anything about a toolbox? One that Pa had?"

"I hardly want to retire now," Mooney continues. "I'm getting on for sixty-five and I've told the directors I'm ready for a holiday, but maybe this latest development will loosen a few more artifacts from other people's shelves. I hope they show up in my time or yours."

Finn pops out, guiltily transparent for the blink of an eye. He nods. "Pa took it with him when he buried Mamie's jewels. I know where he stashed it. If it's still there."

Mooney takes my hand. "Now then, I've recommended you for my post. You've got four more years to prove yourself first choice. Maybe we can get you into a course or two. The board will sponsor you. They've said as much. They... we... that is, I, think of you as a prodigy of sorts. Our very own Titanic child. It's a fair legacy you have there, Lacey. Make it work for you. You've earned a place in my museum ten times over. The ghost business is between you and me and.... well, the ghosts, but think how much more we can dazzle people if we can name names and personalize objects. Take these shoes for instance.

"Er, Professor Mooney," I say. "I have a confession to make. I know who owned these shoes but I'm not at liberty to say. I promised one of the spirits in the gallery."

He's taken aback. "Would they haunt you if you did? It'd be just fine if they haunted the shoes. What a coup. The papers would run with it and we'd be innocent. It's completely out of our control if people see things. It's good business. Rumors sell tickets."

Finn makes a cutting motion across his neck.

"Worse," I say. "The owner of the shoes would *stop* haunting them." He's been searching for them ever since 1912.

I assume the recovery of what Finn and I referred to as 'Mamie's Gold' would be a cinch. A short boat ride and a shovel. But the island is a bank vault. Too much money had been invested to leave a door open to chance strangers. It wouldn't be the first time a plucky sleuth finds something an expert has been searching for and missed. Giving me a free pass was tempting fate. I'm also a woman, which is tantamount to being a vapor as insubstantial as Finn on his thinnest day.

"You can wait," Finn says. "Sure there's bound to be a way past the best of them."

The antique dealer pays me sixty dollars for the jet necklace. It isn't that old but it's signed by a famous carver whose work is highly-prized since his death. It's more than enough to pay the twenty-five dollar fee for a course in Classical Studies 'Introduction to Archaeology' – the prerequisite plateau before one can enroll in a four-year university degree. But I hesitate. I have a good job. Mooney needs me and he's about to retire. A promotion waves at me from down the street.

I have a decision to make. "Come on Finn. I'll stand you to a malted shake," I say.

Finn whines all the way to the soda shop. "Come on Lace, university is what we always wanted. You know, journeys being first steps and all. And you need this course to qualify. Please? We'll find your jewels. I promise. Do I ever ask you for anything?"

His eyes beg at their most adorable. "Fine, fine. I'll register."

If I hadn't followed Finn's lead I would have missed Peter.

42
FOOLS GOLD

FINN

Oh dear heaven. I made a new promise. I'm in trouble.

LACEY – OCTOBER, 1933

The archive lab is where I feel the most calm. The room smells of lemon furniture polish and rubbing alcohol. A cross between a library and a doctor's office. The wooden shelves gleam, dust-free and honey-colored from the natural light from windows nailed shut against damp and mold. The radiators clang clank with rhythmic jazz from the heat rattling their bones. I'm at home. Faded red linoleum in the basement undulates from settled foundations. The building is always settling, making itself more at home on Electric Street.

A tall metal bench as long as a conference table fills the center of the room. Finn's shoes sit center-stage under the spotlight from a goose-neck lamp, bent low on a table littered with paintbrushes of all sizes. A glass beaker of extra-long cotton buds, a pile of lint-free gauze cut into bandages, and a brown stoppered bottle of rubbing alcohol, stand next to a bowl of murky water and two stainless steel kidney dishes filled with used swabs and stained gauze squares. They confirm an intense cleaning session has lasted the morning. A tray of tweezers, scissors, and an array of sterilized dentist picks reminds me of an operating theatre. An autoclave pings like an alarm clock. It reminds us it's lunchtime.

Finn claps his hands and says "it's time for school."

I'm itchy to play doctor with Finn's shoes. "I'd do anything to be in your shoes right now," I say to make Mooney laugh. "It's more fun being hands-on." Curating is not a spectator sport.

Mooney pushes the jeweler's loop on his eyeglasses to ogle the ceiling. He straightens, and his swivel stool squeaks as he looks up, triumphant. He snaps off a pair of rubber surgical gloves and immediately dons a pair of soft handling-gloves. I wear the same obligatory unbleached cotton gloves – an automatic response to being near an exhibit. He resembles a surgeon after a long operation, dressed in a white lab coat. His face is red from concentration. He rubs his eyes from the constant squinting and joins the greater world – a room lined with shelves filled with rows of brown boxes.

Each box is labelled with contents by dates and a number. Mooney's desk is more like a boardroom table placed lengthways against a wall. I covet a souvenir ship in a bottle used as a paperweight – a miniature Titanic, sailing on a painted ocean.

"I've gotta tell ya Lacey," Mooney says. "Goddam it, I love these shoes. If they'd been mine I swear I wouldn't have parted with them. They send a tingle through me whenever I touch them."

FINN

I reply for Lacey as her back is turned away from Mooney. "That's love you'll be feeling, sir."

Mooney surfaces. "How do you reckon?"

"Nice one," Lacey says to me. Then out loud for Mooney: "Love for the Titanic's victims, sir."

Mooney pats her on the shoulder. "I've a confession to make," he says. "I've taken the shoes home once or twice and handled them without the gloves just to feel connected. They transport me. Sometimes I feel the terror of the water but other times I feel happier than I've ever been. It's the strangest thing. But I've got them all locked up tight now. And I promise there'll be no further escapades for me, other than here in the archive room. I'm not taking them home again. Maybe the kid will haunt me. Damn. I'd love that!"

Lacey says her goodbyes. "See you in six weeks, sir. Wish me luck."

Mooney hugs her. "You won't need it. You love Egyptology as much as I love Titanic-ology. Learning isn't a job. When you know... when something grabs you, well, it's not work. But I will toil over your scholarship. Now that *is* work. But you've collected a fair number of references and I like to think my opinion holds some sway."

Lacey feels bad about our eventual caper. She will steal my shoes from Mooney and I will steal away. We're both positioning for the inevitable. It's past the time for us to say goodbye. I still don't know if I'm strong enough.

"I'm a fool to think after all this time I can just take my shoes and leave you," I tell her. "I want more. I want to go to university beside you. No-one will see me. You can have your privacy and now and then we can be roommates." I check her reaction. She's skeptical. "Of course at your discretion. Now, that's a powerful word... discretion."

She looks relieved. "I didn't want to cite the obvious. We're not kids anymore."

"Speak for yourself," I say. We both laugh. Me, on the inside; Lacey for real.

I feel an icy chill when she says "Be serious for a moment. I can't be myself when I know you're listening in. And you can't *not* eavesdrop. Twenty-one is too old for... for being possessed."

"Possession is nine-tenths of the law," I've only been doing my job."

"It's no joke, Finn. Mooney is right. You haven't been doing a job. You've loved it. You loved Mamie and you love me too."

I flicker in and out of body and plunk myself in a chair across the room. My feet don't quite reach the floor. That always throws her. A five-year-old conversing like a professor. I am her confessor and protector, too. We haven't grown apart; we've become inseparable. But it's fiercely uncomfortable for me when men flirt with her. I fluster her confidence on purpose. She's naturally guarded. It isn't fair. It doesn't help that none of them are good enough for her. I'm her big brother. No-one knows more than I that little sisters never grow up.

"Oh Finn. I'd love you to stay," she says. "You could be my study partner. But aren't you missing your homecoming? Won't your time be better spent with your mother?"

I make Lacey sit in a chair and pace in front of her. I am a teacher and she is my student. "I want you to remember one thing, if nothing else *sinks* in, and yes, I mean 'sinks.' Time on the other side doesn't exist. Mam isn't waiting. She's with her sainted Michael. I watch them sometimes. They were a pair, those two. Devoted to each other. They still are. But some day my mother *may* remember she has two other children."

I picture Bridie's exuberant baby hellos when I waved at her. "Words are not the only way to communicate. Babies recognize faces before anything else. Bridie and I... we've known each other before."

"So, does everyone reincarnate like you and Mamie?"

"My mam hasn't. She refuses to leave Michael. And there's Isobel in a lifeboat with her children while she's still alive. Christopher and I will have to work out our latest differences. There are as many consequences for me terrifying him as he's chalked up for his threats to you. Where does Mamie end and May begin? Where do I end and you begin? Look at the stars and imagine drifting there listening and calling, reaching and embracing, shrinking and stretching where time stands still. Sure it's always ten minutes to midnight April 14th or twenty minutes past two April 15th." He glances at the clock. "Or today, at 3:15 in this room, with the rain fair drowning the day. Most of all, it's letting go. And the dead have more to let go of because we remember more."

"Tell me one of your wild Irish stories," I say. "Add as many scary banshees as you want."

"Banshees are more petrified of me, holy terror that I am. But... in a parallel world you and I reached America. Mamie gave birth a month after we arrived, and that time, Isobel helped her deliver a healthy daughter. Mamie named you, Liberty. I grew out of my shoes and you grew up as Bridie's friend, a younger sister to her, with me your older 'brother' who, watched after both his girls. That new girl in Miss Robbins' math class you saw all those years ago, was your best friend, Bridie Cleary.

"And later, after I'm an enormous wizard at school, I helped you both with your homework. And in 1922, the same Tut Fever carried you off into a world of archaeology. But you worked in the great Metropolitan Museum. Of course we marry and we live a long time. And that is the part of our parallel lives which has made me want to stay in this one, even when I have a chance to leave with my shoes. A sense of belonging with another, destined to be together."

Sure I've frozen Lacey into a gobsmacked student.

43

S.O.S.

SAVE OUR SOLES

LACEY – 1933

I feel like a salmon against the current returning to spawn, but for the first time. I've turned the tide. This is all new. I'm rushed along a river of sleepy teenagers in search of an elusive room number. Number 255-B. I worry that I'm a straggler, but by the time I find it, the room is still a sea of empty desks. I am the first. Two aisles of desks are arranged before a podium. A tall man in a tweed jacket is writing on the blackboard. I wait to speak until the name 'Mr. WATSON' is printed in bold letters.

I cough to alert him of my presence. "Hello."

He whirls to face me. He looks the same age as the students, now filing slowly into the room.

"Lovely to have you with us," he says. "Miss?"

"Lacey Waters. I'm early."

He grins and looks even younger. "That means you're keen. Please take a front row seat Miss Waters." He writes something on a pad of paper.

A few seconds pass before it sinks in that he's the instructor.

"I told you, you could teach this class," Finn says. "Tis the blind leading the blind."

There are fifteen of us, two women, and an older professor-looking man in the back with a clipboard. The other girl, a redhead, drops into the other vacant seat beside me. Finn must have left a charm around his own chair. "My name is Tabitha," she says. "Peter's older than he looks."

"Peter?"

She looks at me as if I'm a numpty. "Mr. Watson. He's a grad student. My dad's his mentor. I'm here to begin at square one. Wanna grab a sandwich after?"

I remain speechless so she can be breathless. I'm thankful she isn't Bridie.

"Welcome to Introduction to Archaeology," Peter Watson says. "We have no textbook for this course. I'm going to show you slides and I prefer that you hold your questions until after the lights come back on. Before we get started though, I'm willing to answer a few to clear the air."

A man who looks as if he could be Mr. Watson's father, raises his hand. "Will there be lots of exams?"

"There will be one exam at the end of the six weeks. It's more fun that way." Mr. Watson smiles down at Tabitha with recognition and then at me. "I hope it won't be too dark to take notes."

"How many digs have you been on?" another voice calls out.

"Six, maybe seven. Two in Egypt, the rest... are all local."

The same voice scoffs. "What kind of archaeology is there around *here*?"

Mr. Watson smiles to himself and nods slightly. He's been ready for this question. He launches a well-rehearsed speech, and I'm speechless with wonder. "Oak Island hosts several expeditions," he says. "It boasts pirate loot, too. But eager treasure hunters rarely have the discipline to treat a site with care. They're amateurs. To be a professional excavator, you may as well accept right now that archaeology is a slow tedious business of sifting tons of soil and sand looking for needles in haystacks. After you find a pottery shard it has to be measured and given a number on a grid so we know where it fits in-situ with the overall find. Then we have to draw it and take a photograph. We clean items with brushes, from wide stiff brushes for house painting to #000 sable watercolor brushes. We treat every nondescript bone or shard like a gold bracelet. It's not very glamorous, but the anticipation of a discovery is worth the toil. Sunburned in Egypt or drenched-through in Nova Scotia, the work is the same, other than the mud. Learn how to document all things great and small. And when you're on a dig, take your time and maintain safety regulations. Cave-ins and rockslides are an archaeologist's worst nightmare."

The lights dim and I'm thrilled that my teacher begins with a famous image of Howard Carter's discovery. The explorer's face, illuminated by a single candle, lingers on the screen. "There is no better image to convey the archaeologist's defining moment," he says. "There you have it – the purest wonder of discovery."

Carter's defining moment is followed by the faces of staring eyes inlaid with lapis, and mounds of broken rubble where the familiar sight of wheel spokes still trying to hold the shape of what was once a chariot, together. "This is as good as it gets," Mr. Watson says. He delivers a running commentary of a series of slides of Tut's grave goods.

Each item is presented being removed and meticulously wrapped in bandages. Inside a nearby abandoned tomb, a team of archivists have set up rows of portable tables. Wooden boxes and bales of straw and bolts of white fabric are stacked against the walls.

Outside, sunburned faces and intense expressions under boaters and wide straw brims, peer incredulous, anxious – ever hopeful for a lucky day. Local onlookers, tourists, pickpockets, and the press crowd the gateway in the ground with steps leading to the underworld of a king voted least likely to succeed, in every way.

I'm thinking how systematic it all is when Mr. Watson makes me jump. We are like twins sharing the same thought.

"Everything was placed in this tomb systematically thousands of years ago," he says. "In 1922, Howard Carter reversed the order. What came out first went in last.

"A professional archaeologist has to be a disciplined scientist. In the past, digging was a mad contest for a pot of gold. Now we know history lies in the details. Honoring the details is a prerequisite of archaeology. A thousand years of grave robbers have wiped out ninety-nine percent of all artifacts. They melted down gold statues, hacked priceless sarcophagi into paperweights, and handed out precious heart scarab to anyone with a few shillings. When they ran out of the genuine article they manufactured more. It was more profitable to sell souvenirs to tourists. The landfill under Cairo contains a plethora of sad bones. Some come to light when a building is demolished. There's an ocean of treasure under every modern city built on the ruins of an ancient settlement."

"I'm going to strangle him," Finn says. "That's *my* word!"

The lights come on. I'm a mole blinking in the Egyptian sun. The darkened theatre had been a lovely cocoon. It's a shame to have to join the real world.

Mr. Watson asks for a show of hands. "Does anyone know Howard Carter's famous quote when he first glimpsed Tutankhamen's gold?"

I raise my hand. Swiveling slightly I see that I'm the only one who has an answer. Finn glares from the back of the room. My throat is as dry as the floor of the Valley of the Kings.

"Yes, *er...*" Mr. Watson looks down at his class chart. "Miss Waters."

I begin nervously. "It's dark. A small hole has breached the outer door of the first chamber. It's only large enough for one eye. Dry air from inside the tomb rushes past Carter's face." My nerves even out into plain talking as I continue a scene I've replayed in my mind hundreds of times. "He's barely breathing enough to flicker the candle. Lord Carnarvon asks Carter 'can you see anything?' And Carter replies, 'Things. Wonderful things.'"

Mr. Watson's eyes soften. He nods to me and claps. "Bravo." It's as if he's given me a hug. From that moment Mr. Watson ceases to exist. My teacher's name is Peter and I want to be teacher's pet.

The sound *arragh* comes from the back of the room.

"If you don't get chills from that," Peter says, "you may be in the wrong class. I asked for a quote – a fact, but Miss Waters answered with a story. Without a passion for discovery, archaeology is reduced to gardening. Just digging holes. But the truth is, there's a lot of earthmoving to it. Expeditions aren't called digs for nothing, but you're not digging, you're *uncovering*. All artifacts contain the ghost of a story."

"Or a curse," a boy calls out from the back of the room. "The mummy's curse. Lord Carnarvon died from King Tut's curse." The voice is Finn's.

The next question, shouted from the back of the room, makes me slide down my chair, mortified for my fellow students. "Do you know anyone who died from the curse?" Finn shouts.

Mr. Watson keeps smiling, valiantly. Only those in the first row hear his inward sigh. I close my eyes in sympathy and cover my eyes. That small gesture progresses to an invitation in week two, to have dinner. I'm teacher's pet. Finn is not amused.

Our first date is romantic in the classical definition of romance. We discuss lofty ideals and the emotional connection to minutia so that temples reduced to rubble are once again freshly-painted fired brick and the faint echoes of ancient ceremonies lift into recent conversations. Egypt sings us together. Finn loosens the top of the saltcellar and bad luck ruins Peter's French fries.

It isn't long before I'm sighing over Peter's profile and his voice and his smile. Finn runs around us pretending to be sick, and just plain getting in my way. I feel like a babysitter assigned to a spoiled brat.

I graduate with flying colors. But more importantly, I've graduated from a girl fascinated by an ancient culture to a woman obsessed by a pair of brown eyes. Peter and I become inseparable, and the day arrives when I accompany him to an interview for a new attempt to solve the mystery of Oak Island.

"They need an artist," he says, "and I want to hire you but you're a woman, so behave yourself. Keep quiet and let me do all the talking."

Well, when the truth comes," Finn says, "it's rarely tied in a pretty blue ribbon."

I have to call Finn now, if I want to talk. Most of the time he makes himself scarce. These days he's a distant immature apparition rather than a welcome voice in my head. "I have no desire to watch you kissing Peter," he says. "And I've no stomach for girl-talk. There's no place for me here. But you'll need me on the island dig or is it gig? I hope your darling Peter drops dead. But I'll guard your Titanic loot for you. It's not a large box. It's a few bags within bags inside a box. Bring a pillowcase filled with old sheets that can be used as packing material. A pillow always looks like a pillow even with a solid heart of treasure inside it.

I try to placate him. "I brought toffee," I say. He brings his head up like an animal sniffing for predators.

He's humoring me. "Go on then."

Finn watches me pack my knapsack from the sidelines. "You're just not taking enough books," he says. But I'm concentrating on finding a safe place for my mirror and a new lipstick and I don't see him smiling.

44

OAK ISLAND X

LACEY – NOVEMBER

"Do women ever travel light?" Peter asks when he hefts the bundle I bring with me.

I reel off my list: "Artist's materials, two sweaters, extra socks, an extra blanket, a rain slicker and boots, flashlight, chocolate, and a few books."

"Books!"

"Notebooks, sketchpad, diary. *Those* kind of books."

Peter pulls me into a bear hug and whispers in my ear. "No worries. I'll have you straightened out in no time."

"And a couple of pens." I wait for him to laugh before adding. "And pink slippers."

Finn enters the room carrying a saltcellar. "a wee gift from me," he says.

Oak Island at dawn is a low-lying landmass crouching in roiling surf – a small puzzle-piece of terrain blanketed by fog. There are no tall features. No mountains. It's pretty much one low hill and vast stretches of brambles and scrub more than serious trees. We approach a beach of rocks with a scattering of giant boulders, the other coves being sandy but swamped with knee-deep seaweed and bird droppings.

Its main feature is a blight at its heart where a rickety crane reaches to the sky like the skeletal arms of a murder victim.

Peter takes his team of five to investigate the state of the mineshaft. There are piles of discarded planks like bleached bones. Remnants of rusted tools and equipment litter the excavation's mouth. Pulleys, coils of rotting ropes, and steel cables pose the worse threats.

Peter embodies the persona of a sergeant major. "Our target is lateral," he says, directing a spotlight on a darker patch of earth twenty feet down. "That black soil is more compact. It hasn't been touched for a long time." He determines the rest of the walls are malleable clay, too dangerous for anchoring our harness cables. "We'll have to anchor our cables topside," Peter says. "We have to drill into surface rock to be safe. "We'll do a bit of shoring up now and attack tomorrow at the first decent light. That likely means noon in order for the mist to burn off. Let's hope it doesn't rain again. If it does, we'll be mired in mud, taking site readings for our own survey maps."

At least that promises to be something where I might participate with a hands-on role, if holding a pole while some man cross-references measurements and calculates angles constitutes significant participation. Not that I will be there tomorrow if all goes according to Finn's devious plan.

I sit out the initial groundwork. Being an archaeologist's apprentice girlfriend has its perks. But sadly, it means that the cooking duties are passed along to me without discussion. I sit fuming about a woman's lot, chafing from low self-esteem with Finn rubbing salt in my wounded career.

"A woman's place is in the tent," he says, shaking a finger at me. He hates it when I do that to him so I have to eat my pride. I deserve being paid back. "Don't be forgetting to act out of sorts, now," he says. "That's your ticket out. It's lucky you're a wee actress."

I have that sense of déjà vu from the Halifax explosion façade. "Peter's going to be furious."

Finn chuckles. "Not a chance Missy. He'll be too embarrassed to be cross. You picked yourself a spineless one there, Lace. No worries, they'll all be mortified, so they will."

"Hey, like I *won't be.*"

Finn shrugs. "What can I say? Uncovering buried treasure is tough business."

The men's voices blow back on the wind to where Finn and I chat. It's galling to be boiling water for their coffee, especially after one of the crew has to build the fire. He gives me one of those disgruntled looks that says 'What're you doing here anyhow?' Now and then I catch a swear word over their clattering tongues. Mostly, the echoes of tools sally forth from the concentration of grunt work. Sounds of metal on metal resound from all around me. It takes the better part of four hours before the men break for the day.

Our tent reeks of sulphur and old socks. Under the stars, the outcrops of rock resemble the shapes of animals. The vegetation that blankets the unnamed hill glows in an aura of magenta fire, bathed in a thin layer of golden sunset. But the best thing is being serenaded by loons that sound so close I swear they're the shadows that play on the tent walls.

Finn positions himself between Peter and I which doesn't bother me because Peter is purposely ignoring me to appear professional in front of his crew.

Finn leans on my arm and contemplates the terrain. "It

reminds me of a moon landscape after a million years of rain," he says. As if he's seen the moon.

The main point of interest, after the definitive survey, is locked on the original excavation at the heart of the island – a scar on the face of an unlikely paradise. An unlovely landscape I can barely see but for my own prize. Nothing on the island is far from the central rig. A few army huts have been erected to house the good tools and the barrels of earth. The prospectors who don't want the hard labor, but have paid mightily for their stakes, will stay until the last of the heavy lifting crew are ferried to the mainland.

Only the weather can change the plans to cease activity before sunset. The rowboat disappeared the night Peter rowed us here. It's a mystery how it had slipped its moorings and drifted to shore. But I'm sure it's Finn's handiwork. The campfire keeps five heads discussing the day's lack of progress and the next day's agenda. I beg off early with a headache, and slip into a sleeping bag in the archive tent.

Mooney would have blown a fuse if he'd seen the shoddy way growly workmen sift through the loose soil, smacking clumps of clay with the backs of shovels and plunging their shovel blades into the pile of debris, all the time fussing with their pipes. The continual rebuilding of small fires at the end of briar sticks receives infinitely more concentration. That, and their competitions, blowing blue smoke to see who can form the biggest ring or one that floats the longest. Moronic.

It's evident they define treasure as something involving a large trunk at the bottom of a wishing well and regard the outtakes of earth as nothing worth thinking about. Their minds are focused on stories and local gossip and speculations of this dig being the jackpot that promises a bonus for being on site at the opportune moment.

Finn is right. We don't need Pa's map. Sneaking away to find 'Mamie's Gold' will be easy. I'm almost as invisible as he is as long as the crunch of shale doesn't give me away.

"Not a cat's chance," Finn says. "The sound of rushing water lashing at the boulders on the shoreline will cover our tracks."

He leads me to a cove on the other side of the island by the light of the full moon. A sheer rock face, the highest point of a hill cut in half, drops to a non-beach. Jagged rocks that have been there for hundreds of years make it impossible for the smallest boat to land. It's all rocks. Slabs of granite moved by the hand of a giant stirring them from the seabed. There's no flat place to dig.

One of the largest rocks is a hundred yards off the shoreline. Finn stares at it a long time considering we're on a mission with a lit fuse of time.

"What can you see?"

"A stone iceberg," he says. "Come on, while there's light."

He salutes the moon. I make no comment. Finn is already acting strangely enough.

Finn heads straight for a crevice in the rocks. 'Mamie's 'X' is up a ten-foot climb. He parts the growth of scrap pine saplings coated with seaweed. The salt has stunted their growth; the wind has twisted them into figures of bent old men.

Pa had filled the deepest recesses of the hole with

newspapers. It comes out in a wodge of yellow slime. Finn's arm finally disappears into the hiding place up to his elbow, and he emerges seconds later with a cry of triumph, holding Mamie's Gold.

The leather pouch, found easily, is the size of a large cat. Not too heavy or cumbersome to carry to my designated bunk. The men have been cautioned, not that they needed it, to keep a wide berth of the only female's privacy. Peter would never venture into my territory either. He's on show.

I bundle the smaller bags in the pouch in strips of blanket and heft the weight over my shoulder. I won't be able to let anyone else feel its new density.

First light we hear the grate of wood against rocks and a loud voice shouting all aboard who's going ashore. Food supplies are dropped and I fake feeling faint. Peter looks somewhat embarrassed but no-one wants to know the details of a woman during her 'time.' I'm almost pushed into the boat and Finn says it's like watching the crew on Titanic loading a woman into a lifeboat. He'd seen such things from his sky-view. The men back away, and man who owns the boat refuses to make eye contact with me. Fine. I'm left to my thoughts. Finn sits across from me staring out into the North Atlantic, tracing the rim of the hull with his fingers. The trip takes six minutes. I throw my pillowcase on the rickety pier and hurry after it.

Next afternoon, safely back home, I stoke up the stove to boil water for midmorning tea. Finn waits almost dismissively at the sack of colored bags, a few knickknacks, and some dingy silk lingerie. Neither he nor I are in a hurry. It's as if we know that opening the bags will change us, perhaps more than we care to admit. Money changes everything and there's no doubt some of this swag is destined for funding four years of university.

Finn reads my mind, as always. "Digging is gruesome, so don't expect me to join *your* classes. I've set my heart on studying the classics of literature. I want to write a poem for Bridie – one that will last forever. There'll be a new library of books. You can borrow them for me." He pauses, listening, riveted by a sound only he can hear. Suddenly, he sits up on full alert with panicked eyes. "I've got to go," he says.

I'm concerned. "Where? What did you hear? Is everything okay?" But he evaporates without saying goodbye.

45
EXAMINATION

FINN

I'm riveted by the sound of splintering wood. Back on Oak Island, Peter is being lowered into the mineshaft inch-by-inch. Two men brace themselves against the strain. Creaking beams glisten with an inner fissure of water that dribbles down the rock face, steaming with moisture from the noonday heat. Peter taps a beam and shines his flashlight down below where a rusty pump handle projects from a greasy shallow pool of groundwater like the sword Excalibur. His harness snaps and drops him ten feet – he's a hanged man. I hear snakes. It's gas escaping from a new fissure.

Peter shouts to the men above him. "Get out quick. Go!"

His diggers scramble. In the confusion of swaying cables Peter's flashlight clatters down the well. The sound of broken glass says it has reached bottom. The wooden beams groan like trees in a storm. The shaft is about to collapse into itself as if it had never been.

I'm the silhouette blocking the light at the end of Peter's death tunnel. Beyond me lies heaven. I use the words commonplace in rescues all too familiar by now. "Grab my hand."

Peter grabs hold but his hands are clammy and he threatens to slip into the abyss. I close my eyes and think of a summer sky, and for a brief moment he glimpses a pure slice of blue. He hauls himself towards it, over my arm, until other hands pull him free. The infrastructure implodes and careens into the pit, leaving a solid landfill of smoking debris filled to within a foot from the new surface. The dig is over. I've lost Lacey. Peter has won the hand of my girl.

LACEY

Only twenty-four hours after I leave Peter, he's in my apartment relating his harrowing escape, much chastised after his long grump at my unscheduled departure. "I swear a little guardian angel saved my sorry behind," he says. It reminded me of the headless 'Winged Victory' in the Louvre because I couldn't see its face."

Finn sits in his favorite spot between us, his arms folded in disgust. "Little was it? Headless am I? My arse," he says.

Being fully aware of the near tragedy, I stifle a laugh. "Were there wings?" I ask Peter.

"Funny, he says, "I just remembered something my little angel said. What's a poltroon?"

In the end, Peter turns more to his professional circle of male camaraderie than me to process his experience. They hail him as a hero. But I know who the true hero has been. I too have a guardian angel named Finn.

I have issues to process too. I hadn't much enjoyed being the odd one out on the dig. I was excluded, tolerated at best, and not even with any discernable degree of humor. Playing the 'good egg' had been emotionally draining. I'm angry. Humiliated. Relegated to a role I didn't deserve. I'm like Finn, overlooked and invisible.

That realization of my self-centered nature shocks me. My dishonesty humbles me. It has taken Peter's near-death to remind me that crisis bonds people together like passengers on a doomed ship. I'm terribly ashamed. I've been treating Finn badly. He hadn't deserved to be sacrificed and abandoned to a place in the shadows. No wonder he's acting out. How had he survived for so many years with such good grace?

Peter and his crew had reduced me to the role of mother and I'd found it lacking. I thought of Mamie and Ma and how they mothered selflessly. How Finn's mam devoted herself to Michael. How Finn had felt banished and unworthy of being loved. Finn is the best part of me and I had displaced him with Peter. When it came to the crunch, his mam, Mamie, and I, had all neglected him in turn. I thought of the anonymous mummies of the royal women of ancient Egypt, who had been reduced to background roles of powerlessness, succumbing to the art of feminine wiles for survival, and yet their king's succession relied utterly on their maternal lineage. Even laid in luxurious tombs they rested in unmarked graves.

My career eclipses the exhausting performance of playing second fiddle. I sip my hemlock tea with Mamie's legacy spread before me, spilled onto the table like a cornucopia of bright stars: sapphires and diamonds and pearls and jet and amber... brooches in the shapes of birds and animals and flowers, and a change purse knitted with slivery chains and glass beads.

It's then, drained of romance, that I fall out of love with Peter and into a calm place. The only thing I want is Finn's forgiveness and to be acknowledged as an independent woman – a professional archivist. An historian.

Hours later, when I fall back in love with Peter, it isn't the same.

One thing I *can* do, *will* do, as a rich woman, is buy Ma a headstone. There's no need for her to lie in an unmarked grave up there on her hill. I long to do the same for Finn but he won't hear of it. Let sleeping dogs lie, he says whenever I broach the subject, but he does find the perfect Irish poem to grace Ma's resting place.

We choose a black basalt block with plain gold letters engraved deep, framed in a white lace border. Finn insists on adding a small classic statue of the 'Nike of Samothrace' placed on a low plinth.

"I don't know why but this means something to Ma," he says.

I have to be honest. "Like it or not," I say, "but you've bonded with Peter. Remember that picture you found in my art history text? The 'Nike of Samothrace' has another name – the 'Winged Victory.'"

Finn's gotten mixed up; the angelic messenger means something special to Peter. Ma had never heard of it.

LILIAN ROSE WATERS
1863 – 1933

Come Fairies,
Take me out of this dull world,
For I would ride with you
Upon the wind
And dance upon the mountains
like a flame!

– William Butler Yeats

FINN

I mark a page in Lacey's art history book. Wait until she sees this.

As soon as she meets me I make her sit and listen to me read.

"That Nike statue was found the year Ma was born, so there is some connection, clever clogs! It's all here in black and white. And here's the thing: that goddess – she was a sort of angel. Angels are messengers aren't they? She was the herald of a sea battle coming to tell the people of Samothrace their warriors had prevailed in a great victory and that they were safe. I might have seen her hovering around Titanic if they'd let me on one of the promenade decks after seven-o'clock. Steerage passengers had an early curfew."

"I thought you were never allowed up there."

I tap the side of my nose. "Ah, not the top one, but we had an hour's grace to walk the lower one."

"As above but not always the same as below," Lacey says. "Above stairs and below stairs. Nothing ever changes."

That night, Lacey and I switch roles. She becomes the storyteller of legends and I become the enthralled boy dreamer – hanging on to ancient giants and winged messengers and an entire blue mountaintop of gods.

Mercury has flying shoes, and I'm there with him, standing on a white cliff bathed in sunshine on an emerald the size of forever. His island floats in a sea so blue it hurts the eyes, and a sky so bright I can't open them until the crimson sun drops into the sea. I dream of a green hill. A trumpet sounds like the blast of a dozen steamships. A flock of colored 'victories' fly towards me from the grey horizon, ahead of the rain. When they stop to circle Ballymore, the rain catches up and washes them clean of Greek paint. White wings beat the air turning raindrops into emeralds and rubies and sapphires that fill a red cloth bag the size of a pillowcase.
The River Finn meanders below in a rainbow ribbon that ends in a waterfall that looks like a lazy bolt of blue cloth flung carelessly over a cliff. It's raining diamonds. It sounds like wedding rice on a tin roof.

> *Diamonds bounce off my black umbrella and fill the*
> *rain barrel. One victory touches down to tell me*
> *there's been a sea battle but not to worry. Back inside*
> *the cottage, I brush tiny stars from my shoulder.*
> *Mam has set my birthday tea near the fire. There's*
> *toasted tea cakes, clotted cream, tea and honey, and*
> *jars of colored jams, each with their own White Star*
> *spoon. I place my wet shoes by the hearth and watch*
> *them dry, butter dripping down my chin, licking the*
> *stickiness of strawberries from my fingers.*
> *My heavy shoes are sucked up the chimney and*
> *tumble back down again, filled with a plethora of tiny*
> *ash-grey stars. Once I tip them into the hearth the*
> *shoes sprout tiny wings on their heels, fly about the*
> *room, and land in Michael's corner.*

I visit Lacey's class on reconstructing human bones. Digging for bodies is grim reaper work and ghoulish. I say let sleeping dogs lie. The dead need to have some self-respect. And, in my opinion, it's a wonder there's not more hauntings.

My class in creative writing is as bad. I called it the 'what-if' class. The assignment: find a what-if and expand it into a story. The premise must satisfy the resolution.

Mr. Freeth is our master. I envy him. Ironically he towers above us students academically although every day he stands lower than the rest of us, in the pit of a Greek theatre. We of the amphitheater, in seats radiating up and outward from him, scribble like dutifully trained monkeys.

I sit in a different seat each day. There are always empty places. I wander too. I read over my fellow classmate's shoulders and whisper comments in their ears. I knock their pens on the floor when they ask stupid questions. Me... a muse from the dead with my poet's ways. None of them hear me. Even the girl who sniffs and wipes her eyes when I tell her she's writing a depression her character doesn't feel because she's writing about herself. She needs help.

My premise? What-if Titanic hadn't sunk? I write my opening line, tongue in cheek:

"I have a sinking feeling," the mother said, staring up at Titanic. Her son, Finnegan strained his neck and waved at the strangers on the ship who were excited to be waving to anyone who would notice. Everyone was waving at everyone else. All strangers.
Mrs. Cleary, tore their tickets to ribbons, tossed them like breadcrumbs to the ever-present gulls on the dock and turned for home, dragging Finnegan behind her. Home being a homestead that didn't move under her feet, or lurch sideways, or make her feel smaller than a flea on a mouse. She was poor but she had friends. She had a roof. She had a floor that grounded her. Her house had corners.
Her son Michael, buried deep in the cemetery of Ballymore Church was her anchor. Her son Finnegan, gripping her hand was her lighthouse. The Irish soil was solid and true.
The ground would own her soon enough; she would lie next to her sainted Michael in the churchyard. All this after having a husband who was a fisherman lost at sea."

That seemed to put an end to the story. But no, the mother would have to board the ship, feel seasick and sad, but land in America, falling into the arms of her cousins. She would have a husband too. I would write her a man she loved who loved her. A man who drank as heavily as my own Da. But a man who was king of his time. A man who would work hard and drink hard in New York and sire a few more sons and daughters, and buy his wife a grand house near enough to the sea to smell the salt but far enough away to harken to the call of business. He would cast his nets into the streets of commerce, plying a craft he'd learned well. He would be a carpenter. He would make honest furniture and repair window frames and build doors because, sure enough, everyone needs a door or two.

One day he would build a grand door to rival all the doors in Brooklyn and be offered a commission to build the doors for a tenement apartment that covered an entire city block. He would hire a few assistants and take on an apprentice or two. More doors would follow. He'd be the king of doors. And in his spare time he would create the grandest door for the house built to shelter his exhausted wife and charming children.

Generations would open his doors. His children's children would enter and exit through doors of joy and grief. They would all go to heaven in a pea green boat.

LACEY – 1939

Finn is moving apart from me now, reluctant to play second fiddle as I'd been. And I can't help myself. I'm pushing him away. I want to be alone with Peter. Finn looks sullen but he wants to finish university and so we agree to disagree. "I'll be around he says. "Call me when you're alone or if you come to your senses. Sure you can summon me with this." He places his tin whistle in my hand.

He's jealous. Finn is five-years-old and I'm interested in another 'man.' The logistics of growing up together mean I can no longer have a private life with Peter with Finn in my head. When I confront him, he stays away for twenty-four hours.

Finn returns on a winter night. I'm curled up in the window seat, and I see him arrive as a reflection in the window. I think I'm still daydreaming. But a familiar voice says, "And don't ask me where I've been."

Lazy snow turns faster into a swirl of flakes, all falling into my face, white iron filings to my magnet. I have a vision of Titanic covered in ice-blue hoar frost. Icicles drip from her railings. I envisage this quite often now.

"It's a premonition," Finn says. But I can't see how, since the Titanic disaster has already happened. He corrects me. "It's a presentment. You're reading the future."

"Oh," I say, "I guess so." My mind returns to my fantasies, unmoved. I forget Finn is in the room.

I have no pending classes but I do have a paper to write. I've been sitting scrunched up with a pad of paper penning the names Mrs. Peter Watson and Lacey Watson over and over as if I'm in detention writing lines. *I will not moon about in class. I will not moon about in class.* The snow is wonderful. Downy flakes reflect the lamplight and twist into a yellow whirlpool. I'm dozing in Fairyland and about to let the hypnotic tornado take me to Oz. I click my heels. There's no place like Oz.

Finn's spirit shines in the corner and distracts me. "I know you're right," he says, "but spirits have dreams too. You forget that. My heart isn't five. I'm the same age as you."

My mind does a belly flop. I have a world of friends and colleagues but Finn only has me. Even though he drifts away for weeks at a time on ethereal excursions, I am his anchor in the living world. Finn isn't a ghost haunting the house where I live. He is *my* anchor. And I am his house.

"There's something called Karma," he says. "Events happen in the world to balance other events. Disasters, births, deaths... suffering. Time moves like the seasons even though some summers last several lifetimes and some winters a thousand years. The Titanic was a short window of time and thousands of souls are still being overwritten to compensate that singular event."

"Are you saying everyone – man, woman, and child on Titanic knew each other before?"

"Certainly not. Sometimes it's only two or three. A family. Dying together neutralizes hundreds of events at once. Except..." he pauses.

"What?" I ask.

"Well, once people have a collective experience, they're connected."

"You mean..."

"I mean Titanic created a new country of rules. Death is busy work. Like the ripples from the sinking ship, the passengers, and their friends and relatives who lived-on, the White Star Line, and every person since who's altered by the tragedy, terrified or inspired, has something to work out. Those ripples will never cease rippling. The survivors help the victims across both worlds. Everyone who feels the nightmare has radiating terrors to work through. I'm just a kid whose life froze in subzero water. I had to die to remember all the people I once was. It's a pattern seen from above and even then it's so vast and complicated I still dive in and out to learn. That's where I go. I don't think there's an end to it. I actually come back to you to relax. It's been a grand comfort for me to keep a home with you. You're learning how to be an archaeologist of the past but I'm learning how to be everyone I've ever been, all at once. Soon, I won't have that harbor. Without you I'm a ghost; with you I'm alive."

I swing around and pay attention. "You and I... we... have things to work out?"

He shakes his head with his eyes closed. "You can't *imagine* how deep we go. After a person dies they can wait years for even a chance of a chance to heal. It takes infinite patience to experience an infinite world. Heaven isn't one place; it's a million places of past and future. Like one of your ancient pots. Shards separated by miles and years – in a whirlpool of forgiveness and resistance."

I gasp. "How odd. I was just thinking of a whirlpool watching the snowflakes."

"What a coincidence," Finn says, smugly."

"Sarky."

"As it happens, you're very close, but it's more *sparky*. Moments of male and female playing tag. Each spark is you and me and everyone else together for eternity. Well, it's not as dopey as it sounds."

"Out brief candle?"

"You and I were born as twins. The Titanic sparked a thousand-million such fires. She won't be forgotten."

"I won't forget you. You're a miracle. You're my miracle. I've never doubted that for a moment."

Finn looms larger in the reflection and wavers as if he's under water. "I guess that's you letting me go then."

I examine a speck of lint on my sleeve that isn't there.

"Please don't put it like that. That's not fair. Don't you think I haven't..."

His face lengthens like a funhouse mirror. "What? Felt sorry for me?"

I look away, embarrassed.

Finn seems remarkably cool. "I've learned a lot about love from living with you," he says. "Teachers and students turn into friendships. Friendships turn to love. And IF you're incredibly lucky, it turns back to friendship again. So I guess we're still friends."

"You saved Peter by the skin of his teeth," Teacher says. "In other words, dear heart, by the skin of the skin of the skin of *your* teeth."

"I did."

Take a reward," he says, proffering a scattering of moonbeams that fall at my feet and turn into pale cards.

The card I draw has five words: Ask Lacy on a date.

But Peter is ahead of me. He asks Lacey first. She blushes and says yes. The three of us are going to 'The Wizard of Oz', one of Lacey's favorite books made into a moving picture. It's my last chance. Peter can be our chaperone. It's my last hurrah.

46
THERE'S NO PLACE LIKE HOME

FINN

CHRISTMAS EVE, 1939 – 7 P.M.

Who knew that when the theatre lights were raised my life would change. The story is a powerful 'what-if' but I can't be fashed about a wee girl and her dog, Toto. If the munchkins are meant to be leprechauns they're far too big.

At the end, I realize how a girl's destiny can change from a bump on the head. It makes sense. I identify with Dorothy because she has a powerful pair of shoes and a mission to get home.

Lacey is more interested in Peter. She snuggles into him and pretends to be scared of the winged monkeys. She's an actress all right. I hear her thoughts from my seat, three rows up. One thing I realize is it's only me who's keeping me anchored. My going-home-shoes are within reach. It's time to click my heels together and say a few magic words. Death is the strongest magic. It equals birth. Going back, or is it forward, means I will have to redream my story in fearless fragments at the back of a queue for rebirth. If there's still time.

But maybe I can remain Lacey's guardian for as long as we both shall 'live.' Being already dead has its advantages; it's not as if I'm going to die. But it's still giving in. I promised Mamie. And then it slams me hard, sure as if I'd hit a blue mountain. I've been keeping an enormous secret from myself.

Mamie is right about time repeating itself. I check into the vast storehouse of knowledge about such things. The date and time that Lacey hands me my shoes must coincide with 'Titanic Time.' There's no place like home!

47

HARDSHIPS

LACEY
NEW YEAR'S EVE, 1939 – 11:50 P.M.

The fireworks excite the stars in the midnight sky. Peter kisses me. "Happy New Life, sweetheart," he says. "Marry me."

"Go on then Dorothy, it's time I went home, anyway," Finn says from inside my heart, and I break down sobbing.

Peter looks hurt. "That's okay, you don't have to decide right now," he says. "I can wait until next year."

Peter floats away in a bubble. I can see his lips moving but there's no sound. I'm radiantly happy, looking in a full-length mirror. My wedding dress is white lace. Bridie hands me a bouquet of orange blossoms and rowan branches. Molly Cleary kisses my cheek and gives me something old and blue – a length of faded blue ribbon. Something borrowed is my mother's jet necklace. Something new is how I feel about marriage. But, there's my Peter, overflowing with the joys of our future. He's so far ahead of me that I may never catch up.

Just when I feel settled and useful, just after Peter talks of marriage and children, he talks of being the sole breadwinner too.

"You won't have to work," he says. As if that's a grand thing.

I stare at him in utter disbelief. He's been my supporter through to graduation. What did he think I was doing?

"I don't believe what I just heard," I say. "You know how I feel about Egypt."

"You can write papers. Travel there with me a few times and when the babies start coming you can turn my reports into a cracking thesis. You can write a book. Both our names will be famous."

The gild is off the lily. The expression on my face makes him laugh. "Come on Lace, if we work as a team we can go far. A man and wife academic partnership, eh? What could be better than that?"

"But I want to wield a shovel and get sand in my shoes."

"I'll build our kids a sandbox," he says.

"Kids? Motherhood is a big step. I haven't traveled the world yet."

Peter reaches for me in that lovely way he has of seducing and adoring me in equal measure. He's my best friend. "Oh!" I gasp at my thought. "Oh, God, Finn, I didn't mean that. You're my dearest friend. If you only knew what it was like to be a grownup and fall in love you'd understand."

"I understand more than you think," Finn says from a few feet away. "From my wee mountain of eternity I can see quite far. In fact, I've been a husband myself a few times. I've even been a wife. I've born children and borne hardships."

"Relationships require sacrifice." I throw back, to hide my embarrassment.

I'd rarely heard Finn angry but he erupts at my thoughtless flippant remark.

"SACRIFICE?... RelationSHIPS! What about OUR relationship? What about my relationship with your mother? And my parents?"

FINN

My 'eternal mountain' was never a boast. I'm not a braggart and it wasn't the Himalayas; it was a wee hilltop in Ballymore. It was colored by the insight gained from the height of memory and the width of time. I never thought of the sum total of human knowledge as being as deep as the sea. That would have been too near the mark. But perspective is as farseeing as a fortune teller without the tricks. From my hill I can see the end of Lacey's life, and more importantly, 'see' she needs her privacy to get there. If she marries, I hope it's Peter, but I see her as a spinster, in love with her work – one of the suffragettes on the frontlines of science. Not a plain housewife who craves the life of a kept chatelaine, buried under the weight of 'any day now' promises, but a woman who deliberately sidesteps domestic bliss for a chance to change the world.

LACEY

Finn watches me rub preservative wax into the wood of the Titanic's deckchair. "I have reservations," I say. "Mooney has been like a father to me. I owe him his prime exhibit. Can't you leave your shoes with me and haunt the museum when it opens?" I was semi-serious. It was supposed to make Finn smile.

He sighs himself down into the chair and I abandon my task. I lean against the wall, a woman tough as old boots with my arms crossed, and confront my alter-ego. Finn's five-year-old-legs reach half the length of the deckchair which makes him look less commanding.

"How many sacrifices *does* it take to fill the Atlantic Ocean?" he says.

I go and kneel beside him. "Think how many people will feel the story of your shoes. That's a grand legacy. You'll be remembered after I'm gone. Consider it a tribute to all the children who died. Your Bridie. All the babies."

Finn sits up. There's a strange light in his eyes. He points his finger at me. "Lacey, you're a smart lass, so listen." He clears his throat. "Now then, I have no intention of haunting a museum any more than I intend to hang around your new life dragging a chain or babysitting your kids. Your life is not a spectator sport. I have things to do. Things to prepare."

I know the look in his eye. "But?"

"But I learned something at university. What-if I could leave a *different* legacy? I could even dance at your wedding. I've fair mastered the Irish jig."

"No need to be sarcastic," I say. "If you've got a proposal, I'm listening."

"Proposal is it! Proposal she says. Marry me Lacey. I'll build you a sandbox." *Hmmpf.* "Some proposal. But I *do* have a solution."

"Will Mooney survive it?"

"Mooney will *get over* it. Loss is part of life. He's a soldier." He winks. "A tough egg. Sometimes boiled eggs are overcooked the exact amount of time for a reason."

"I'm all ears."

"That's the trouble you only listen with your ears."

"And my heart. I listen with that too."

"Then you understand what I need to do. If you love Peter, say yes. I'll be gone for a wee while, maybe longer. You figure out how to steal my shoes without Mooney suspecting you, and listen to that heart of yours. Is it in Egypt or with Peter or with a pair of old shoes?"

I'm packing artifacts into boxes in the lab. Straw litters the floor along with bales of cotton. Finn's shoes are ready for the new building, the next stage of the museum. Mooney's office is mine for the asking. He's off in a meeting. The building for the museum seems in order. We have six months to make a floor plan. Finn returns with a smug grin. He's holding a bundle wrapped in butcher paper the size of a small steak.

"Happy New Year," he says. "I may have forgotten to say that. I was in a bit of a slump."

"You shouldn't be."

"Happy New Life. It's what you and Mooney always wanted. Titanic shoes."

"What?" I peel off the paper and inside is a pair of baby shoes. Scuffed and brown with three buttons on each shoe. Michael's shoes. The holy relic of Ballymore.

Finn heaves the sigh of one being relieved of a great burden. "They were lost at sea," he declares. "They're my brother's but I wore them too. In a sense Michael was with us on the Titanic. Mam never left him behind. It was unthinkable to believe he was not always with her. So, these are Titanic shoes right enough. Bequeathed to me, mine to give, and for the world to take. So fair exchange, says I."

"How? Where?"

"Mamie brought them to me. She said Michael sent them as a peace offering."

"What did you give *him*?"

"I may have released him from his corner. Sure it was me who put him there."

April 10, 1940 – 8:20 A.M.

I present Finn's baby shoes to Mooney on the anniversary of Titanic leaving Ireland. Like his namesake, he's over the moon. I'm able to provide a fake provenance for the holy relic of Ballymore, along with the indisputable evidence of a rescue worker. Pa's friend Jimmy McPhee, the one who years ago, took Finn's shoes and his and Mamie's bodies off to their final journey to the Fairview Cemetery, was always blathering about the rescue days and how he had a few 'bitties' of souvenirs put by as keepsakes. The newspapers had interviewed him back in the day, and afterwards he heeded Pa's advice to stay silent. No-one was going to miss a few gewgaws. Pa had the bigger sin. His souvenir was an entire baby.

McPhee died in the Halifax explosion but his tin toolbox survived. Ansel had borrowed it for a quick repair. God must have told him to hide Jimmy's sins. Finn had witnessed the day Ansel had discovered the treasures wrapped in oilskin under the tangle of nails and screws. In the box had been the article snipped, dry and yellowed, along with a greasy document with Jimmy's signature declaring his guilt, and his will declaring, after his death, that his Titanic indiscretions would be preserved as a few anonymous donations. Along with Michael 's shoes, the objects in the box included a spoon with the White Star logo impressed in the handle, a pocket watch, wire spectacles, and a pair of child's booties knitted from sky-blue wool but it was impossible to discern a shape from the clump of mouse-chewed wool droppings as far as I could tell.

I'm in awe that Mamie and Finn were buried side-by-side.

I hold Finn's shoes in my hands long before midnight. I sit hugging them for an hour before Finn materializes by the empty case. It won't take long before Mooney will order a stronger case with a killer lock and Michael Cleary's baby shoes will have a new home. The sign will read an anonymous child from the Titanic and it will be true.

From this night, ten minutes to midnight will chime rather than the hour. I set Finn's shoes on the floor. He dances a jig around them. To him it's a celebration. To me it's a death. There's still time.

"Do you hear that?" he says.

"The ticking of a clock," I reply.

He puts his hand on my shoulder and I hear what he hears – the sound of a ship's bell, and the frantic voices of the officers on the bridge. I see what they see. A blue mountain of ice looming on the right. I wince, preparing for the impact, but I feel nothing but a slight shiver of powdered ice, falling like snow. Finn removes his hand and the room is warm.

As soon as Finn touches the shoes they changes. They untwist and shine uncrushed, brown as a fox and lovely. The laces are tidy. But the insides of the heels are still stained rusty red. Finn shows me his raw blisters before he pulls on the shoes he remembers. I watch, hypnotized.

Finn's fingers are stained brown from boot polish. I smell its friendly scent. I see Molly Cleary, shaking her head with a soft tsk tsk. *"Clean hands make a better impression than..."* she pauses to laugh and rubs her eyes. *"Arragh. The truth is, I don't give a shiny shoe what anyone thinks anymore,"* she says. *"As long as my three children are with me."* Finn holds up his hands to show me. He looks like a prisoner surrendering.

"Don't be getting those new shoes dirty," I say. "I feel like Ma."

"You sound like Mam," Finn says. He touches my shoulder again. I feel the shoes on my own feet. Slightly damp but warmed by Finn. My toes explore. The hard leather pinches them. I lift my foot to take a step and pain shoots from my ankle into my head. "God, Finn, did it feel like this?" It's unthinkable to be walking the corridors of a fated ship in torturous shoes and then drown at sea. It isn't fair.

It's the night of April 9th the day before Titanic leaves Queenstown. Somewhere an ice flow moves into place. It's all staged by Titans waving their hands over the ocean and a fairy ship and a diamond shard of ice. The ship is loaded with ants. It blasts a steamy farewell into the Irish day and I watch her dip past the shape of Spike Island.

The next day I say yes to Peter. Am I being a coward?

48

GRADUATION

I wear my red dress to match the balloons. It's a private party. Peter has many friends. I invite Joe and Mooney and Finn as my 'standup' family. A few telegrams arrive from London. Mooney let them know I wouldn't be returning. I am to be married. I write to May but she can't come. She's a newlywed herself, already pregnant, and terrified. Apparently she nearly died when she was born and has carried that fear within her. I'm beginning to believe everyone dies a little when they're born. Travel is ill-advised. She will visit me by train when the railroad allows. Thankfully we live on the same side of the Atlantic.

Finn is becoming more transparent for longer periods. It's as if he's suffering from depression and has shut a door. It's becoming harder to reach him. Once in a blue moon he rallies and tries to kid around, but then, he's a kid. As old as he is, he's my baby brother. We're like a pair of old shoes, he and I. But he's hiding something.

It is another 'thin' day. Finn moons about aimlessly kicking stones on a deserted stretch of shore where we still occasionally enjoy spending time together. I find the perfect spot for our picnic and spread a blanket near the water. "I had a dream about May last night," I say. "She was handing out toffee in the servant's hall at Fabersham. Do you think it's Mamie trying to get in touch?"

"I do."

"Have you seen her again? Do you discuss me? What does she think of me getting married?"

Finn eyes me impishly. "Did you bring ginger beer?"

I imitate one of his cryptic answers, hopefully to make him smile. "I did."

I packed all his favorites: hard boiled eggs, bread and butter, scones, fig jam, and a thermos of sweetened tea. It isn't until after this repast, when Finn is tossing bread to the gulls, that he finally speaks his mind. As usual, his words come from a deep place where they've been harbored. Not rehearsed but mulled over until the right out-of-the-blue moment.

"Strange as it may seem, a ghost can be haunted," he says.

He's trying to catch me out. "Ah, but Mamie said you *weren't* a ghost."

"Am I not?"

For a while I'm not sure anymore. "Ghosts don't do new things. They're stuck repeating an old event in a place they think still exists," I say.

He gives me a look of incredulity and shakes his head. "Oh, do they? You're an expert now, are you? And what about your mother? ... and I don't mean Ma."

Okay, he's testing me. But I know I'm fairly close to being right from the smirk on his face. He tries to hide it as boyish smugness. He's pleased with me. "Ma died willingly," I say "and Pa was always keen on meeting God, so neither of them stuck around. Mamie wasn't a ghost either; she was sort of a sleepwalker."

"The last thing one sees prior to death can influence their next life," he says. "That goes double for the last sounds one hears, especially voices. I heard Bridie crying and the crack of exploding flares. Mamie heard Isobel calling for Georgie before she lost contact with her forever. She woke up in a cradle in Atlanta, dressed in a miniature white nightgown of the finest cotton with lace at her neck and wrists. You love the math. Atlanta --- Atlantic. Go figure."

I nearly choke on a bite of apple. "And Atlanta is *in* Georgia!"

He gives me a thumbs up. "Old memories carry over like dandelion seeds and sprout in dark places as often as in the sun," he says. "Strong smells and colors return like surprises. I get homesick for the joy of breakfasting with a princess. I'm revisited by a persistent teacher."

I hand Finn a special treat wrapped in wax paper. "You mean that man-in-the-moon of yours?"

"Precisely, Miss Waters. An insistent presence, who, just when I think he's long ceased to care, there he is. He can be annoyingly maternal." Finn gets a wistful look in his eye. "Mamie taught me about spoons and honey and how to lop the tops off boiled eggs without getting shell in the yolk. She was a *mothering* as opposed to a *smothering* sort of teacher."

"Does your teacher know Mamie?"

Finn attacks the wax paper like a boy on Christmas morning. "He seems to know things about everyone I ever knew, so yes. Ooh, lovely toffee."

Finn, my adorable chameleon, is able to change colors from boy to man and back again as lightly as a breath of wind. When he speaks again, it's the small boy savoring a cheek full of toffee, but his words break my heart.

"I've never liked fireworks," he says.

Mamie, heading for the new world is proof of living reincarnation. She was reinventing herself from the old world, dead to her. New York would have only been a port of call. Had she and Izzie reached their destination I had no doubts they would have continued their friendship and likely my mother would have eventually gone to Atlanta.

At the bottom of May's letter is a postscript in a different hand... same ink.

Dearest darling girl,
Concerning the firsts and lasts of life – first I must apologize
for the way I sprang my attack on Christopher without you
knowing. But, Finn was right. To achieve the desired effect,
you had to be surprised.
You and I shared tea once. As I recall it was a windy day on
Titanic. Finn and I had a few days and some stolen moments
where he was more like a zoo animal with me feeding him as
much love and confidence as I could. His life with you hasn't
been an easy incarnation for him. You are still his big sister.
He needs your help more than he'll dare to ask. Let him go.
Let him go with love. But push him out to sea.
And for the last, I'm sorry I had to leave you. I am so proud
of both of you.
love Mamie

Mooney startles me with a package. "Something for your hope chest," he says.

It descends in front of me as I sit at the head table wondering if Finn is off visiting his family. I wonder if Mamie is there to greet him while May sleeps.

I shake the package. "Maybe it's a tin whistle," I say for Finn's benefit, hoping he'll hear me.

Mooney sheds a tear as I open his gift. It's a model of the Titanic in a bottle.

"Made that one myself," he says. "I guess I know what my retirement hobby will be."

I hold the bottle up to the light, imagining a miniature Finn waving from the prow. *Oh, Finnegan. Where for art thou Finnegan?* He chuckles from the dining room in steerage. I squint into the bowels of the ship and spy the ghost of a child in a bib, eating a boiled egg. "We're all soldiers," he says, waving a spoon at me. He had been a confident boy king on a throne. He wears a cloth cap and holds a salt spoon in each hand – his scepter and flail. The perpetual charmer. I see him as Mamie must have that first day. He's so easy to love.

Hope would be a fine thing, he used to say. My hope for Finn is for him to be released from his guilt – an innocent genie, now trapped inside a ship in a bottle.

"How does one get a ship OUT of a bottle?" I ask Mooney.

"I think it involves a hammer," Mooney says. He fills two glasses with champagne and makes a toast. "May you and Peter have a happy life together."

I make a counter toast. "Who knows what feasts and famines lie ahead. What will soar or what must be buried at sea? There's always going to be icebergs in the water," I say, but I smile.

Back home I put my feet up, happy to be alone. Peter is off on a pub crawl with his latest group of students. My feet are chilled. I half expect to have blisters on my heels. I enjoy a lovely hot soak in bath bubbles that smell of magnolias. After I towel off and wrap myself in a robe, I pull on a pair of knitted blue slippers. Suddenly I dissolve in tears. I could be the child who wore the blue booties. My blue slippers could be the reincarnation of Bridie's socks. I must be mad. Finn's pale crestfallen face wavers in front of my eyes.

It's not a time to be maudlin. Finn has found his shoes. I have a fiancé. Michael has a shrine to his memory. The toys on the unknown child's grave continue to amass. Magic jackdaw switcheroo has made my old boss happy – an eye-for-an-eye... a pair of shoes for a pair of shoes. I'm Cinderella with the dream of a prince but the promise of glass slippers cuts my heels raw as any blisters. That's what promises do.

Museums can be fierce about their shoes and ancient baby toys. I'm ever mindful that a dehydrated pharaoh was once a newborn wrapped in fine linen, howling for his mother. My time-slip brother, Tutankhamen, a teenage survivor for over three-thousand-years, was once a babe in arms. Signs pointed to a young man who struggled with a spinal birth defect, but Finn said no, he'd been a vital king. During warrior games an axle of his chariot had been sabotaged. Finn saw him hurled under the wheels of another chariot. And so... massive traumatic injuries. Tut left his twisted body linen-shrouded in mystery. Who were his murderers? Who were *his* teachers?

Museums celebrate the survivors as well as the victims. Tut's mummified stillborn children radiate more life than his million-dollar death mask. A single piece of toffee would have been agony for his poor Egyptian teeth.

FINN – April 14, 1940

I sit on the Halifax wharf staring at a tugboat guiding a cargo ship out of the harbor. I need my timekeeper. "I'm here," I call out. "According to Mamie, I'm almost out of time."

Teacher is pleased. His voice spins around me weaving a golden spiral. "Top of the class, Finn," he says. "You have seventy-two years left. Make the most of your promise. That's barely a heartbeat in the scheme of things." An invisible hand clamps me on the back. "I'm that proud to be your ... teacher."

"You can hug me if you like," I say. "I'm lucky to have you for a mentor."

"No, you're all right," he replies. "I have to go. It's time to put the fear of God into a new protégé."

His voice condenses into the corner that's fair bouncing with white light. "I'll miss you," he says.

I am an *eedjit*. How hadn't I guessed the truth? "It's you, isn't it?" I say to the light, "You're Michael. You're the man-in-the-moon."

"I am."

"You were in the museum. I thought you were Christopher. You tricked me."

The light dims and a boy steps forward, sporting a school uniform and tattered shoes. He lifts one to show me the hole in its sole. He shrugs. "Mam was saving her pennies. You were on your way, you see, and she wanted you to have new baby clothes. I was used to making do with a pair of Da's hand-me-downs. Apropos isn't it? Holes in holy shoes and all, what with the business of soles and souls."

"I'm guessing the money went towards our tickets," I say.

"The money was used to bury me."

Silence.

Michael kicks a large stone that leaves a familiar mark across the battered toe of his shoe. "Mam gave up after that, no matter what I said. I told her I wanted to stay, but she heard what she wanted to hear. Just as you saw what you wanted to see. She only heard the word stay. She made me promise to take care of you if anything happened to her. So I went with you on the ship. You know how we spirits sense an impending death? Well, you know yourself from when you saved Lacey and Rose, that Christmas. You knew what was coming in a great swirl with no actual details. With Titanic I sensed danger but it might have been you falling overboard. I knew I had to be on hand to pick up the pieces. When I found out about the disaster I could do nothing except keep my promise. By the way, it's the devil of an imagination you have. But for the life of me..." he stops himself with a grin, "for the *life* of me, why couldn't you imagine I was a decent brother? That I was on your side while on the 'other side'? That I would be on your side when we were both dead?"

"Did you hate me?"

Michael relaxes for the first time. He crosses his arms and widens his stance as if gaining his balance on board a ship. "A firstborn child is a bit of a shock," he says. "Our parents were that in love they were blind to everything other than each other. And bit by bit, as soon as I could walk, I pulled Mam away from Da out of jealousy. I had a set of lungs on me and I knew just when to cry. Later, I was the smarty-pants from school. I had to fake reading to her. I probably amassed an uncommon deal of sins for making up the bible as I went along."

"A plethora of sins," I say.

"Mam was afraid to love you."

"She had boiling water but she never made me the boiled egg. We had eggs once in a while."

Michael gives me a pained look. "Did you ever see the likes of an eggcup in our kitchen? They didn't sell such things in Ballymore. Mam looked when she remembered. I was with her, tagging along, but she always saw me out the corner of her eye, and used the money to buy a candle for me in the church, instead. And the price of butter was over the moon. Mam loved stories," Michael says, "so I gave her a rare few I can tell you. In any case, I made sure I was larger than life. I was the 'too big for his own boots,' lad. I never understood that until I watched you. A wise teacher learns from their student."

"Get away with you. What did I ever teach you?"

Michael walks towards me with his arms outstretched. "You rescued me from that corner? I'll take that hug now, you great poltroon."

LACEY

It's ten to midnight and I can't sleep. My car takes Finn and I to Pier 21. Finn stares out the window and tries to find the moon. He turns to me, all smiles. "There's no moon," he says. "School's out."

The pier is deserted. Finn takes my hand and leads me to the far end. His hand grips mine harder with each step but I don't cry out. He's scared. He's just a scared kid. At ten to midnight his body trembles and he lets go of my hand. "Just so you know, I won't look back," he says. He takes two steps and falters. He shrugs, turns to face me, and blows me a kiss. As he turns away from me he disappears, and I fall to my knees, sobbing. I feel a pair of little arms about my neck as he kisses my cheek goodbye.

In lieu of flowers I've brought a life preserver as an offering. The ring shape reminds me of a Remembrance Day wreath laid on a cenotaph. Throwing a life preserver to a drowned boy is surreal. Finn once said that staying buoyant was fine if the water isn't freezing and that only the salt stops the Atlantic from being the most enormous skating rink in the world.

"Grab this," I shout into the wind and toss my offering into the water. It's like tossing my hat into the ring. Suddenly I know where my heart wants to be.

I return home to find Finn's shoes in a box. He's left a note. He's gone to heaven without his shoes.

Dear Lacey,
You'll be pleased to know that I've grown too big for
my boots. No worries, my darling girl. I'll love you
forever. And I haven't left you entirely. I could never
do that, but I'm over the moon to be gone.
Mam will have to take me as she finds me.
Teacher sends his regards.
Meet you in New York. – love F.C.

I break off my engagement, move to New York, and find work in the Metropolitan Museum, cleaning floors. Outsiders are suspect. Women are suspect. But eventually I catch a break, and I'm promoted through the ranks until, there I am, a permanent fixture entrusted to handle the Egyptian collection. And all the time, I wait for Finn. Years go by. Will he finally make it to New York?

49

ICEBERG AT TWELVE O'CLOCK

LACEY – 1950

Finn finds me ten years later. With us it's always April regardless of the season. He never says, but something big has happened in our time apart. He returns happy. He's mellow. My Peter Pan has found his rightful place, and what's more, he's content to never grow up. I never ask about his 'Neverland' or why he still runs about barefoot or mention lost boys or pirates. In return, he never asks me to sew our shadows together. My willow-the-wisp friend comes and goes, and when he stays for a while it's out of brotherly love. We make each other no promises. And then, after I retire, we return to our birthplace like a pair of determined salmon.

HALIFAX – SEPTEMBER 2, 1985
countdown – 27 years to 2012, centenary

Things discovered sweep the headlines. Once more I'm carried off in a spin of intrigue. Finn is subdued. We watch the underwater footage of Titanic berthed in sludge. She appears through the turquoise murk – a manmade cave of stalactites and stalagmites caught in the headlights of a baby submarine, all the while serenaded by whale-song and violins. Her hull drips with fronds and tendrils, reminding me of a weeping willow. And what cause for widespread weeping she had unleashed.

That night, Finn and I watch our old favorite, 'Fantasia' where a wizard's apprentice, becomes overwhelmed after casting a spell ran amok. It's a story of power out of control. I recall being a mousy girl, arranging my enchanted mops and brooms at the end of a long day, and how they danced away into a dream of Egypt under an irrepressible spell.

Later, I dream I'm a mouse conducting a symphony. I wave my baton over Titanic's grave. The ship's whistle blast sounds like a distant fog horn. Jets of bubbles stream from the crushed funnels. The halves of the ship reconnect in a film played backwards. The spill of debris rises into the rightful order of things. The sides of the ship turn to glass. Inside, waiters deliver champagne and brandy to dining tables laden with salt spoons resting in tiny silver bowls with legs. Blind minnows swim through the stems of red roses in silver vases, and the crystal ropes of the chandelier swing a hypnotic dance, luring light-sensitive creatures into its arms. Transparent ghosts waltz and float, carried along a maze of corridors, their long dresses and capes billowing in the water. On the promenade deck, men have to hold onto their top hats. Mamie reclines on a deckchair dreaming of her unborn child. Molly Cleary and Michael pass by her, strolling arm-in-arm, she in her blue hat; he in his blue sweater. They cast a pair of baby shoes over the rail. Two shoes spiral upward, drawn to the surface, glowing with light.

A pulsating gold line runs around the circumference of the hull as if it were painted yesterday – a living vein demarcating above and below, life and death. Above, the toffs wine and dine. Below, in steerage, children race down Scotland Road, and little Bridie sucks her thumb, sleeping next to Finn in an upper bunk. I observe it all – an overexcited little girl, nose pressed against an aquarium window, mesmerized by the undersea silence of slow-motion.

Finn is restless. He falls asleep in his favorite armchair and mumbles something about a dragon in his sleep. He calls out. "Don't look back."

Just as the Titanic is discovered and given a new lease on life, I'm diagnosed with the 'new consumption.' It's advanced and terminal but I'll not lose my faculties. I will 'drown' in my bed, gasping for breath as sure as Finn's brother, Michael.

Finn holds my hand. "Death isn't so bad. I'll hold your hand just like this, until the end."

"Didn't you tell me death was a grand beginning?" I say. "I'm afraid you'll have a long drawn out wait."

He pats my hand, folds his arms in mock severity, and glances at his wrist where a watch would be if he'd had one. He taps the watch's invisible crystal and brings his wrist to his ear. "*Jaysus* woman, is it much longer than seventy-three years that you'll be?"

He climbs onto the bed and hugs his knees, a leprechaun at the foot of my bed, grinning. A fairy trickster after my heart. *"Lacey, Lacey, give me your answer do. I'm half crazy, all for the love of you,"* he sings.

Rain on the window reminds me of the watery lens of the underwater cameras – a square porthole. Out there the world is wet for miles. I rest on the warm bedrock of electric blankets and sedatives. Finn's hand squeezes mine, again. It's safe, here inside the lullabies of whales. I'm adrift in a lifeboat that rocks like a cradle. It's a cod barrel filled with lace.

"I'll be glad of your company. Tell me again what death is like."

"I can only tell you of mine," he says. "My daddy made it easier for me." He nods slowly. "He was a good father."

Some days I'm back in Moon's Maritime Museum, holding Finn back from destroying a door. Some days I'm polishing the glass of a mummy case in the Metropolitan Museum. I move back and forth from museum to museum, from leather boots to beaded sandals. I never visited Egypt the country, but Tutankhamen delivered it to me whole and romantic. I never did feel the sand of Sakkara beneath my toes yet I can see the sand, slightly pink under the haze of an eighteenth-dynasty sun. Pink sand reminds me of something important. I don't remember what for the life of me.

I stayed a spinster, Peter and I became friends, and to cite a cliché, I danced at his wedding. He named his son, Finn, to honor my 'invisible friend' who saved both our lives. Prospectors still dig for pirate treasure on Oak Island, ever hopeful of a miracle. It's good to have a dream.

I've had enough miracles for a lifetime. I've been lucky. Finn was my miracle. I was his.

Lately I'm less aware of distances. I overreach for things and knock them over. Nurse Taylor laughs and calls it dropsy. I need Finn's glasses, improved with thicker lenses. I see strangers out of focus at the edge of my room. Nurse Taylor and Finn are the only ones who come close enough for me to recognize.

Finn is always smiling. He's the one who suggests I make my way to the night kitchen so we can share a feast of biscuits and hot chocolate. I don't trust myself with boiling milk but I steal down the stairs and dutifully search the cupboards. I check the top cupboards first. No biscuits. But I forget to close the door. When I come up from the lower cupboard I hit my head. It's a shock but not painful.

"Is it stars you're seeing?" Finn says, laughing. I laugh too. He is such a sweetheart.

Taylor gasps when she sees the blood on my forehead. "Lacey, what on earth," she says, and fetches a cold compress. I close my eyes and see the museum's Titanic deckchair and a woman reclining there. "Hello child," Mamie says. "I've missed you."

I'm dizzy but Finn assures me it's nothing to worry about. "Sure it's only a wee scratch," he says. "We can buff that out with a little shoe polish, sure as a rainy day."

countdown – 26 years to 2012, centenary

It's the night of April 14, 1986, tomorrow I'll be seventy-four, and I'm restless.

Taylor lays out my flannel nightshirt. "It's almost midnight," she says. "It's way past your bedtime."

The flannel nightshirt lies on the bed like an empty stranger. "I want to change into the nightgown," I say. There's no hesitation, Taylor knows the one I mean. She opens a drawer and pulls out a soft bundle wrapped in silver tissue paper with a blue ribbon. She holds up Mamie's gown in front of her to show me how beautifully it drapes. It slinks lazily down to the floor. We both smile. I tell Taylor it once belonged to my mother, and that my practical stepmother had intended to cut it up for handkerchiefs but when she tried to put scissors to fabric she lost heart. By Tailor's expression she's heard the story before, but she's kind so she smiles and says, "Fancy that."

The embroidered initials I.F. are no longer pure white but a creamy shade of ivory. Whose were they? Was it a princess? They remained a mysterious watermark – a question scrawled by a quill dipped in buttermilk.

I stay Taylor's hand from fussing with my pillows. "Listen. Can you hear that?"

She pauses to humor me again and shakes her head. "No Miss Lacey, I don't hear anything."

"The engines have stopped."

"Sweet dreams," Taylor says. "If you need me, just ring. I've put your slippers by the bed."

"If you live in Egypt you don't need shoes," I say. "The sand is pink you know."

The clock shows 11:55 p.m. "Well I never," Taylor says. "No shoes at all? Fancy that."

I scamper out of bed, reach under it for Finn's shoes, and place them at the foot of my bed.

I close my eyes. Finn is there, arms crossed, looking unconcerned. "Sweet dreams," I say.

He answers. "Bedbugs."

The waters close in on everything and he disappears.

I'm a newborn in a night nursery. Mamie, in a starched white apron and a lace cap, tucks me in and kisses my forehead.

"Goodnight my darling girl," she says. "God bless." She blows out the candle and closes the door.

"Lacey Waters," Finn whispers from far away. "Take my hand."

"I'm too tired." I see white seafoam floating on the sand. The Atlantic has a lace hem.

It's 2:20 a.m. by the clock, when Finn's voice wakes me again. "Sweet dreams," he whispers. "Hurry up, we don't want it to leave without us. Don't forget your slippers."

"And don't be forgetting your shoes," I say to him like a mother hen. "Sure you'd forget your head entirely if it wasn't screwed on." My voice is different, with the musical lilt of the Irish.

I whisper my final words for Finn alone, shamelessly misquoting Yeats' poem. The one Finn chose for Ma's gravestone. *"Come Fairy sprite. Take me out of this dull world, for I would sail with you upon the wind and dance upon the ocean like a flame!"*

Finn and I watch Peter Pan from front row seats in a darkened theatre. It's about to begin. Nana the dog, barks madly at the window. Tinkerbell is a finger of moonlight that plays over a night nursery, searching. A ship in a bottle on the mantelpiece glows from inside. I grab Finn's hand and whisper "This is going to be exciting."

"Tis."

The houselights flicker.

"It's only a paper moon... sailing over a cardboard sea... but it wouldn't be make-believe if you believed in me," Finn sings.

I nudge his arm. "That reminds me. You have to clap if you believe in fairies."

"Get away with you now."

A scenery backdrop descends to reveal a painted pirate ship on the horizon. An invisible stagehand turns on a wind machine and the stage floor ripples like a flag. My hair blows into my eyes. When I'm able to see again, the real Atlantic Ocean undulates into the horizon and I smell the salty memories of childhood.

Our young toes are inches from the water and every few seconds they're gently lapped by the surf. The water is lovely and warm. A lone seagull circles around us crying like a newborn baby. Finn's new shoes are tied together and slung over his shoulder. I carry my slippers in one hand. My age spots are gone and I'm wearing a diamond wedding ring too big for my childish fingers. It reminds me of a chunk of ice. "Look Finn says," pointing out to sea.

Fifty yards away floats an empty lifeboat with the number five painted on its side. A bouquet of five red balloons is tied to its bow. The next thing I know, I'm swimming towards it. Finn is already in the boat calling to me. How did he get there so fast? "Grab my hand," he shouts, reaching for me. "Don't look back."

But I don't listen. Safe in the boat, I feel compelled to look back at the shore. Something white is there in the foam and a seagull is circling it, dive-bombing for a closer look. I enter the body of the seagull and spy a lace nightgown stuck to the sand like white seaweed. Next to it is a double set of footprints filling with pink seawater. Pink sand.

Finn shouts my name and I'm back in the lifeboat. He takes my hand. "Don't ever let go," he says.

AUTHOR'S NOTES

What is great about writing fiction is how quickly inspiration arrives when strolling through an art gallery or a museum. What's sad about writing historical fiction is that the everyday human details of obscure individuals are unfairly eclipsed by the famous. Some identities are misappropriated; others are relegated to the historical background, but most are lost completely. That's why I like to mind-travel to fifteenth-century Florence to track down missing art, and breathe life into unrecorded lives. Finding forgotten people often begins at the end – their grave sites and locations of buildings that no longer exist.

When I moved to Nova Scotia I did what I always do in a new place. I explored the local heritage. I visited the Titanic graves, moved by toys left in the rain for the unknown child. Some were wrapped in cellophane to keep them dry, and I thought, no, they should succumb to weather to make sense. I couldn't help but connect the similarity, albeit climatically opposite, to the childhood toys of Tutankhamun left in his tomb for his afterlife pleasure.

Quite often the graves of heroic figures exist only in memory. Leonardo da Vinci's remains were desecrated for building renovations after the French Revolution; Mozart was buried in a mass grave; and then there's the opposite – the tributes to unknown soldiers and the monuments honoring entire clans on a battlefield. Beautiful architecture is often confiscated and turned into offices or worse, parking lots. There's often no place to pay one's respects above a final resting place. Only a few privileged divers will ever gaze at Titanic from a submarine window.

Curiosity inevitably lured me into archive territory

because happily, museums are time-machines that lead to encountering the shoes of an unknown infant who perished (or survived) on April 15, 1912 during the sinking of the Titanic.

Baby shoes are a common enough item. In another era they're often bronzed and turned into a whimsical paperweight. But these were not the shoes of an ordinary child. Fate marked this child for unlikely celebrity. All I could see was the living child, kicking and gurgling. A real being whose mother worked those shoes onto wiggling toes in the morning and eased them off at night.

I sat in the replica deckchair from Titanic. Later, it was easy to slip into a fantasy where one of my characters drank tea, sheltered from a brisk crosswind on one of the promenade decks – a woman also sheltered from the event that would soon devastate her life. Tea in a deckchair would never be the same. For her or for me.

Drifting through rows of model ships, I accidentally came upon the 'Franconia' – the Cunard ship that brought me from Southampton to Nova Scotia, when as a child, not much older than Finn, I came to Canada with my mother in 1956. I still recall being left to wander the decks alone, with my mother too seasick to leave our cabin. I remember the stewards in their white uniforms, who smiled and gave me bread and jam in their common room. I had the run of the decks. A loose kid exploring an ocean liner, unsupervised at sea. Such a crazy thought. No guardians. Certainly, no nanny. I'm barely one generation removed from my ancestors who had been in service.

My great-grandmother was a cook's helper in a stately home; my great-grandfather was a carriage driver. On occasion, when my mother lived with her grandmother, she was 'allowed' to play with the 'lord and lady's' children. My mother, born in 1922, was ten when the Titanic sank. It was also the year the tomb of Tutankhamen was discovered by Howard Carter. Both of these events blended together seamlessly as I wrote Finn and Lacey's extraordinary love story – two children on Titanic, destined to marry, who were torn apart by the events of April 15, 1912.

The things we realize later often trigger the most thought-provoking ideas. My own Atlantic crossing passed over the wreck of the Titanic, twenty-nine years before it was found, and King Tut was to become an ongoing obsession for me from an off-chance elementary school presentation.

Other girls my age wanted to be teachers and ballerinas but, like Lacey, I caught the Egyptology bug early, and later I referenced Egyptian art heavily during the time I studied for a Fine Arts Degree. *I invite you to visit my website to view those paintings:* http://veronicaknox.com

My lifelong love of Egypt began at the age of seven when a school friend of mine brought a 'show-and-tell' item to class. That item put a human face on a culture already consuming my imagination. She showed a few seeds of grain, proclaiming them to be from King Tut's tomb. The other classmates were indifferent. Not me.

Now there's no knowing if it was a true artifact. The likelihood is well, unlikely, but the seeds she uncovered in a folded white tissue were as powerful as Jack's magic beans. I touched them. They transported me to the time when a person first placed them in a jar. I imagined their hands sealing the lid and other hands breaking the seal, and new light exposing unplanted seeds, transplanted to a cold country thousands of years and miles away from the eighteenth-dynasty.

A few museum seeds sprouted into my story of Titanic's child-ghost searching for his lost shoes and a new identity while trying to reunite with the girl he was destined to marry.

Finn's valiant sojourn through a reincarnation attempt gone wrong, accepting the consequences for his mistakes to recover his lost destiny grew from a time capsule of artifacts: a deckchair, a pair of shoes, and the archive photographs of a luxury ship and her passengers who survive in romantic memories.

Things in a museum are more than artifacts. Behind each human relic is the ghost of a life.

~ *Veronica Knox* - April 15, 2023

ABOUT THE AUTHOR

V Knox writes 'metaphysical' novels for imaginative bookworms who savor exploring the realms of creative history and Paranormal Romance. Her invented genres of choice are 'Cozy Outer Limits', 'The Fine Art of Haunting' (her 'Ghosts in the Gallery' series), and Time-slip Adventures for Middle-grade readers of all ages.

Veronica obtained a Fine Arts degree from the University of Alberta where she developed an imaginative take on art history that led to an untapped source for stories. She discovered that inanimate objects were rarely bereft of life and that paintings have juicy secrets to tell.

She explores the creative inner worlds of autistic savants and master artists, and in one case, the unknown child in the Titanic cemetery. She explores the discrepancies between reality and lucid dreams, fishes the depths of the subconscious, the afterlife, reincarnation, the anomalies of parallel lives and dimensions, the classic psyche of 'the ghostly lover', reconciles historical facts with surreal fiction, and has written seventeen 'outer limits' novels.

Veronica remains intent on listening to the ethereal echoes from objects in museums and the voices of the Italian Renaissance – the artists as well as their anonymous subjects and companions. She grants them second chances to air their grievances, tell their stories, and together they set the dreariest history books on fire.

WEBSITE & CURIOUS ART HISTORY BLOG

If you enjoyed
'Violet Seaborn's Unfinished Soul'
please help me spread the word.
Thank you

Veronica Knox – May 27, 2023

SILENT K PUBLISHING — Vancouver Island, Canada
https://veronicaknox.com

OTHER BOOKS by V KNOX

The 'LISABETTA' Trilogy:
a fictional biography of the 'MONA LISA'
'LISABETTA' – *a stolen glance*
'LISABETTA' – *a stolen smile*
'LISABETTA' – *a stolen sister*

'WOO WOO'

The posthumous love story of Miss Emily Carr

The 'BEDE' Series:
A middle-grade novel for ages ten to twelve:
'TWINTER' – *the first portal*
'TIME FALLS LIKE SNOW'
'TOMORROW AGAIN'
'SNOW BEHIND THE DOOR'

'ADORATION' – *loving Botticelli*

The 'PEARL' SERIES:
historical paranormal romance
'THE INDIGO PEARL' – *book one*
'PEARL BY PEARL' – *book two*